A World War II Th...
Courage, L...

LIBERATION

Emilio Iodice

Wall Street Journal Best Selling Author

Dedication: To the ones I love and who love me. To my grandchildren, Sofia, Helena, Lukas, and Anna. May they discover themselves as they turn these pages and find that only love, passion, and compassion conquers all.

To the women and men who suffered and perished for freedom and those who continue to do so.

I shall pass this way but once; any good that I can do or any kindness I can show to any human being, let me do it now. Let me not defer nor neglect it, for I shall not pass this way again.

Etienne de Grellet, Quaker Missionary

Registered with the U.S. Copyright Office.
Registration Number 1-8505719731

Also by Emilio Iodice

Profiles in Leadership, from Cæsar to Modern Times

A Kid from Philadelphia, Mario Lanza, the Voice of the Poets

Sisters

Future Shock 2.0, The Dragon Brief, a fiction thriller about 2020, based on fact

Reflections: Stories of Love, Inspiration, Remembrance, and Power

Electing the President, 2016. The Most Important Decision You Will Ever Make

When Courage Was the Essence of Leadership: Lessons from History

The Commander in Chief: The Qualities Needed of Leaders of Freedom-Loving Nations in the 21st Century, Lessons from American History

Table of Contents

Acknowledgements

Family and friends are precious. Their value shows up in this book with love, encouragement, and assistance. Such was the case with Liberation.

I am grateful to those who helped me fine tune my words, thoughts, and phrases as readers, reviewers, editors, and advisers.

My cousin, Carolyn Aversano, read each page and helped me see the trees in the forest, so every syllable made sense.

Alessia Ardesi and Alberto Castelvecchi, my good friends in Rome, showed faith and trust in me and this work with their ideas, contacts, and inspiration.

Professor Silverio Lamonica did a masterful translation into Italian and has my endless gratitude.

My thanks to photographer Carlotta Di Felice and artist Isabella Raffa, who helped create the cover and several internal images, and to Federica Prosperi, who organized the manuscript and prepared the Italian edition.

Thanks go to my editors and publisher, who produced this work.

My eternal gratitude to the voices and souls who gave me the stories at the heart of Liberation.

Author's Note

Liberation was inspired by actual events. It is a work of fiction, based on fact.

As a boy, growing up in an Italian section of the South Bronx, I sat around family tables listening to stories. They were about adventures of young people, immigrants, Italy, and, most of all, World War II.

Scenes became real as I listened to heroes and heroines nonchalantly relate incredible acts of bravery as if part of daily life.

I learned about them from the characters themselves.

I corroborated each story and episode by speaking with those in Italy who lived and participated in the events. I uncovered details that added ingredients of drama and love.

I swore to keep their accounts secret and to tell them in the form of fiction, only after their passing.

I kept that promise.

Names were altered and no last names were used, for privacy and confidentiality.

The protagonists provided the "skeleton" of each story. I added the rest.

Events and dialogue were recreated to capture lost details.

The characters in this book actually lived, loved, and died.

Silverio, Lucia, and Antonio existed, as did Don Lorenzo, Giovannina, Don Gabriele and others. Carlo, Helena, Joe, Tom, Sofia, Lukas, and Anna came back to life with different names.

I am grateful to Silverio and his wife, Lucia, for many things, and two in particular.

One, for telling me their story and those of their friends and family. I recorded them as honestly as time and space have allowed.

The second is personal: They were my parents.

World War II archives of the OSS, CIA, the U.S. Department of Defense, and primary and secondary sources were consulted. Eyewitness accounts of facts, plans, strategies, battles, and their outcomes were related as they happened.

The people in *Liberation* changed the lives of millions.

They changed mine. They made me a better person.

I traveled to another era.

I felt emotion, fear, and terror.

The stories reminded me of my Jewish friends and their families who I grew up with and shared the journey of life.

I dedicate this work to them and to the memories of those they lost.

I wrote this book in Rome, where I live.

The people I described during the Nazi occupation lived in my neighborhood, walked on my streets, and breathed the same air of the Eternal City as I have.

I put myself in the shoes of the victims and imagined the minds of the villains and the acts of heroes and heroines.

The champions in this work survived the worst of times by love, suffering, bravery, compassion, fearless leadership, and deliverance from fear and injustice, all performed in the shadow of secrecy.

They fought anti-Semitism, discrimination, hate, and prejudice.

Today, these evils still live among us, like demons.

This book is a tribute to the silent "Unknown Warriors" who freed us from the shackles of oppression and fought the devils of bigotry and arrogance — and asked for nothing in return.

Their sacrifices should inspire us to fight the fiends of intolerance before they overcome us.

Hear their voices, and remember what they say.

Thoughts before We Begin

*Love is liberation. The only way beyond time, to unravel the knot
of existence, is to love.*

Frederick Lenz

*Love is the only answer to every question. It is the only thing that will serve
you in every situation. It is the route and the destination. It is… liberation.*

Rasheed Ogunlaru

There's no path to liberation that doesn't pass through the shadow.

Jay Michaelson

*Within yourself, deliverance must be searched for because each man makes
his own prison.*

Edwin Arnold

*A secret pride in every human heart revolts at tyranny. You may order and
drive an individual, but you cannot make him respect you.*

William Hazlitt

*My dream is of a place and a time where America once again is the last
best hope of earth.*

Abraham Lincoln

We are a country where people of all backgrounds, all nations of origin, all languages, all religions, all races, can make a home. America was built by immigrants.

Hillary Clinton

America isn't Congress. America isn't Washington. America is the striving immi-grant who starts a business or the mom who works two low-wage jobs to give her kid a better life. America is the union leader and the CEO who put aside their differences to make the economy stronger.

Barack Obama

A Providence protects idiots, drunkards, children, and the United States of America.

Otto von Bismarck

Be courageous. I have seen many depressions in business. Always America has emerged from these stronger and more prosperous. Be brave as your fathers before you. Have faith! Go forward!

Thomas A. Edison

America was not built on fear. America was built on courage, on imagination, and on an unbeatable determination to do the job at hand.

Harry S. Truman

Now, as a nation, we don't promise equal outcomes, but we were founded on the idea everybody can succeed. No matter who you are, what you look like, where you come from, you can make it. That's an essential promise of America. Where you start should not determine where you end up.

Barack Obama

We are never defeated unless we give up on God.

Ronald Reagan

Let us ask ourselves, 'What kind of people do we think we are?' And let us answer, 'Free people, worthy of freedom, and determined not only to remain so but to help others gain their freedom as well.'

Ronald Reagan

With confidence in our armed forces – with the unbounding determination of our people – we will gain the inevitable triumph – so help us God.

Franklin Delano Roosevelt

The American Army – including thousands of Americans of Italian descent – entered Italy not as conquerors, but as liberators. Their objective is military, not political. When that military objective is accomplished, the Italian people will be free to work out their own destiny, under a government of their own choosing.

Franklin Delano Roosevelt

You ask our aim. I can answer in one word: Victory. Victory at all costs. Victory despite all terror. Victory, however long and hard the road may be. For without victory, there is no survival . . . . If the British Empire and its Commonwealth last for a thousand years, men will still say, "This was their finest hour."

Never in the field of human conflict was so much owed by so many to so few.

Winston Churchill

Winston Churchill, House of Commons, 4 June 1940

"We shall go on to the end, we shall fight in France, we shall fight on the seas and oceans, we shall fight with growing confidence and growing strength in the air, we shall defend our island, whatever the cost may be, we shall fight on the beaches, we shall fight on the landing grounds, we shall fight on the fields and in the streets, we shall fight in the hills; we shall never surrender."

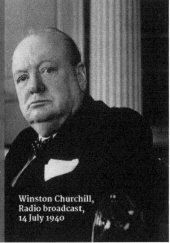

"This is no war of chieftains or of princes, of dynasties or national ambition; it is a war of peoples and of causes. There are vast numbers, not only in this island but in every land, who will render faithful service in this war but whose names will never be known, whose deeds will never be recorded. This is a war of the Unknown Warriors; but let all strive without failing in faith or in duty, and the dark curse of Hitler will be lifted from our age."

Winston Churchill, Radio broadcast, 14 July 1940

Preface

T hree families meet at Kennedy Airport. They are on the same flight to Rome. It is 1971. They discover something uncanny: All are bound by World War II in a dramatic saga, captivating and surreal. They reminisce about what happened.

~

A thousand miles from home, outside a World War II prison camp in Mississippi in 1944, Silverio faces three ghostly figures mounted on horses wearing white outfits with red crosses, brandishing fiery bottles of gasoline, bullwhips, pistols, and shotguns.

Their mission: to kill him.

Hundreds of miles away, in Wheeling West Virginia, a love affair grows between Carlo and Helena. Helena is a beautiful girl whose parents come from the same hometown in Italy as this handsome young man. He is an Italian soldier captured in North Africa and is a prisoner in an American camp in Alabama.

To consummate their love, they face tremendous challenges, including their own fears.

In a secret place near Washington, DC, brothers Joe and Tom train to join the Office of Strategic Services. They are to aid partisans during the invasion of Italy.

The men learn communications, sabotage, and how to murder silently and efficiently.

Unbeknownst to them, Joe and Tom become heroic figures of liberation and struggle to save the innocent before the forces of evil reach them.

And then they meet Sheila...

This is their story.

Liberation

Courtesy of the U.S. Library of Congress

A World War II Thriller of Love, Compassion, Courage, Leadership and Redemption

Inspired by True Stories

Heroism is its own reward.

Often, it is about ordinary people doing extraordinary things, although our memory of them and what they did may evaporate with time.

Here begin three unforgettable sagas of bravery, love, and courageous defiance to tyranny.

CHAPTER 1 ▬▬▬▬▬▬▬▬▬▬▬▬▬

JFK, 1971

"Alitalia flight 611 to Rome will depart from Terminal one, at 9:50 PM.

Passengers are requested to go to gate 12 for boarding," came the announcement from a loudspeaker barely heard over the no ise of crowds assembled at John F. Kennedy Airport. Thousands of travelers gathered in the departure area to fly to places across the globe.

"Papa, you and Mamma have two hours to get to the gate. Don't be so nervous," said Silverio's son. "I know, but it's been a long time since me and your mother were on a plane," responded Silverio. He was perspiring. His hands were trembling. His anxiety was not about flying. It was about returning to his roots, returning to his past.

He feared all he held dear had vanished. Friends and relatives were gone. His father and sister were dead. A few cousins and an aunt were still there. Questions revolved in his mind: Did anyone remember him? Would he be welcomed or thought of as another "Americano" who returned to claim his property rights and inheritance? Would he be recognized at all? He left the Old World at sixteen and landed in New York without a cent in his pocket and only a pair of socks and underwear. He was slim and handsome with long, curly hair. Now, he was prosperous and well-dressed, but also old, overweight, and balding.

For Silverio, the moment was a scene from a movie.

Getting on a plane and going back to his birthplace was a dream — and a nightmare.

It was June 1971. Thirty-four years had passed from the last time Silverio and Lucia were in Italy. So much happened to these immigrants from a small island in the Mediterranean. They longed to see families and friends again. Memories flooded their minds as they kissed their son and daughter-in-law and began the long walk across JFK to the terminal and gate. "Did you pack my pain killers?"

asked Silverio as he pushed the luggage cart. "Yes, and also those little blue pills the doctor said you should take for your prostate," explained Lucia. She was tranquil and happy. Two sisters and two brothers were still alive. They lived on the island. Another sister was in Rome. Lucia was excited to return home.

She left Italy a young lady of twenty-three and now was a middle-aged woman of sixty. She was twenty pounds heavier and her youthful figure was gone. The experience and pain from decades of hard work, disappointments, suffering, and six miscarriages did not make her resentful and angry. Instead, Lucia was wise, calm, and optimistic.

'So much has changed — and so much is the same,' she thought.

Her life in America was bittersweet, filled with sacrifices and satisfaction. Still, she counted her blessings. She had her health, a good husband, and two loving sons and grandchildren. Her family in Italy had endured war, famine, bloodshed, and sorrow. Lucia recalled moments of anguish and joy. Words from countless letters from her loved ones flashed in her mind's eye as she and Silverio reached the gate.

They took seats and waited. A couple stood close to them looking at their boarding passes. Another pair sat next to Silverio and Lucia, going through personal effects to double-check that they had all they needed for their nine-hour journey to Rome.

"I got a nice letter from Don Lorenzo yesterday," said Lucia. "He was a little boy at our wedding and today he is the pastor of the church. My uncle, Don Gabriele, raised him and helped him through the seminary," explained Lucia. "Thanks to Don Gabriele, I married you," said Silverio, holding Lucia's hand tightly and looking at her with eyes of love. "You remember the letter I wrote to your uncle asking him to help me convince your father?" asked Silverio. "I do," remarked Lucia with tears in her eyes. "I wish my uncle was still with us. He died right after the war. It still breaks my heart to think he is gone. At least Don Lorenzo took his place. He is anxious to see us again," beamed Lucia.

The name of the priest caught the attention of the couple nearby. A gentleman in his mid-fifties, with dark hair and brown eyes asked Lucia a question. "Excuse me, did you say Don Lorenzo?" "Yes, he is my cousin on the Island of Ponza," responded Lucia. The man was stunned. "He is your cousin? We are on our way to see him," he said. "My brother and I were with him in the war. My name is Joe. This is my brother Tom. We are taking our wives to Italy for a vacation and to show them where we fought. Our family came from Ponza, but we were born in New York," explained Joe.

"Wait a minute," said Lucia. She looked closely at the brothers. Their faces were familiar. "You are Maria's boys. She and I grew up in Ponza together. We are cousins. I was at your baptism," she said with a smile. Silverio and Lucia introduced themselves. A lively conversation began.

"We are going for the feast of San Silverio on June 20th," explained Tom. "Our parents always told us about it. It was our special connection to the traditions of the island as we grew up in Little Ponza in the South Bronx. We loved the procession, the mass, and all the stands with food, toys, and games," said Tom, with nostalgia. "My favorite was the one with sausage and pepper sandwiches," chimed in Joe. "And what about those women who fried the dough right in front of you to make zeppoles? That was a work of art," insisted Tom.

"I was the President of the Society of the people from Ponza in the U.S. and I put together our feast every year," stated Silverio, proudly. "Now I know why you and your wife are so familiar. We saw you at the novenas when we went to Our Lady of Pity Church," explained Joe. "During the war, we reminisced all the time about life in Little Ponza," said Tom. "It was a wonderful place that was safe, secure, and pure family," replied Joe. "We celebrated the feast with your family and relatives at our house in 1944," said Lucia.

"While you were fighting," said Silverio, "I was filling ships with munitions to send to the front. I even visited a cousin who was a prisoner of war in Mississippi." Suddenly, a tall, very handsome man standing next to Silverio and Lucia flinched and looked at him.

"You do not recognize us, do you Silverio? My wife, Helena, and Gabriela and Richard were at that dinner on the feast day of San Silverio in the Bronx in 1944.

"I was captured in North Africa in 1943 and spent three years in a POW camp in Alabama." Carlo presented his wife, Helena, and her cousin Gabriele and Richard, her husband. "We are going to our family town near Avellino with my brother Luigi and his wife Antonietta," he said. "My cousin, Gabriela, married a boy whose family came from Ponza and lived near us in Wheeling, West Virginia. We are going to visit his family and go for the feast on the island," said Helena. Lucia looked carefully at Richard. "You are my cousin Fanny's son," she said, hugging him.

Everyone seemed related.

"What an amazing coincidence," remarked Silverio. "Here we are, three families who shared, in some way, similar experiences in World War II, now on our way to Italy, on the same flight, to go to the same place for the same event. If we wanted to arrange this, it would have been impossible," he said, as they all laughed while recalling those frightening and ominous memories still vivid and fresh, even if they happened thirty years earlier.

The plane landed six hours later in Dublin to refuel. The three families went to a restaurant to eat and continued to talk.

Silverio recalled his memories of Joe and Tom.

During the 1930s the boys worked on his truck when he was a peddler selling fruits and vegetables in Italian neighborhoods. Each night, the boys brought home a box of food and some money. It meant a great deal during those difficult times. Joe and Tom's mother was Lucia's first cousin. The families were close.

"Silverio, we learned about generosity from you," said Joe. "We carried food to widows, and you never asked to be paid," stated Tom. "We looked to you as the kind of leader we wanted to be. When we went into the service, we thought of your courage and kindness. It helped us through tough times," explained Joe. "Especially when we went to Ponza. We made difficult choices, and you inspired us," asserted Joe.

While the families chatted, Silverio sat back, closed his eyes and remembered....

Emilio Iodice

CHAPTER 2 ━━━━━━━━━━━━━━━━━━━━━━

THE POSTMAN

The night shift was grueling. Twelve hours loading crates of bombs and bullets and live ammunition onto ships bound for theatres of war was exhausting and terrifying. Silverio was weary. He felt most of the blood drained from his body. The day before, a box of explosives slipped from a forklift. The blast was heard across the waterfront. The vehicle and driver were blown to bits. It was not the first time it happened. It would not be the last.

Silverio knew the man. They were friends. He grieved for his widow and children.

It could have been him.

Thoughts of the dangers of the docks and of his wife and child circled his mind as he left the Brooklyn Navy Yard to reach the South Bronx. It was a long drive in the dark. World War II was being fought on two fronts, and America needed all its resources to defeat the Axis powers. It was the fall of 1943. Thousands of ships were being loaded with supplies for the war effort. Millions of workers like him were struggling to bring the nation and the Allies to victory under arduous conditions filled with risks and peril.

Finally, he reached home. It was a small apartment on the second floor of a large tenement, with a kitchen and two tiny bedrooms. The bathroom was a toilet bowl and chain, and a little sink. A bathtub was in the corridor for12 families to use. Hiking up the two flights was like climbing a mountain for a man as weary as Silverio. His wife heard him come in. It was long past midnight. She got up to serve him dinner, which was a warm plate in the oven.

"How are you?" she asked. She saw the lines of fatigue in his face. Silverio's hands were swollen and cracked from lifting boxes and bales. "I'm okay. Tired and hungry. I need to get some rest. I have to get up to go to the market in a few hours to stock up the store with fruits, vegetables, and canned goods. I am on the night shift tomorrow, so

I can spend the day in the shop," he responded with a sigh. He had a small Italian food store in the North Bronx that he and his wife ran.

After a quick meal, Silverio tucked his son in, kissed him, and went to bed. His head throbbed with pain. He fell into a deep sleep when he touched the pillow. Six hours passed. He was awakened by a loud knock on the door. The sound rippled through the apartment and increased his headache.

Silverio got up from his warm bed. He was in his pajamas. He looked through the peephole. It was the postman. Silverio lifted the chain from the lock and slowly opened the door. He yawned. The postman pulled an envelope from his canvas bag and handed it to him. It was a registered letter. The postman asked for his signature to confirm receipt. Silverio signed.

He sensed something was wrong.

He looked at the envelope with concern. A wavy, black "Postage Free" emblem was stamped on the right side emblazoned with "U.S. Army Official Business" on the left. A dark eagle was in the center of the insignia. Beads of sweat poured down Silverio's hair and face as he ran his hand over his curls. Worry wrinkles formed across his forehead. Silverio's imagination flew as he wondered what was enclosed in that yellowish, brown paper.

"Sorry," said Sam, the postman. Stains and holes covered his blue uniform from years of use. Deep lines crisscrossed his face. His mustache and hair were grey from age and anxiety. His back was curved from the weight of his postal sack.

Sam had delivered mail in his neighborhood for thirty years. Each inch had been walked over again and again. The postmen knew the names of those born, raised, and deceased in a three-mile radius of his territory in the South Bronx. Every family was his family. Every child was his child.

"All I do these days is bring telegrams or registered letters like that one. The news is always bad. I fought in World War I, and now we have World War II. I won't be around for the next one, I hope. This is the worst time of my life. Some days, I can't handle it. This morning a naval officer arrived at the post office, who must personally deliver ten letters to families in our area. We are helping him locate the homes. It's awful.

"I brought a dozen messages today, just in our neighborhood. You know the Minelli's down the street? I was at the baptism, communion, and weddings of all their children. Their son Joey is fighting in Europe somewhere. I'm sure the letter was about him. He was a fine boy, and now he is missing in action or dead. If he is lucky, he may be wounded. I hope your letter is not like the one I gave them," he remarked as he walked on to the next house to deliver another note that would break someone's heart.

Normally, Silverio was fearless.

He overcame challenges in the face of formidable odds. From the first moment he set foot in America, he confronted one obstacle after another. At sixteen he landed in New York, without a penny in his pocket, and no one to greet or help him. He spoke not a word of English. He felt illiterate and helpless. Silverio came ashore the day after the Stock Market crashed. Millions suddenly lost their livelihoods as the Great Depression began.

He was determined to survive and succeed despite the harsh times and challenges. Within weeks of his arrival, he started his own business as a peddler of fruits and vegetables. This young immigrant from Italy was courageous and hard working. Business thrived. Yet thousands were suffering and hungry. The economic collapse of America overwhelmed one family after another, like a tidal wave of despair that reached around the world.

Silverio helped anyone and everyone, especially widows. He provided food and clothing for hundreds of families. Jobs were found for young men, and orphans were put through school. Silverio was a leader in his community and admired for his character, honesty, and bravery. But this simple man from Italy was living in unpredictable times. Despite his fortitude, he could not see what was up ahead. He was thirty. After years of sacrifice, he saw progress and peace in his life.

Now all could change with the opening of an envelope.

CHAPTER 3 ━━━━━━━━━

CIVIL DEFENSE

W orld War II was raging in the Atlantic and the Pacific. Most of Silverio's relatives and friends were in uniform. Some were wounded and in military hospitals. Others came home in coffins, or were lost on a battlefield, or were under the soil of a faraway grave.

US Civil Defense Mock Newspaper Article Simulating an Attack on New York,
Courtesy Fallout Shelter, NYC, 2016

Silverio was concerned, since so many depended on him. This young man from Italy was trusted to safeguard his people in time of war. He was the head of Civil Defense in his locality in the South Bronx. His neighborhood was a microcosm of the Island of Ponza, but in America. Thousands from this small rock in the Mediterranean settled in the Big Apple, near Yankee Stadium.

Civil Defense contingency plans were created if New York City was struck. Silverio knew them. Even the bombing of the Bronx was simulated. Authorities imagined the shelling of the zoo, where thousands of creatures could be released to terrorize the population. If New York was attacked, a plan was put into effect to kill all potentially dangerous animals in all the wildlife reserves of the city before another assault occurred.

The Normandie Burning in New York Harbor, February 9th, 1942,
Courtesy New York Historical Society

Fear grew that Axis spies had infiltrated the United States and planned similar incidents like the burning of the French ocean liner Normandie in February 1942. It was the largest and fastest ship afloat. The vessel found itself in the port of New York when hostilities broke out. When America entered the War, it was converted into a troop carrier named "The USS Lafayette" in honor of the great Frenchman who fought in the revolution to free the United States from England.

Poster promoting the Normandie, 1935,
Courtesy French Line

The official version of losing the *Normandie* was "accidental." Apparently, a welder using a blow torch unintentionally ignited bales of burlap, which led to the disaster. Concern rose that German spies carried out the attack on the world's most famous liner right in the heart of America.[1]

German U-boat Attacking a US flag vessel outside New York City,
Courtesy Library of Congress Department of Prints and Photographs

Numerous cargo ships were sunk outside the port of New York by German U-boats. An enemy strike on the city was considered imminent.

To safeguard the homeland, the government needed loyal civilians to assist in the war effort. Constant surveillance and observation was required. Civil Defense officials were the eyes and ears of the country. At sundown, they made sure lights were out. People were to be off the streets in the dark and organized into shelters during drills. Industrial parks, railroads, power stations, and neighborhoods were patrolled. Suspicious movements were monitored and checked.

Emblem of the Federal Civil Defense Administration

Each night Civil Defense workers perched on rooftops to watch the skies with binoculars. Two-way radios alerted the authorities if they saw anything out of the ordinary flying, sailing, or on the ground. Any questionable information was reported.

"That plane is not on a scheduled flight from any of the airports at this hour," Silverio told Antonio. He was watching the skies with his cousin and best friend. They were on the roof of their building. Several pigeon coups and chimneys kept them company on this cold evening in the South Bronx. Silverio had a book of flight schedules. He looked at it with his flashlight. He double-checked the information. "A four-engine aircraft just flew overhead that is not on the list for this hour," Silverio reported to the Central Command unit office near Yankee Stadium. The Center was opened 24 hours a day, seven days a week. "It's military," said someone on the other end. "OK, we will record and report it," and hung up abruptly. Such was the routine for Silverio each night after work. For four hours, he manned the rooftop to see if anything was out of the ordinary to prevent the enemy from reaching the shores of America.

The United States was a land of trust. It was open to all, even to its enemies. Germans and Japanese went to colleges and universities in America. Some were hosted at military facilities and educated along with American military officers.

In 1921, a Japanese Naval Officer studied at Harvard University and later at the U.S. Navy War College. He was familiar with American history, culture, and the armed forces. Eleven years later, as a captain, he read a press report about a military exercise held on February 7th, 1932, at Pearl Harbor in Hawaii, where the Pacific fleet was stationed. The article explained how an air strike on the American fleet could succeed. Nine years later, the officer applied the same techniques when he directed the Japanese attack on Pearl Harbor on December 7th, 1941.

His name was Admiral Isoroku Yamamoto. [1]

---

1   The First Attack: Pearl Harbor," February 7, 1932, https://www.military.com/navy/pearl-harbor-first-attack.html, 1920-1929, Chronology of Courses and Significant Events. U.S. Naval War College. *Retrieved May 29, 2010.*

The trial of Nazi Saboteurs, 1942, Courtesy History.com

CHAPTER 4 ━━━━━━━━━━━━

ESPIONAGE

"The largest invasion of American soil during World War II came in the form of eight Nazi saboteurs sent to the United States on a doomed mission known as Operation Pastorius. The men – all naturalized American citizens who were living in Germany when the conflict began – were tasked with sabotaging the war effort and demoralizing the civilian population through acts of terrorism. In June 1942, U-boats secretly dropped the two four-man crews onto the coast of Amagansett, New York, and Ponte Vedra Beach, Florida. Each team carried up to $84,000 in cash and enough explosives to wage a long campaign of sabotage.

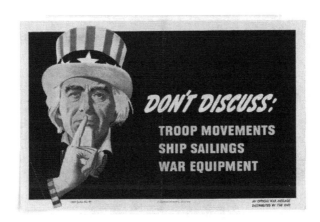

World War II Poster, *Courtesy Library of Congress*

The men had orders to attack transport hubs, hydroelectric power plants, and industrial facilities. But before a single act of sabotage could ever take place, the mission was compromised when George John Dasch, one saboteur from the New York group, turned himself in to the FBI. Dasch was heavily interrogated, and after two weeks the FBI successfully rounded up the remaining saboteurs. Six of the men were executed as spies, while Dasch and an accomplice were jailed for six years before being deported by President Harry Truman."[1]

---

1 "History Stories, 5 Attacks on US Soil During WWII,"
https://www.history.c5om/news/5-attacks-on-u-s-soil-during-world-war-ii

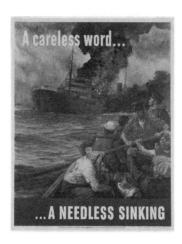

World War II Poster, *Courtesy Library of Congress*

The incident added to the growing paranoia in the country that extended to each metropolis and hamlet in the nation. Personnel in all fields were warned to be especially careful if they were involved in sensitive operations such as where Silverio was working.

World War II Poster, *Courtesy Library of Congress*

He was a longshoreman at the Brooklyn Navy Yard, loading live ammunition onto vessels bound for theatres of war. Silverio was strong, with broad shoulders, big calloused hands, and powerful arms and legs, which gave him the perfect physique for a man destined to haul boxes of bombs and bullets for twelve to fifteen hours a day. His "hook," which he used to grab cargo, was made of tempered steel and weighed five pounds. He could handle it like a tool or a weapon, if need be.

This young man from an Italian rock in the Mediterranean loved America.

He was trusted.

He was ready to give up his life for his adopted land, even if it meant dying on a dock loading ammunition for the war effort.

Emilio Iodice

CHAPTER 5 ▬▬▬▬▬▬▬▬▬▬▬▬▬▬▬▬

THE ENVELOPE

Despite his roles in Civil Defense and on the waterfront, Silverio knew that his status could change at any moment. Wartime telegrams and messages from the government contained frightening news or instructions to report for active duty. What was in that letter marked "Official U.S. Government Business?"

Perhaps he was being drafted to serve in the armed forces. Would he be sent to some distant beach to die under explosions and gunfire? Perhaps someone he loved was dead or missing in action or was a captive in an enemy camp or wounded in a far-off hospital...

The secret was in that envelope.

No matter what, he would face it and deal with it.

His name and address were typed in bold letters on the front. There was no mistake. It was for him.

He opened it.

As he tore the envelope paper, his heart pounded. Inside was a short, handwritten letter in Italian. Another note was typed in English. Silverio was confused. He read:

> *Dear Cousin:*
>
> *It has been seven years since we have seen each other, and I hope you and your family are well. The last time we embraced was in 1937 as you left Ponza with your bride to return to America. I never imagined what could happen in a few years. The war began in June 1940, and two years later I was sent to the front. I went to North Africa as part of the Afrika Korps with the Germans. In May 1943 after months of battles, we surrendered to the Americans. We were exhausted, thirsty, and dying of hunger.*

Thousands of Germans and Italians were rounded up to be sent to prisoner of war camps. We were treated well by the Allies. They nourished us and cared for our wounded and dying.

We were sent to Tunisia and put on a boat to America. After ten days, we landed in the South of the US. We were interrogated and then separated. We were put on a comfortable passenger train for two days and then loaded into buses until we reached a camp in Como, Mississippi. I am writing to you from there. This is the first opportunity I have had, and I am grateful to the Americans for allowing me to send you this letter. I have written to my family in Ponza, but I have no news on how they are. Please come to see me. I am nostalgic for my family and for signs of home.

Your beloved cousin,

Bruno

The letter was accompanied with instructions for visitors to prisoners of war (POWs). Attached to it was a brief letter:

Dear Silverio:

It is extremely important that you come to see your cousin at our camp soon.

I need your urgent assistance.

Sincerely,

Colonel Gregory J. McCarthy[1]

Commandant

Camp Como, Mississippi

---

1   Author's Note: For the sake of practicality, some elements of this story have been fictionalized to fill in gaps that could not be fully substantiated. The name of the commandant of the camp is one of them.

The Commandant of the POW (Prisoner of War) camp wanted to see him?

The words, *"extremely important,"* rang in his mind like a bell.

What was the reason? It sounded ominous and menacing.

Silverio was alarmed. He had a job, ran a store, supported a wife and a 4-year-old son, and worked nearly 24 hours a day to feed his family, send money to his parents in Italy, and cover his debts. Silverio was still paying medical bills for his father with bronchial pneumonia from 10 years earlier. How could he take off from work to go to Mississippi? And where was Mississippi? It was 1200 miles away, over 2000 kilometers, and in the Deep South. It would take two or three days to drive there, if he was lucky.

He had to travel to the *Deep South* to reach Mississippi, where they hated Italians, Catholics, Jews, Blacks, and anyone who was not a White Anglo-Saxon Protestant.

It frightened him.

"You must be crazy," exclaimed his cousin Vincenzo. "You have a job, a business, a family, and you're going to drive more than a thousand miles to visit Bruno? Send him a letter and tell the commandant that you can't go. That is the most dangerous part of America. They hate anyone from the North, and especially us. Haven't you seen newsreels about the Ku Klux Klan? They're everywhere in the South, and you will probably run into them," insisted Vincenzo.

Silverio had seen movies of the Ku Klux Klan burning crosses, lynching blacks, and attacking anyone they felt was different.

Silverio was *different.*

He was born in Italy and was a Catholic who spoke broken English, and who looked and sounded like a foreigner, even though he was a loyal American. Now he had to risk venturing into the shadows of Mississippi to reach his cousin, because the commandant of a POW camp in Mississippi asked him to come.

CHAPTER 6 ━━━━━━━━━━━━━━━

CARLO

While Silverio was reading his message, another letter in Italian was being opened in Wheeling, West Virginia:

> *My Dear Brother Luigi,*
>
> *I hope these few words find you and the family well. I am fine, and, thanks to the Lord and the prayers of our family, I have survived the War.*
>
> *I am in a prison camp in the US state of Alabama. My entire division surrendered to the Allies at El Alamein. We were taken as prisoners of war and sent across the ocean to this place that we share with Germans. Before our general decided to lay down our arms, we were told by the Fascists and the Nazis that the Americans would either execute us or put us in slave labor camps. They wanted us to fight to the death.*
>
> *We were told that the Allies would torture and brainwash us, and we would not see Italy again. Those were lies. The Germans forced us to give up our water and food and left us to die in the desert. Many of my comrades perished in my arms. We were famished and dehydrated to the point of death. The condition of our troops was terrible. We were saved by the American army. They immediately took care of us. We were given food and water and those who were ill and weak were hospitalized.*
>
> *In the camp, we have been treated with respect and dignity. We eat abundantly and sleep in decent barracks with hot and cold running water. We are forming soccer teams, and the Americans gave us jobs. I bake bread and pizza, just like I did at home. They even pay me.*

> *We were told those of us with family in America can be reunited with them. I have asked permission from the camp authorities to visit you and the family.*
>
> *Your prayers, dear brother, saved my life.*
>
> *I miss my family much and long to embrace you again, after all these years.*
>
> *With all my love,*
>
> *Your devoted brother, Carlo*

Luigi could not believe what he had read. His brother was alive and well and on his way to see him! He sat down in shock. Overcome with emotion, Luigi cried tears of joy and thanksgiving.

Luigi had raised Carlo like a son. The boy was special. He was the baby, and he even looked like Luigi, who was handsome, dark, and tall. He changed his diapers, taught him how to speak, eat, walk, and play soccer. They did chores around the farm together. Carlo followed him everywhere and hung on Luigi's words, like listening to a philosopher or a teacher.

Luigi immigrated to America from a small town outside of Avellino in 1930 with his wife and daughter. He was the oldest of five brothers and three sisters. Their parents, Maria and Agostino, were poor farmers who could barely feed themselves, let alone eight children. They had a small house, without running water or electricity. Luigi helped the family survive. He rose at dawn to tend the animals, clean their stalls, plow the fields, and then went to school. At age twenty, he realized his future was to be like his father: born poor and die poor. Luigi went to America to have a better life or to die trying.

"Antonietta," said Luigi with tears in his eyes. "Carlo is alive! He is in Alabama. My baby brother is coming here!" he wept. He held the letter as if it was a piece of sacred parchment. "Oh my God, our prayers were answered!" exclaimed his wife. She made the sign of the cross.

Luigi had married "the girl next door." Antonietta lived on the adjacent farm. She came from a large family. She was not attractive, yet she had a solar quality, was happy, and worked while singing and even dancing. Large, dark brown eyes and black hair gave her a Moorish look. Antonietta was strong, hardworking, and skillful. Like many women of that era, she knitted, made clothes by hand, and was a splendid cook and homemaker. She had all the qualities of a fine wife and mother. She willingly left her farm family to be with her husband.

Luigi and Antonietta were too poor to have a reception to celebrate their wedding. They saved for their passage to America and spent their "honeymoon" on a freighter bound for Baltimore. It was uncomfortable, but they were happy and optimistic. They were bound for the New World and new beginnings. In Wheeling, they lived with relatives until they could rent their own apartment. Luigi drove a truck. He and his wife learned to speak, read, and write English well and became citizens. They were patriotic and loved America. Luigi earned enough to start his own general store and send money to his parents in Italy. He sold everything, from nails to cheese, and flour to textiles. It was a good living in a growing town that produced coal, steel, and iron.

Carlo was drafted at 18 to fight in "Mussolini's War," as Luigi called it. Now Luigi's "baby brother" was on American soil. Ten years had passed since they had seen each other. When Luigi left, Carlo was heartbroken. Luigi was his idol. Carlo would spend hours listening to him about his dreams of America and raising a family to live in freedom and prosperity, instead of the tyranny and poverty of the Fascist regime.

"I will be back in no time," lied Luigi to Carlo as the little boy cried at the departure of his brother. "You will never come back!" cried Carlo. He was devastated. As Luigi boarded the ship in Naples, Carlo wept and ran after the vessel as it left the dock, like a puppy following the boat of its master, until it disappeared over the horizon. He sobbed for days. He believed he would not see his brother again.

The boy never recovered from the loss.

Carlo waited for Luigi's letters. He hid them in a secret place, like precious jewels. He read and reread them, and imagined the life his brother was leading. On Carlo's birthdays, Luigi sent him a dollar. He wrote on each bill, "Dearest Carlo, Happy Birthday Little Brother, Love, Luigi." When Carlo went to war, he had eight U.S. dollars he carried in a belt under his clothes.

He felt the love of his brother would protect him from harm.

CHAPTER 7

ANTONIA AND MICHELE

Luigi's aunt and uncle went to the U.S. in the 1920s. Antonia worked as a cleaning woman and a cook. She did laundry until she saved enough to open a boarding house for Italian coal miners. She was a beautiful woman with a statuesque body, and she was intelligent and clever. She ran the small hotel with care, hard work, and dignity. It was a job filled with sacrifices and challenges, but it was better than living in an overcrowded town in southern Italy without money and without a future.

"I have saved $120," said Antonia with pride to her husband, Michele. "My job at the mine is going well. With my promotion, we will buy a refrigerator and a washing machine," replied Michele. "I can stop washing by hand and won't have to change any more ice in the box," beamed Antonia. She hugged her husband and kissed him. After years of hard work, the couple was enjoying the fruits of their labor.

In America, the couple sacrificed, yet earned well. Antonia's dream was to return to Italy with a trunk filled with dollars and gold coins and open a store. She was married in the church of the Assumption in their town. Her uncle was the pastor, and he presided over the wedding. It was a simple ceremony. Her wedding dress was her great-grandmother's, and it was worn by twelve women before her. It would be passed down to other brides for generations.

She was 16 when Michele proposed to her. He was two years older and was strong and healthy, and he was from a good family, like Antonia's. He was tall with wavy, black hair and dark, brown eyes that smiled when he smiled. Michele watched Antonia grow from a little girl to a woman. She blossomed like the violets and wildflowers that covered their land in the early spring. Antonia was raised with the values of marriage, family, and being at the side of her husband as he struggled to provide for her and their children.

Michele rose from a simple miner to become a boss. He worked for years and learned every aspect of coal mining. He supervised teams of Italians and trained them. It was backbreaking and dangerous.

Each day, Michele never knew if he would come home alive.

Accidents were a daily occurrence.

Courtesy Fitchburg Sentinel, 1907

Mine disasters happened frequently. In West Virginia, memories were still fresh of the coal mine explosion of 1907, when over 500 miners died. Coal mining was a perilous job.

Miners had no rights, earned poorly, and risked their lives constantly.

Families were forever in fear.

Michele and Antonia were deeply in love and devoted to their only child, Helena. She was gorgeous. She had dark eyes and black hair that gleamed with the sun of the Mediterranean. She was lively, quick, intelligent, and pleasant. She was the joy of her parents.

Antonia and Michele were content.

Then tragedy struck.

Coal Miners, *Courtesy miningfacts.com*

Michele's life was the mine and the company that owned it. The community depended completely on it. Miners and their families shopped in company stores. They went to doctors and lawyers who worked for the mine. Churches were supported by the company.

Even the undertakers worked for the mine.

During the first third of the 20th century, concern grew about worker safety, but little was done. The New Deal tried to help miners. Yet by the mid-1930s, there was no workman's compensation, pensions, or government inspections of mines.

Miners' salaries were low, but work was steady, unless something unexpected happened. For Michele and Antonia, the unexpected came on their daughter's eleventh birthday.

The couple could not have other children. Fertility problems affected Antonia after the baby was born. They thanked God for Helena. She was affectionate and good in school. They were proud she was a citizen by birth. It was a conquest. Antonia and Michele naturalized after a long, complex, process. Helena was at their side when they swore allegiance to the Constitution.

The morning before Helena's birthday, Antonia explained to Michele about the party she planned with a few Italian families and their children. Michele was a happy man. He was delighted with his wife and little girl. The next day he would leave the mine early and bring home beer and homemade wine. He and Antonia would give Helena a gold bracelet. On the back, it read, *With Love, Mamma and Papa*. "Tomorrow, we will have a dozen children over," said Antonia with a warm smile. "This needs to be a special birthday for Helena. She is growing so fast and is becoming more beautiful each day."

Antonia was amazing. She ran the boarding house single-handedly, keeping control of twenty young, virile men who suffered from nostalgia for Italy and the sweet companionship of a woman. Antonia was strong and kept her distance. Her boarders respected her and her husband, and admired them for their ability and hard work.

Michele and Antonia were kind and generous. They were mother and father to the Italians. They helped them settle into their new life and resolve problems ranging from health to immigration, sending money home, and dealing with American law.

CHAPTER 8 ━━━━━━━━━━━━

THE MINE

The night before the party, Antonia had a horrible nightmare. She saw death. A dark rider, clothed in black, was on a horse snorting flames and smoke. He galloped to their house and tossed a skull through the window.

Antonia woke screaming. She leaped from her bed. She searched for her husband. It was dawn, and he was on his way to the mine. She ran out of the house, but she could not reach him in time to prevent what she saw in her heart.

Michele led 150 miners into the mine's deepest shaft. They were to shore up the walls of a section that had collapsed from water infiltration. Several crews repaired the damage while others dug out fresh coal. A deadly risk of coal mining was methane gas. It was odorless and colorless.

Every mine had birds in cages taken down the shaft. If a bird died, they knew there was gas and would immediately evacuate.

"Willy, you take these men to number four. Check those beams and reinforce them. Don't take any chances. If you see water in number five, let Joe know so we can send down the pumps. Johnny, take the rest of the crew to number six and start digging that new vein. Pile it on the sides until we have enough to send on the train," ordered Michele to his team.

After several hours, Michele's men were settled and operating in the key areas of the mine. All was proceeding normally.

Suddenly, a miner raced to him with a birdcage.

The animal was dead.

Carbon monoxide and methane gas were seeping into the shaft. An explosion could happen at any moment.

Michele gave orders to suspend all work immediately and evacuate the area. Like the captain of a sinking ship saving his passengers, he loaded the lifts with his men and sent them to safety. Seconds after the miners reached the surface, a spark from the elevator motor ignited the gas and set off a massive explosion in the center of the mine.

The blast happened when all the men made it to the top, except one.

Michele.

Mine Explosion, *Courtesy History.com*

Antonia heard the loud boom of thunder two miles away.

Her heart stopped.

She raced to the mine. Helena ran with her. When she reached the site, she saw a plume of smoke and fire shooting up from the pit, with flames soaring a hundred feet into the air. She ran to the shaft, but she was stopped by the miners. "Michele! Michele!" she shouted. One held her tightly. He told her what had happened.

She fainted as Helena stood speechless, trembling with fear.

What took place was a great blur for Antonia. Michele's body was brought up from the hole. The coal company doctor examined the body. He determined death was caused by an accidental detonation of gas that led to the collapse of the shaft. The firm was not at fault. It was an occupational hazard. The company paid for the undertaker to do a minimum burial procedure. Within two days, the love of Antonia's life was gone. The coal company mailed her a check for $50. They considered it a generous gift. Yet, for a man who gave them his most precious possession, his life, it was a mockery.

CHAPTER 9 ▬▬▬▬▬▬▬▬▬▬▬▬▬▬▬▬▬▬▬▬

HELENA

Antonia was devastated. She was inconsolable. She tried to continue to work, but her mind gave way to depression. She knew she had to live for Helena, but her mental state deteriorated. It affected her physical condition, and she aged rapidly. Within two years of losing Michele, she died of a massive heart attack. Husband and wife were buried side- by-side in a Catholic cemetery in Wheeling. It was filled with Italian coal miners and their loved ones who never were able to fully realize the American Dream.

Helena was an orphan.

Michele and Antonia were wise enough to prepare a will leaving their modest home, land, proceeds from life insurance, and some money and mining stock to their daughter. It was not much, but it was enough to pay for her education at a Catholic school for girls. They left everything in a trust fund managed by their lawyer, which she could not touch until she was 21.

Antonia's brother, Alberto, took in the young girl as part of his family with three other daughters. Helena quickly realized her situation differed from her cousins. Her aunt, Carmela, complained there was never enough food to feed another mouth. Helena became a Cinderella-like servant who worked for her keep.

She grew into a ravishing beauty who attracted envy and hatred from her new family. Her hair glowed like obsidian. She had fair skin and large, black eyes. The young girl entered adolescence with the stunning looks of a Greek goddess.

"That miserable lawyer of yours won't let you touch your money until you are 21. All he does is pay for your schooling. And what about your room and board?" scolded Carmela. "We have to feed you and care for you and we get no money. As soon as you are an adult, either you pay us each month, or you get out of here," she insisted, while her husband looked on with fear. Alberto dreaded his wife. He loved his niece, but he could do little to protect her against a woman only interested in money. He earned well by selling mining equipment, but it was never enough for Carmela. "And make sure you clean the carpets and wash the porch and steps before you go to school," she commanded. Helena obeyed.

Each day was an agony. Her escape was school and a dream of fleeing when she reached maturity. The years passed. She missed her parents. She clung to a photo taken on the day of their wedding. She was twelve months from her 21st birthday and freedom.

Helena was working part-time in a bakery and earning enough to continue her education after high school. She took a correspondence course to be a secretary and administrative assistant. She also qualified to be an elementary school teacher. On the way home from work, one day, she met her cousin Gabriela, who was the daughter of Luigi and Antonietta. The girls had gone to the same Catholic schools and were close.

 "My father received a letter from his brother yesterday," said Gabriela. "He is an Italian soldier in a prisoner of war camp in Alabama. He is papa's youngest brother, and he has asked permission to leave the camp to visit us. He may come at the end of this month," she said. "What is his name?" asked Helena.

"His name is Carlo," said Gabriela, "He is very handsome. Mamma says he looks like Rudolf Valentino. Can you imagine? We are all so excited to meet him. I have a picture of him. Doesn't he look just like Valentino?" Helena studied the photo. Carlo was the image of the Italian silent film star. He had wavy black hair, sharply cut features, and large dark eyes. He seemed to stare at her. "Carlo is a nice name," said Helena.

She repeated his name in her mind.

She imagined the sound of his voice.

Her heart fluttered.

It was a sensation she would only understand when she came face to face with the man who would change her life.

CHAPTER 10

SILVERIO'S DECISION

The farthest Silverio had driven was to Boston and Detroit. Those were trips in the North. He knew people along the way.

Mississippi was like the planet Mars.

It was unknown and terrifying.

He did not want to go. But Silverio knew something vital was at stake, so he had to act.

The commandant warned him that a dramatic event was to happen. Silverio sensed it in his bones. The American officer needed his help. Silverio felt responsible to Italy, America, and his family to help him, no matter how high the risk.

"Don't go," pleaded Lucia. "Please don't go. I feel something will happen to you. Who will take care of me and our son if you have an accident or those people in the South hurt you?" She wept. Tears poured down her cheeks. Her lips were trembling. They had been married 6 years. Each day was a struggle to pay bills, raise their 4-year-old boy, run their store, and deal with the heartbreak of war.

Four months earlier, the ferry, *Santa Lucia*, going from the mainland to Ponza was shot at by Allied aircraft. The machine-gun fire was a warning for the boat to no longer leave its port. The Fascist government painted the passenger vessel battle grey and mounted a gun on it that no one could operate. They thought it would be a deterrent. Instead, it turned an innocent liner into a deadly target.

The next day, the *Santa Lucia* was ordered to leave for Gaeta. Two hours into the voyage, British fighters machine-gunned the vessel. The passengers hid below deck. Moments later the aircraft released torpedoes that struck the ferry. The ship exploded and sank in less than a minute. Over 100 people died, including Lucia's brother, Benedetto. The boy who grew up with Lucia, whom she loved dearly, was entombed in a watery grave between Ponza and the Island of Ventotene.

Her nephew, Salvatore, was a prisoner in a German concentration camp. Lucia adored him. She watched him grow up with her father in Ponza. He was his first grandson and had his name. The boy was handsome, brilliant, wise, and charming. Salvatore could fish, swim, and read and write at an early age.

Now, like so many other soldiers, he was starving in a Nazi prison.

Lucia knew he would not return home.

Her brothers were all in uniform, fighting on the high seas or in Africa. Each day a message arrived in Little Ponza about losing a loved one who was either fighting for America or fighting for Italy. It was horrible. All Lucia had left were her son and her husband. "Write back to them and say you can't go because of your job and us," she insisted.

Silverio was tortured. He understood the risks even better than his wife. He had no choice. His relatives and friends were against him.

He believed God wanted him to go.

"I have to leave," he told Lucia. "Something deadly is going to happen at that camp. I may be the only person who can save the situation. Lives are in danger. I will be careful. I will call you. Nothing will happen. Everything will be fine. I will return home safely, I swear," said Silverio as he held his wife in his arms.

In his heart, he knew it was an empty promise.

CHAPTER 11 ━━━━━━━━━━━━━━━━━━━━━━━━━━━━━━━━

POWS IN AMERICA

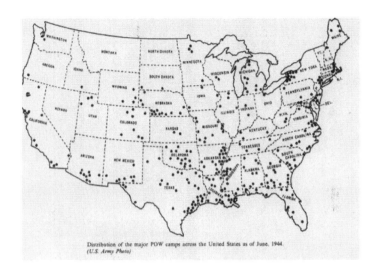

Distribution of the major POW camps across the United States as of June, 1944.
(U.S. Army Photo)

Information about prisoners of war in the U.S. was slowly emerging. By 1943, there were over 1,000 camps across the continental United States. Hundreds of thousands of German and Italian soldiers were interned, in sites from California to New York, and from Illinois to Texas. Nearly every state of the union had men who had been captured on the battlefield.

America abided by the 1929 Geneva Conventions, which it signed along with Germany, Italy, Japan, and other countries. The accord was clear in the way former combatants were to be treated. Once they laid down their arms, they were to reside in decent facilities; be fed and clothed properly; not forced to work in war-related industries; and not tortured, either physically or mentally. They were to be treated humanely and with dignity.

Following the defeat of the Afrika Korps, tens of thousands of German and Italian prisoners were shipped to the U.S. and landed in Norfolk, Virginia. They were assigned to various camps, including

German prisoners of war, including members of the Afrika Korps,
marching through Aliceville, Ala., in 1943.

Camp Clinton and Camp Como in Mississippi.

"At Norfolk, the prisoners who were assigned to Clinton expected a slow freight train to carry them to their destination. Instead, they boarded a sleek, comfortable passenger train. Two days later they arrived."

Camp Clinton, one of four major POW base camps established in Mississippi, was unique among the other camps, because it housed the highest-ranking German officers. Twenty-five generals lived there, along with several colonels, majors, and captains. The generals had special housing and were given special treatment. Lower ranking officers had to content themselves with small apartments.

For example, General Hans-Jürgen von Arnim was interned in Camp Clinton, after he surrendered to the British in North Africa in May 1943. Von Arnim had been appointed by General Erwin Rommel to head up a division and later replaced Rommel in his role as head of German forces in North Africa. Arnim lived in a house in Camp Clinton and had a car and driver.
Some swore that General von Arnim attended movies in Jackson, Mississippi, because the movie theater was the only air-conditioned place in town. Food was not a complaint from the prisoners. Most

were prepared by German cooks with ingredients furnished by the U.S. Army. A sample breakfast was cereal, toast, corn flakes, jam, coffee, milk, and sugar. A typical lunch was roast pork, potato bread, carrots, and ice water. Supper might be meatloaf, scrambled eggs, coffee, milk, and bread. Beer could be bought in the canteen.

Individual barracks fielded teams for sports as diverse as horseshoes, volleyball, and soccer. Athletic contests among the barracks were highly competitive, and tournaments selected the winners. Prisoners at Camp Shelby, for example, reported the outcome of athletic events in the camp's newspaper, *The Mississippi Post.*"[1]

The installations were small towns with libraries, movie theatres, hospitals, doctors, and dentists, educational, religious, and recreational facilities, and opportunities for the prisoners to work and be paid. They received the daily, national minimum wage of about a dollar a day. Jobs were in agriculture, like the cotton fields and forestry. They were paid extra to do odd jobs.

Many prisoners of war took considerable savings with them by the time they were sent back to Germany or Italy.

1   "German Prisoners of War in Mississippi, 1943-1946," By John Ray Skates, Mississippi History Now, http://mshistorynow.mdah.state.ms.us/articles/233/german-prisoners-of-war-in-mississippi-1943-1946

CHAPTER 12 ━━━━━━━━━━━━━━

POWS AND THE ENEMY

Allied prisoners of war were by no means treated with the same dignity and respect by the Japanese and the Germans.

American Prisoners liberated from a Japanese camp, *Courtesy US National Archives*

Instead, the Germans and the Japanese were notorious in the way they persecuted and tormented POWs.

Japanese beheading POW, *Courtesy Pinterest*

Japanese brutalities against former enemies included starvation, torture, random executions, and even medical experiments.

U.S. Olympic star, Lou Zamperini, was an officer in World War II who was captured by the Japanese. Laura Hilenbrand chronicled Zamperini's story in *"Unbroken."* In its review of the book, *The Boston Globe* focused on his time in captivity:

"Zamperini's journey into four consecutive Japanese POW camps with names like Execution Island and Punishment Camp is compelling — until the descriptions of torture overwhelm. POWs lived in deathly shacks filled with lice, rats, and snow in winter, and floors covered in 'wiggling maggots' in summer. Gruel was thin, and servings were often cut in half as punishment for any infraction. Zamperini shared his meager servings with other POWs. Evil overseers named the Weasel, the Quack, and the Bird were sadistic tormentors who administered unbridled beatings and unjust punishments to Zamperini. 'Punctuating the passage of each day were beatings... Dozens of men were lined up and clubbed in the knees.' Zamperini was enslaved on coal barges and in salt mines where 'the salt liquefied in his sweat... burning fissures in his skin.' He cleaned a pig sty with his bare hands... POWs also lived while knowing about Japan's 'kill-all" policy: All prisoners would be executed if rescue became imminent." [1]

The Germans did not respect the rights of POWs, and they committed atrocities against non-combatants from the start of the War in 1939 until the end in 1945.

"Immortalized in the film *The Great Escape,* the mass breakout from POW camp Stalag Luft III on March 24-25, 1944, was swiftly followed by terrible retribution – the cold-blooded murder of 50 recaptured prisoners, on Hitler's direct orders." [2]

Over 3 million Soviet prisoners were killed during the German invasion of Russia. Most died of deliberate starvation and summary executions. Numerous incidents were reported and documented

---

1   "To Hell and Back," *The Boston Globe,*
http://archive.boston.com/ae/books/articles/2010/11/14/harrowing_account_of_wwii_pow_who_survived_a_brutal_captivity/

2   Simon Read, "The Great Escape murders: How the Nazi slaughter of escaped heroes led to one of post-war Europe's biggest manhunts." Mail Online, Published: 22:00 GMT, 2 March 2013 | Updated: 16:43 GMT, 18 March 2013, https://www.dailymail.co.uk/home/moslive/article-2285629/Nazi-killers-How-Great-Escape-murders-led-post-war-Europes-biggest-manhunts.html

300 Polish Soldiers Executed by the Nazis on September 9th, 1939,
Courtesy Polish Military Bureau in Berlin, 1950

51

Allied Airmen who attempted to escape from Stalag Luft III were executed. *Courtesy Mail Online*

during and after the war. War crime trials were held to prosecute those involved.

"On January 20th, 1943, a young Polish farm worker from Ebersbach, near Wurttemberg, Germany, was hanged because of sexual relations he had with the farmer's daughter. All slave workers from five kilometers around were rounded up and brought in to witness the penalty for such a crime. About the same time, ten German women in Augsburg were jailed for terms of four to ten months for having sexual relations with French prisoners of war. In Duisburg, a twenty-two-year-old woman was sent to a concentration camp for the same crime; her twenty-six-year- old Polish friend was sent to the camp at Neuengamme and hanged on June 18th, 1942. Between May and August 1942, the Gestapo dealt with 4,960 cases of forbidden relations between Germans and foreign slave workers." [3]

Even the Allies were accused of isolated incidents of killing defeated soldiers instead of taking them prisoners. As the war ended, millions of German soldiers surrendered to the Allies to avoid falling into the hands of the Red Army. The human avalanche resulted in prisoners being kept in poor conditions until the final German surrender, which would allow them to return home.

3   George Duncan's "Lesser Known Facts of World War II"
http://members.iinet.net.au/~gduncan/1943.html#lesser_known_1943

Axis prisoners of war in the U.S. were respected and allowed privileges, in addition to being properly nourished, clothed, and housed. By the end of World War II, over 425,000 prisoners of war were on American soil. Most were German.

Italians numbered over 51,000. They were organized in 21 camps in 18 states.

CHAPTER 13 ━━━━━━━━━━━━━━━━━━━━━━━━━━

ITALIAN POWS IN AMERICA

Italian Prisoners of War at a US internment camp, c. 1943, *Courtesy, US National Archives*

Most Italians were sympathetic to the Allies, particularly since millions of their fellow countrymen were living in America. Some Italian POWs accepted the option of enrolling in Italian Service Units, because Italy had joined the side of the Allies in 1943. Some went into combat, while most stayed behind in POW facilities and were given jobs that allowed freedom of movement, with permission.

Diehard Nazis and SS officers were not trusted. They posed special problems and had to be under constant surveillance. Some former SS officers, for instance, fought openly with other Germans to force them not to cooperate with the enemy. Doctrinaire Nazis demanded that the battle to defeat the Allies should go on.

Italian officers, inculcated with Fascist values, often refused any form of cooperation. Some common soldiers, who grew up under

Fascist poster calling for revenge against the Allied takeover of Italian East Africa, 1943,
Courtesy, Italian National Archives

Mussolini and swore allegiance to the ideals of Il Duce, wanted to continue the struggle, even though Italy surrendered in September 1943 and joined the Allied side against the Germans.

Italian prisoners faced a crisis of conscience.

Would they betray the Germans, who they fought alongside with, or would they resist? Would they cooperate with the Americans or continue to fight them even on the native soil of the United States? Most Italian and German prisoners submitted to their situation and lived their time as POWs peacefully.

Some did not.

Those who continued to swear allegiance to the Axis cause were considered non-compliant and called "NONS." They were sent to special camps where they were subject to control and observation.

German Prisoners of War in Mississippi, 1943, *Courtesy, National Archives*

Several facilities were in Mississippi.

In Como, Mississippi, many Italians and Germans who declined to comply with the rules of disengagement were interned. For them, the conflict went on; they refused to conduct themselves nonviolently and insisted that they would escape if given the chance. They were treated with the same respect as other POWs and were extended most of the same basic benefits, but they were kept under special surveillance.

German Prisoners of War, 1943, *Courtesy, Arkansas History Commission*

For example, prisoners were given a daily allowance of about 10 cents in "chits," which were coupons that could be used in the camp canteen to buy many goods, from food, beer, and cigarettes to cosmetics and toiletries.[1]

Most POWs gained weight and improved their health during their time in America. By the time they returned home, they were cured of battle scars and wounds. Italian prisoners, who received special permission to leave the camps, visited relatives across the US.

Some fell in love.

There are numerous tales of women who went to Italy after the war, were reunited with their POW lovers, got married, and returned as couples to the U.S. [2]

Even Silverio heard stories of some prisoners being allowed special opportunities to be with family members, particularly during holidays.

---

1   Camp Como opened in June 1943 and held over 2600 German prisoners and numerous Italians until it closed in November, 1945. Chits were issued in 1, 5, 10, and 25 cent denominations, http://worldandmilitary-notes.com/pow/como-mississippi-usa-pow-camp

2   Stories like these and others are part of a splendid documentary prepared by the Istituto Luce, "Prisoners in Paradise, Historical Narrative and Scholarly Analysis," by Camilla Calamandrei, which can be found on this Amazon site: https://www.amazon.it/Prigionieri-Paradiso-Camilla-Calamandrei/dp/B0041KXHPA/ref=sr_1_6?ie =UTF 8&qid=1530782284&sr=8-6&keywords=prigionieri+del+paradiso

Camp Como Chits, Courtesy, *World Military Notes*

Liberation

CHAPTER 14 ▬▬▬▬▬▬▬▬▬▬▬▬▬▬▬

CARLO LEAVES THE CAMP

"**H**ere are your train and bus tickets. Make sure you have your camp ID with you. This is a letter from the Commandant. It allows you safe passage from Alabama to West Virginia and back. You have an allowance of $10 for your expenses. Your pass expires in exactly 10 days. If you are not back by then, an all-points bulletin will be sent to the FBI to arrest you. If you violate the rules, you will be put in a special cell and lose your privileges. Do you understand?" explained the Sergeant to Carlo. "I do, and I am grateful to you for allowing me to visit my brother," he responded with a broad smile.

Carlo's teeth were white and perfect, which made him photogenic and gave him a movie star image. He was delighted to be alive, to be on U.S. soil, and now about to see his brother again. He had been in the camp for three months. In that time, he changed physically and mentally. He was stronger and healthier than ever. Carlo's battle wounds were healed. A grenade blast shattered his upper and lower leg muscles. He barely stood when he arrived at the camp. The doctors and the rehabilitation team cared for him. He recovered his ability to walk without pain. Now an Italian American soldier was helping him call on his family in the U.S.

The Sergeant was from Brooklyn. His parents were from a small town near Palermo. His first language was Sicilian. He was selected to work at the camp because he spoke "Italian." His dialect was understood to a large extent by the prisoners who came from all parts of Italy. At the camp, there were translators in German, but most were Italian.

Carlo packed a travel case with his clothes and personal effects. He was given a new suit, shirts, and ties. With the money he earned in the camp bakery, he purchased two cartons of cigarettes and three bottles of perfume. He also bought a few U.S. Army insignias as souvenirs for Luigi's young sons. He wondered why he instinctively bought the third bottle of perfume. The first was for his sister-in-law, Antonietta, and the second was for his niece, Gabriela. But who was the third one for?

Something compelled him to acquire another gift — but for whom?

The Sergeant drove him to the train station. Carlo wore simple clothes for the 600-mile trip to Wheeling. He would change into his new suit shortly before arriving. The Sergeant gave Carlo a bag with a bottle of water and some sandwiches. They had grown fond of each other in the four months since Carlo's arrival. "Take this little book with you, Carlo," said the Sergeant. "It has English phrases translated into Italian, and vice versa. It is done phonetically so you can easily pronounce the words, if you need to speak English." Carlo was filled with emotion at the compassion and kindness of this soldier, who was but a little older than he was.

For him, the Sergeant represented America and the strength of a great nation that could be magnanimous even to its enemies.

Carlo boarded the train and waved goodbye to the Sergeant. A tear of gratitude ran down his cheek. As the train moved, goosebumps ran up and down his spine.

He suddenly felt he was on a rendezvous with destiny.

CHAPTER 15 ━━━━━━━━━━━━━━━━━━━━━━━━━

SILVERIO DEPARTS

Silverio decided he would leave immediately for Camp Como. He showed the letters to his supervisors on the waterfront and in Civil Defense. He was given two weeks of leave. His store was left in the hands of his brother. He set about carefully preparing for his trip.

A valise was packed with new clothes for Bruno. Boxes of food were prepared with homemade Italian salami, sausage and cheese, and cakes and sweets. It was enough for a small army. He wanted to bring some of his wine, but feared passing state lines with alcohol, especially in the South. He took $100 in cash and rolls of coins for phone calls. Silverio always had a pocketknife with him.

For some strange reason, he stored two baseball bats, some short and long lead pipes, and his longshoreman steel hooks under the compartment of the spare tire in the Cadillac. He wondered why he felt obliged to bring these things with him.

He would learn soon enough.

1931 Cadillac, Courtesy, Fleetwood Metal Body Co.

Silverio loaded up his car. He had a 1931 Cadillac convertible. It was a stunning auto, painted metallic green, with gorgeous, white-walled tires. The car was a dozen years old but in excellent condition, with a powerful 12-cylinder engine that could pull a vehicle ten times its weight. It had huge wheels and a truck-like suspension system. Silverio used it for everything, from loading fruit and vegetable crates to touring with the family. It was his most precious possession.

He would now depend on it to take him to Mississippi.

CHAPTER 16 ━━━━━━━━━━━━━━━━━━━━━━━

ANTONIO

Silverio asked his cousin, Antonio, to accompany him. Antonio also worked in the Brooklyn Navy Yard. Silverio had introduced him to his supervisors, who gave him a job. He was tall, handsome, and very strong. Antonio could not drive, but he was a brave and loyal relative and friend.

He also loved his cousin's wine.

Antonio always assisted Silverio in the crushing of the fruit and the bottling, after fermentation was completed.

One year, Silverio asked him to fill his glass jugs.

The procedure was simple. Antonio was to take a rubber hose, put one end in the barrel and the other end in his mouth and suck out the air. Almost immediately, the brew would pour from the tube into the bottles. The method was repeated after a jug was filled and another took its place. Antonio swallowed a mouthful of wine before inserting the spout in the flask. By the time he completed fifty gallons, he had consumed five liters. He was drunk. He staggered out of the cellar and into Silverio's back yard. It was filled with snow. A blizzard was underway, covering everything in sight.

Antonio disappeared.

The next day, his wife called Silverio and asked where her husband was. "I thought he went home, after he filled the bottles in the cellar," responded Silverio. Another day passed and his cousin could not be found. Early in the morning of the third day, Silverio was about to call the police when he was struck by an unforgettable vision.

His station wagon was in the driveway covered in snow. Silverio shoveled to liberate the car. A door suddenly opened. Antonio stumbled out. "Good morning Silverio," he said. His words were slurred and hard to understand. While Silverio watched in amazement, his cousin wobbled to the metro station and took the train to Brooklyn.

It was the last time Silverio asked Antonio to help him bottle wine.

CHAPTER 17 ━━━━━━━━━━━━

THE COAL THIEVES

Courtesy, the Library of Congress

Silverio and Antonio were grateful they had jobs.

It was not always this way.

The endless years of unemployment and misery of the 1930s left permanent scars on minds and hearts.

When the Great Depression began, blacks, minorities, and immigrants were the first fired and the last hired.

Millions lost their jobs after the Wall Street Crash of 1929. The dark shadow of hunger and misery fell on America as people starved, because they could not buy food or froze because they could not buy coal to heat their homes.

"You remember the winter of '33, Antonio?" asked Silverio? "How can I forget it," he replied. "My teeth chatter when I think about how cold it was and how poor we were. It snowed so much in December that you could not see the cars anymore. They were buried. My wife and kids were hungry and freezing. I was out of work for two years. We got some food from a soup kitchen and the church, but it was not enough.

"We went to bed famished and woke up starving. Then you knocked on the door. I can still feel the weight of the box filled with vegetables, fruit, cheese, bread, pasta, and salami. We needed coal for the boiler, but we had no money to buy it. We got into the truck and drove down to the rail yards. There were piles of discarded coal everywhere. We took as much as we could. It took an hour. The truck was filled with twenty bushels. Then we heard, 'Hey, you! What are you doing there?' It was a railroad guard. He took out his gun as he ran toward us. I was afraid. We jumped into the truck. It would not start. I got out and cranked it up, again and again. The guard was a hundred feet in front of us when he began shooting. Just then the engine turned. I got in and we drove. I heard the shots and almost fainted. Three bullets went through the windshield past our heads," explained Antonio. His voice trembled. "We got out of the yard just as the police cars showed up."

"We had enough coal to keep us warm for the winter," said Silverio, smiling. "And the bullet holes are still there."

Courtesy, the Library of Congress

CHAPTER 18

JOE AND TOM

Maria sat weeping, as if her sons were dead. Her husband, Enzo, was at work. She opened the two letters. They began, "Greetings from the President of the United States." Her boys, Joe and Tom, were drafted to fight. Joe was 21, and Tom had just turned 20.

It was four months after the Japanese bombed Pearl Harbor. The voice of President Franklin Roosevelt reverberated in her mind as he asked for a declaration of war against the empire of Japan. The echo of Benito Mussolini proclaiming war on America a few days later was like an arrow in her heart and gave Maria recurring nightmares of her sons dying on a battlefield.

Joe was a plumber and Tom was a mechanic. They were splendid sons. Honest, handsome, healthy, and hardworking is the way she described them in her letters to her family on the Island of Ponza in Italy. Now the United States was at war with her homeland. It was dreadful. Her boys grew up with Italian values and traditions. They spoke the language at home, knew all about the food, music, and lifestyle of the Old Country, but Joe and Tom were Americans.

Like most children of Italians born in America, they struggled to preserve the wonders of their ethnicity while assimilating into the New World. It was difficult, and now with her homeland at war with the country she loved, it became a torment for Maria.

Her boys would soon be in uniform and on their way to a camp for training, and then on a ship to land on a beach, to suffer and die.

She felt they were gone, and she would not see them again.

"Arnie and Ralph were shipped out this morning," said Joe to his brother as they opened a second bottle of beer. "Ralph said they're on their way to Texas for basic, and then who knows where," responded Tom. In the neighborhood, Giuseppe and Tommaso were known as Joe and Tom, which was the typical American way of abbreviating names. "I know our papers are in the mail," said Joe somberly. "Mamma and papa will go crazy," replied Tom. The men sat outside the tenement building in the Bronx, where they had spent most of their short life.

"Father Francis at Our Lady of Pity had a mass this morning for the boys and girls from the neighborhood who are in uniform," noted Joe. "They said the church was packed. The parents and families were crying. Sister Agatha told me that there were fifty soldiers and sailors at the ceremony. Most will be shipped out this week. I wonder who will come back. We went to school with at least half of them. I saw Lorraine in a WACS uniform yesterday, going to the bakery. She looked more beautiful than ever. She smiled at me. I remembered the first time I kissed her behind the statue of the Our Lady in the schoolyard. You remember the way Father Pat yelled when he saw us. He said, 'And you kissed her right behind the Virgin Mary. Aren't you ashamed of yourself?' He blew up when I said, 'But Father, Our Lady didn't see a thing!' Wow, I miss those days," reminisced Joe. Tom laughed. He looked up to his older brother and hung on his words.

"Where do you think they'll send us?" he asked Joe. "You know, Ron, the truck driver down at 152nd Street?" responded Joe. "He enlisted in the Marines the day after Pearl Harbor and just came back this week from Paris Island, North Carolina, where he did his basic training. He told me yesterday he thinks he's going to the Pacific to fight the Japs because his orders are to report to the Naval Station in San Francisco," explained Joe.

The thought of the War was on their mind and that of nearly every American. Everyone would participate. Some would fight at the front. Others would stay home to secure the shores of America. And still others would pray to hope loved ones would return safely and the ordeal would end soon.

Tom and Joe were inseparable. They grew up a year apart and were like twins. Neither needed lots of friends. Family, God, Country, and Ponza were what they learned about.

So little and so much was known by them about this rock in the Mediterranean, where Maria and Enzo were born.

Ponza was a gorgeous fishing village filled with history, adventure, and brimming with the values of Italy and the attachment to a clan, the soil, and the sea. Ponza's seafood was the best in the world, they were told. The people of Ponza were smart and clever, and the men and women were strong, healthy, and had incredible survival skills.

Most were exiles sent to live on a rock in the sea where they created gardens, built a city, constructed ships to sail the seven seas, and were among the most skillful mariners in history.

Tom and Joe came from this stock. Talents of generations were in their blood.

As they faced the struggles ahead, those skills would help them survive.

CHAPTER 19

THE CHURCH

Silverio fueled the Cadillac, checked the oil and brakes, and had a mechanic inspect every aspect of the car before embarking on the longest trip he had ever taken. Energy was rationed during the War. Silverio took enough extra tanks of gasoline to get to Mississippi. He wanted to avoid stopping at gas stations in the South.

It was cold and damp. There was a thin layer of snow on the ground and the roads were icy. At 60 miles an hour, he might make it to Mississippi in two or three days.

Altar of San Silverio, Patron Saint of Ponza in Our Lady of Pity Church, *Courtesy, Ponza Racconta*

Before leaving, Silverio needed to talk to God. He went to Our Lady of Pity Church in the South Bronx. Silverio lived a block away from this holy place, in the heart of Little Ponza. "Almighty Father," he prayed. "You, who have created the universe, please protect us on this voyage. We know there is danger before us, but with you at our side, we will be safe. Thank you for the many blessings you give me and my family. Please allow me to continue to help others, especially in this time of need," he pleaded.

The young immigrant from Italy went up to the statue of San Silverio, his patron Saint. He stood before this martyred pope. "San Silverio, please stay with me and Antonio as we cross America to reach our cousin in Mississippi. Be our guide and bring us safely home." He lit a candle and bowed his head. He took a picture of the Saint to keep in his car. Emotion filled his heart and mind. He wiped tears from his eyes as he slowly made the sign of the cross and left the sanctuary.

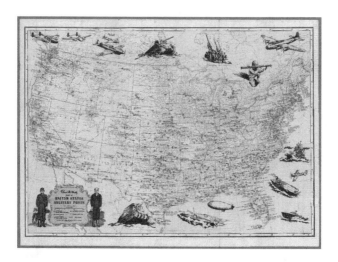

Map of US Military Facilities and roads in 1943, *Courtesy, Rand McNally Corporation*

He got into his Cadillac and drove. It was 4 AM. The city was dark and gloomy. Fine, freezing rain covered New York with a thick fog. Silverio had prepared his windshield by rubbing an onion over the glass. The acidic juice created a thin layer of protection from the elements. He left before dawn to avoid heavy traffic. The city was desolate as he coiled his way through small streets and boulevards toward the George Washington Bridge.

Few highways existed in the U.S. in 1943.

Most thoroughfares were state roads. The largest was four lanes, with two going north and two going south. They passed through the main streets of villages with traffic lights, railroad crossings, and other obstacles to slow any traveler trying to traverse a part of the continental United States.

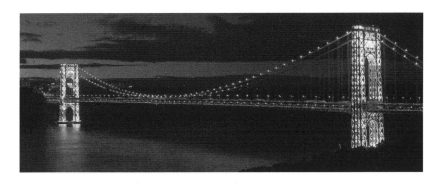

The George Washington Bridge, *Courtesy, New York Port Authority.*

Within an hour, Silverio saw the string of lights illuminating one of the largest bridges on earth. His father, Raffaele, worked on it in the late 1920s and was there when the George Washington Bridge opened in 1931. He helped prepare the giant cement columns sunk deep into the muddy bed of the Hudson River. Raffaele was skilled in building cofferdams structured to keep water out while the posts were constructed. It was a complex and perilous job. Twelve men died erecting the bridge. Raffaele never forgot their sacrifice. Neither did Silverio as he crossed it.

New York City at Night, *Courtesy, Associated Press Photos*

CHAPTER 20 ━━━━━━━━━━━━━

THE TRIP BEGINS

As he left the great viaduct, Silverio glanced across the river and stared at the spectacular scenery of the City of Lights. New York was like a gigantic Christmas tree filled with millions of stars. He wondered if he would see it again as he continued his journey into darkness.

Silverio drove while Antonio studied the maps. He had a map of one of the Southern States that reached into Mississippi. Routes were drawn in black ink following each roadway to his destination. The charts were filled with dark lines leading ever southward and slowly bending west by northwest, spanning rivers, mountains, and hills, forests, and towns, large and small. It was a labyrinth of winding motorways with frequent stops in hamlets where people would stare at the New York license plates as the car passed through one community after another.

Sunrise over Philadelphia, *Courtesy, Philadelphia Inquirer*

Silverio and Antonio reached Philadelphia.

The sun seemed to rise like a golden ball above the clouds as they continued their voyage. Pennsylvania was filled with leafless trees as the grip of winter settled in. He drove past endless farms and over greyish green hills and into valleys dotted with white and blue homes and churches, and through main streets packed with general stores and quaint shops that looked like pictures from postcards.

US Capitol Building, *Courtesy, Washington Tourism Commission*

Just past 10 AM, he arrived in the nation's capital. He decided he needed a break. Silverio drove to the Capitol Building, which housed the Senate and the House of Representatives.

The White House, *Courtesy, White House website*

He stopped near the White House. He imagined his hero, President Franklin Delano Roosevelt, was inside with his wife, Eleanor.

Eleanor and Franklin Roosevelt, *Courtesy, FDR Library*

He admired and respected the Roosevelts. He listened to FDR's speeches and "Fireside Chats." He watched newsreels of Eleanor helping the weak and fighting for the poor. Eleanor and Franklin guided America through the Great Depression, and now the War. FDR supported unions, the rights of workers, and passed the first minimum wage and child labor laws. Eleanor fought for minorities and women. She was Franklin's eyes and legs as she traveled to battlefields to be with the troops to comfort the dying and the wounded.

In January 1941, President Roosevelt delivered the State of the Union address to Congress known as "The Four Freedoms Speech." FDR spoke of the basic values that all people everywhere were entitled to:

> *In the future days, which we seek to make secure, we look forward to a world founded upon four essential human freedoms.*

> *The first is freedom of speech and expression — everywhere in the world.*

The second is freedom of every person to worship God in his own way – everywhere in the world.

The third is freedom from want – which, translated into world terms, means economic understandings which will secure to every nation a healthy peacetime life for its inhabitants - everywhere in the world.

The fourth is freedom from fear – which, translated into world terms, means a world-wide reduction of armaments to such a point and in such a thorough fashion that no nation will be in a position to commit an act of physical aggression against any neighbor – anywhere in the world.

That is no vision of a distant millennium. It is a definite basis for a kind of world attainable in our own time and generation. That kind of world is the very antithesis of the new order of tyranny which dictators seek to create with the crash of a bomb.

After the U.S. entered the War, artist Norman Rockwell was commissioned to do four paintings depicting the Four Freedoms to be used as posters throughout the United States.

Liberation

CHAPTER 21 ▬▬▬▬▬▬▬▬▬▬

THE LINCOLN MEMORIAL

Finally, Silverio reached the Lincoln Memorial. He parked the car and went up the steps. He told Antonio all about Lincoln. Silverio had read a biography of the 16th President of the United States in preparing for his citizenship test.

He was fascinated with this amazing leader. As he approached the statue of Lincoln, he said, "This was a common man who came from the poorest of the poor. He educated himself and struggled all his life. Lincoln was a man of integrity. He believed in things that most people were against. He fought for animal rights and the right for women to vote. He didn't drink, or smoke, or hunt, yet he was a hard worker and did every job imaginable to survive. Still, he became a good lawyer who had strong values. Lincoln would not defend someone he knew was guilty of a crime or take money for his services from the poor. Even as President he stayed humble, simple, and compassionate. He fought to liberate people from bondage and led the U.S. through the Civil War, realizing that he would give his life for the country."

Memorial to Abraham Lincoln, *Courtesy, nationalparks.org*

Silverio looked at the Gettysburg Address and the Second Inaugural Address. He took off his hat and read those most memorable words:

> *That this nation, under God, shall have a new birth of freedom, and that government of the people, by the people, for the people, shall not perish from the earth.*

> *With malice toward none, with charity for all, with firmness in the right as God gives us to see the right, let us strive on to finish the work we are in, to bind up the nation's wounds, to care for him who shall have borne the battle and for his widow and his orphan, to do all which may achieve and cherish a just and lasting peace among ourselves and with all nations.*

Tears welled up in his eyes as he turned and left the monument. *"That government of the people, by the people, for the people, shall not perish from the earth.* Antonio, this is what this war is all about, and what America is fighting for," exclaimed Silverio as he descended the great staircase to reach his car.

Following a breakfast of sandwiches and strong espresso from a thermos, Silverio and Antonio continued their trip into the South. As they drove through Virginia, they reduced their speed to 50 miles an hour. Silverio did not want to risk having a highway patrol car stop him. He went even slower through North Carolina.

It was nearly midnight.

Silverio and Antonio were exhausted.

They pulled over to a side of the road and slept.

CHAPTER 22 ━━━━━━━━━━━━━━━━

TENNESSEE

Screaming seagulls flying from the coast woke them. It was dawn. Silverio and Antonio had made excellent progress.

Now they had to carefully plot their route as they turned west into Tennessee. The roads were poor, uncomfortable, and filled with farmers with mules and carts. They literally meandered at less than 30 miles an hour to cross the state. It was beautiful countryside, filled with lakes, rivers, and hills. Finally, they reached Knoxville after seven hours of driving. They wanted to pass Nashville and Memphis and enter Mississippi from the north, since Como was close to the border with Tennessee.

Silverio put his foot on the accelerator. He was tired and irritated after snaking along for hours through backwater farms and towns. The four-lane state highway toward Nashville seemed like a giant boulevard compared to the dirt and gravel roads he had left behind.

Within seconds the mighty motor of his Cadillac was pushing the vehicle over 70 miles an hour. Silverio felt a sense of exuberance and power.

After an hour of progress, something frightening happened.

Courtesy, Tennessee Highway Patrol Authority

Out of a wooded area came the sound of loud engines: motorcycles.

Two state police officers were following them. They put on flashing lights and sirens.

Silverio's nightmare had come true: He could see Antonio and himself behind bars in a bleak Tennessee cell awaiting a trial before a tough Southern judge who hated Northerners.

CHAPTER 23

ARRESTED

Silverio pulled over. One officer stopped right behind the Cadillac and recorded the license plate. He spoke into a radio with the information. The other officer pulled up in front of the car. He and his partner were dressed in black woolen uniforms with dark grey shirts, black ties, and long, polished jackboots. They reminded Silverio of Nazi storm troopers. They wore thick, protective glasses wrapped around their faces like masks and grey police hats with gleaming badges, blazing with eagles. Black leather gloves protected their hands from the elements.

Both men were tall, with broad shoulders and muscular arms and legs. One was at least 6 feet 4 inches in height. Silverio nicknamed him "The Giant." Their faces were sparkling white with tinges of pink, reflecting North European blood. Their eyes were piercing and expressionless. The two men seemed like brothers. The only difference was their height and a rough scar on the cheek of one officer. Silverio nicknamed him, "Scarface."

Silverio opened his door to get out. Suddenly, Scarface shouted, "Stay in your vehicle and do not move!" He took out his revolver and approached Silverio. The Giant did the same on the other side of the car. Their guns looked like cannons. Silverio heard them cock the triggers on their firearms. They pointed their pistols at the two men. Scarface yelled in a strong Southern drawl, "Now, both of you get out of the car with your hands up! Put them on the hood and bend over!" They did as they were told. Silverio's knees became weak. Antonio turned pale white with fright.

He felt he would faint at any moment.

The patrolmen frisked them thoroughly. They emptied their pockets. Scarface found the pocketknife and set it aside along with their wallets and even their handkerchiefs. Then they investigated the Cadillac. "What's in the trunk of your car?" asked the Giant. Silverio's mouth was dry from fear. He could barely speak. The Italian thought carefully before answering this huge man who looked like he should be in a circus. He wanted to make sure that he told the entire truth so there could be no misunderstandings of their motives. "It is filled with food and clothing and two tanks of gasoline," said Silverio. Scarface looked at his partner with an expression of skepticism.

"Show me your license and registration," he said. Silverio had his documents in a leather folder. Besides those for his vehicle, he had his Civil Defense ID card and a copy of his U.S. citizenship. The officer looked at his papers and handed them over to his partner.

"Unlock the trunk," said Scarface. Silverio did as he was told. The patrolman opened the boxes. The pungent scent of cheese and salami struck his nostrils like bullets. He cringed. He looked at the tanks of gasoline and fuel oil and examined the tools and bottles of water Silverio had packed.

"You were going 70 in a 50 mile an hour zone," he said. "You're carrying gasoline over the state line, and you're transporting cured meats and other prohibited items. You have a deadly weapon in your pocket. Explain to me why I shouldn't lock you up right now," he insisted. Silverio told him the purpose of his journey. He showed the letters to the patrolmen.

Scarface went over to the giant. "How do we know these guys aren't Italian spies?" he whispered. "We don't know," said the giant, "but we can check it out in Nashville. Let's take these guys in." Scarface agreed. The patrolmen took their possessions and documents and ordered, "Get back in your car and follow us," he said. Silverio obeyed. "What's going on?" asked Antonio. "I think they're going to either arrest us or check our story, one or the other, or both," stated Silverio.

He started the engine and followed the motorcycles, wondering where they were going — and if he would ever see his family again.

Liberation

CHAPTER 24

BEHIND BARS

In less than an hour, they were at the police headquarters in Nashville. "Get out of the car!" barked Scarface. As soon as Silverio and Antonio were out of the vehicle, they were handcuffed with their hands behind their backs. Scarface banged Silverio's head against the hood of the car until his face was covered in blood. They were taken to the station and seated in a chamber that was cold and grey with blank walls.

An older officer came into the room.

His face was red and puffy with freckles, age lines in the forehead, and a heavy double chin. He had a special badge on and a more elaborate uniform, which he could barely fit into. He held a black Billy club in his right hand. Yellow bars decorated his cuffs, and golden stars were attached to his collar. He was the Chief of Police. Scarface and the Giant followed him.

He looked sternly at Silverio and Antonio.

His grey eyes were intimidating, frightening, and captivating, like those of a snake about to attack its prey.

He stood erect and faced them like a general. The Chief banged the Billy club on the table. Silverio and Antonio jumped with fear. "Now boys," he said with a heavy Southern drawl, "you have violated enough Tennessee laws to put you behind bars for at least five years. Our prisons here are a little different than those up North. Here we have chain gangs, and men break rocks and work on roads and stay in cells with little creature comforts. Yankee city slickers like y'all would have a hard time, if you know what I mean. So, unless you come clean and tell us what you're up to, I will bring you today before the judge, who I promise will put you in the State Penitentiary tonight." Silverio knew the man was serious. He also knew that he had exceeded the speed limit and that they could use that and other things against him.

"Sir," he responded politely, "my cousin and I are honest men. We work on the waterfront in New York, loading ammunition onto ships to help America win the War. I work in Civil Defense to protect my neighborhood. We left New York to visit our cousin, who is a prisoner of war in Como, Mississippi. The Commandant sent me a letter asking me to come." Scarface had Silverio's briefcase with the letters and other documents. He turned them over to the Chief. "Please call the Commandant and ask him," he pleaded. The Chief took the papers, along with Silverio's passport and driver's license. He left the room.

The immigrant prayed and asked San Silverio to help him out of this terrible ordeal.

CHAPTER 25 ▬▬▬▬▬▬▬▬▬▬▬▬▬▬▬▬▬

THE TUNNEL

"We need five more days of digging. Once we pass over the water main, we should be under the fence. At 2 AM on the sixth day, we will start to move. Captain Weber will go first, followed by SS Senior Storm Commander Leader Schmidt, and then the enlisted men in groups of ten, with each group led by a sergeant or corporal. The Italians will be led by Lieutenant Molinari and backed up by the Fascist unit leader," whispered SS Senior Leader Fischer.

He laid out a drawing written on a brown paper bag. It was a map from the central barracks to a fence and then a wooded area. Instead of an above ground road, it was a tunnel. It was over 100 feet long and stretched under the main building to the perimeter of the camp that bordered on a forest.

"We will head north through the woods, which will lead us to the railroad tracks. We will proceed south along the line until we reach the first station. We will hide among the trees and wait until the first train stops," explained Fischer.

The plan was to mount the train by entering the cars in the rear. The Germans and Italians would head toward New Orleans, where they would secretly get on neutral ships heading to Europe, so they could continue the war effort. This was plan A. Plan B dealt with partial success. If they could not get to New Orleans, they would attack the American rail system by trying to derail trains.

They would kill, if need be, to carry out their plans and continue the war effort on American soil.

The SS officers wanted desperately to find a southern escape route to get out of the U.S. and reach Latin America. They feared post-war tribunals, in which they would be tried for war crimes. The Germans needed the help of the Italians, since the Americans trusted them.

The key person the Italians listened to was a corporal who was also the head of the Fascists.

His name was Bruno.

CHAPTER 26

RELEASED

Silverio and Antonio remained handcuffed in that dark room for over four hours and were not allowed a break, except to go to the bathroom. Neither a glass of water nor a cup of coffee was offered. 'Perhaps I should have listened to Lucia,' Silverio thought. Doubts about his ability to deal with what he was facing flashed before his mind. He knew he was doing the right thing, but was it proper to risk his life and that of Antonio's for a secret mission he knew nothing about?

It was nighttime when Scarface opened the door. "The Chief checked your story, and it is okay. We will release you and not give you a fine for speeding if you leave Nashville first thing in the morning. You can stay in the boarding house across the street tonight," he said.

Silverio put out his handcuffed wrists. Scarface reluctantly removed the shackles. The cuffs had cut deeply into Silverio's skin. He was bleeding. Silverio took his handkerchief and tied it over the wound. The officer took a brown paper bag and poured their belongings onto the table. The patrolman grabbed them by the arms and escorted them out of the building. He pushed them through the door. "I want you out of town tomorrow morning, and if I see you again I will make sure you will regret that you ever set foot in Tennessee," he declared.

Silverio and Antonio went to the hotel and got a room for the night. A "Whites Only" sign was on the front desk. A bathroom with a shower was in the corridor to be shared by the guests. The men bathed and tried to sleep. They were restless and worried because their journey was not over. They slept for about three hours. Fear and anxiety kept them awake most of the night. Then they heard sirens and garbage trucks moving in the city center near police headquarters.

"Antonio, if you want to go back home, I can bring you to the bus or train station in Memphis. I don't want you to risk your life. You have a family, and I don't know what is ahead of us for the rest of this trip." Antonio looked at him. "We grew up together on the island. You arranged for me to come to America. You got me my first job in this country and took care of me and my family when we needed help. Do you really think that I would leave you alone, now, in this hell hole?" Antonio responded.

Silverio embraced him as tears welled up in his eyes.

Silverio used the hotel pay phone to call Lucia. From Tennessee to New York it was a long-distance call. It cost $1.25, which shocked Silverio. "Everything is fine. We are not far from the camp. The trip has been good. No trouble whatsoever," he lied.

It was eight AM when they started toward Memphis, over 150 miles away. Silverio saw motorcycles and cars parked outside the police building.

There was no sign of Scarface or the Giant.

He hoped he would never see them or this place again.

Memphis, Tennessee, Riverboat, *Courtesy, Library of Congress, Federal Arts Project*

CHAPTER 27 ━━━━━━━━━━━━━━━

THE FOREST

The road to Memphis seemed interminable. Silverio moved along at less than 35 miles an hour to save gas and avoid any problem with the authorities. He kept his eyes peeled for police cars and anyone in uniform. The men were exhausted after their adventure in Nashville. They needed rest. Silverio pulled off the road to sleep. When they woke, the sun was setting.

By the time they reached Memphis, it was almost dark.

The streets were filled with mud. Trolley cars cut across the town, and horse and mule-driven carts were everywhere. Silverio looked at the riverboats docked along the Mississippi. Bales of cotton and sacks of coal were being carried by hand into the steamers.

Most workers were black. During their journey, Silverio and Antonio talked about how awful the blacks lived in the rural South.

People resided in shacks and shanty towns. He could tell the homes had no hot or cold running water, plumbing, or heating. He rarely saw a schoolhouse or a library in the areas populated by blacks.

"Someday these poor people are going to fight for their rights. They can't vote, go to good schools, or have decent jobs. I hope to be alive to see the day that they are liberated from segregation," he said to Antonio.

By the time Silverio reached the border, it was 9 PM.

There were few lights on the roads and no homes or boarding houses. According to the map, it was only 50 miles more to Como. Silverio had no choice but to continue to drive into the shadows of Mississippi.

The main road narrowed.

It turned into a wooded area with muddy dirt paths.

Rain pelted the car. Visibility got less and less. Silverio hesitated to stop because he was afraid his auto would sink deep into the mud, and he would be trapped.

After two hours of zigzagging through forest paths, Silverio and Antonio felt desperate. Perhaps they had made a mistake? Should they have turned left 10 miles back, instead of right? How come this road was not on the map? Was the chart accurate?

As they continued to twist and turn in the darkness, they saw the carcass of a vehicle abandoned in the woods. It was a little older than their car.

Silverio and Antonio wondered what tragic story was behind that lost auto in a forest in northern Mississippi.
The only illumination came from the headlights of the Cadillac. Suddenly, a group of greyish brown figures darted across their path.

Silverio stopped.

He could not distinguish what was happening.

He heard barking.

Without warning, a giant wolf jumped on the hood of the car and was growling at the windshield. The predator's icy white teeth, grey eyes, crimson tongue, and silvery fur glistened in the darkness.

The men were terrified. Several animals were gnawing at the doors to get in.

Two were on the roof.

A pack of ravenous wolves was trying to enter the car and attack them! Silverio immediately pushed his foot on the accelerator. The car darted into the forest. Branches of trees and bushes crashed into the vehicle. The creatures fell from the auto. The beasts raced after them and continued to pursue the Cadillac for nearly an hour.

"Those monsters wanted us for dinner," said Antonio, trembling. Silverio prayed out loud. "San Silverio, God Almighty, please help us get out of this awful place!"

They continued to drive when they saw a tree had fallen across their path. Another challenge. It was raining hard. The air was cold, and a heavy mist was settling into the forest. Silverio stopped and put on the brakes. It was a large oak that must have been at least fifty years old. The wind and the rain brought it down, right in front of their car.

It was heavy. The men were strong, and it took an hour to move it far enough from the road so the car could pass it.

They were soaked and freezing, when Silverio saw something in the distance.
It was a light.

"Antonio, look," he said. An illuminating figure shined through clouds and trees and cut across the darkness. It was hard to distinguish.

It seemed like a bright star in the heavens.

The men immediately got into the car and drove toward the glowing object.

CHAPTER 28

OFF TO WAR

"**M**amma don't worry, we'll be fine," said Joe as he embraced his mother.

Maria could not be consoled.

Enzo stood frozen. His sons were drafted, which he had expected. He fought in the First World War in Italy. A photo of him in uniform was on a dresser table. Now he pictured his boys in greenish-grey clothes with U.S. Army insignias. Then he saw them in battle grey with helmets in foxholes, dodging machine-gun fire and sleeping in the rain and mud. Enzo recalled the agony of battle, the sound of ear-piercing explosions, and the suffering of soldiers fighting in a faraway land for ideals they would never see come to light.

"Why did they start this war? What do Mussolini and Hitler want with my boys? You have to risk your life for what?" Maria cried hysterically. Tom and Joe knew they could not reason with their mother. She could not understand they were leaving the warmth and love of her arms to liberate nations enslaved by tyrants. Her boys would fight to save America from the Nazis and the Japanese, who were determined to end freedom and conquer the world.

"Mamma, we need you and our family to pray for us and take care of everything here until we come back," said Tom trying to help his mother deal with the situation.

She caressed the faces of her sons.

Maria wiped the tears from her eyes with her apron.

"Sit down, and I will prepare dinner," she said as she slowly regained her composure. "We have to report tomorrow to the Armory in Manhattan for our papers and physical," said Joe to his father. "Once we have the enlistment documents, we can go to our bosses to hold our jobs until we come back," chimed in Tom.

Maria heard the conversation and repeated, 'Come back' in her mind, again and again.

After 20 minutes, the family sat at the small kitchen table for a meal of pasta, chicken cutlets, and homemade wine.

"Oh God," prayed Enzo as they held hands, "please protect our boys as they go to war. Take care of them and bring them home to us soon. San Silverio, please be at the side of Joe and Tom each day and night and keep them out of harm's way." They made the sign of the cross and ate.

Silence filled the room, as if they were having their last supper together.

CHAPTER 29 ━━━━━━━━━━━━━━━━━━

THE CROSS

For some strange reason, the Cadillac seemed to fly by itself.

Silverio was excited.

The gleaming silhouette in the distance gave him a sense of hope.

It grew larger and brighter as they pushed through the woodland.

Suddenly, they came to a clearing. Fog had fallen, and the only thing they could see was the shimmering object that hung like a candle in the mist. The forest was behind them.

Silverio stopped the car. The two men got out to see beyond the haze. As they emerged, the vapor disappeared as warm winds pushed aside the steamy air and revealed the glittering outline of what Silverio's soul was searching for.
"Antonio, it's a cross!" cried Silverio.

"It is, and it's not far from here. Do you think it's a church?" said Antonio with hope in his voice. "We have to find out," said Silverio.

They drove across the clearing.

A greyish building emerged with colored glass windows. On the structure was a cross lit up by white neon lights.
Silverio drove up to the front of the sanctuary.

He stopped the car. It was 3 AM. The men were spent. They needed a place to rest. Silverio took out his flashlight and walked up to the entrance. Over the door of the building were these words:

> *I was hungry, and you gave me something to eat, I was thirsty, and you gave me something to drink, I was a stranger, and you invited me in. Matthew 25:35*

Courtesy, Mississippi Department of Archives and History
http://www.mshistorynow.mdah.ms.gov/articles/96/religion-in-mississippi

Silverio and Antonio knelt and made the sign of the cross. They thanked God for bringing them to this holy place with the light of his grace.

Silverio knocked several times.

He heard footsteps, then the turn of a key, and then the door opened. Out of the darkness of the portal emerged a black man. His hair and beard were white and trimmed. He held a green lantern, illuminated with an oil wick. He wore striped pajamas with patches on the elbows and legs. The light shined on his face. It was filled with deep lines from suffering. The man was tall, handsome, with dark skin and bright eyes, and shimmering white teeth.

"Come in, my sons," he said. "I have been waiting for you."

It was very cold. They were shivering. The chapel smelled musty, with a tinge of burnt coal. Silverio and Antonio took off their hats as the man escorted them through the dim church into a small apartment. It had a living room with a sofa and two armchairs and a little coffee table.

The furniture was worn, and paint was peeling from the walls.

Behind the lounge was a kitchen with a white and grey wood-burning stove and an old cedar table. The smell of cooked bacon hung in the air. The man led them to a bedroom with a large poster bed covered with a white, embroidered spread filled with shapes of stars. A pitcher with water and a basin was on a tiny table. There was no bathroom in sight.

"Please rest here tonight," said the man. "I am grateful Jesus brought you to our doorstep. Sleep, and when you awake, we will talk. God bless you."

He lit two candles in tin trays filled with wax, and placed them on a dresser and left the room. Silverio and Antonio were speechless. They gently took away the lovely bedspread and covered themselves with a thick woolen blanket. The bed was divine. It seemed to be a cloud, as the travelers fell into a deep sleep that overcame them from the fear and fatigue they had experienced only hours before.

Past 9 AM, the sound of someone chopping wood, opening doors, and chirping birds aroused the travelers from their slumber. "Good morning," said the black man as they emerged from their room.

"In the back, we have an outhouse, if you need to use it. I will get some water from the well for you to wash with," he stated with a broad smile. He was dressed in a grey jacket with a white shirt and a collar. His trousers and shoes were worn like those of a farmer or backwoodsman. Twenty minutes later, the visitors and the black man were seated at a table laden with fried eggs, ham, and thick slices of cornbread, a bowl filled with butter, and cups of coffee.

The pastor took their hands in his and prayed, "Oh Almighty Father, thank you for bringing your children to our humble place of worship. Please help them as they continue their journey and protect them with your divine wisdom and grace. Thank you for this food which we are about to share as brothers and members of your holy family. Amen."

Silverio and Antonio made the sign of the cross and looked at the pastor for a signal on when to eat. He nodded his head, and they ate with gusto. They had never tasted better eggs, and the fried ham and buttered cornbread seemed like the food of the gods.

Perhaps it was hunger or gratitude, but the men felt they were in a shrine created by the Lord to save them.
"I am Isiah Jefferson, pastor of the First Baptist Church of Como, Mississippi. Ours is a poor congregation of colored people who love the Lord Jesus Christ and see in Him the road to salvation. You are welcome to stay here if you wish. I was expecting you. Several nights ago, the Holy Spirit illuminated me in the form of a dream and told me God's children were on their way to our chapel in the wilderness, and I was to welcome them and help them complete their mission," explained the pastor with soothing words accompanied by a warm, friendly smile.

"Thank you, Reverend," said Silverio. "My cousin and I are grateful to you and our Father in heaven for your hospitality and generosity."

He then explained why he had traveled over a thousand miles to reach this town in the soul of Mississippi.

Liberation

CHAPTER 30

FDR

While Joe and Tom were on their way to a fort in Georgia to do basic training, a group of Italian American leaders was meeting with President Franklin Delano Roosevelt. They had traveled from various parts of the country and were in close contact with Italian communities across America. As they entered the Oval Office, several generals and admirals were leaving with the President's Personal Secretary.

FDR in the Oval Office, *Courtesy, FDR Library*

The Commander in Chief had a black armband on, in mourning for the men and women killed at Pearl Harbor. As the United States entered the War, casualties from the land, sea, and air mounted.

An invasion of troops in Europe, North Africa, and the islands in the Pacific were in the planning stages. Sooner or later, American soldiers would attack Italy.

"Mr. President, I can assure you of the loyalty of Italian Americans in the war effort," began the head of the delegation, one of the most important bankers in the U.S. "As you know, Italian Americans are in every walk of life, from the professions and sports to industry and even politics". "I know," laughed FDR. "One of my closest friends is Mayor Fiorello LaGuardia of New York. He never ceases to tell me about his heritage," said the President with a broad smile.

"Tens of thousands of the sons and daughters of Italians living in our country have enlisted or have been drafted. They will fight for the United States no matter where they are sent, even if it is Italy. They are Americans, first and foremost. You can imagine, Mr. President, that the parents of these soldiers and sailors are concerned about the fate of their former homeland, especially after we have rid them of the Fascist regime. We ask you to consider, as the fighting becomes more intense, to make plans to safeguard the vital cultural treasures of Italy, which are the patrimony of the world, and to avoid as much needless bloodshed as possible," he concluded.

The President puffed on his cigarette in a long silver holder. He stared at the delegation. "I assure you our quarrel is not with the people of Italy," he said. "It is with Mussolini and his band of criminals who have joined with Hitler in this terrible conflict. We will do all we can to preserve the country's marvelous art treasures and to end the Italian involvement with the Nazis. I promise that when we restore peace, we will rebuild Italy and help return its economy to prewar conditions," FDR concluded. He shook hands with each member of the delegation, had his photographer take a photo, and bid them farewell.

"We can't ask for more than that," said the banker to his colleagues as they left the Oval Office.

"We have a long and bitter time ahead. Things are not going well in the Pacific, and we are just getting our act together in Europe. No country in history has succeeded in winning a two-front war," said a business leader.

"The key thing is that they are already planning to rebuild Europe after the war is over," stated a judge.

"That is assuming we win," responded the leader of the group as they went their separate ways after the meeting.

CHAPTER 31

SOFIA

"**M**y love, this is for you," said Joe. He gazed into Sofia's light-brown eyes.

She felt he was peering into her soul.

Tenderly, he placed a thin golden ring on her finger.

A chill ran through the young girl. She felt it was their wedding day. The place where they sat was special. It was a park bench, but for the lovers it was an enchanted room. It was their nest, their meeting place, and where they exchanged words, embraces, kisses, and promises.

On that simple seat surrounded by trees, Joe told her, "I love you," for the first time.

They had been in love since grammar school. "Do you remember the first time you kissed me?" she asked. "It was the second grade, and we were walking across the street from the church when a car almost hit you. I pulled you away and held you close, and kissed you."

Since that moment there were many "first times."

They recalled their first dance, first date, first walk in the park, first night at the drive-in movie, and the first time they pledged eternal love.

"I love you with all my heart and soul," Joe said sweetly.

She and Joe were made for each other. They were born in the South Bronx in the same year, in the same hospital, and baptized in Our Lady of Pity Church. Ponza was the shared homeland of their ancestors. Maria, Joe's mother, was Sofia's godmother. The families were close. Holidays were celebrated in each other's homes and, occasionally, the parents chatted about their children coming together.

Sofia was blond with a snow-white complexion and long, flowing hair that glistened and shined like strands of gold. She was beautiful.

With high heels, she reached Joe's shoulder.

Her smile, happy and pleasant personality, and slim figure enhanced her beauty. She was perfect. Charming, outgoing, intelligent, and religious, Sofia was a splendid daughter, a loyal friend, and madly in love with Joe.

At school, they called her "Veronica Lake," because she looked so much like the famous movie star.

"Let's get married right away. We can go to City Hall, get a license, and do it!" she said, with tears running down her cheeks.

"I love you, Sofia. Are you sure you want this? What if I come back wounded, with an arm or leg missing, or if I return with battle fatigue and am put in a mental hospital?" Sofia put a finger to his mouth.

"I don't care how you come back, as long as you do come back. I will be here waiting and praying for you until I can hold you again."

They kissed deeply. The world melted away. All they felt was their bodies intertwined in rapture.

Joe and Sofia were married the next morning.

CHAPTER 32 ━━━━━━━━━━━━━━━━━━━━━━━━━━━━━━━━━

THE KU KLUX KLAN

Secret meeting of the Ku Klux Klan, *Courtesy, Library of Congress*

As Silverio told his story to the black pastor, a group of men was gathering in a house five miles from the church. "Got word from Nashville that some Yankees are coming our way," said Billy Bob. "Heard that they were Italians, and the boys in Nashville think they're spies," responded Andy. Both men were huge in height and build, and they had reddish-blond hair. One had a face filled with pink freckles. Their necks were thick with muscles, and their arms were covered with hair. They worked as lumberjacks, cutting trees in the dense Mississippi forests and hauling the timber to the river to be floated south for Louisiana paper mills.

They had avoided the draft because they were involved in a vital peacetime industry.

They also knew the head of the local draft board.

A few minutes into their conversation, they heard a car door being opened and shut in front of their house. Fred, who ran the local gas station, walked into the room. "Saw a Cadillac with New York plates outside the nigger church this morning. Bet it's been there all night and that nigger pastor is housing those Yankees everyone is talking about," said Fred. His eyes were silver-blue, like those of a fox, but his intellect was closer to that of a sloth.

The three men had much in common.

They grew up Episcopalians in the same town, went to the same school, dated the same girls, were active in their community, and were loyal members of the Northeastern Mississippi Ku Klux Klan.

"Let's call Jack," suggested Fred. "It's time we give those niggers and nigger lovers a lesson," remarked Billy Bob. He lifted the phone. "Jack, we got a problem here in Como. A nigger pastor took in some Italian spies last night. We got the word from the team in Tennessee. The authorities in Nashville let the spies go. We think it's our patriotic duty to teach them and that nigger about American democracy, Mississippi style," said Billy Bob with conviction.

Jack listened carefully. He was a man with power. Jack was the County Sheriff and the Grand Dragon of the Ku Klux Klan for Mississippi. "What do you have in mind?" asked Jack. "Think an old-fashioned Klan barbecue is what the doctor ordered," replied Billy Bob, laughing. "When would you like to hold your 'barbecue,' Billy Bob?" replied Jack. "There's a full moon tonight, and I think it would be perfect if we brought in the delegation at 9 PM sharp," responded Billy Bob. "You have my blessing brother. Go forward with the sword of righteousness for God and country," said the Grand Dragon, who oversaw 'the invisible empire' for the entire state.

Billy Bob hung up. He was delighted. As the Grand Titan of his district, he had to maintain law and order and respect the principles of the Klan as written in their book entitled the Kloran. The heart of the precepts was that of white supremacy. The three men raised their hands and recited their common pledge:

We avow the distinction between the races of mankind as same as has been decreed by the Creator, and we shall ever be true in the faithful maintenance of White Supremacy and will strenuously oppose any compromise thereof in any and all things.

Billy Bob turned to Fred, "We're going to need some of your high octane tonight. And Andy, don't forget the ropes. I'll bring the whip."

CHAPTER 33 ━━━━━━━━━━━━━━━━━━━━━━━

THE KLAN PREPARES

T he pastor told Silverio the POW camp was two miles from the Church. He suggested they rest another day, and then he would accompany them to the facility. That morning, Antonio repaired the small generator the church used to keep the neon lights on in the cross, since the chapel had no electricity. Silverio fixed pews and helped the pastor fill up the kitchen with enough firewood to keep the stove burning all winter. He took a large piece of cheese from his Cadillac's trunk and gave that, along with a $5.00 donation, to the pastor for the poor of the church.

Reverend Jefferson was a good, kind man.

His grandfather was a slave. His parents were tenant farmers. He struggled to study to be a Baptist Minister and earned a scholarship to a black college to complete his studies. He talked about his parishioners. They were farmers and workers who labored along the river. Some cleaned the homes of white people. They lived slightly better than when they were in bondage.

Segregation assured a complete separation of the races and cut off opportunities for a normal life for millions of blacks trapped in the shadows of discrimination and isolation in the South.

Ku Klux Klan Rally, c. 1920, *Courtesy, Library of Congress*

Darkness descended on the town. It looked like a black curtain. It covered the trees, roads, and houses. Out of the night moved three startling forms. They looked like ghosts searching for death and destruction. A full moon emerged and lit up their white gowns. Red crosses glowed on their chests. The figures and the animals they mounted seemed bonded into one frightening shape. The horse and the man appeared like a medieval creature prepared to siege a city or battle a regiment of enemies.

But they had set out to murder a defenseless minister and turn his humble chapel into ashes.

It was not the work of valiant knights, but of cowards who hid their faces as they committed the most heinous of crimes. The criminals were confident and secure in their task. They had done this before and had sharpened their tools of mayhem with precision.

Three bottles of gasoline stuffed with rags would be enough to torch the church. A horse whip was perfect to scourge the black pastor and teach the Italian spies a bloody lesson. The glorious night would finish with "a necktie party," with the minister swinging from the old oak.

A loaded shotgun and three pistols completed the arsenal of war of the three Ku Klux Klan members.

CHAPTER 34

IL DUCE'S WAR

"**B**elieve, obey, and fight." Mussolini's words echoed in his mind as he thought about his decision. Bruno was driven by pride and patriotism. Italy surrendered to the Allies, but Il Duce would not accept defeat. Mussolini was courageous, gave Italy an empire, built new roads, highways, schools, created millions of jobs, and transformed a backward nation into a world power.

How could this end so quickly?

Fascism was Bruno's religion from birth.

He was taught that Italians were a superior race who had civilized the world. The Roman Empire represented the glory of the past, and Benito Mussolini had brought it back to life. Il Duce claimed that they would defeat their enemies, if they stayed united and were not afraid to die for him.

After Italy capitulated, Mussolini formed a new government in the north to continue the struggle. He called on Italians to fight wherever they were. "I would rather live a day like a lion and not a hundred as a lamb," said Mussolini. His sayings were on buildings across Italy. Bruno repeated Il Duce's proverbs to his fellow soldiers. Most would not listen. They were exhausted from the war and the failures of Fascism.

Like Bruno, millions of Italians grew up believing they could conquer the world and that glory would come from war. Instead, the pride of Italian youth was hurled into the mouth of hell. First, they conquered Ethiopia with poison gas against spear-carrying natives, sacrificing 10,000 Italian lives and hundreds of thousands of Ethiopians. Il Duce sent them to fight in the Spanish Civil War, where 6,000 died. Now, Mussolini dragged the nation into a war against the world in which millions would die or be wounded.

He lied about imaginary victories and boasted about the marvelous alliance with Germany. Instead, Italian forces faced defeat and humiliation, and the Nazis were not allies, but psychopathic criminals who Mussolini spoke of as if they were gods.

Italian soldiers in German prisoner of war camps were tortured, starved, and murdered.

A far cry from the compassion and respect Americans extended to prisoners of war.

Italians were interned with Germans in Camp Como. Some were members of the SS and the Gestapo. The SS, or Protective Guards, began as Hitler's private police force and became the private army of the Nazi Party. The Gestapo was formed to use cruelty and terror to identify and punish political opponents of the regime.

Arrogant and cunning, SS and Gestapo leaders criticized German officers and soldiers who cooperated with the Americans, accusing them of betraying the Fatherland. They pressured the Germans and Italians to refuse privileges and tried to convince them to escape.

Bruno was trapped between his Fascist ideology and his desire for peace. Some soldiers followed him because he was a strong, honest leader. The Nazis knew this and compelled him to organize the Italians to escape or revolt. "It is your duty to Il Duce and ours to the Fuhrer to fight these plutocratic pigs that preach democracy but instead are tools of Wall Street who suck the blood of the people. Only National Socialism and Fascism can save humans from this scum," insisted the Gestapo leader to a gathering of POWs.

An Italian corporal translated the Nazi's harsh language into his native tongue and repeated it to his comrades.

He tried to capture the spirit of sacrifice demanded by the German, but failed.

His heart was not in the task.

CHAPTER 35

THE ATTACK

"**R**everend, this is excellent," remarked Silverio. The pastor responded, "Southern fried chicken is what we are famous for in this part of the country. I hope you like the cornbread. I bake it myself three times a week. My people bring me food in the fall and winter but, in the spring and summer I have a nice garden." "I will send you some tomato and hot pepper seeds from New York," said Antonio. "I grow three varieties of eggplants and squash. Last year, I had bushels of string beans. It's because I fertilize the soil with cow manure," explained Antonio. "We use whatever the chickens give as fertilizer," said the pastor with a broad smile. The three men laughed. They finished dinner at about 8 PM.

The black minister shared the little he had with the strangers.

"Reverend, do you know anything about the camp?" asked Silverio. "Yes, I do. I hold services on Sunday for the prisoners and the guards. The Commandant was criticized by the local whites for allowing a black man into the base. He swept that away and said that God was color blind and so was he. Since most inmates cannot understand our language, my services have a translator for the Germans and the Italians. The base auditorium is always full for Sunday services. I don't know if it's because the prisoners want to come or are forced to. I doubt anyone would compel them to hear a colored Baptist preach the gospel." He laughed.

"The prisoners are fine," continued the minister. "They are well fed and look healthy and fit. I was told they play soccer and basketball, and are learning to play baseball. Some work in the motor pool and the camp greenhouse, where they grow a little bit of everything. They get paid for the work. I'm sure they will take home some money when this war is over."

Close to 9 PM, something happened. "I hear hoofbeats," said Silverio. The three men froze. Lights were flashing in the front of the church. Reverend Jefferson rose from his chair with terror in his eyes. He peered out the window. He put his head in his hands and cried. "It's them!" he said. Silverio and Antonio looked through the tinted glass.

A large wooden cross was burning on the lawn of the church.

Three men, mounted on black horses, were clad in white hoods and gowns and were galloping in a circle around the cross. "Antonio, it's the Ku Klux Klan," Silverio said with fear in his voice. "They've come for me. They will burn my church and hang me," exclaimed the minister. "Well, I ain't gonna die without a fight," he insisted. He got up and clenched his fists. "Your fight is our fight, Reverend. We will do all we can to stop them," responded Silverio. The black man put his hand on Silverio's shoulder. "You best clear out of here. The Klan takes no prisoners or witnesses. They're liable to hang you along with me," he said. Silverio looked at Antonio.

"We're not going anywhere. We face pretty tough guys on the docks, and we're not afraid of a couple of ghosts," said Silverio with conviction.

"Come out, nigger!" boomed a voice from the darkness. "We're gonna teach you a lesson! You're entertaining Italian spies, and you and them will pay for your treason!" shouted the lead Klansman. "Italian spies?" exclaimed Silverio.

He turned red with anger.

"Antonio, let's get to the car, right away. Reverend, you stay here. We will take care of this," he said as they ran out of the building to the Cadillac.

CHAPTER 36

SILVERIO & ANTONIO MEET THE KKK

Silverio opened the trunk, lifted the spare tire, and took out the bats, pipes, and hooks. The two men fastened the hooks to their belts. They snuck out the back of the church and, like cats, quietly slid to the rear of the three Klansmen who were positioned in front of the house of worship. One had a coiled whip, another had a shotgun, and each had a bottle of gasoline with rags stuffed into it. "Come out, nigger, before we smoke you out!" the Klansman bellowed.

Silverio and Antonio hid behind a large bush to the rear of the horsemen. They could smell the stench of the animals mixed with the pungent odor of gasoline. Each Klansman took out their bottle. They galloped to the fiery cross and lit them. Then they circled back into a military-like formation.

All three were directly in front of the church with the burning bottles lifted high above their heads.

Silverio and Antonio darted to the back of the horses. Like seasoned baseball players, they swung their bats and struck each animal's rear.

The horses shrieked, buckled, and leaped into the air.

The men were simultaneously thrown from their mounts.

They hit the ground hard. The gasoline bombs broke and burned.

Within seconds, the outfits of the three would-be murderers were blazing. The gowns of the Klansmen were covered in flames. They looked like human torches and screamed as they tried to put out the inferno.

One lifted the shotgun and pointed it at Silverio, who threw a lead pipe at him with tremendous force. It struck the Klansman in the neck.

He collapsed, unconscious.

Another took out a pistol and fired.

Silverio was hit in the shoulder as Antonio sunk his hook deep into the man's arm before he could get off another round.

The three men wailed in agony. Silverio and Antonio went to the well and dumped buckets of water on the criminals.

The Klansmen lay on the ground, wounded, defeated, and disgraced.

CHAPTER 37

CARLO'S NIGHTMARE

"Get up, move, march," said the voice in harsh German. His nightmare was vivid. He saw the khaki-colored uniforms, the tall men with stoic faces, expressionless eyes, holding machine guns and attack dogs on leashes.

"Take off your belt and hand over your canteen and your rations," ordered the German soldier.

Carlo could not understand the command, but he knew what the German wanted. The Italian army was being stripped of their weapons, food, and water as the Germans marched to the sea in North Africa.

They would leave their "allies" to die in the desert.

Carlo saw the soldier drink his water. The canteen was nearly empty when the German poured the rest of the water into the mouth of the dog. Carlo was angry and mortified.

He was parched. Italian soldiers were dying of thirst and hunger. His nightmare was filled with images of gunfire, sand, fear, and suffering. He smelled the odor of decaying bodies in his dream.

His comrades died in his arms.

The Italian army marched 100 miles to reach the Egyptian port of Alessandria. The entire Afrika Korps was in retreat from the onslaught of the English and the Americans. The planes and tanks of the Allied armies had defeated General Rommel, the legendary "Desert Fox." Now they were rushing to surround the enemy forces and annihilate or capture them. Carlo recalled the shouts of Gestapo leaders demanding that the Germans fight to the death for the Fuhrer. Fascists commanded the same for Il Duce.

He awoke sweating and trembling. "Wheeling, next stop!" shouted the conductor. The announcement roused Carlo from his slumber. The train ride was long and boring, with numerous pauses in villages and cities. He slept with intervals of meditation and prayer along the way.

The kind Sergeant had given him a heavy woolen coat and a broad-brimmed hat. Wheeling was in one of the coldest parts of West Virginia. He would need the coat and hat to protect him from the elements. Carlo straightened his tie, drank some water, and splashed cologne over his unshaven face.

For eight hours he had pondered the past chapters of his life.

The thoughts moved through his mind like a movie. As a boy, he learned so much about farming, hunting, and fishing in the local streams and rivers. Luigi taught him how to live and survive. He discovered how to use a rifle, bait a hook, raise animals, till fields, cook, and bake bread.

He recalled being forced to join the army and basic training. So many thoughts seemed like distant memories fading away as his mind tried to erase one horrible recollection after another.

Carlo missed his brother and his parents. Family was the center of his life. Now, after seven long years, he would see Luigi again.

The train whistle blew. The train slowly came to a stop.

Clouds of vapor rose from the wheels and surrounded the train.

Carlo peered out the window as the mist gradually evaporated. The platform was filled with people. American Army soldiers and sailors and many passengers descended from the cars. He searched the crowd. He wondered if Luigi would meet him as he said in his letter. Maybe he was delayed, he thought. Perhaps he had to work or deal with some emergency.

Just then, he saw his face. Their eyes met.

Carlo's heart pounded as he dashed from the train to embrace his brother.

CHAPTER 38 ━━━━━━━━━━━

THANKSGIVING

"**L**uigi told me his brother was captured in North Africa just as the Italians and Germans were escaping," observed Alberto as he knotted his tie. "Antonietta says Americans put him on a nice train from Alabama to get here and gave him new clothes to wear. He has eaten well and works as a baker," responded Carmela. She was patting talcum powder to her cheeks and straightening her hair. "They pay him to work. This country is generous, even to those who want to destroy it. God bless America," remarked Alberto.

His family was invited to Luigi's house for dinner to celebrate Carlo's arrival.

It was also Thanksgiving.

Carmela was a splendid cook. She baked a large cake covered with cream for the occasion. Alberto prepared a gallon of his white wine. It was the color of gold and tasted of liquid grapes. "I have a good mind to leave her here," said Carmela in an angry voice. "She still hasn't finished cleaning the attic," she insisted. "It's Thanksgiving and it would look bad if we didn't take her. Antonietta and Luigi like her, and she is close to Gabriela," explained Alberto as he fastened his suspenders. "All right, but she doesn't deserve it," answered Carmela.

'This is the one. No, this color goes better with my makeup. The red one is too loud. Okay, the beige dress is perfect,' thought Helena as she went through the clothing left to her by her mother. She carefully examined each garment to make sure there were no stains or holes.

She lived in the basement of Alberto and Carmela's house and shared a room with the furnace, a pile of coal, boxes of canned goods, jars of tomato sauce, and jams and jellies. She had just enough space for a small bed and a few suitcases holding the precious belongings of her parents.

A broken mirror decorated the wall. She used it to apply her mother's rouge and lipstick. "What do you think, Mamma?" asked Helena, peering into the photo of Antonia. Helena was gorgeous. Her breasts were large and round for her age, while her hourglass figure rivaled that of film stars. Her face was angelic, with perfect features and soft white skin, with a touch of natural pink. Her eyes were large and black, as was the color of her hair, which was filled with lovely curls. Her heart-shaped lips were even more inviting after being colored with a soft lip balm.

Helena's loveliness was part of her soul.

Her personality was beautiful. She was happy and playful, even when mistreated by Carmela and her cousins. She was intelligent and excelled in school, and she worked hard. The young lady was delighted to be included in the Thanksgiving celebration. Luigi was a distant relative who had known her parents well. Gabriela, Luigi's daughter, was her best friend.

Now she would meet Carlo, who she thought so much about, but did not know why.

CHAPTER 39 ━━━━━━━━━━━━━━━

SAVING THE KLANSMEN

Silverio and Antonio hauled the Klansmen into the church. They were unconscious. It was midnight. "They're badly burned. This one is bleeding heavily from his arm," said the minister. "They need immediate attention. There is no time to take them to the local doctor." Silverio stopped the loss of blood from the gunshot wound in his shoulder with a tourniquet. The bullet went through his flesh and came out the other side without hitting the bone. The pastor disinfected the deep gash and applied a bandage. The shoulder was swollen, but it did not prevent Silverio from using it to move the men so they could be helped and saved.

"Thanks to you, Antonio, the one with the neck injury is alive after you resuscitated him. His larynx may be damaged, but he will be okay," stated the pastor, who knew a lot about medicine. He exposed the charred skin. Second and third-degree burns covered parts of the bodies of the three men. The pastor washed and medicated the injuries. He used a natural salve, prepared from local herbs, on the scorched tissue.

Silverio had taken bottles of penicillin with him from New York and included them in his first aid kit for the trip. He recalled the words of his doctor and pharmacist, who both said he would never need them for his journey. Still, he felt compelled to bring them, but did not know the reason until that moment. The pastor was grateful that they were available.

The patients developed high fevers, which he treated with aspirin and the penicillin. By noon the next day, one Klansman regained consciousness.

"Where am I?" asked Billy Bob. He looked up and saw the face of Reverend Jefferson. He jumped when, suddenly, severe pain gripped his upper and lower body like a vice. "Please don't move. You are here in our church, and we are caring for your wounds and those of your companions," the pastor said with a smile.

The Klansman laid back. He looked around the room and at the face of the pastor and the two Italians.

"We tried to kill you, nigger, and we were gonna horsewhip you Wops," he uttered with weakness in his voice. "Now you're taking care of us? Why?" said Billy Bob. "I was gonna burn your church, and you are not angry or taking vengeance?" he asked.

"My son, Jesus would do what we are doing. He loved his enemies and would have healed them just like he healed so many others. He forgave his oppressors and murderers, just as we forgave you. The important thing is that you get better and resume your life. The next time your heart is filled with hate, ask yourself, 'What would Jesus do?' He has all the answers," said the black minister in a voice laden with love and compassion.

Billy Bob rested back on the pillow and stared at the ceiling. He was confused, but he knew that something had happened that was changing his life.

CHAPTER 40 ▬▬▬▬▬▬▬▬▬▬▬▬▬▬▬▬▬▬▬

CARLO'S TRIP

Carlo nearly fell from the train to reach his brother.

He ran as fast as he could.

The two men locked themselves in a powerful embrace. They wept tears of joy. They held on for minutes as if they feared to lose each other again.

Finally, Luigi looked at his baby brother, now a man. He could not believe this moment. He was filled with emotion. "You look wonderful!" said Luigi. "The Americans have been good to you, little brother. You have rosy cheeks, and you are dressed like a gentleman. I am so happy you are here," he said, as more tears welled up in his eyes. Carlo was speechless. The two brothers could not stop weeping. They embraced again and held onto each other as they left the train station.

Gabriela was waiting for them in the car. She leaped on her uncle with joy and kissed his cheeks. He had the musky fragrance of a man who was virile and strong. She was so happy to meet him. She embraced him with the exuberance of a little girl and was fascinated by this younger image of her father, whom she adored. Gabriela chattered like a teenager meeting a rock star.

"Mamma has been cooking for two days," she said.

"She prepared homemade ravioli with her own sauce. She says the tomatoes here are not like the ones in Italy. Here, they are watery and not as sweet as the ones she had in her hometown. Her sauce is filled with special cuts of meat and sausage papa made. I just started to taste his wine this year, and it is wonderful! I like the white better than the red. After the ravioli and the meat, we have a turkey. It's huge! We have a dozen people coming.

Everyone wants to meet you. Welcome to America, Uncle Carlo!" she said with enthusiasm.

Carlo was enthralled. He was with his family.

For the first time in years, he felt safe.

CHAPTER 41 ━━━━━━━━━━━━━━━━━━━━

THE SHERIFF

The Klansmen were awake. It was 5 PM the day after the attack on the black church. The pastor organized a makeshift bed for each. His small apartment was now a hospital, working to save the lives of men who tried to slay him and burn down the house of God. Their burns were serious. They could not be moved and were wrapped in bandages, literally from head to toe. Silverio made a strong chicken soup with carrots, potatoes, and onions. The minister spoon fed each patient. He made sure they had plenty of water to drink. Penicillin was administered twice a day, along with aspirin to deal with the pain.

Shortly before sundown, a black car drove up to the church and screeched to a halt, as if there was a crisis to deal with. The insignia of Panola County Sheriff was engraved on the doors of the vehicle. A tall man with broad shoulders opened the car door and went up to the back of the church, where he knew the pastor resided.

In his holsters were two pearl-handled pistols.

He had on a thick black leather jacket lined with wool, and sunglasses to hide his blue eyes, even though the sun was nearly gone. His tall grey hat had a well-polished badge.

Harnessed to a fence were three black horses watered and fed. A pile of partially burned white robes littered the lawn. Jutting from one garment was a red cross. Several broken bottles were on the ground as part of a dark circle next to a pile of charred wood. The smell of gasoline was in the air.

A bullwhip hung from the fence near the animals.

The sheriff grew tense. Anger welled up inside him.

He went up to the door and banged on it with all his might. He grabbed the knob. The door was locked. He was about to kick it in when he heard the deadbolt turn. The pastor opened the portal.

The Sheriff looked coldly at the black man.

"Jefferson, I'm looking for three men who have been missing for two days. You know anything about it? And who do those horses belong to?" he demanded. "Come in, Sheriff," the pastor said with a smile. The Sheriff walked rapidly into the apartment. He put his hand on one of his pistols. The sound of his boots thundered off the oak boards of the floor.

As he passed through the kitchen and into the apartment, his mouth dropped open. He took off his hat and glasses. Three men were wrapped like mummies lying in makeshift cots, spread out across the room. "What the hell..." he said.

Silverio and Antonio were helping the pastor to care for his patients. They were washing their legs and arms with water, soap, and sponges, like trained nurses. The Sheriff had a hard time distinguishing the faces of the men. He went up to Billy Bob and looked carefully at him. A white bandage partially covered his head and one eye. "What's goin' on here, Billy?" asked the Sheriff. The Klansman whispered into his ear what happened. The Sheriff was shocked. He went over to Silverio and Antonio. "And I suppose you Wops are the ones who spooked their horses last night. I could bring you in for assault and attempted murder," he said with an air of authority. The two longshoremen from New York felt it was best to remain silent.

Billy and Fred sat up in their beds when they heard the Sheriff's words.

"Jack, leave them alone. The pastor and them could have killed us and dumped us in the swamp. The gators would have had a feast. Instead, they saved our lives," insisted Billy.

The Sheriff looked puzzled. He was also angry.

The KKK was defeated on his soil.

It was not an ordinary incident, especially since the Sheriff was the Grand Cyclops of the Ku Klux Klan.

CHAPTER 42

LUIGI AND ANTONIETTA

Luigi's boys, Federico and Gianmarco, were waiting on the porch for the car. Once they saw the auto pull up into the driveway, they dashed to greet their Uncle Carlo. The twins were seven. After Gabriela was born, Antonietta lost three babies in four years. The twins were saved by a cesarean section, which was a dangerous procedure. They were typical boys, filled with energy and curiosity, and constantly playing.

Antonietta was still wearing her apron and drying her hands as she ran to greet Carlo. She had gained 20 pounds since she left Italy and looked older, but she was still jovial and filled with energy. "We left you a boy, and now you are a man! You look wonderful! You must tell us everything! My parents and family are surviving, and Luigi will tell you what we know about this terrible time. And I have prepared a meal fit for this special day of Thanksgiving! We thank God you are home with us!" she said with a happy smile, caressing his face with her hand.

The boys took Carlo's suitcase to the upstairs guest room. Antonietta showed him around the house, while Gabriela continued to cook in the kitchen. It was a split level, with a staircase leading to a porch and the front door. Upstairs were three bedrooms. On the ground floor was a foyer, with living and dining rooms, and the kitchen. The furniture was not fancy, but it was solid and attractive. Luigi was good with his hands and had constructed the dining room table, which could fit 16 people. They had a full basement, with another table and kitchen, where Antonietta did her laundry and jarred tomatoes and marmalade, and eggplants, just like she did in Italy.

The family often ate in the basement in the summer, since it was cooler than the rest of the house. One section of the underground room served as Luigi's wine cellar. Each September, he bought boxes of California grapes to make his own brew. It was a wonderful experience that involved the entire family.

Antonietta was especially proud of her gas stove and oven, and her refrigerator and washer. "This is America, where they do everything to make life easier," she said. "We have a toaster and a coal furnace for heat, and all the house is wired with electricity. I have a vacuum cleaner. We even have a light on the two porches and in the garden." She loved her house, and she and Luigi were pleased with the progress they had made.

"Here you work hard, very hard. You are almost always working, but at least you see some money, and the government gives you services for your taxes. In Italy, we worked seven days a week and were always poor," she explained.

After Carlo freshened up from his long trip, his brother sat him down in the living room. "I have not received a letter from Mamma in three months," said Luigi. "The last one I got was through the Red Cross. Mamma said she had no word about her boys and was desperate for news. She and papa are alive, but the town was bombed and lots of homes destroyed. The only food they have is what they stored last winter in the barn. I wanted to send packages and money, but there is still no way to reach them. I am worried. You remember the Aiello's. They had the farm next to Antonietta's. The Allies bombed the house, and they lost everything. The two Greci boys are dead. You went to school with them. One was killed in Taranto, and the other in Salerno. Our neighbors here have their son in the Army, and he's fighting in the Pacific. Their daughter is a nurse in the Navy," Luigi went on discussing how families were suffering from the War.

Carlo was silent. He was numb. He wanted to forget what he had been through, but now felt forced to talk about the events leading to his capture, which had plagued him with recurrent nightmares. He wanted to enjoy the peace of silence. In his dreams, he still heard the roar of cannons and the thunder of bombs dropping like raindrops from the clouds. Machine-gun fire and the whizzing whistle of approaching bullets seemed like they were happening at that moment.

He saw the disfigured bodies and faces of his companions in uniform. He heard their voices as they begged for water and food. Dreadful visions of combat stayed with him night and day, and now all he wished for was to be surrounded by his family and enjoy a meal cooked at home, and not in a mess hall with a hundred other men.

Carlo and Luigi got up to go to the kitchen. The scent of the baking turkey was like perfume to Carlo. His niece, Gabriela, was cutting celery and fennel to make a salad. She chatted about the family from their hometown who were coming to dinner.

They had a niece named Helena, she said. "She's my best friend and she's gorgeous, and she looks like the movie star, Ava Gardner," said Gabriela.

Carlo had seen a film with the actress, but her image was far from his mind. "Unfortunately, Helena is an orphan. Both parents died when she was very young," asserted Gabriela.

The word "orphan" was like an arrow to his heart.

Carlo had seen many families shattered in towns in North Africa. Camps were filled with boys and girls who had lost their parents. They were starving to death. As a soldier, he tried to provide food and shelter for children. Some orphans had died in his arms.

He was in no mood to meet another on this special day.

CHAPTER 43

BRUNO

Bruno remained undecided. The Nazis had prepared the plans, and the tunnel was dug. All that remained was to escape. The Germans were ready. The Italians were yet to be convinced to join them. There was strength in numbers. The only person trusted by the Nazis and the Italian soldiers was Bruno. He believed Italy was fighting a just cause and was liberating the world from democratic capitalism that favored the few over the many.

The Gestapo officers said the Americans were weak because they were a mixed breed of bastards and would ultimately be defeated by the "master race" and its allies. They preached that the camp was a good example of what fools the Yankees were. Enemies were not to be dealt with as equals or with respect.

Instead, since they were defeated, they should be treated little better than slaves.

SS leaders intimidated anyone who collaborated with the Americans. There were beatings of German soldiers and death threats against the Italians who would not cooperate with the prisoners against their captors. SS Senior Leader Fischer was the enforcer. He demanded discipline and no cooperation with the Americans. He would use any measure necessary to bend the German and Italian soldiers to his will.

"Hold him down," Fischer commanded as two Gestapo leaders pinned a German sergeant to his bed. Fischer took out a leather belt like a whip. The SS members exposed his back and buttocks. Fischer beat the man with vigor. His aides muffled his mouth with a rag so that no one could hear his screams. He lashed him until blood seeped from multiple wounds. The soldier squirmed violently with pain. Fischer continued until the sergeant lay still and unconscious.

The SS leader perspired from his task.

He put away his belt, like an artisan stores his tools.

"If you continue to work with the Yankees in the laundry, I will beat you to death. Let this be a warning to you and the others," he whispered in the ear of the wounded soldier.

"Tell the other soldiers and the Italians that if they refuse to join us in the escape, I will kill them."

CHAPTER 44 ▬▬▬▬▬▬▬▬▬▬▬▬▬▬▬▬▬▬▬▬▬▬▬▬

HEALING THE KLANSMEN

"I wanna take you boys to the hospital, where they can fix you up," insisted the Sheriff. "I don't think they should be moved at least for a few days. Their burns are serious, and they need to rest. No one will bother them here," explained the pastor. "Listen to the nigger," remarked the Sheriff. "Are you a doctor? Do you know what you're doin'? These guys might die from infection if they don't see a real doctor soon."

The pastor explained the treatment and how they were progressing after the incident. "And what about these Wops?" cracked the Sheriff, turning to Silverio and Antonio.

Silverio got up from his chair. He walked up to the Sheriff who was at least a foot taller than him.

"Stop calling us Wops," he said. "And stop calling the pastor a nigger," he stood up to the Sheriff with determination.

He looked him in the eyes.

The Sheriff put his hand on his Billy Club. The wooden baton had metal tips on both ends. "Jack, we're fine and getting better," spoke up Fred, for the first time. "We don't want the whole town to know what happened," chimed in Andy. "If we go to the hospital or to the doctor, people will ask questions," said Billy Bob. "You could help us by telling our boss at the mill that we are on a 'special' assignment for you and will be back in two weeks," he insisted. "Tell our kinfolk the same thing. If it comes from you, no one will say anything," remarked Andy "You could also help the Italians. They need to get to camp Como," noted Billy Bob. "Silverio, show Jack the letter," he said.

The Sheriff read the message from the Commandant and digested what the Klansmen had said. "Okay. It's a deal. Silverio, tomorrow I will see to it that you get to the camp. Pastor, you need anything?" he inquired. "Sheriff, we could use fresh bandages, iodine, and more penicillin. Andy has a cough. He may be getting bronchitis. Get some good strong cough medicine. We are down on food so meat, potatoes, chicken, and vegetables and oranges, and cornmeal, are what we need for the next few days. We could use a few sacks of coal for the stoves." The Sheriff was sorry he asked. "Okay, but I'm warning you, Jefferson, if something happens to any one of these boys, you will regret the day you were born!" he declared with anger in his voice. "I understand," replied the pastor. He gave him a warm smile. "Jesus is with us, and now he brought you to help heal the bodies and the souls of these men." The Sheriff promised to return first thing the next morning.

He put on his hat and glasses and marched out of the church. The Sheriff got in the car and felt disgusted with himself and with the situation. He was not a religious man, but he went to church on Sundays for political reasons. He was up for re-election and needed every vote he could get.

Perhaps there was a reason all this was happening. Maybe the minister was right. The Sheriff believed in Jesus and Divine Providence.

Maybe the hand of God was involved, after all. He did not know, but he would soon discover the truth.

CHAPTER 45 ━━━━━━━━━━━━━━━━━━━━━━━━━━━━━━━━━

BREAKING BREAD WITH THE KLANSMEN

"Get that stuff out of the trunk and back seat," ordered the Sheriff to Silverio and Antonio. They hauled bags of food and medication into the church. It was only 6:30 AM, and the pastor's patients were just waking from a sound sleep. The minister decided that they could have something solid to eat. He prepared bacon and eggs and slices of buttered corn bread, and coffee. "Join us for breakfast, Sheriff," said the pastor. "Don't mind if I do, Reverend," he responded. 'Brought some of that fancy coffee that these city slickers drink in the North," he said with a smile. "Got you a case of condensed milk, and I will bring you some ice for your ice box later today. I know you can keep the meat outside, but those coons and bears are all over the place these days. I have a suitcase with undergarments for them, and some shirts and jeans along with the bandages and medicine you wanted. Bring you the coal this afternoon."

Silverio and Antonio gingerly brought each Klansman into the dining room. They could barely walk. Their feet and leg burns were painful. The men were slowly seated at the table. A large pan filled with scrambled eggs and bacon was before them along with a stack of buttered cornbread and jars of jams and jellies. The Sheriff sat at the head of the table as if the place were set especially for him.

After the pastor and the Italians found their seats, the black minister joined hands with the Sheriff, and everyone followed suit. "Almighty Father, we thank you for this food from your garden of love. We thank you for our brothers who are with us today and are healing miraculously because of your grace. May your divine light shine on us in friendship and brotherhood," he prayed.

It was the first time the Sheriff had ever touched the hand of a colored man.

"Amen," the men responded simultaneously. "You make great cornbread, Jefferson," said the Sheriff. "Can you cook good grits and fried chicken?" he asked. "His chicken is fantastic," chimed in Antonio. "We've eaten more grits than anyone in Mississippi," said Silverio. "We have it three times a day. It's good, but it's coming out our ears," he said with a grin. They all laughed, especially the Klansmen. The pastor was happy the spirits of his patients were improving.

Everyone ate well. It was a meal they would never forget.

The Klansmen returned to their beds. "I fixed things at the mill and with your families. No one will ask questions," said the Sheriff. He turned to the Italians. "As soon as you have your gear together, I will take you to the camp," said the Sheriff. Silverio and Antonio had their suitcases ready.

"Thank you for your kindness, Reverend," said Silverio as he embraced the black man. "You and your cousin saved me and my church. I will never forget you," he said, with tears in his eyes. "Maybe the KKK will think twice before they tangle with Italian longshoremen again," boomed Silverio in a voice all could hear. The three men hugged and shook hands. The pastor waved to them as they got into the Cadillac. "He's a good man," said Silverio. "A few more days with him and I'd become a Baptist," responded Antonio.

CHAPTER 46 ━━━━━━━━━━━━━━━━━━━

CAMP COMO

Silverio followed the Sheriff's car. He and Antonio had washed and shaved and put on their best suits with a white shirt and tie. They expected to meet the camp Commander and wanted to look presentable. It was early, and there was no one on the back roads of northern Mississippi. The sun was up and seemed to shine directly in front of the car. Late November was chilly and humid in this part of the country, and the men needed to wear their warm coats to protect them from the cold.

The brilliant colors of fall were everywhere. Trees, bushes, and shrubs with red, green, and yellow leaves were scattered along the muddy roads. Bright orange pumpkins were strewn over fields, surrounded by bales of hay and scattered farm machinery. A few houses with horses, chickens, and pigs dotted the landscape. The mooing of cows seemed to welcome them.

It was a short drive to reach the compound, which rose out of nowhere. Forests had been cleared for hundreds of acres around the complex. The camp was encircled by miles of simple wooden fencing, not over three feet high. There were no towers with guards and machine guns. In the middle were countless rows of cottages and barracks, and square and rectangular structures with pyramidal roofs. It seemed like a resort filled with bungalows for honeymooners. But the jeeps, armored vehicles, and automobiles they could see parked in several areas of the camp quickly swept away any thought that this was a vacation spot. A green helicopter sat on a cement pad. Trucks and artillery were in and around the buildings.

Prisoner of War Camp in Mississippi, *Courtesy, US Army*

Inside, several troops in strategic locations patrolled with automatic rifles. Soldiers manned the perimeter with long guns and spotlights. Men in grey outfits walked in and around the campgrounds, without guards or dogs restricting them.

Military Police officers guarded the main entrance, which was a tall metal gate. The MPs were dressed in army green and white, with beige-colored helmets. All were exceedingly tall, with huge, muscular frames. Pistols, protected with white leather covers, were in holsters attached to their belts. They wore long jackboots and green, mirror-like sunglasses that hid their eyes and gave them the look of massive robots. It was easy to see these were not ordinary soldiers, but that they were carefully selected for an important role.

The Sheriff drove to the opening. A guardsman came forward and saluted him.

"The car behind me has two men from New York who received this letter from your camp Commander," he said, showing him the document. The corporal read the message and returned to his station. He lifted the phone.

"Lieutenant Black here," was the response. "Sir, I have the County Sheriff here with a green Cadillac with New York license plates. The Sheriff showed me a letter from Colonel McCarthy to one of the people in the car. The letter asks him to come to the camp," explained the MP. "Hold on, Corporal," responded the Lieutenant. He knocked on the door of the Commandant and went in. He told him what he had learned.

"Let them in right away, Lieutenant. Meet them downstairs and bring them to my office," said the Colonel, rising from his chair.

CHAPTER 47 ━━━━━━━━━━━━━━━━

THE COMMANDANT

After a conversation that lasted five minutes, the MP came back to speak with the Sheriff. "The Commandant will be glad to meet them, Sheriff. He asked for you to accompany them," he explained. The Sheriff knew the man in charge of the camp well. Some of his enlisted men had run into trouble in town, and he and the Sheriff had an understanding about how to deal with it. Most problems were about women and drinking. Soldiers would get into fights and the MPs, along with the Sheriff's deputies, would arrest them. The Sheriff always let them off if nothing serious had happened.

The MP opened the gate and waved the cars to enter. The Sheriff drove to the main building. It was shaped like a large barn. The building was white, with stairs and multiple floors filled with offices and coal-burning stoves. Chimney pipes popped out of the roof. The clicking of typewriters and men walking across floorboards could be heard from the outside. Silverio followed and parked beside the Sheriff's car. "Come with me," he said. Lieutenant Black was waiting for them at the entrance. "Morning, Jack, how are you?" asked the Lieutenant, politely. "Could be better, Tom," responded the Sheriff dryly.

The Lieutenant led the way as they climbed the stairs to the second floor. A door with a white porcelain knob faced them. Office of the Commandant, Camp Como, Mississippi, was engraved on a plaque attached to the portal. The Lieutenant knocked and opened.

Colonel Gregory J. McCarthy stood before them. He looked somber and grave.

The Colonel extended his hand. Silverio and Antonio shook it with respect. The Sheriff looked on. "Didn't expect these New Yorkers to have a special escort, Sheriff," said the Colonel. "Wanted to make sure they got here safely, Colonel. Got to know them, let's say, through mutual acquaintances," responded the Sheriff somewhat sarcastically. "Best be movin' on, Colonel. Have some fires to put out. If you need me, you know where to find me," he stated as he went to the door. "You Yankees behave yourselves now. You are now in the hands of the U.S. Army," he remarked as he left the room.

"Please sit down," said the Colonel. "Can I get you some coffee?" he asked. The Italians accepted. He lifted the phone, "Lieutenant, make a fresh pot of coffee and bring some of that corn bread they brought in this morning." Silverio and Antonio looked at each other. They had eaten enough cornbread to fill a bakery. What they really wanted was some Italian cookies and pastries. They hadn't eaten pasta or pizza for 5 days.

Silverio thought that if he didn't have some spaghetti soon, he would need it intravenously.

"Thank you for accepting my invitation, Silverio. I know it has been a long and difficult trip. I understand you had some problems in Tennessee, but I assure you that your being here is important, and you will have both my gratitude and that of the United States of America for any sacrifice you have made in assisting us," explained the Colonel with an air of formality and seriousness. Silverio nodded his head in agreement.

He listened carefully to the Commandant, even though he was still confused on why he was there, except to see his cousin.

CHAPTER 48 ▬▬▬▬▬▬▬▬▬▬▬▬▬

THE PLANNED ESCAPE

"**S**ir, you have a familiar accent," said Silverio. "Are you from the East Coast?" he inquired. "I was born and raised in the Bronx near Gun Hill Road. I went to Theodore Roosevelt High School and the Military Academy at West Point. My mother is from Caserta, near Naples," he responded with a smile. "Our island was once in the province of Caserta, and we speak Neapolitan," said Silverio.

Antonio slapped his leg and laughed. "I was the custodian at Roosevelt High School when I first came to America. I remember having trouble with lots of the boys who were always trying to make out with girls in the basement. Now I know why you looked so familiar," he said with a broad smile. The three men laughed as if they had known each other forever.

After the coffee, the cornbread, and pleasantries, the Commandant got down to business.

"This camp has thousands of German and Italian prisoners who were captured mainly in North Africa. As you can see from the fencing, this facility is relatively open. The inmates are not confined in any manner, except they cannot leave the camp without permission and a purpose. The reason could be to work at the nearby farms, visit the town library, or just take a walk on Main Street. In each case, they depart with trust and must return to the camp at a certain time. If they do not respect the rules, they lose their privileges. The prisoners basically run the place themselves. They cook, clean, build, and repair. It is more of a community than a prison.

"Now, the internees are divided into three groups. The 'NONS' are those who refuse to cooperate and still believe they must fight. The German SS, the Gestapo, and the Fascists give us the most trouble. We inter them with other inmates to not make them feel isolated, but we keep our eye on them. The regular Italian soldiers are fine. The Italians are our most trusted POWs.

"They and the Germans, who have taken a peaceful route, basically manage the facility under our supervision. Cleaning, cooking, and repairing is done by them. Most prisoners also have paid jobs in town, in stores, or on ranches. We have soccer and basketball teams and libraries stocked with Italian and German books and several movie theatres. An international Red Cross Office is also on the base so the POWs can write home and receive mail. We are teaching English to whoever is interested. As you can see, our location is like a small town," explained the Colonel. He showed how the camp policies were based on the Geneva Convention, which the U.S. respected.

"Despite our best efforts to treat the POWs with dignity, we are still at war with the countries they come from. We know that some believe the struggle must continue, even in captivity. The Nazis are planning an escape or an insurrection," he said bluntly. "We can't allow it. We would have to use deadly force to stop it. Anything of this sort could affect morale and could cost lives."

He stared at Silverio. He raised his voice for emphasis.

"I need your help to prevent this."

CHAPTER 49 ▬▬▬▬▬▬▬▬▬▬▬▬▬▬▬▬▬▬▬▬

CARLO'S PRAYER

Carlo finished showering and shaving. He splashed some cologne on his face and pressed toilet paper to his chin to absorb the blood of a small cut. He was surprised how smooth his cheeks had become after months without shaving and washing during the North African campaign. The camp provided common bathing facilities, but that was nothing compared to being in a home where he could properly take care of himself.

Before going down to dinner, he had to think and rest.

Reality was covering him like a shadow.

He needed to understand where he was and where he was going. Silence helped him bury the past months and years, which had changed his soul from a farm boy to a man who had seen enough for a lifetime.

He lay down, closed his eyes, and reflected.

Luigi had changed. He was older, stouter; signs of age and worry were etched in his face. He was no longer the big brother who took him by the hand to milk the cows, fish in the streams, and gaze at the stars and dream about the universe. Luigi was an American entrepreneur, a solid family man, and deeply rooted in the soil of the New World. He had found himself and discovered a meaning for his life and his children.

Carlo felt like a cork thrown into the ocean. He was taken by the waves and currents from one shore to the next with no control.

He felt powerless, and he was paralyzed by images and feelings of the turbulent past.

He dreaded facing his family and their friends assembled to celebrate an American holiday and his homecoming. Carlo was frightened to talk about the war and what he had seen and done. He killed men and launched bombs into towns, where children and women were blown to bits. Bodies were strewn amidst the rubble. Images of toys, cradles, and bloody baby clothes flashed across his mind, like scenes from a horror movie.

The terrible memories had chained him into a form of mental bondage.

The trauma of war, defeat, and imprisonment snuffed out his sense of freedom. *Home* was now a strange word.

What would he go back to? Was the family house still standing? Were Mamma and Papa alive? Where were his brothers and sisters? Italy was in ruins and so was his future.

Questions and thoughts as these weighed on Carlo's mind as he dressed for Thanksgiving dinner.

Before putting on his clothes, he knelt in front of a cross in the room. He closed his eyes and prayed. "Almighty Father, thank you for protecting me and bringing me to the home of my brother and his family. Please take care of them, Oh Lord. They are good people. Now, as I face a new life, please deliver me from the burden of the past. Help me find a way into the future to deal with the challenges ahead. I feel so alone and afraid, but I know if you are at my side, all will be well."

For several minutes, Carlo knelt in silence, with his head bowed, sweeping away all negative thoughts.

He rose, feeling better after his petition to his Creator.

A fresh shirt was laid out on his bed. It was white and went well with his red tie and dark blue suit. Carlo was surprised at how well it fit. The Sergeant had thought of everything. His kindness was amazing.

A car arrived and parked in front of the house. Carlo heard voices and doors opening. He looked out of the second-floor window. A man, a woman, and three girls left the auto and came up the path. The last person was a young lady. It was cold and windy. She darted to the front door to avoid the freezing air. She moved like a breeze as she hugged her coat tightly to her body. In a glance, he noticed how her hair shined as it fluttered in the wind and how she straightened her back, stood poised and erect as she entered the house, like a princess.

Carlo's heart pounded, and he did not know why.

He left the room. As he walked down the stairs, he heard the wooden planks creak.

Helena removed her coat.

She raised her head at the sound of Carlo's steps.

Her eyes met his.

He stopped, frozen and speechless.

She smiled.

Something inside him trembled.

Passion rose in his heart as he fixed his eyes on the most beautiful girl he had ever seen.

Emilio Iodice

CHAPTER 50 ━━━━━━━━━━━━━━━━━━━━━━━━━━━━━━━━━━━

THE OSS

"**L**ieutenant, we want to be assigned to the same unit," said Joe to the officer in charge. He stared at the young man with his light green eyes. He was from the South, and he did not like hyphenated Americans or northerners. His great-grandfather was a Confederate general, and his ancestors were southern aristocracy who still flew the Confederate flag and believed that the South was not defeated in the Civil War, but that it was overcome by an occupying power.

The Lieutenant had sworn allegiance to the Constitution of the United States of America. It was the only country he had. He was a patriot and would die to defend America, even if he felt its values were flawed.

As the Lieutenant pondered the fate of these Italian Americans from the Bronx, Joe thought about all that happened since he and Tom had been inducted and sent to Georgia for basic training.

At the Armory in New York, they went through the process of having their height and weight recorded, being given a general health checkup, having a brief examination of their teeth (you had to have at least 12), and being given a review of past illnesses and convictions for crimes, if any, as well as taking a test for literacy. During the War, thousands of young men were rejected because they could not read or write or had flat feet.

Ten weeks of basic training involved getting up before dawn, marching for 25 miles, learning how to shoot a rifle and throw a hand grenade, dig a foxhole, and crawl under barbed-wire fences with machine guns firing live bullets above them.

Joe and Tom passed, but they felt they could not capture even a tree with what they had learned.

"You both speak Italian, according to your records," the Lieutenant said to the young recruits. "Yes, sir. It was our first language," responded Tom. "If you want to be assigned to the same unit, I can send you to OSS," he explained. Joe and Tom did not know what the officer was talking about. They assumed it was more military jargon. "That's fine, sir," replied Joe.

In less than an hour, the two soldiers were in front of a Major. There was no title on his door. His office was a grey metal desk with maps of the world pinned to the walls, plus a bookcase and a phone. A photo of FDR was prominently displayed on a wall, along with an American flag.

The officer wore a regular Army uniform and had numerous commendations pinned to his chest. He was of medium height. His blond hair was cut to the edge, military style, and he had a ruddy complexion from years of being outdoors. A photo of a woman with children was the only decoration on his desk. A small pile of folders was in front of him.

He was raised in the Northwest of the United States. The woods and fields of Oregon were an excellent place to raise someone who would have to maintain a clear mind and concentrate on a mission with the precision of a high-powered weapon.

"The Office of Strategic Services was formed after Pearl Harbor," he said. "OSS was created to coordinate and collect intelligence information in one central unit; to engage in spying; wage wars of propaganda; perform acts of sabotage and help anti-Nazi resistance fighters and anti-Jap guerrillas. We train special intelligence units to land behind enemy lines and support partisans who are fighting to liberate their country from the Nazis or the Fascists before we invade. I need native language speakers in Italian to join my company. Do you understand?" he asked.

The young soldiers from the Bronx were puzzled. "You mean you want us to be spies?" asked Tom. "That's only part of the job. It requires gathering information, organizing and supplying foreign fighters, and conducting sabotage missions to keep the enemy off balance," he explained.

"So we won't operate with the regular Army and we'll be involved only in separate operations?" asked Joe. "Precisely. You will be specially trained in communications, psychology, history, geography, handling of explosives, and understanding the enemy. You will be sent behind enemy lines to help partisans liberate Italy. We select only qualified volunteers because of the skills required and the risk involved. Are you interested?"

Joe looked at Tom. The young men nodded. "We're in, sir."

CHAPTER 51

SILVERIO'S CHALLENGE

"**S**ilverio, your cousin is the leader of the Fascist movement in the camp. The Gestapo looks to him to indoctrinate and organize the Italians. We know the Germans are planning an escape. They have dug a tunnel and expect to make a run for it any day now. I want you to persuade Bruno to not participate. If he and the other Italians do not participate, then either the Germans will go alone or drop the idea. We do not want to harm anyone, but we will use deadly force to stop them from leaving the camp. We know the plans of the SS. They are determined to strike at civilian and military installations in and around the camp and to transport themselves out of the country. We will not allow this to happen.

"Italy is now on the side of the Allies, and we need them to rid the country of the Nazis and the Fascists. Mussolini's puppet government in the North has created a civil war and divided the population and the armed forces. We can't have this happen while the Italians are POWs here in America. Instead, we want them to live peacefully, work and earn money to take back to a liberated country, and help rebuild it into a democracy," concluded the Colonel.

Silverio now understood the seriousness of his task and the gravity of his mission. Persuading Bruno was only part of the equation. There were hundreds of thousands of enemy prisoners of war on U.S. soil. An escape or an uprising in one camp could touch off a chain reaction in others, once the news got out.

The security of America was at stake.

CHAPTER 52

THE BROTHERS' TRIP

It was a long train ride from Savannah, Georgia, to Arlington, Virginia. Joe and Tom had never traveled beyond New York and New Jersey. In a matter of months, they crisscrossed the eastern part of the United States, which was the size of Western Europe. Millions of young men and women would have the same experience during the War years.

It would change them forever.

As they moved across plains and slinked through valleys and circled mountains, the boys from the Bronx feasted their eyes on America in all its beauty, variety, and power. Here were rich farms bursting with fruits and vegetables to feed the teeming millions in cities like Atlanta, Philadelphia, New York, Miami, and Boston. New ports, airports, and roads were being built from Bangor, Maine, in the north to Key West in Florida. Steel mills and factories were working three shifts a day to fabricate guns, bombs, bullets, tanks, planes, and ships that would cross the oceans to defend America in the greatest conflict ever known to man.

America's strength and determination were seen in the faces of the common folk along the way. Victory was assured in the hearts, souls, minds, and hands of the people of the United States.

"I fear all we have done is to awaken a sleeping giant and fill him with a terrible resolve," said Admiral Yamamoto after he planned and executed the Japanese attack on Pearl Harbor. He could not imagine how prophetic his words would be.

Joe and Tom understood it clearly as their journeys continued.

They were now members of the Office of Strategic Services. A special training center was organized outside of the nation's capital. The brothers were on their way to a new adventure.

They would be taught how to operate the most sophisticated communications systems in existence, learn about explosives and sabotage, collect and use intelligence, study European history and geography, understand human psychology and the philosophy of the Nazis and Fascists.

They would also be taught how to kill quickly, silently, and efficiently.

CHAPTER 53

ANNA

Tom reminisced during the long ride.

His mind flew to the echo of a sweet, saintly voice. It was now part of him.

It first happened when he was in the eighth grade at Our Lady of Pity School. Each Sunday morning, he and Joe would go to the 9 AM mass. It was obligatory. For a 14-year-old boy, it was hard to concentrate on the religious ritual while thinking of the next baseball game that the New York Yankees would be playing.

During the service, Tom heard an angelic echo flow through the air.

It enthralled him.

On a balcony, high above the rear of the church, was the organ and the choir. A young girl sang in Latin the "Ave Maria."

Tom could not understand the words, but he sensed passion and emotion as the sound literally captivated him.

He turned and saw locks of blond hair and a face out of a beautiful painting.

She had mahogany-colored eyes, and a smooth light skin with perfect features. She was the soloist. She smiled as she chanted a melody that carried her remarkable singing across the chapel and reached into the heart of Tom like Cupid's arrow. After the mass, the boy ran to the gallery.

He walked up to the girl with the golden locks. "You sang so beautifully. I got goosebumps. I am sure if angels exist, they sing like you," said Tom to Anna. She blushed, stretched out her hand, and introduced herself.

From that moment on, Tom was enveloped in an ever-deepening love for this amazing girl.

Anna's family was also from the island. Like Tom, she was born in America. Her parents worked. Her mother, Concetta, made dresses, and her father, Alessandro, worked as a laborer in construction sites, like most men who came from Ponza. It was a hard life. Anna was a splendid daughter and an only child. She helped do chores and took care of any problems dealing with English, since her mother and father could barely read or write Italian, let alone their new language.

She was born gorgeous.

Her looks surpassed that of her parents. Her baby face grew more appealing with age as it filled out but kept the glow of innocence and youth as she grew into her adolescence. In school, she was the first in her class and often "the teacher's pet" for her charm and ability to take responsibility. At events, she danced and sang like a young star from the silver screen. Anna was naturally talented, attractive, and kind.

Boys fell for her at first sight.

The moment that she met Tom, she felt the first sensations of love. She could not define what was happening, but she knew she had to be with this handsome young man who exuded energy, joy, and courage. He was irresistible.

Anna discovered love was caring, being together, and dreaming.

From the second they embraced, Tom and Anna were inseparable. They pledged eternal devotion and planned their lives together.

Then the War came.

Now the man in her life was in uniform, bound for destinations unknown to her or him. The day he left for basic training, Tom took Anna in his arms. "Darling, when I return, we will get married, save for a house, and have a family. But, if something happens to me, you are free to marry someone else. I love you so much, and all I want is your happiness." He kissed her face filled with tears.

"You will come back, and I will wait for you. If you don't come back, there will be no space in my heart for anyone else. Do you want me to be a spinster? Tom, please be safe. I love you and can't live without you!" cried Anna as she hugged and kissed him as if she would never see him again.

He gave her a bracelet. Etched on the inside was his name with the words, "I love you. I will always love you. No one can ever love you more."

Tom still sensed the flavor of her lips on his as he sat back in the train on his journey into the mysterious world of military intelligence.

CHAPTER 54 ▬▬▬▬▬▬▬▬▬▬▬▬▬▬▬▬▬

LIBERATION OF THE KLANSMEN

Two weeks had passed. The Klansmen were nearly recovered. Physically, their wounds had healed. Psychologically, the men went through a transformation.

No longer were they the fierce crusaders of white supremacy.

A cornucopia of emotions changed them.

Humiliation, at their failed vengeance against the black pastor. Amazement, as those they hated saved them from the ravages of a fiery death, showing mercy and compassion.

Kindness and love softened their spirits and opened their hearts and minds to God.

Each evening, the pastor read passages from the Old and New Testament to his patients just before bedtime. The Klansmen were a captive audience. Even though they attended church services, they never before had actually reflected on the words of the Good Book.

Now, as they convalesced in an African-American church, they listened to the voice of the Lord. Godly words penetrated their souls and liberated their minds from hate, prejudice, and intolerance.

> *Keep on loving one another as brothers and sisters. Do not forget to show hospitality to strangers, for by so doing people have shown hospitality to angels without knowing it. Hebrews 13:1-2*

> *You shall love the Lord your God with all your heart and with all your soul and with all your mind. This is the great and first commandment. And a second is like it: You shall love your neighbor as yourself. Matthew 22:36-40*

But I say to you who hear, Love your enemies, do good to those who hate you. Luke 6:27

Owe no one anything, except to love each other, for the one who loves another has fulfilled the law. For the commandments, "You shall not commit adultery, You, shall not murder, You shall not steal, You shall not covet," and any other commandment, are summed up in these words: "You shall love your neighbor as yourself." Love does no wrong to a neighbor; therefore, love is fulfilling the law. Romans 13:8-10

So, whatever you wish that others would do to you, do also to them, for this is the Law. Matthew 7:12

This is my commandment, that you love one another as I have loved you. John 15:12

Therefore, let us stop passing judgment on one another. Instead, make up your mind not to put any stumbling block or obstacle in the way of a brother or sister. Romans 14:13

Bear with each other and forgive one another if any of you has a grievance against someone. Forgive as the Lord forgave you. Colossians 3:13

Above all, love each other deeply, because love covers over a multitude of sins. Peter 4:8

Learn to do right; seek justice. Defend the oppressed. Take up the cause of the fatherless; plead the case of the widow. Isaiah 1:17

You, therefore, have no excuse, you who pass judgment on someone else, for at whatever point you judge another, you are condemning yourself, because you who pass judgment do the same things. Romans 2:1

The Klansmen heard the voice of the Lord. Each phrase and thought was part of them. Their souls, hearts, and minds were lifted to heaven and the Almighty.

CHAPTER 55 ━━━━━━━━━━━━━━━━━━

THE KLANSMEN GO HOME

Town folk inquired about the Klansmen and rumors started. The Sheriff decided it was time to get them out of the church. He needed to do so when no one could see them exit the chapel.

It was 2 AM.

The Sheriff drove up to the back of the building. He waited in the car with his radio off. He would take them home, where they could complete their recovery. No signs of infection showed up and their faces appeared like they had been in the sun longer than necessary and not engulfed in flames.

"Billy, you and the boys need to take off your bandages tomorrow and let the wounds dry. Continue the antibiotics and the aspirin for another day. I suggest a week before you go back to work. Drink a lot of water, and no alcohol, for ten days. If you need anything, let me know." said the pastor as he helped each man get on his feet.

Billy hugged him and cried. He wiped away his tears and said, "Reverend, I know I am speaking for all of us. We came here with hate in our hearts. We came to hurt and kill you. We came to destroy your church. Instead, you forgave us and showed us mercy when we were down. You healed our wounds when you could have left us to die. You gave us love and kindness. We have changed. We are liberated from the poison that was in our hearts. Isiah Jefferson, we are no longer your enemies but now your lifelong friends and protectors, so help us, God."

The pastor was moved by their words. "Here is a little gift for each of you," as he handed them each a Bible. "Read God's words and those of Our Lord every day. They will bring you comfort and guidance as you start your new journey of deliverance. From this day forward, Jesus will be your co-pilot and at your side, always."

As they left the church, the men realized that the grace of God had saved them and they had a new mission in life. It was to give a message of peace and love to combat animosity and bitterness.

The Sheriff opened the door of the car. The pastor helped them get in and sit comfortably. The Sheriff started the vehicle. The men peered at the minister as they departed.

The black man waved to them in the darkness as the car disappeared into the night.

"Jack," said Billy, "thanks for all you did for us.

As of today, I am no longer a member of the Ku Klux Klan."

CHAPTER 56

THE CALL TO LUCIA

"We finally made it to the camp. We should see Bruno tomorrow," explained Silverio to Lucia over the phone. "The Commandant gave us a nice room and invited us to have dinner with him. The trip took much longer than we expected because of the roads and the traffic. Everything is fine, and we should be leaving in a few days." Lucia knew her husband well. He would not tell her if anything was wrong, to avoid worrying her.

"The baby is good and is walking and talking a lot," she said. Silverio and Lucia felt lucky they had a son as handsome as Ralph. He was four years old and very intelligent for his age. "Everyone is asking about you and Antonio in the community. Your boss at the Navy Yard called. Mr. Lynch from the union told him not to worry and that you would be back soon. The store is okay, but we need to order the trees to sell at Christmas when you come back," she responded. Silverio had left his world behind as he journeyed into the shadows of Mississippi.

Now it was slowly coming back to him, in his mind.

His son Ralph was born in 1939. He was named after Silverio's father, Raffaele. The couple wanted more children, but Lucia could not have a normal birth because of the tightness of her hips. From 1939 to 1944, she lost four babies, each of which she carried for nine months. All but one was delivered stillborn. A baby girl lived a month and then died. It was a traumatic experience. Lucia still remembered the church service and the burial of her infant in an unknown grave somewhere in New York. Each event was a terrible shock to this young lady from Ponza, whose mother brought eleven children into the world.

Lucia thought about this as she held her precious son in her arms. She prayed each day that God would grant them one more child as healthy and handsome as Ralph.

"Section C, where your cousin lives, has 800 Germans and 200 Italians," explained Lieutenant Black as he escorted Silverio and Antonio on a tour of the camp. "The Gestapo and Fascists are held in that subdivision so we can keep a special eye on them. We have 12 areas with over 5,000 prisoners. Each is self-contained with its own food, housing, recreation, and entertainment facilities. We hold religious services on Sunday with Catholic, Protestant, and Jewish chaplains. The SS officers protested that a Jew was in the camp. We told them that in America we have freedom of religion. Some of our Italian inmates and our troops are Jewish, so we hold Saturday services for them.

"Our sports include soccer games, where all the units play each other and then have an annual championship. They have basketball courts and three baseball fields, four libraries, and six movie theatres. As I've said before, the inmates run the camp under our supervision. So far, we have had no real trouble except for an occasional fight. The SS officers intimidate the Germans and the Italians. If we get evidence of this, we will discipline them," he stressed as they concluded their visit to the camp.

"I understand," said Silverio to the Commandant as he cut into a tender steak. "We toured the camp today and can see the gravity of the problem. If they break out of Section C, it could affect the rest of the camp. I will do all I can to stop Bruno from organizing the Italians," he said. "I hope you succeed. Many lives are at stake," responded Colonel McCarthy. Silverio and Antonio listened carefully as the Colonel went on about the entire issue of prisoners of war in America.

"As you know," explained the Colonel, "we abide by the Geneva Conventions, which state that prisoners of war are to be treated humanely. What you see at this camp is repeated in a thousand facilities throughout the U.S. The POWs are, to a large extent, given the same privileges of any American citizen except they know that they are interned and have much of their liberty controlled until the war ends. We are doing this because it is the right thing to do from a humanitarian and democratic viewpoint. Also, we know these men will return home someday to rebuild their country. We will help reconstruct Germany, Japan, and Italy, and we hope they will be our allies and not our enemies. We want these men to know us as being fair, honest, and just. As they go back to the lives they led, we want to work together to build a peaceful world after this tragedy is over."

CHAPTER 57 ━━━━━━━━━━━━━━━━━━━━━━━

THANKSGIVING DINNER

Gabriela stood up at the dinner table. Everyone was seated to listen and then eat. "This morning, the newspapers had President Roosevelt's Thanksgiving Proclamation, which I will read to you," she said with pride:

> God's help to us has been great in this year of the march towards worldwide liberty. In brotherhood, with warriors of other United Nations, our gallant men have won victories, have freed our homes from fear, have made tyranny tremble, and have laid the foundation for freedom of living in a world which will be free.
>
> Our forges and hearths and mills have wrought well, and our weapons have not failed. Our farmers, victory gardeners, and crop volunteers have gathered and stored a heavy harvest in the barns and bins and cellars. Our total food production for the year is the greatest in the annals of our country.
>
> For all these things we are devoutly thankful, knowing also so great mercies exact from us the greatest measure of sacrifice and service.
>
> Now, therefore, I, Franklin D. Roosevelt, President of the United States of America, do designate Thursday, November 25th, 1943, as a day for expressing our thanks to God for His blessings.
>
> May we on Thanksgiving Day and on every day express our gratitude and zealously devote ourselves to our duties as individuals and as a nation. May each of us dedicate his utmost efforts to speeding the victory which will bring new opportunities for peace and brotherhood among men.

Everyone but Carlo clapped. He did not understand parts of the message and the meaning of the holiday.

"Thanksgiving is a special day for us in America," explained Helena, sitting next to him. "We give thanks for all the blessings we have received as a people and a nation. It goes back to the time of the American Revolution when George Washington declared the first day of Thanksgiving," she said.

Luigi was at the head of the table and Antonietta at the other end. Carlo was to his right and the other guests were placed randomly. Helena and Gabriela helped Antonietta bring in the food. When everyone was seated, Luigi asked them to hold hands.

"Oh God, please bless this which you have generously given us," he prayed. "Protect this great country from harm and bring peace to Italy and the entire world. Thank you, Lord, for saving my brother Carlo and bringing him here to us, his family, and take care of our parents and loved ones who are trapped in this war and are so far from us. Through Christ, our Lord, Amen." All made the sign of the cross and passed around the antipasto. It was the start of a huge Italian-American feast.

Plates of cold cuts and cheese were followed by ravioli, meat in a red sauce; a 20- pound turkey with stuffing; a large Virginia ham with pineapples; accompanied by sweet potatoes; Italian greens, peas, carrots; then assorted nuts; bowls of fruit; pumpkin and apple pies; Italian pastries and chocolates, all washed down with bottles of homemade red and white wine, ending with glasses of grappa, anise liqueur, frozen limoncello, and espresso. Dinner began at 7 PM and ended past 11 PM.

Carlo ate moderately.

His mind was elsewhere.

All he could think of was this gorgeous girl that sat inches from him.

He absorbed her fragrance. She was scented of honey and fresh wildflowers.

When she asked him to pass the salt, their fingers touched.

Electricity flowed.

The slight touch of her skin pierced his heart with passion.

By accident, he brushed his leg against hers as she pulled

away reluctantly.

The two young people were absorbed with each other.

It was love at first sight.

Carlo was liberated from his war demons by the vision, voice, and glances of Helena, as each precious moment revealed more of her inner and outer beauty.

CHAPTER 58

HELENA AND CARLO

"**N**ext month I take the exam to be an elementary school teacher in Wheeling," said Helena to Carlo as they finished Thanksgiving dinner. "I love children, and it is an excellent job with superb benefits." "You will be a wonderful teacher," responded Carlo. "I am sure children naturally trust you and fall in love with you." He wanted to say, "As I have," but held his tongue. "Teaching pays $95 a month and includes a West Virginia state pension and health benefits. Next year, when I turn 21, I will inherit the trust fund my parents left me." Helena spoke as if she was making plans with her lover for the rest of her life. She could not explain why but it came naturally to her.

"I don't know how long I will be at the camp, but I know I can visit here every other month. I am the senior camp baker and a trustee. The Americans have given me special privileges, including the chance to see my family," Carlo said in a tone of growing excitement. "May I see you again, Helena?" he asked. She responded immediately with love in her eyes. "I can meet you tomorrow morning at Luigi's store since I have to buy groceries for my aunt."

Carlo calculated minutes until the next morning when Luigi would take him to see his shop and meet Helena again.

"Something is going on with those two," said Antonietta as she rubbed two fingers together. "She is a lovely girl and would make a splendid wife," responded Luigi as they finished washing and drying the dishes and cleaning up the kitchen after the Thanksgiving meal. "This war will end and Carlo will go back to Italy. In the meantime, they can get to know each other. Who knows, if they get married, he can come to live here.

"I have an idea. Tomorrow I will tell him," said Luigi with excitement in his voice.

The dinner ended. The families went their separate ways. Carlo kissed Helena on her cheeks to say good night.

His blood boiled as she left him.

Her fragrance, her look of love, stayed with him through the night.

Carlo slept restlessly.

During the meal, the cacophony of voices and sounds melted away. He could only hear and see Helena. He erased the past and only saw a future with her.

He could not define it or understand it, but he knew that he had to be with the woman he loved, no matter what.

'He touched me,' thought Helena as she lay on her small cot in the basement, "and now nothing will ever be the same," she mused as she went to sleep with Carlo's smile in mind.

"She acted like a brazen hussy with Carlo," said Carmela to her husband in an angry voice as she combed her hair in front of the mirror before retiring for the night. "He said almost nothing during dinner and spoke only with her. I couldn't hear their conversation because of the noise, but I saw the looks on their faces. They are in love. It makes no sense. He has no future ahead of him. What can he offer her? Italy is in ruins. He will go back to no job and probably no home," she insisted.

"Love always finds a way," responded her husband with a smile, as he crawled under the covers.

CHAPTER 59 ━━━━━━━━━━━━━━━━━━━━━━━

GROWING UP A FASCIST

Silverio and Antonio waited anxiously. A small room with a table and three chairs was set up for the visitors. Silverio pondered what to say to his cousin. Should he be direct, vague, forceful, or perhaps weave the issue into a larger conversation?

" 'When in doubt, always revert to common sense,' "

The last time he saw his cousin was when he was married in Ponza, in 1937.

Young Fascists, c. 1937, *Courtesy, Les-Chemises-noires*

Bruno wore his Fascist uniform to the wedding. He was proud. He grew up with the ideals of the strong dominating the weak, a master race governing the world, war and conflict being a natural phenomenon, and the ends justifying the means.

At the reception, Bruno insisted that all give the Roman salute and say, "Long live Il Duce!"

Silverio wondered how much his cousin changed. Seven years had passed. He went from a boy to a man, to a soldier, and now to a prisoner.

Silverio was against the way Fascists raised young people to think, act, and be like them.

While he waited for Bruno, he wondered about the difference between Mussolini's Italy and Franklin Roosevelt's America.

'Children,' Silverio thought, 'should be taught empathy and not prejudice. This is why we came here. In the United States, we deal with all types of people. Our sons and daughters must grow up understanding others as much as themselves. We should teach them to respect differences, protect the weak and mistreated, and never look the other way.

'We want them to tell the truth.

'It is hard. Yet, if they learn to do the right thing, not to lie and to fight for justice, they will never fall under the spell of a dictator. Our children will want freedom over tyranny, and they will sacrifice for it.

'In America, they will be challenged. They will face obstacles. Problems will make them strong and into models for others. As they grow, we must show love and affection. They must know that, because they exist, it gives us happiness and a meaning for our lives and theirs.'

CHAPTER 60 ━━━━━━━━━━━━

MEETING BRUNO

An MP went to the barracks and called for Bruno. He was laying on his bed reading the Italian American newspaper, "Il Progresso," which was published every day in New York City. His edition was three days old. It gave the news about the war and showed photos of Italian American soldiers killed in action in Europe and the Pacific. There were articles about death and destruction in Italy under the German occupation.

Since the fall of Mussolini, a few months earlier, the Nazis took over the country. As soon as King Victor Emanuel III declared that his nation would join the Allies to defeat Hitler, a wave of atrocities engulfed the country. Jews were rounded up and sent to concentration camps. Those who avoided arrest were held in seclusion by Italian sympathizers and by priests and nuns. Thousands of Jewish children claimed to be Catholics so they could be hidden from the Gestapo in convents and monasteries throughout Italy.

Bruno wondered if the news he was reading was propaganda from the government, just like it was in Italy.

"You have visitors," said the MP. Bruno got up from his bed, straightened his clothes, combed his hair, curled his mustache, and trimmed his beard. The camp barber styled and groomed him elegantly. His goatee was neatly clipped, and his long hair was cropped to make it look clean and distinguished. The barber gave him a small bottle of cologne that he used every day. After North Africa, he looked sick, ragged, shabby, and poorly kept, with a filthy mane and long whiskers not touched for nearly two years. Now, he and the other prisoners visited the stylist twice a month.

Bruno wondered who his visitors could be. He had written to Silverio in New York, but did not expect him to come to Mississippi, especially when he realized the trip was over 1000 miles.

The time in American captivity had changed him.

His war wounds in his leg and arm were healed by the camp physicians. He put on weight. Exercise, hearty food, and tranquility restored his health. He missed his Fascist and army uniforms, which were tattered and damaged. They were replaced with a grey outfit with POW stitched on the right leg. The clothes were simple and comfortable, and they were washed and ironed twice a week, along with his bed sheets and pillowcases.

He disliked the cuisine. It was not Italian. No wine or olive oil, pasta, cheese, or green vegetables. Instead, most of it was meat and potatoes, lettuce, cucumbers, tomatoes, oranges, apples, and pears. Twice a week, slabs of steaks were served. Other days chicken, pork, and even catfish fillets trucked in from New Orleans were prepared. Beer was available in the canteen for a few chits.

Bruno was tall and handsome, with a perfect set of teeth. When he smiled, they glistened and made him even more attractive. His sense of humor was gone with the weight of his decision.

He wanted to the escape. It was patriotic.

The Italians were waiting for his advice.

If he decided on the side of the SS, most of the Italians would follow him. Many realized that a break in their section could cause a prison riot in the rest of the camp.

Bruno knew this.

He continued to be torn between loyalty to Mussolini and gratitude to the Americans who treated him and his comrades with honor, respect, and compassion. These thoughts ran through his mind as the MP opened the door to the waiting room.

Silverio and Antonio stood up when he entered.

Bruno froze. He was stunned. The three men smiled with joy.

He ran to embrace his cousins. He could not hold back his tears. A waterfall of joy, sorrow, anger, confusion, and pain broke loose in his weeping. He sobbed for minutes at seeing Silverio and Antonio again.

A sense of freedom was growing in his soul. Insecurity was giving way to the love of family.

He realized they had come from across the country to see him.

"You look splendid," said Silverio after he composed himself.

Bruno sat down and reflected. "The Americans treat us well. I can't complain. I am lucky to be here instead of buried in an Egyptian desert. The conditions are good, and I am working in the camp motor pool fixing jeeps, trucks, and cars. I have $75 saved up. The food is typically American, and I miss what we had at home." At that moment, Silverio put a large parcel on the table, which had been inspected by the MPs.

Silverio opened the cardboard box. It was filled with cheeses, preserved meats, 2- gallon tins of olive oil, cartons of pasta, bottles of homemade tomato sauce, jars of pickled eggplant, peppers and tuna, and enough cakes and cookies to fill a small shop. Bruno took in the scent of the food as if it was an exotic perfume. He picked up a piece of provolone and salami and looked at them as if they were rare treasures.

Silverio cut slices of cheese and ham. He offered some to the MP guarding them. Bruno ate with relish. Forgotten were the thoughts of war, escape, and conflict.

The taste of Italian delights was synonymous with the peace and prosperity that his cousin Silverio had found in America. "All made in the USA," said Silverio as he carved more cheese and some salami. "It's as good as home," remarked Bruno. "Home?" questioned Silverio. "The only news from Ponza is bad. Ships and boats sunk, no government left to run things, most men are in uniform, and the island is starving," he explained. "When the Americans liberate Italy, they will bring food for the people," said Silverio with pride. "This country has been good to us. We work, eat, and raise our families in security and peace. We need to bring this hatred and conflict to an end so that Italians and Americans can be friends and build a great future together."

"Mussolini made us great and gave us an empire," responded Bruno. "If it hadn't been for this war, he would still be in power. The military and the king betrayed him. Hitler will win the war and restore him to power and get rid of the traitors," insisted Bruno with passion.

Silverio realized his cousin was filled with Fascist dogma and dreams of greatness.

His task to convince him not to escape might be impossible.

CHAPTER 61

OSS BASIC TRAINING

Emblem of the OSS, *Courtesy, National Park Service*

"**C**ongressional Country Club," was on the sign, as Joe and Tom's bus passed into the lush green park surrounding one of the most exclusive places in the Washington, DC, area.

It was remote and secluded, and it was the training center of the OSS.

A battery of physical and mental tests had been completed. They were chosen because they had high school diplomas, technical skills, were intelligent, creative, and showed imagination, bravery, and ruthlessness. Most of all, Joe and Tom spoke Italian. At the center, they received documents with false identities and badges to keep them anonymous.

Missions, locations, and everything about them was confidential.

Joe and Tom were assigned separate cabins with simple sleeping and bathing facilities. The area had a recreation hall, a cafeteria, and classrooms with audiovisual equipment. Shortly after they arrived, they were assembled in a large conference room along with 60 other recruits. A manual stamped "Top Secret" in bold, red letters was given to each trainee. It outlined the program and provided material to study and digest.

"For the next 90 days, you will undergo education in demolition, special weaponry, and safety and security," barked the head of OSS training. "Our goal will be tremendous, detailed planning, followed by violent execution. It will be intense and dangerous. You are not to discuss among yourselves or the outside world anything that happens here. All letters will be censored before they are mailed to family and friends. Any infraction will be considered a violation of the Espionage Act," he declared. That same session included a slide presentation by a British Major. In a heavy English accent, he described the latest technology developed by the UK in plastic explosives.

"Nobel 808 is what you will use for sabotage missions," he explained. The officer put on gloves and safety glasses. He gently opened a black, metal box. A square, green wad of putty weighing a kilo was taken out. It looked like unbaked clay and scented of almonds. "It is light, malleable, adaptable to numerous environments, and deadly. It must be handled with extreme care," he noted as he displayed a set of slides explaining the chemical composition of the material.

A film showed how the British used tripwires with the plastic explosives to blow up viaducts, derail trains, and destroy enemy communications.

From the classroom, the trainees went into field operations to apply what they learned. As the days progressed, Joe and Tom came to know about hand grenades made by the Germans, French, British, Italians, and Japanese. The Nazis used "stick grenades." The Germans called them "door knockers." The U.S. explosive was named "the pineapple" because of its shape.

Variations of these deadly weapons gave the recruits a feel for the difference in weight, destruction inflicted, and how to carry, store and use them. German, Italian, and Japanese ordinances were examined. Trainees had to show as much dexterity in using enemy arms as their own.

OSS Demolition Training, *Courtesy, National Park Service*

Along a fifteen-acre field, the OSS novices set off many bombs and simulated placing charges on bridges, dams, railroad lines, in and around barracks, and under vehicles, trucks, and tanks. To pass, they had to prove skill in each part of the program.

If they failed, they returned to a regular army unit.

A special pistol firing range was created. Colt 45 automatic handguns and other arms were used to learn "quick firing" methods to shoot from the hip in "point and shoot" actions. A key exercise was to attack a building occupied by Nazis. The structure was dark. The recruits would enter and hear realistic sounds of Germans talking. Suddenly, paper-mache enemy soldiers with revolvers would pop out.

Basic survival techniques were taught, like using a compass, reading maps, and living in wooded areas or mountains with little or no food. Photography, cryptography (the coding and decoding of messages), document forgery, and methods of disguise were taught to OSS recruits. At the end of the course, there was a "graduation party," which was a final psychological test to determine if the trainees revealed secrets.

Physical training was mandatory. It was severe and perilous. Combat exercises included wrestling, ju-jitsu, and fighting with knives, pipes, and many forms of lethal devices. Ropes were set up to climb over obstacles and water traps. Perhaps the hardest hurdle for Joe and Tom was the parachute jump. It was simulated by jumping from a platform over a sand pit.

The real test would come when they had to leap from planes.

Tom was deadly afraid of heights.

CHAPTER 62

SILVERIO'S DREAM

Silverio told Bruno of their thousand-mile odyssey to reach him. Bruno was stunned at the threats his cousins confronted. "After Tennessee, Antonio and I thought of giving up and returning home. We were worn out and sensed more hazards ahead. The night we slept at the boarding house in Nashville, I had a dream. Perhaps it was fear, or fatigue, or a premonition. I can't explain why I dreamed what I did. San Silverio and our grandfather, Giuseppe, came to me. They were together. Our patron Saint was dressed in his red robes and gold crown. He looked deeply into my eyes like he wanted to reach my soul.

"Grandpa talked to me. 'You must see Bruno. He is in peril. He must decide. It could lead to his destruction and that of others. Stop him before it's too late.' San Silverio raised his miter and made the sign of the cross to bless me. I woke sweating and worrying. I did not understand what the dream was about. I explained it to Antonio. Then we knew we had to complete our mission," explained Silverio. Beads of perspiration poured down his forehead as he recalled the wolves, Scarface and the Giant, and the night with the Ku Klux Klan.

Bruno bowed his head in silence. Giuseppe was a god-like figure in his life. While his father spent months fishing on the high seas, Giuseppe took Bruno in and raised him like a son. His grandfather was kind, strong, intelligent, and wise. Giuseppe did not want Bruno to be a Fascist. "Avoid them, my son," he would say. "They preach war and violence and will bring our country to its knees." Bruno did not listen. Millions of young people wore black shirts and imbibed Fascist doctrines of pride and nationalism like a religion. It dominated their thoughts, lives, and choices.

Il Duce attracted youth like moths to a flame. He was a spell-binding orator. His speeches were broadcast over the radio and seen in movie theatres every day. When Mussolini spoke, speakers were hooked up to broadcast it live in piazzas around the country.

People hung on his every word.

His voice and delivery were hypnotic.

Benito Mussolini Declaring War on France and the United Kingdom, June 10th, 1940, *Courtesy, Istituto Luce*

On June 10th, 1940, Il Duce stood on his balcony in Piazza Venezia in Rome to give an historic address. Giant amplifiers were set up by the Fascists on the Island of Ponza and all over Italy. They were placed in the front of City Hall and outside the three churches on the island. Thousands gathered to hear Il Duce pronounce these words:

> *We go to battle against the plutocratic and reactionary democracies of the West who, at every moment, have hindered the advance and have often endangered the very existence of the Italian people… This gigantic struggle is nothing other than a phase in the logical development of our revolution; it is the struggle of peoples that are poor but rich in workers against the exploiters who hold on ferociously to*

> *the monopoly of all the riches and all the gold of the earth; it is the struggle of the*
> *fertile and young people against the sterile people moving into the sunset; it is the*
> *struggle between two ideas… And we will win, in order finally to give a long period*
> *of peace with justice to Italy, to Europe, and to the world. People of Italy! Rush to*
> *arms and show your tenacity, your courage, your valor!*

Giuseppe was standing outside the place he was married in to hear the speech. He listened carefully to what Mussolini said. The words went deep into his soul. Giuseppe fought in the First World War and realized what was ahead for Italy and his grandson. After the speech, he went into his small garden to plow the soil. Suddenly, he felt pains in his left arm and chest.

He suffered a major heart attack.

As he lay dying, the old man struggled to say his last words to Bruno: "My son, do not take any unnecessary risks. Italy will lose the war. We will be swallowed up by misery and famine. We cannot win against the whole world. Entering this battle was an evil decision. Our nation will pay a high price for Mussolini's sins. Promise me you will return home and take care of your mother and sisters. I love you, my son. Remember, your family comes first." Bruno held his grandfather's hand. He nodded with eyes filled with tears as the man he adored slipped away from him.

Giuseppe's words and Silverio's dream gave him the last pieces of the deadly puzzle he had to solve.

CHAPTER 63 ━━━━━━━━━━━━━━━

LUIGI'S STORE

1936 Buick Roadmaster, *Courtesy. New York Public Library*

"I bought this used, just before the war," explained Luigi to Carlo as they cruised in his 1936 Buick Roadmaster. "Imagine, it has over 120 horsepower, a radio, heater, cigarette lighter, a clock, whitewall tires, tinted glass, and leather upholstery. Look how it handles the road. The suspension system is fantastic." The car was a symbol of the progress Luigi had made. "Who had a car in our town in Italy? Not even the richest family had one. Only the Fascists had autos," he asserted. Luigi turned on the radio.

Music filled the car as the notes of the William Tell Overture seemed to sweep away the air and replace it with a sensation of sweetness, hope, and then a galloping feeling of energy and power. "It's Arturo Toscanini and the NBC Symphony Orchestra. Listen to him. Mussolini drove him out of Italy. Now he is fighting to liberate our country and give it back to us," expressed Luigi with pride as he turned a corner and parked the car in front of his shop.

General Store, *Courtesy, Needham History Museum*

"General Store" was etched in large, golden letters on a slab of green, enameled oak that hung over the door. Signs advertising specials and prices of goods covered the inside of two large window displays on both sides of the entrance. Tins of vegetables, condensed milk, and small sacks of flour were carefully placed in view for passersby to observe.

As he and Carlo entered, Luigi unlocked the door and turned a sign that read "Open."

A pungent odor of vinegar greeted him. The smell was from a barrel of pickled cucumbers that stood prominently in front of the counter that Luigi went behind to put on his apron, turn on the lights, and check the refrigerator. Hundreds of canned goods stood on shelves that went from one end of the store to the other. A section had Italian styled products with tins of tomato sauce, cooking oils, jars of beans and peas and dried sausages, and cheeses. Boxes of pasta, crackers, and containers of cookies lined one shelf. One section had cigarettes, cigars, and pipe tobacco.

Glass vessels of candy, lollipops, and licorice covered the countertops. Several scales and a cash register were placed in a part of the store. Another area had dry goods and tools, and even oil lanterns, nails, screws, and canisters of paint with brushes. Carlo was amazed at the variety and the abundance.

A bell was fastened to the top of the door of the shop, and each time the door opened the bell would tingle.

Carlo was examining some cans of corn when he heard the chime.

As he turned to see who had entered the portal, a breeze carried to him a hint of honey and wildflowers.

For the rest of his life, the tender sound of tiny bells pealing would remind him of the perfume of the girl he loved.

Helena entered the store with a radiant smile that lifted the young man into a new dimension, as his heart pounded and his cheeks flushed with passion.

CHAPTER 64 ━━━━━━━━━━━━━━━━━━━━━━━

TOM'S FEAR

"I can't do it, Joe. I just can't. I get sick every time I'm up there," explained Tom as he failed another simulated parachute drop. Joe insisted, "Listen, Tom. If we fall from three stories or thirty stories, the result is the same. You've got to get used to this, or we will be thrown out of OSS and be sent back to the regular Army. At least here we have a chance to call our own shots and work on our own assignments. With the army, we'll be tossed on some beach to be eaten by machine guns. We have to learn to jump from a plane to survive. There's no other way."

Six months had passed, and Joe and Tom had completed basic OSS training and were deeply involved in learning the art and science of being paratroopers. Their initial mission would involve dropping behind enemy lines.

First, they had to be in the best physical shape possible, and, second, they had to learn to deal with heights, aircraft, parachutes, and all that was involved before, during, and after the jump. A team of expert paratroopers, known as the Pathfinders, came from Fort Benning, Georgia, to train the OSS teams.

"Visualize success," asserted Captain Williams of the Pathfinders. "Think of effectively landing, which will be the outcome. Overcoming fear of heights is as much psychological as it is physical. The important thing is to breathe heavily and oxygenate the brain. You should always remember that if you have done everything by the book to prepare, you will succeed, unless something unexpected and unplanned for happens. You have a 95% percent chance of landing on your feet; a 10% possibility of getting shot by enemy fire; a 1% risk of being hit by a plane or falling on another paratrooper; and a .005 % probability that your chute won't open. A good 50% likelihood is that you will miss your landing mark by at least a mile, but you will make provisions for that and other contingencies," explained the Captain of the Pathfinders.

Slowly, Tom overcame his problem, yet he understood that the real test was when he finally made his first jump. Five weeks of constant training were followed with simulated leaps from planes. One replicated jump used an actual parachute. It was like a ride at Coney Island in Brooklyn. He was placed in a harness and dropped. After a hundred feet, the parachute would open by itself, and he would feel the jerk of the device catching the wind and bringing him down.

With the encouragement of Joe and excellent instructors, Tom enjoyed the experience, as if he was a boy again in a New York amusement park, but he knew it was not the real thing.

The Pathfinders explained how to use a special, top secret radar system called "Eureka," which transmitted location information to designated aircraft via a system named "Rebecca." It was the latest form of radar, and it was essential to helping paratroopers land in the proper location. Joe and Tom realized they would face dangerous missions. Dropping behind enemy lines to prepare the way for an invasion required the utmost training and skill, especially since they would be alone.

Finally, it was time to go to war.

In January 1943, Joe and Tom went to England. By the time they arrived, the British had been fighting the Nazis for over three years. Despite victories, the outcome was still not clear since the Germans controlled most of continental Europe. The U.S. and the British were struggling on two fronts, but they had achieved promising results:

- The Allies had captured Burma from the Japanese.
- The Russians launched an all-out offensive on Stalingrad and Leningrad.
- British forces were attacking Tripoli, the capital of Libya, an Italian colony.
- The Royal Air Force bombed Berlin.
- Jews in the Warsaw ghetto rose against the Nazis.
- American flying fortresses started carpet bombing Germany.

- Churchill and Roosevelt met in Casablanca and declared they would only accept "unconditional" surrender from the Axis powers.

"Italy is the 'soft, underbelly of Europe,' according to our Prime Minister," asserted the British general in a heavy English accent to briefing OSS operatives sent to London for strategic planning training. "The North African campaign is moving forward successfully, now that you Yanks are actively in the war," remarked the officer enthusiastically as he looked at Joe and Tom.

"An invasion of the continent is a huge risk, which is why we are examining hitting the enemy where they are most vulnerable. Italians are poorly equipped and lack resources for a prolonged effort. We have seen their forces in North Africa, and we realize that much of their equipment goes back to the Great War. We destroyed their fleet in Taranto shortly after the war began. Defenses in the bottom of the boot are especially feeble. Our need is to strengthen the work of Italian partisans in the south; weaken military supply movements; and sabotage factories, power stations and refineries. We have a good mapping of the transport arteries in southern Italy, from Sicily to Naples, and we have established contacts with the opponents of the Fascist regime who are fighting to bring down Mussolini. We will give them all the help we can with supplies, intelligence, and logistics support," he emphasized.

The general stared at Tom and Joe.

"It is risky and deadly, and that will be your job."

CHAPTER 65

THE WALK IN THE PARK

"Good morning, Helena," said Luigi as he came from behind the counter to welcome her. The young lady barely heard his voice. Her eyes met Carlo's, and she felt her knees grow weak as a strange sensation overcame her. Helena's bosom became tense as her heart beat faster at the sight of Carlo's smile. "Good morning," she affirmed, looking at Luigi and Carlo simultaneously. Carlo ran to her like a flash and hugged her.

Her warm form in his hands made him tremble as he held her in a brotherly embrace and kissed her cheeks chastely.

A short sigh came from Helena as he let her go.

"I have this list of things to buy, Luigi," she mentioned as she tried to compose herself. She handed him a sheet of paper. "I will prepare everything and deliver it tonight on my way home after we close the shop. I wanted Carlo to see the store before he returns to the camp next week," he proclaimed.

The thought of the man she loved returning to captivity forced Helena into a near panic. The reality of their situation was setting in.

Carlo and she were in love, yet he was a prisoner until the end of the war, when he would be sent home. A hundred thoughts raced through her mind as she looked at this handsome young man.

"Why don't you go and take a walk in the park? It's a nice day and not too cold. In the meantime, I will prepare something for lunch," declared Luigi, with a sly look in his eye. Helena instinctively held Carlo's hand as they crossed the street to reach a path surrounded by trees bathed in the colors of autumn. Oaks and poplars were decked in red, orange, and yellow.

A crimson leaf floated in front of the young man. He caught it.

"For you," he said as he squeezed her hand. She looked at it as if it were a sacred relic and held it up to the sun to see its contours and veins.

"It's beautiful," she proclaimed as she put her first gift from Carlo in her purse. "I will always cherish it."

The lovers walked for a few minutes in silence. Endless thoughts were exchanged as they gazed at each other and walked hand in hand for an hour. Her touch was familiar to Carlo.

Helena's hand was like holding his own, as if her skin and body were a part of him. The young girl had the same strange sensation. A park bench welcomed them. Sunlight bathed it with a warm, autumn glow. No one was in sight. Carlo brushed away some foliage from the seat as he gently sat Helena like she was a princess mounting her throne. He settled beside her and reached into his coat pocket. A pink box with a red bow emerged.

It was French perfume.

The young man presented his gift with quivering hands, not knowing what her reaction would be. Helena was surprised and delighted. She opened the package. A small, heart-shaped bottle was nestled in red velvet. She picked it up with care and opened it. As she twisted the cap off, a whiff of orange blossoms filled the chilly November air. "It's wonderful. I love the fragrance!" she exclaimed, smiling as she dashed a few drops on her wrists and neck.

Carlo felt the perfume take on a special bouquet as it united with Helena's skin.

For some reason, neither could ever explain, Carlo took her in his arms and kissed her.

It was the deep, passionate kiss of timeless lovers, and not of a couple that barely knew each other. Carlo caressed her face and looked into her eyes. He held her as if he would never let her go.

"I love you," he said breathlessly. The air left his lungs as the power of love absorbed him. Helena was overcome with a fervor that seemed perfect and ancient, as if they had loved before. An imaginary magic carpet appeared and carried them away into a mystical place that only lovers find.

"I have adored you for a thousand years," he uttered as if his heart had a voice. "I searched for you in my dreams and my travels. I looked around every corner to find you, and here you are. My dream is here beside me," he whispered as he kissed her hands. She was speechless, as she absorbed the beautiful words of the man she cherished.
"I love you, I love you, I love you, Helena," he repeated again and again. "I have always loved you. This happens once in a million years. Love at first sight. The moment I saw you I realized that I had loved you in past lives, for decades, centuries, for a thousand years!"

The words raced from his mouth with such emotion that he wept.

Helena was overwhelmed. All reason and control disappeared in the white-hot fire of love. "I feel the same, Carlo. I cannot explain it. The second your eyes met mine, I was carried away with love for you. I know you. I have always known you," she declared.

He stared profoundly at her. "Will you marry me, Helena?" he murmured with a deep and passionate sigh.

CHAPTER 66

BRUNO'S FEARS

"**S**ilverio, I have been through hell. North Africa shaped me. I became another man. I witnessed death and destruction. We were not equipped to fight. Our guns were old and needed spare parts. Our uniforms were made of wool when we had to fight in the summer. We were constantly low on ammunition, water, and food. I went into the war with enthusiasm. Il Duce told us that we were fighting to find a 'place in the sun,' stop the great powers from oppressing Italy, and to spread the doctrine of Fascism to the whole world. I trusted him. I volunteered. I believed Mussolini was always right. I was wrong, deadly wrong," explained Bruno with his head in his hands.

Silverio and Antonio comforted him.

"Soon all of this will be over. The Allies will win the war. America will rebuild Italy. You can go back to Ponza," asserted Silverio in a calm, quiet voice.

Bruno suddenly leaped from his seat. It was as if he had a revelation.

Italian Children in Fascist Uniforms, *Courtesy, Istituto Luce*

"Don't you realize that everything I believed in since I was born was a lie? We are not a 'pure race' as Mussolini claimed. We are the product of millions of slaves released from captivity after the fall of Rome. We are a poor country with no resources. Invading Ethiopia and the Spanish Civil War cost us dearly. Now we have been humiliated on the battlefield, and every town and village in Italy is occupied by the Nazis. They betrayed us. They promised it would be a quick war. Instead, Hitler invaded Russia, and the Japanese attacked America. Italy is caught in the vice of the Allies and the Axis. Right here in this camp, I feel the pressure from the Germans and those loyal to Mussolini to participate in a plan to escape. Why should we? The Americans have treated us well. We have peace and tranquility when all we received from the Nazis was blood and tears," exclaimed Bruno.

"Then tell the bastards that you and the Italians won't participate in any breakout," insisted Silverio. "Convince your comrades that the war is over and not to do anything against the Americans. If anyone tries to escape, they will be shot," he maintained.

"But I am a Fascist, and I swore allegiance to Il Duce, who demands that we fight to the death. How can I betray him and my principles?" declared Bruno.

"You are not betraying anyone. You were deceived like millions who thought that the Fascists would improve the lives of all Italians. It was a lie based on violence, hatred, and war.

"Remember what our grandfather Giuseppe used to say: 'He who rides the back of the tiger, ends up inside.' Mussolini and the Fascists mounted the tiger and now they will end up inside," affirmed Silverio. He stared at his cousin.

Bruno was struggling with his convictions, his conscience, and the reality that he was a prisoner of war and a prisoner of himself.

CHAPTER 67 ▬▬▬▬▬▬▬▬▬

THE PURPLE CAPSULE

"The Research and Analysis branch of the OSS has prepared considerable information on southern Italy, especially from Naples down," explained an American OSS official to Tom and Joe. "What you have is a complete map of the Italian railway, road, and port system. It includes telegraph and telephone stations, postal facilities, and government offices. Most importantly, it shows with a high level of accuracy all the oil, coal, and gas facilities, and small and large airports, and military installations. We have the code names of Italian partisans who you will work with. Your mission will be to make life miserable for the Germans and the Italians and to detour troops, supplies, and artillery by blowing up bridges, derailing trains, and sabotaging highways," he explained.

1943 Invasion of Italy, *Courtesy, US Department of Defense*

By May 1943, the Allies had taken hold of North Africa after months of bloody battles. General Erwin Rommel,[1] the legendary Desert Fox, had been defeated and his army captured.

The Allies controlled the Mediterranean and the supply lines from the Middle East and Asia. For the British, the Mediterranean was essential. It was the road to the empire in the east and the route for colonial soldiers and sailors to join British forces. Bases, airports, and maritime installations were constructed to launch an invasion of the continent from the south. Tens of thousands of American and British Common-wealth troops were assembled for one of the largest invasions in history.

Plans were made for a full-scale attack on southern Italy.

Tom and Joe had spent over a year in training. Without ever having visited the country, they knew the detailed history, geography, and topography of Italy. Every major city and nearby towns were studied. Emphasis was given to enemy facilities and understanding their plans. They learned how to use all sorts of new lethal weapons like lightweight machine guns, pistols with silencers, and small grenades that exploded on impact. Besides knowing Neapolitan, which was the dialect of Ponza, they learned basic Sicilian and proper Italian.

"You will not wear uniforms. It means, if captured, you will not be treated as a prisoner of war. There will be no trial or imprisonment. You will be shot as a spy. Before being executed, you will be tortured to give the enemy as much information as possible. I can assure you that their methods are horrible," stressed the officer. The recruits were handed a sheet of paper. "This gives you an idea of the techniques that the German Occupation forces use:

---

1   Rommel was an early supporter of Hitler and his seizure of power. The General was implicated in the July 20th, 1944 plot to kill Hitler. Since he was a national hero, Hitler wanted to avoid a trial. Instead, he ordered Rommel to commit suicide with the assurance that his reputation would remain intact, his family cared for, and he would receive a state funeral. On October 14, 1944, he was visited by two generals and given a cyanide pill. The official reason for his death was from injuries in the field of battle. After the funeral, his body was cremated. He once said, "Don't fight a battle if you gain nothing by winning."

- Putting people's hands in boiling water until the skin and fingernails came off like gloves
- Stamping on a man's foot for ten minutes with a special steel boot and repeating the process for two weeks
- Pressing a hot poker into the hands
- Hanging persons by their hands behind their backs until their shoulders were out of joint
- Gashing the soles of their feet and making the victims walk on salt
- Pulling teeth and drilling into teeth and gums
- Cutting and twisting off ears
- Running electric current through the victims' bodies and other fiendish devices too horrible to describe[2]

"Part of your equipment is in this special box," said the Captain with seriousness in his voice.

In the container was a brass cartridge shell with a chain to make it look like a necklace. The officer put on a set of gloves. He picked up the casing and carefully screwed off the lid. He emptied it.

A purple capsule tumbled out.

"In the event you risk capture, this will save you from the anguish of torture at the hands of our enemies. It is cyanide and will induce death within three minutes. You are to wear this necklace always. I hope you never have to use it," he concluded somberly.[3]

---

2   The Holocaust Historiography Project, Nazi Torture and Medical Experimentation, https://www. historiography-project.org/1946/01/01/nazi_torture_and_medical_exper/

3   In the last few months of WWII, it is estimated that over 7000 Nazi officials committed suicide to avoid falling into the hands of the Soviets or the Allies and facing post war tribunals for war crimes. This number is what was reported. Unreported information would give higher numbers.

CHAPTER 68 ━━━━━━━━━━━━━━━━━━━━━━━━

THE GOLDEN BAND

Carlo and Helena stayed in the park for several hours. The setting was beautiful. It was filled with trees and grass.

Wheeling Park, *Courtesy, Wheeling Historical Association*

Squirrels and pigeons greeted them. The place was quiet, peaceful, and seemed made for couples to linger, talk, and do what lovers do. A lake was filled with swans and ducks. It was crowned with a golden bridge that invited them to cross it. They held hands as they strolled over the water.

Carlo and Helena stopped. They looked at their reflections in the lake. Images of smiles, embraces, and a warm kiss were what they saw and would remember. Lost in the reverie of love, the couple did not notice the storm clouds gathering above them. Thunder rolled in the distance, but they could not hear it.

Forgotten were family, obstacles, and challenges. For them, the war was over. All they could think of was their love and a life together.

"Yes, I will marry you," said Helena as she stared into his eyes and peered into his soul.

She saw a man who was sincere and kind, and who loved her. He kissed her again and held her as if never to let her go.

Carlo felt liberated from the past.

Gone were the ghosts of battle. Worries of the future evaporated. Helena was his life, his today and tomorrow. She was his port in the storm.

He reached into his pocket. He took out a gold paper band. It was the wrapper from a cigar he found in Luigi's store. "Please accept this as a symbol of my love."

He placed it on her finger like a wedding ring.

She smiled as tears welled up in her eyes. It was no longer a meaningless piece of paper, but a precious image of Carlo's love. Helena gently closed her hand around the ring to protect it.

They kissed again and sealed their devotion, forever.

As they embraced, rain fell. It was chilly. The drops covered them in a cool mist, but they felt only the warmth of their bodies. Gradually, the downpour grew intense. It took several minutes for them to realize they were being soaked. Carlo took out his handkerchief and placed it over Helena's curls as they ran to the shop. The bells of the door tingled. She took the handkerchief and placed it in her purse.

"There you are," said Luigi. "I began to worry. I prepared something for lunch." A platter was filled with ham and cheese sandwiches, pickles, and potato chips. Helena and Carlo were famished.

No thoughts of food had passed by their minds as they traveled on their magic carpet of love.

As she reached for the tray, Luigi saw the paper ring.

He smiled and winked at his brother.

CHAPTER 69 ━━━━━━━━━━━━━━━

BRUNO'S DECISION

"Have you made up your mind?" demanded the head of the Gestapo.

"We won't go," said Bruno, firmly.

"What? Are you serious? You are a fool. The Fuhrer has a secret weapon that will eradicate London and New York. Washington will be in ashes. We will destroy them. You and your companions will be sent to slave labor camps to work for us once we have taken over. You are an idiot!" screamed the Nazi.

"The war is over for us. The Americans are treating us well. We are tired of fighting and running. All we want to do is wait for this to be over and go home," insisted Bruno.

The Nazi leader was furious. He paced back and forth. "It changes nothing," he yelled at the German officers listening to him. "We will proceed with our plan. We do not need these cowards. Leave them with the Yanks!" he shouted as he turned to Bruno.

"I should cut your throat, you lousy grease ball!" screeched the Nazi. "If I find out you or one of your spineless companions told the Americans about our plan, I will strangle you with my bare hands!" he said as he spit in Bruno's face.

A moment later, a loud whack was heard in the barracks as the Nazi flew back from a powerful blow to his face. Bruno punched him so hard that he dislocated the German's jaw. As the Nazi lay unconscious, Bruno rubbed his sore knuckles and walked away. He crossed the main courtyard and entered a building that housed guests.

He knocked on a door.

Antonio opened it. Silverio was sitting in a chair reading a newspaper. Bruno walked in and sat down on the sofa. He was trembling. His hands were shaking.

"What's wrong?" asked Silverio. "I just told that miserable Nazi bastard to jump in the lake. We will not go. I convinced the other soldiers to not participate in the escape. After I told the Nazi, he threatened me and spit in my face. I was beside myself with rage. I hit him so hard, I wanted him to fly to the moon. I probably broke his jaw. He will be out like a light for the next day or two. I am not sorry for what I did, and I would do it again," asserted Bruno.

Antonio had a flask of brandy. "Drink some of this. It will make you feel better." Bruno downed two mouthfuls. His face grimaced as he swallowed the alcohol. His knuckles were bleeding. Silverio opened a first aid kit and took out some disinfectant and band aides. "You never know. That Nazi could have poisonous blood," he said as he smiled and medicated and wrapped Bruno's hand.

"Listen to me," demanded Silverio. "Everything will be fine. You did the right thing for you and the other Italians. Let the Germans try to escape. They will pay for it. This war will end. The Americans will win it, and you will go home. All will be well. Believe me," insisted Silverio with conviction.

Bruno embraced him. He was a free man. He was liberated. The evil pact made by Mussolini with Hitler was broken.

The devil had been sent back to hell.

Minutes later, Bruno returned to his section of the camp to join with the other Italian prisoners of war. Silverio went to see the camp Commandant. As soon as Lieutenant Black saw Silverio, he stood up and saluted him and immediately opened the door to the office of Colonel McCarthy.

"It's over. My cousin convinced the other Italians not to escape with the Nazis. Apparently, the breakout is set for tomorrow," explained Silverio. "Bruno and the chief Nazi had some words, so to speak. You may have a German with a broken jaw in the infirmary today," said Silverio with a broad smile.

The Commandant laughed. "Great. I understand. I will never be able to thank you enough," said the Colonel. "I ask only that you stay two more days. We will have a convoy of troops, artillery, and trucks bound for New York. You can be part of their caravan. I promise no one will bother you until you get home," stated the Colonel, smiling.

CHAPTER 70 ━━━━━━━━━━━━━━

THE PARACHUTE JUMP

Joe and Tom had written several letters to their mother, wife, and fiancée. Each had to be cleared by the OSS censures. No mention was made of where they were or what they were up to. Most letters were filled with affectionate thoughts and assurances that they were well. Now a critical point arrived in their training. It could mean life or death. They were to parachute from a plane for the first time. For days and weeks, they jumped from towers where inflated parachutes simulated the fall.

Shortly after dawn, on a cloudy British morning, Joe and Tom and other OSS recruits were loaded into a military truck and taken to the Royal Air Force airport at Ringway, near Manchester. It was the paratrooper training camp of the RAF (Royal Air Force).

Tom was trembling and perspiring heavily.

Despite the extensive training, he was afraid.

Joe was concerned. His younger brother was strong, athletic, and had flown through the OSS program. The last obstacle was this one, and it grew menacing to Tom as the minutes passed.

"It's going to be all right. The jump is higher and longer than the one we did in the simulations, but the same thing," insisted Joe to his brother. Tom was not convinced. He knew the difference. They would be in an aircraft bouncing in wind, hundreds of feet above the ground. There was no safety net below. If something went wrong, he would fall to his death. His heart pounded. His blood pressure fell. He turned pale.

By the time the truck reached the base, he fainted.

Joe put Tom's head between his legs to get the blood rushing to his brain. He revived. "He will be alright, sir, he just needs a few minutes to catch his breath," said Joe to the RAF Jump Master who met them at the base.

"I can't have anyone passing out on me on the plane. It would add an element of extreme danger to the operation. If your brother can't do this, then I will cross him off the program, immediately," he said decisively. Tom heard the warnings. Joe gave his brother a glass of water. Tom gulped it down.

"Come on, Tom," said Joe as he helped his brother up. "Let's get the show on the road. I am going to jump in front of you. After they pull your ring, follow me by jerking on your ropes in my direction," he said reassuringly.

Joe always felt a sense of responsibility to his kid brother, now more than ever. Tom regained his composure. The calm voice of Joe gave him strength.

The team spent the next two hours preparing their parachutes and gear. It was painstaking work, but vital. The canopy had to be carefully folded so it would release easily once its bag opened. They donned helmets to protect them from the snapping cords of chute as they descended. High boots were worn to break the landing shock. A machine gun, a pistol, ammunition, and a demolition kit were part of their arsenal.

They got on the plane. Tom and Joe heard the engines roar and felt their teeth vibrate. It took off. The aircraft was as cold as an ice box, but it lacked air. It vaulted in the wind as it climbed. It seemed to fly vertically. The recruits were tightly strapped to the sides. They leaned heavily against each other as the flying machine rose to a 90-degree angle.

Suddenly, it leveled off. Some men felt nauseated.

Tom prayed. "Almighty Father, please help me succeed today. Protect me and my brother as we jump from this plane. San Silverio, guide us, and assist us in this challenge."

He had a picture of his patron Saint in his pocket. He searched for it and held it tightly. For a moment, he imagined God and San Silverio were up in the clouds with him and near him. "You okay?" asked Joe.

Tom nodded and raised his right thumb to indicate that all was go.

It was not.

When the aircraft reached three hundred feet, the Jump Master opened the cabin door. It suddenly seemed narrow and ominous to Tom. "Could my gear get caught on the edge of the door as I jump?" he worried. "Can I make it through that narrow hole?" Tom saw the grey and white clouds and felt a burst of cold air slam against his face.

"Stand up," commanded the Jump Master. The soldiers stood up. "Attach your static lines!" he yelled.

The line was a cord attached to the aircraft on one end and to the top of the jumper's D-Bag (Deployment Bag, where the canopy was packed), on the other end. As the parachutist fell from the plane, the line became taut and pulled the D-Bag out of the container. The line and the D-Bag stayed with the plane as the paratrooper left the aircraft. Once the D-Bag was out, the canopy opened and the weight of the jumper plus the upward, rushing wind exposed the chute.

All this happened in four seconds. [1]

Joe and Tom were seventh and eighth in line. Tom trembled as he placed his hook on the static line. He fumbled with it. Joe grabbed it and attached it to the line. Tom was perspiring. He was out of breath. "Jump," screamed the Jump Master. Tom watched as one man disappeared out of the door after another. In seconds, Joe was before him. His brother touched him and nodded as he leaped from the plane.

---

1   Static Line, https://en.wikipedia.org/wiki/Static_line

Tom hesitated.

He was at the door. He saw clouds under his feet. Fear gripped him like a vice. He felt a sharp pain in his stomach.

"Jump, jump!" commanded the Jump Master.

Tom closed his eyes and fell from the plane.

His body froze with panic as he tumbled in the wind. The static line pulled his ring and the chute shot from its pack. Tom felt a jolt. The parachute jerked him upward with a sudden snap that startled him. He opened his eyes and saw the plane traveling far into the distance. Below were a dozen chutes floating in all directions. He looked for his brother, but it was useless.

The ground seemed to rush towards him. He could see the leaves of grass and trees dotting the landscape. Tom held tightly to the cords of the chute. As he hit the ground, he felt the air knock out of him. He laid flat on his stomach for minutes.

Sweat poured down his brow and into his eyes.

He made it. He was alive.

"Oh God, thank you. San Silverio, thank you," he said, repeatedly.

CHAPTER 71

THE LETTERS SENT HOME

"**M**amma, we got letters from Joe and Tom." Sofia ran up the stairs to see Maria. She was now part of the family and was with her in-laws every day. She waved the letter like it was a flag as she ran into the kitchen. She tore it open, sat down, and read it to Maria. Her mother-in-law stopped what she was doing, dried her hands on her apron, and listened:

> *Dearest Mamma and Papa:*
>
> *Tom and I are well. We just completed our training and now will be deployed. We are on the other side of the ocean. It is cloudy and rainy, but we are fine. We have never been healthier.*
>
> *The food is not like home, but we are now used to eating steaks and potatoes and lots of eggs. We miss your cooking and Papa's wine. Here they don't celebrate holidays as much as we do. Easter came and went. Tommy and I went to church and had our own Easter meal with roast lamb. They don't know how to cook pasta, and we think all the time of Mamma's pizza rustica, cassatiello, and zeppole. Please say hello to all our friends, especially the Mazzellas and Contes. We miss everyone very much.*
>
> *With love, your sons, Joe and Tom*

Maria made the sign of the cross. She dried the tears from her eyes.

"Thank God they are all right. My boys are together. Joe will take care of Tommy, and they will take care of each other," she said as she went about her chores.

She stayed busy to not get depressed.

When she was not in the house, Maria visited Our Lady of Pity Church. She asked God and San Silverio to bring her boys home. She prayed for all the men and women in combat fighting for America and Italy.

Each day was an agony.

Families were in terror to receive a message that a son or daughter was a new casualty of the war. The postman was the most frightening figure in the neighborhood. He brought the tragic news or delivered the latest message of love.

Sofia opened Joe's letter to her. She was careful and tore the envelope slowly to not damage the paper inside. She read it alone in the living room.

My Darling and Sweetest Sofia:

Each moment I miss you more. No one can imagine my feelings of being away from you. I see your face in every sunrise and hear your voice before I go to bed. Your photo is with me, night and day. I dream of coming back to your arms and living our life together. I know God and San Silverio will protect us.

I have been through a lot, but all is well. I am healthy and stronger than ever and am ready to take on any challenge. Your love will bring me back to you.

My nightly and morning prayer is this:

"God, thank you for all the blessings that you have given me. I have a wonderful family, a brother I love, and parents that love me. Most of all, thank you for bringing Sofia into my life. I love her so much. Please protect her and me and allow us to be together again in peace and love so we can raise our children in the light of your grace. Through Jesus Christ, Our Lord, Amen."

I love you, Sofia.

With a kiss, your Joe

Sofia's tears fell on the paper and smudged the ink. As she tried to brush them away, a heart shaped itself onto the page.

She looked at it and caressed the image.

She kissed it and knew it was a symbol of Joe's love.

CHAPTER 72 ━━━━━━━━━━━━━━━

THE GREAT ESCAPE

Darkness fell on Camp Como like a black cloud. It was two AM. All the inmates seemed asleep. Guards patrolled the buildings and heard snoring, coughing, and prisoners getting up to go to the bathroom.

Nothing appeared to be amiss, but it was.

One section of the compound housed the most German soldiers, along with members of the Gestapo, and the legendary SS part of Hitler's special army of loyal Nazi criminals and assassins.

They were awake.

For months, the Germans dug a deep tunnel under their barracks. They covered it with floorboards, to avoid detection. At night they excavated. In the daytime, they stored the soil in the legs of their trousers and then released the contents on the ground during recreation. Stolen spoons and simple utensils were their tools. Wire robbed from parts of the camp helped create a string of lights to illuminate the passageway. It was an arduous task. The tenacity, persistence, and determination of the Nazis fueled the tunnel project.

Now it was ready.

Three hundred men were planning a daring escape.

The burrow stretched two hundred feet from the building to the edge of a forest. The prisoners would crawl like groundhogs through the passageway. Once they exited the shaft, they would re-group, and dash into the woods. Divided into units of 50, they would go in various directions, once they were far enough from the compound to avoid capture. German officers would take charge of every company, except the one with the SS. The Germans planned to get to the railroad lines and hop on freight trains going toward New York.

They expected to join the German army as it invaded the East Coast of the U.S.

The SS officers had another scheme. They would travel as a team. Their objective was Memphis. Once they reached the port on the Mississippi, they would board a ship bound south to New Orleans. They earned enough money working for the Americans to sustain them until they reached South America and safety. It was a bold and cunning strategy.

"Follow me," commanded the head of the SS as he entered the hole and climbed down the ladder into the tunnel. He could barely speak. His chin was dislocated from Bruno's blow. A German officer with some medical training snapped his jaw back into place. His face was swollen and throbbing with soreness. A makeshift bandage wrapped around his head and chin provided support, but it kept slipping off. Each time he opened his mouth, sharp spasms of pain struck him like flaming arrows.

The tunnel was ten feet below the floor. One man after another went with him. Wooden boards were mounted to the roof of the shaft and supported by columns to prevent the tunnel from collapsing. In less than two hours, the entire German garrison was empty. To avoid detection from the MPs, the inmates put pillows in their beds, and covered them with blankets, to simulate someone sleeping. The prisoners crawled quickly through the hole. The lack of air in the tunnel could cause someone to pass out. If this happened, the entire column would be blocked. The string of lights bounced off them as they slithered like snakes through the narrow cavern.

Suddenly, a bulb burst and nearly blinded a prisoner.

The explosion echoed through the chamber. "What happened?" asked an officer from the back of the tunnel. "Nothing," whispered a Gestapo leader. "Keep moving and do not stop!" he commanded.

It was 4 AM. All the prisoners made it through the passageway. They gathered at the perimeter of the forest and regrouped.

As they congratulated themselves and organized into escape units, the sound of aircraft motors pierced the night air.

Two military helicopters hovered above them.

Huge lights from the flying machines came on. They were directed on the Germans and looked like powerful rays of sunshine that blinded them. The men covered their eyes with their hands to protect themselves from the illumination. Out of the forest, hundreds of U.S. Army troops emerged, carrying machine guns. An officer with a bull horn blasted a message: "Do not move. You are surrounded. Anyone who tries to run will be shot." The prisoners froze and raised their hands above their heads.

The Commandant was on a truck with binoculars. Silverio and Antonio were with him. The Great Escape was over.

CHAPTER 73

REPENTANCE AND FORGIVENESS

The bell rang from the church to signal services would soon begin. Reverend Jefferson donned his white robes, with a black and white collar. The church was clean. It had been washed and dusted by several of the female parishioners. It was a special Sunday. The pastor felt the grace of the Holy Spirit with him.

Today, he would speak of *forgiveness*. The Lord came to him in a revelation and told him that *forgiveness* was the gift that God gave to man and that man must give to each other. *Repentance* and *forgiveness* were two sides of the same coin.

As a man repented, he was also forgiven.

"Good morning, Mrs. Patterson, how is your mother?" asked the pastor as he greeted his flock. "She is at God's door." she said with tears in her eyes. "I am sorry. I will visit her today," said Reverend Jefferson. "She would like that very much, Reverend. You have a special place in her heart," said Mrs. Patterson as she held the pastor's warm hand. The Minister welcomed each of his parishioners. He knew them by name and family.

He was their Shepard and guided them through the difficult life of black families in the south.

"How are you, Mr. Quinn?" asked the Reverend. "Don't know how to respond, pastor. My two sons, Jacob and Lewis, were drafted last month. They are off to Biloxi and then to basic training before going into action." The Minister had seen many families lose their sons to the war.

He wondered if America would ever show gratitude to the thousands of black men and women who fought and died for it.

The United States was the only country they had, but was it worth giving up their life for a nation that segregated and oppressed them?

It was a question the pastor could not answer for himself. "They are in my prayers, Mr. Quinn. God bless you," said the pastor as he walked back into the church.

He went to the pulpit. "Let us begin, my children, by thanking the Lord for all that He has done for us. Let us raise our voices and sing his praises with *Amazing Grace*." The congregation rose. As if with one voice, they sang the beautiful verses of this worthy hymn:

Amazing grace,
How sweet the sound
That saved a wretch like me
I once was lost
But now I'm found
Was blind, but now I see

'Twas grace that taught
My heart to fear
And grace my Fears relieved
How precious did
That grace appear
The hour I first believed

Through many dangers
Toils and snares
We have already come
'Twas grace hath brought
Us safe thus far
And grace will lead us home

When we've been there
Ten thousand years,
Bright shining as the sun,
We'll have no less days to sing God's praise
Than when we first begun

Amazing grace,
How sweet the sound
That saved a wretch like me
I once was lost
But now I'm found
Was blind, but now I see

As the congregation sang, five white men entered the church and sat in the back. Billy Bob and the former Klansmen took a pew in the rear of the church. The men reverently removed their hats. Silverio and Antonio sat next to them.

The pastor beamed a warm smile to his visitors. They nodded respectfully. He climbed the pulpit and opened the Bible. He knew every verse by heart. He could recite the Old and New Testaments from memory. He began his sermon. "God Almighty, Creator of Heaven and Earth, we thank you for your love. Most of all we thank you for your forgiveness. Yes, you have forgiven us, and we have forgiven our brothers and sisters with the grace of your love," he said with his eyes closed.

"Amen!" roared the congregation.

"We forgive our brothers," came a voice from the crowd.

"Hallelujah!" shouted another. In a few moments, the entire church was animated to hear the word of the Lord.

"Today, God will speak to us from the Good Book. He will tell us what forgiveness is and how we should love our enemies and treat them as brothers and friends," said the pastor.

"Let's hear his voice!" cried someone. "Hear the Lord. Speak to us, Oh God!" screamed another. The Minister recited passages from the Bible. He closed his eyes. His voice grew deep with power as if the Almighty was speaking through him:

He has not dealt with us according to our sins, nor punished us according to our iniquities. For as the heavens are high above the earth, so great is His mercy toward those who fear Him; as far as the east is from the west, so far has He removed our transgressions from us. Psalms 103:10-12

"Come now, and let us reason together," says the Lord. "Though your sins are like scarlet, they shall be as white as snow; though they are red like crimson, they shall be as wool." Isaiah 1:18

I, even I, am He who blots out your transgressions for my own sake; and I will not remember your sins. Isaiah 43:25

Billy Bob felt the warm power of the Lord overcome him as the voice of the pastor penetrated his heart.

Let the wicked forsake his way, and the unrighteous man his thoughts; let him return to the Lord, and He will have mercy on him; and to our God, for He will abundantly pardon. Isaiah 55:7

For if you forgive men their trespasses, your heavenly Father will also forgive you. But if you do not forgive men their trespasses, neither will your Father forgive your trespasses. Matthew 6:14-15

And whenever you stand praying, if you have anything against anyone, forgive him that your Father in heaven may also forgive you your trespasses. Mark 11:25

Judge not, and you shall not be judged. Condemn not, and you shall not be condemned. Forgive, and you will be forgiven. Luke 6:37

The pastor's voice grew louder. He sensed the energy of God within him.

Repent, therefore, and be converted. Turn away from sin and darkness, from the power of the devil, to the living God. We repent from our former sins, cast off our old life – a life which enjoyed living in the passing pleasures of sin – and lay hold of a new mind – a mindset determined to resist... that your sins may be blotted out, so times of refreshing may come from the presence of the Lord. Acts 3:19

He has delivered us from the power of darkness and conveyed us into the kingdom of the Son of His love, in whom we have redemption through His blood, the forgiveness of sins. Colossians 1:13-14

As the Minister completed his sermon, he felt as if his strength was gone. He was exhausted. The Lord used him as an instrument to send a message to his flock and to the white men who were his guests.

When he finished, the crowd rose and sang "The Battle Hymn of the Republic:"

Mine eyes have seen the glory of the coming of the Lord
He is trampling out the vintage where the grapes of wrath are stored,
He has loosed the fateful lightning of His terrible swift sword
His truth is marching on.

Glory! Glory! Hallelujah!
Glory! Glory! Hallelujah!
Glory! Glory! Hallelujah!
His truth is marching on.

I have seen Him in the watch-fires of a hundred circling camps
They have built Him an altar in the evening dews and damps
I can read His righteous sentence by the dim and flaring lamps
His day is marching on.

Glory! Glory! Hallelujah!
Glory! Glory! Hallelujah!
Glory! Glory! Hallelujah!
His truth is marching on.

I have read a fiery gospel writ in burnished rows of steel,
"As ye deal with my condemners, so with you my grace shall deal;"
Let the Hero, born of woman, crush the serpent with his heel,
Since God is marching on.

Glory! Glory! Hallelujah!
Glory! Glory! Hallelujah!
Glory! Glory! Hallelujah!
His truth is marching on.

He has sounded forth the trumpet that shall never call retreat
He is sifting out the hearts of men before His judgment-seat
Oh, be swift, my soul, to answer Him! Be jubilant, my feet!
Our God is marching on.

Glory! Glory! Hallelujah!
Glory! Glory! Hallelujah!
Glory! Glory! Hallelujah!
His truth is marching on.

In the beauty of the lilies Christ was born across the sea,
With a glory in His bosom that transfigures you and me:
As He died to make men holy, let us live to make men free,
While God is marching on.

Glory! Glory! Hallelujah!
Glory! Glory! Hallelujah!
Glory! Glory! Hallelujah!
His truth is marching on.

"My children," concluded the pastor, "as you leave our house of worship, please welcome our guests who have joined us today in friendship and love."

The members of the congregation greeted the white men and shook their hands as if they were part of their family.

Outside the Church, Billy Bob went up to the pastor. "Reverend, I ask you to forgive me my sins. Pardon my transgressions against you and your people. Consider me your friend. From this day forward, I will worship with you and yours, if you will have me," he said with deep sincerity. The pastor could see tears in his eyes.

"My son, this is your home. It is God's house, and He welcomes you. He has taken away your sins. You are forgiven. You are free. You are liberated. Come home, come home."

He embraced him.

"Reverend, we are here to thank you and to say goodbye," said Silverio. "You showed us the way people should treat others. We learned a lesson we will never forget. Please bless us as we begin our trip home." The pastor gave Silverio and Antonio a warm hug.

Billy Bob took Silverio and Antonio's hands in friendship. He said with a smile, "You know, I never met any Italians before and never met any northerners, either. You were the first. I can tell it's different in your part of the country, but I picked up something from you: 'All men are truly created equal,' and have the same rights to live and be happy. I love this country and will fight for it. I want to thank you for saving my life and changing me. I am a new man today."

He handed them two key chains. "The state flower of Mississippi is the magnolia. Please accept these as a token of my gratitude."

The Magnolia, State flower of Mississippi, *Courtesy, MS.GOV.*

The brass key rings had the image of a white blossom. "Thank you. This means a lot to us. We also want to give you something to remember us by," said Silverio. He handed them a photo of the statue of San Silverio at Our Lady of Pity Church in New York. "He is a powerful Saint. Whenever you are in trouble, talk to him. He will help you," said Antonio. The Italians from the North, and the former Klansmen from the South, bid farewell.

The men were proud to be different, yet Americans.

As they left the church, Silverio and Antonio looked back at the cross that brought them there. The pastor was in the door, waving with a broad smile shining through his white beard. They knew they would never see him again, yet that face would stay with them forever.

CHAPTER 74 ━━━━━━━━━━━━

THE PARTING

"I have to return home," said Helena to Luigi and Carlo. "I have chores to do," she said sadly, waiting for a word from her lover. "Tell Carmela I will deliver everything tonight when I close the store," stated Luigi. Helena was about to go to the door when Carlo stopped her.

"I need to see you tonight, tomorrow, and every day, Helena," he said breathlessly.

"Tomorrow morning, I will take the bus and get off at the stop across the street. We can meet there at 10 AM and go to the park," she responded with the look of love. "Wonderful. I will be waiting for you," he kissed her cheek, and she disappeared as the bell tinkled over the door.

Helena floated up the street. Her mind was wrapped in a heavenly cloud of love.

She could not think clearly.

"Parting is such sweet sorrow, that I shall say goodnight, till it be tomorrow." She recalled those words from Romeo and Juliet.

Parting was not sweet. It was sorrow. "Can this be what love feels like?" she asked herself. She longed to be with him. Away from Carlo seemed unnatural.

She felt lonely, lost, as if a part of her was gone.

Aimlessly, she mounted the bus. "Have you forgotten something?" said the driver. Helena looked at him as if he were invisible. "You have to pay the fare," he said. She woke up from her dream and reached into her purse for some coins and dropped them in the turnstyle. She sat down. She felt out of breath. Slowly, she composed herself.

" 'What is happening to me?' she thought. 'I have lost all control. Leaving Carlo took away my oxygen. I can barely breathe.' " A sense of emptiness engulfed her. She was deeply in love and, without him, felt confused and alone.

"Helena is a wonderful girl. She would make a perfect wife," said Luigi. "I can tell you are in love. Ask her to marry you. Do not let her get away," said Luigi with encouragement in his voice. Carlo wanted to say, "But we have only just met. We do not know anything about each other. How can I propose after meeting her only once? It does not make any sense. What can I offer her? I have no money, no job. I am a prisoner of war. I have no future. Once the war is over, I will have to return to Italy. The country is devastated and in ruins. Our family home may be gone, and we would be destitute. What can I offer this fantastic girl who I am madly in love with?"

Instead, Carlo said, "Luigi, I proposed to her today. I love her with all my heart." Luigi jumped with joy.

"Little brother, I am the happiest man in the world at this moment. You cannot understand why, but you will."

CHAPTER 75

BRUNO'S LIBERATION

Bruno sat next to Silverio and Antonio. The three men had coffee in the camp canteen. The Cadillac was packed and ready for the journey back to New York. A convoy of troops, trucks, and artillery was assembling at Camp Clinton, fifty miles away. It would stop at Camp Como so Silverio and Antonio could join the caravan.

"Your visit changed my life. You helped me make the most important decision I've ever faced. It was the right one. Thank you. I can never repay you. Once the war is over, I can start again. I have my maritime engineer's license. I know I can get a job on cargo ships and oil tankers," he said emotionally.

He felt a special bond to his cousin.

If it had not been for him, he would have joined the escape and now would be in solitary confinement. He would have lost his privileges, especially the right to work off the base and earn money.

"Cousin, you do not owe me anything. God, San Silverio, and our grandfather sent me here to save you. We must thank them. I am proud of you. All will be well," he said as they rose from the table and embraced. "We have to get on the road. I promised the Commandant we would say goodbye," he told Bruno as he and Antonio left the canteen.

Bruno cried as he watched his cousin leave the room.

He dried his tears, composed himself, and walked slowly to the camp chapel. It was plain and had no decorations or statues. The church was interdenominational. There was an altar at the end of the building. It had a pulpit and a Star of David on the left and on the right was a cross. Ten rows of chairs were laid out in the center.

Bruno sat in one close to the front of the church. He kneeled. He made the sign of the cross. His thoughts flew to images and sounds. He saw the face of his grandfather.

He recalled his voice. "Bruno, come home, my son," he would shout to get him to return after playing with his friends. Giuseppe prepared snacks Bruno adored: bruschetta, covered with the sweet, ripe tomatoes of Ponza, crowned with his grandfather's olive oil; a piece of goat's milk cheese and a bowl of fresh figs picked from Giuseppe's tree.

It was heaven.

Sunset over the island of Palmarola, *Courtesy, Emilio Iodice*

The boy sat on the balcony and gazed at the sun setting over the island of Palmarola, while Giuseppe told stories of fishing adventures. "You remember the time we lost that giant grouper?" he would say. "It must have weighed 10 kilos." Giuseppe's voice was vivid and fresh. Bruno felt a special bond to this old man who was the center of his life.

"Grandpa, thank you for saving me. I am sorry if at times I did not listen to you. Please forgive me and stay with me as I move on with the rest of my life," he prayed.

CHAPTER 76 ━━━━━━━━━━━━━━━━

THE CONVOY

"Silverio, I have prepared four letters for you and Antonio. I am mailing them today," said the Commandant. "The first is to Mayor Fiorello H. La Guardia of New York. It cites, 'Your heroic sacrifice to come to Camp Como and help prevent a prison escape that could have resulted in considerable loss of life.' The second letter is to the Commandant of the Brooklyn Navy Yard, mentioning 'Your patriotism and willingness to risk your lives to help the U.S. government prevent a tragic event at this Camp.' The third is to the President of the International Longshoreman's Association, congratulating you, 'For your distinguished service, which is an example of the courage and sacrifice of the members of his Union during this critical time in the war effort.' Finally, the last letter is to the President of the Society of San Silverio in New York, noting 'The amazing effort you and Antonio made to save lives, which should make the people from Ponza especially proud.'"

Silverio smiled. He and Antonio thanked the Commandant for his generosity. "Colonel, you can save the postage on the last letter and give it to me, since I am the President of the Society of San Silverio." The three men laughed. "If you had not come to Como, the Italians would have joined the escape. Thanks to you, we knew when it would take place and were able to stop it. If not, many lives would have been lost. A chain reaction of escapes and insurrections could have come to pass once the story got out of a successful break," he insisted.

A rumbling sound vibrated through the Commandant's office.

The building shook as a hundred huge military vehicles thundered through the compound.

"Silverio, that's your parade out there, waiting for you to join it," said the Commandant as the three men shook hands.

CHAPTER 77

LUIGI'S DREAM

"**L**ook, isn't it incredible?" said Luigi with enthusiasm. Carlo and his brother were looking at a store next to Luigi's shop. It was closed. A "For Rent" sign was in the window. "We can turn this into a bakery. In the back, they have plenty of space for stock. The basement is huge. There we can put the oven and all the machines to make dough. This could be a gold mine. No one in town makes good Italian bread, and no one makes pizza," said Luigi. Carlo visualized the dream. He saw the oven, the dough, the bread, and the pizza. As a first-class baker, he could also make many cakes and pies and fancy Italian pastries.

"It's wonderful, Luigi, but where will I get the money to convert this store into a bakery? It would cost a fortune," he said with a worried look on his face. "I will supply the capital. We will be partners. You don't have to worry about anything. I will take care of all the details. In the meantime, I will take out a long-term lease on the store. I can use it as storage until you come back. What I want you to do is to promise me that once you go home to Italy, you will arrange to marry Helena and come back here," said Luigi firmly.

Carlo looked at his brother. He smiled and then laughed and hugged him. "Thank you, Luigi. I promise I will return. Once I am in Italy, Helena can come, and we can get married there, and then I can return as a legal immigrant. We don't know when this war is going to end, but I am still here and, if the camp allows me, I can come every other month and stay a week. I can even help you in the store. What do you think?" Luigi was ecstatic.

"My dreams are coming true, Carlo! I always wanted you here with me. This is a good country. We can raise our families in peace and happiness and give them a chance at a good life. You will be happy in America, little brother." They celebrated with a glass of homemade wine as they closed the General Store. The groceries that Helena ordered were in Luigi's car.

When they arrived at the house, Carlo brought the box to the door. Helena heard the bell ring and dashed upstairs. She was in the basement doing the wash and ironing her uncle's shirts. She opened the door quickly and sighed at the sight of Carlo. "Can I come in," he said. "Where would you like this?" he asked with a broad smile. "In the kitchen, please," said Helena as she showed him the way. "My darling, I have something important to tell you," said Carlo anxiously. He wanted to explain his plan to return to America and open the bakery. "Thank you, Carlo, for bringing the groceries," exclaimed Carmela, who walked into the kitchen abruptly. "Luigi knows to put it on my account, and I will pay next week. Can I offer you some coffee?" she said, looking at the way Helena was staring at Carlo with eyes of love.

Carlo wanted nothing more than to linger with Helena, but he realized that it would be better to leave, especially with the roving eyes of Carmela around. "I appreciate it, but Luigi and I have to move on. Please give my regards to your husband," said Carlo as he hugged Carmela and kissed Helena's cheeks. As he hugged her, he felt the contour of her warm body. Carlo got into the car, and they drove away.

"He is very handsome, isn't he?" noted Carmela with raised eyebrows. "He is very nice," responded Helena.

She wanted to hold on to their secret, so that no one could spoil it.

CHAPTER 78 ━━━━━━━━━━━━━━━━━━━━

THE CONVOY DEPARTS

"**S**ir, please pull in between the two lead jeeps," said the Sergeant to Silverio. "As we travel from city to city, we will have interchanging police escorts up to the border of each state. That way we will not have to stop at traffic lights or intersections. It is important to stay in our formation. We should be in Camp Le Jeun in North Carolina by late tonight. We will stay at the camp, and then start toward New York first thing in the morning. If all goes well, we should be in Fort Hamilton in Brooklyn by 6 PM tomorrow." The soldier's words were sweet to Silverio and Antonio's ears. They could already see their apartments and families, and they could smell the perfume of homemade cooking.

"I sure could use some of my wine right now," said Antonio, as he settled into the front seat of the car. "I think we will both get drunk as soon as we get home," responded Silverio as he started the engine of the Cadillac. He drove the car behind the lead jeep.

The Captain in charge of the convoy came to the door of Silverio's car and saluted him. "Sir, if you need anything, anywhere along the route just honk your horn. We will do a rest stop in about three hours in Tennessee," said the Captain. "Thank you, Captain," responded Silverio. "We will be fine and appreciate being part of your caravan going back to New York." The officer smiled. "Colonel McCarthy told me about what you did in Camp Como. This is the least we can do to show the gratitude of your country," he stated with pride.

Chills ran up Silverio's spine when he heard the word, "Tennessee." It was hard to forget what had happened in Nashville. The loud voices of Scarface and the Giant and the intimidating words of the Chief of Police echoed in his mind. The mistreatment, handcuffs, and the grey, windowless room where they were confined gave Silverio feelings of anger and horror. Soon this would be behind him, and he would be home in the arms of Lucia and his son Ralph.

He could imagine nothing happening between now and then.

CHAPTER 79 ▬▬▬▬▬▬▬▬▬

ITALY'S RACIAL LAWS

"In 1938, the Italian Fascist regime under Benito Mussolini enacted a series of racial laws that placed multiple restrictions on the country's Jewish population. At the time the laws were enacted, it is estimated that about 46,000 Jews lived in Italy, of whom about 9,000 were foreign born, and thus subject to further restrictions, such as residence requirements. Large Jewish communities existed in Rome, Venice, Trieste, Florence, Ferrara, Turin, and other cities. Largely urban, Italian Jews were traditionally secular and very integrated, often intermarrying with non-Jews." [1]

The Fascist government "forbade Jewish children to attend public or private schools, ordered the dismissal of Jews from professorships in all universities, and banned Jews from the civil service and military, as well as the banking and insurance industries." [2]

In 1939 and 1940, more onerous laws went into effect that revoked licenses of Jewish shopkeepers and peddlers, and bond and stockholders were required to turn over their accounts to non-Jews. The government also confiscated bank accounts to prevent funds being transferred outside the country. [3]

---

1   The Holocaust in Italy, The Holocaust Museum, https://www.ushmm.org/learn/mapping-initiatives/geographies-of-the-holocaust/the-holocaust-in-italy.

2   Paul Vitiello, "Scholars Reconsidering Italy's Treatment of Jews in the Nazi Era," New York Times, November 4th, 2010, https://www.nytimes.com/2010/11/05/nyregion/05italians.html

3   Ibid. Vitiello

CHAPTER 80 ━━━━━━━━━━━━━━━━━━━━━━

BOMBING OF ROME

In July 1943, the Allies bombed Sicily to prepare to invade Italy. On July 19th, 1943, 500 Allied bombers dropped over a thousand tons of explosives in the working class neighborhood of San Lorenzo, in the city of Rome. 3000 people died. Six days later, on July 25th, 1943, the Grand Council of Fascism voted against Il Duce, which led to his ouster by King Victor Emanuel III. As soon as Mussolini left the royal residence, he was arrested and taken to the Island of Ponza in exile, where he remained for a short time. Later, he was rescued by the Germans, who helped him form a new government in the North of Italy.

On September 8th, 1943, the King announced that his country would join the war on the side of the allies. As the King escaped from Rome, the Germans began a swift occupation of the country.

They also rounded up Italian Jews.

A month before the deportation of Jews, the Nazis "demanded that the Jewish community of Rome pay over 50 kilograms of gold as a ransom. The Jews were given 36 hours to come up with the metal or face the immediate deportation of 200 of their members. Chief Rabbi Israel Zolli went to the Vatican for help. Indeed, he was advised that the Jewish community could borrow whatever amount of gold was needed, to be repaid after the war. Some sources say the Vatican capped its offer at 15 kilos of gold, worth over $600,000 in today's market prices. In fact, it did not become necessary to take a loan from the Church. Citizens of Rome, both non-Jews and Jews, streamed into the city's synagogues to turn over such items as gold jewelry, watches, and cigarette cases to help with the ransom.

"Unfortunately, the gold payment only delayed the inevitable. On October 16th, the Germans entered the city's Old Jewish Ghetto to round up the Jews. By then, however, most of the Jews had gone into hiding. About 4,000 found sanctuary in various Roman Catholic institutions, including within the Vatican itself." [1]

Over a thousand Roman Jews were deported to concentration camps. Few returned.

"Trucks pulled up on the cobblestoned piazza beside the Portico d'Ottavia (the Jewish Ghetto), the neighborhood was sealed, and 365 German soldiers fanned out through the narrow streets and courtyards. Families hid at the backs of their shuttered shops. The able-bodied and quick-witted jumped from their windows or fled along the rooftops. The unlucky were hounded from their homes at gunpoint and herded into the idling trucks." [2]

Priests, nuns, and monks sheltered Jews in Italy to prevent the Nazis from finding them. They were given new documents with new names, and they "converted" to Catholicism to avoid being arrested by the Germans.

One priest saved a group of families.

He was stationed in Castellonorato, a small mountain town near Formia, which faced the Island of Ponza. His name was Don Lorenzo. As the Germans broke into Italian churches, convents, and seminaries, Don Lorenzo searched desperately for a way to protect his flock before the Nazis could find them. Unbeknownst to him, two Italian American boys, whose parents came from Ponza, were on their way to Italy to help him.

1   "The Haaretz," by David B. Green and Ruth Schuster. The original version of this article was published on October 18, 2012. https://www.haaretz.com/jewish/.premium-this-day-nazis-deport-roman-jews-1.5193435

2   David Laskin, "Echoes for the Roman Ghetto," July 12, 2013, New York Times. https://www.nytimes.com/2013/07/14/travel/echoes-from-the-roman-ghetto.html

CHAPTER 81 ━━━━━━━━━━━━━━━━━━

BRITISH DECEPTION

"On April 30th, 1943, a fisherman came across a badly decomposed corpse floating in the water off the coast of Huelva, in southwestern Spain. The body was of an adult male, dressed in a trench coat, a uniform, and boots, with a black attaché case chained to his waist. His wallet identified him as Major William Martin, of the Royal Marines. The Spanish authorities called in the local British vice-consul, Francis Haselden, and in his presence opened the attaché case, revealing an official-looking military envelope. The Spaniards offered the case and its contents to Haselden. But Haselden declined, requesting that the handover go through formal channels—an odd decision, in retrospect, because in the days that followed, British authorities in London sent a series of increasingly frantic messages to Spain asking the whereabouts of Major Martin's briefcase." [1]

German intelligence in Spain quickly discovered the incident. Helped by Spanish authorities, they were determined to see the contents of that briefcase. Inside was a sealed envelope with a Top Secret message. Using a thin metal rod, they wound the contents of the envelope, removed it, read it, photographed it, and returned it without breaking the seal. The information was astonishing. Major Martin was a British courier. "He was carrying a personal letter from Lieutenant General Archibald Nye, the vice-chief of the Imperial General Staff, in London, to General Harold Alexander, the senior British officer under Eisenhower in Tunisia. Nye's letter spelled out what Allied intentions were in southern Europe. American and British forces planned to cross the Mediterranean from their positions in North Africa and launch an attack on German-held Greece and Sardinia. Hitler transferred a Panzer division from France to the Peloponnese, in Greece, and the German military

---

1   Malcolm Gladwell, "Pandora's Briefcase," The New Yorker, May 10th, 2010, https://www.newyorker.com/magazine/2010/05/10/pandoras-briefcase

command sent an urgent message to the head of its forces in the region: 'The measures to be taken in Sardinia and the Peloponnese have priority over any others.'" [21]

The Germans felt they had discovered what they had frantically been searching for through their elaborate intelligence operations: the Allied plans for the invasion of Europe. The Nazi high command was delighted. They thought that the contents of the envelope would change the course of the war. They were wrong.

"The Germans did not realize – until it was too late – that 'William Martin' was a fiction. The man they took to be a high-level courier was a mentally ill vagrant who had eaten rat poison; his body had been liberated from a London morgue and dressed up in officer's clothing. The letter was a fake, and the frantic messages between London and Madrid a carefully choreographed act. When a hundred and sixty thousand Allied troops invaded Sicily on July 10th, 1943, it became clear that the Germans had fallen victim to one of the most remarkable deceptions in modern military history." [2]

Following the successful invasion of Sicily, the Allies pointed themselves to the middle of the Italian boot to get closer to their objective: Rome.

---

2   Ibid. Gladwell

Allied invasion of Sicily, Explosion of Liberty Ship Robert Rowan after hit by German bombers, July11th 1943, *Courtesy, US Army Signal Corps*

CHAPTER 82 ━━━━━━━━━━━━━━━━━━━━━

THE ORDERS

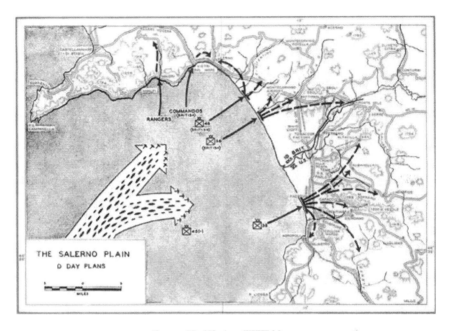

Courtesy, The US Army WWII Museum

"You will land here on August 25th and unite with partisans behind enemy lines," explained the Captain to Joe and Tom as he pointed to a map showing the elements of the Allied invasion of Salerno, near the city of Naples. It was one of the largest amphibious landings in history. "We need every road blocked, every rail line blown up, and every bridge that the Germans can use to be destroyed before our boats hit the beach on September 3rd. You will go ashore near Amalfi and proceed north to Nocera Inferiore. Partisans will meet you outside of town and from then on you will be on your own to carry out your mission with them. The password is *'Aristotle was here.'* The partisans will greet you with that word. Your response is, *'So was Plato.'* The details are in your packet. Any questions?"

Joe and Tom studied charts, roads, rivers, railroads, highways and knew every bridge and tunnel in a 20-mile radius of Salerno. Targets were mapped out to the minutest detail. Plastic explosives, pistols, and communication devices would be part of their arsenal. The bulk of what they would need would be parachuted in. "After you have made contact with the partisans, and we know your coordinates, we will fly in crates of detonation equipment and ammunition and weapons," explained the officer.

The two young men from Little Ponza in the Bronx had passed the rigorous OSS training. From Britain they were flown to North Africa to join regular Army and Marine units to coordinate activities. A key role was cooperation with opponents of the regime to fight together to make sure the invasion succeeded. A dossier with the names and profiles of each member of the partisan team was provided. Joe and Tom studied and memorized details from the color of their eyes and hair to their height, weight, and some other features. Italian partisans came from different political persuasions. Some were Christian Democrats, or Socialists. And many were Communists.

What they had in common was hatred of the Fascists and the Nazis.

CHAPTER 83 ━━━━━━━━━━━━━━━━━━━━━━━━

THE BEACHHEAD

Courtesy, Wallpaper BlogSpot Photo by Emily O'Brien

Light winds buffeted the sea along the western coast of Italy in the wee hours of the morning of Wednesday, August 25th. It was not a typical late summer night, in the Mediterranean of 1943. The sea was filled with blood and debris, from the war growing more intense. Sunken ships and bombs lay across the seabed.

German and Fascist patrol boats scoured the coast in search of Allied craft attempting to land.

On this night, the sea was calm and the enemy was nowhere in sight. The invasion of Sicily, several months earlier, forced the Germans to reposition their forces to prevent the advance of the U.S. Fifth Army, which was fighting its way up the boot.

An American submarine carried two members of the Office of Strategic Services within five miles of a beachhead not far from the city of Salerno. "Up periscope," said the Captain. He slowly turned the device 360 degrees. "A fishing vessel dropping nets; small boats pulling toward the shore; no military craft. Down periscope. Prepare to surface," he ordered. Tom and Joe were dressed in civilian clothes. They had backpacks with flashlights, flares, small arms, grenades, two kilos of plastic explosives, and K rations to sustain them.

Courtesy, Office of Naval History

The submarine rose into the surf. It bounced about in the waves as a sailor opened the hatch and removed a self-inflatable raft from a canvas bag. Within minutes, the rubber boat was ready. Two small oars were attached to the inside of the craft. "Thank you, Captain," said Joe as they saluted and climbed out of the hatch. A full moon illuminated the men and flung silver shadows on the sea. They jumped into the boat and rowed to shore. The winds changed, and they felt the small vessel being pulled by the currents in all directions.

They looked at the sub as it disappeared into the mist.

The brothers were alone.

Moonlight cast rays on the sandy shore, making it appear close. Instead, it was miles away and the currents were pulling the raft out to sea. They rowed harder. Soon their rhythm set the rubber boat in the right direction.

Tom thought of all the parachute training and the stress in taking one jump after another, just to be put into a dinghy to land on an Italian shore.

And he did not know how to swim.

It took 90 minutes to reach the beach. Joe and Tom were perspiring heavily. It was past two AM. No one was about. They felt lucky, as they leaped from the raft, deflated it, and dug a hole in the sand to hide it. With their back packs securely fastened, they started on their 23-kilometer journey to Nocera Inferiore to meet the partisan garrison. The location was a church in the outskirts of the town. Joe took out his compass. He rotated it in the light of the moon to see the arrow pointing north. Suddenly, they heard breaking twigs.

Someone was walking toward them.

They hit the ground. The men raised their heads cautiously and saw tall bushes lining the beach move.

A dark figure emerged.

The brothers pulled out their pistols, unlocked their safeties, cocked their triggers, and pointed at the shape coming closer to them.

CHAPTER 84 ━━━━━━━━━━━━━━━━━━━━

RETURN TO NASHVILLE

The fleet of military vehicles moved smoothly past Memphis as it left Como and drove into the heart of Tennessee. At the border, two city police autos with flashing lights met them. One took the front of the caravan and another the rear. Silverio lit a cigar for the first time since the start of his journey. He felt good. The Commandant at Como saw that his Cadillac had plenty of fuel for the long journey home. Mechanics looked it over, changed the oil and a fan belt, and tightened a few bolts and screws to make sure it was in perfect condition for the trip. The car had been washed and polished. It glowed in the sunlight like a mirror as they drove toward Nashville.

On the outskirts of the town, the Memphis police cars departed. Suddenly, Silverio and Antonio heard a menacing sound that sent goosebumps through their skin.

They looked at each other.

Two Nashville city police motorcycles approached the lead vehicles. The convoy slowed down and came to a halt as the police officers ordered it to stop.

The motorcycle duo drove up and down the caravan examining the vehicles and their drivers.

Silverio saw Scarface and the Giant.

They looked larger than life as they came up to his side of the Cadillac. "Well, well, if it isn't those Italian spies we took in a while back. Someone told us you would be coming back our way today," said Scarface with sarcasm. "We thought the boys in Mississippi would take care of you, but it looks like you're getting a free ride home. I'll bet these soldiers don't know a thing about you," he exclaimed.

"Get out of this car," demanded Scarface. Silverio and Antonio obeyed.

Scarface took out his handcuffs while the Giant pointed his pistol at them.

"What's going on here?" demanded the Captain of the convoy. "Officer, why did you stop us? And why are you interrogating these civilians who are part of this taskforce?" he asked. "And put that revolver away," demanded the Captain. The Giant did not obey.

"Sir, these men are suspected Italian spies. We had them in our custody ten days ago when they were released. We told them never to return to Nashville or we would arrest them, which is what we will do, with or without the blessing of the U.S. Army," insisted Scarface.

"You will do nothing of the sort," asserted the Captain. "Get the Chief of Police on your radio and get him down here, now," commanded the Captain.

Fifteen minutes later, the Chief descended from his car wearing the same uniform he had on when he interrogated Silverio and Antonio. His face was red and swollen from drinking bourbon and beer.

"Captain, you have no jurisdiction here in Tennessee. These men will be arrested and put in jail awaiting a trial. We warned them never to set foot in this town again, and they violated our accord and have broken a number of Tennessee laws," exclaimed the Chief in a loud voice.

He grinned and nodded to Scarface and the Giant smiling like cats that ate the mice.

"These two men are heroes and patriotic Americans who have saved lives for our country and risked their own in doing so. Medals and commendations are what they deserve. Not to be put in jail!" exclaimed the Captain. He went on and told them the details of how they stopped the escape from Camp Como.

"If you touch as much as a hair on their head, I will have General Marshall, the Chief of Staff himself, get on the phone with the Governor. I promise you will be fired and out on your asses within an hour after that call!" insisted the Captain with anger and determination.

He was bluffing.

He had no way of reaching the general, but he was trying to convince the Chief to back off.

Instead, the Chief's face turned red with anger. He would show them who was in charge in his city.

He clenched his fists and pulled his revolver from his holster.

The motorcycle officers flashed their pistols and joined him in defiance as they walked up to the Captain with fire in their eyes.

CHAPTER 85 ▬▬▬▬▬▬▬▬▬▬▬▬▬▬▬▬▬

HANDCUFFS

$\mathbf{A}$s the Chief and his henchmen approached the Captain, he nodded to a Sergeant, who heard the conversation. Three soldiers leaped from a truck with machine guns.

In seconds, high-powered automatic weapons were focused on the Nashville police team. They raised their hands as the Sergeant cuffed them.

A Lieutenant approached.

"The three of you are under arrest for interfering with a war time military convoy, for intimidating an officer of the U.S. Army, for willfully delaying the advancement of vital supplies for the war effort, and threatening to falsely arrest two civilians who were in service to the U.S. Government!" exclaimed the officer, who was an attorney with the Judge Advocate General Corps (JAG).

The Chief, Scarface, and the Giant blanched white.

"You can't do this, Captain! We will accuse you of protecting Italian spies!" shouted the Chief. A black car had driven up to the convoy a few minutes earlier. Two men in dark suits presented themselves with badges in hand. They were agents of the Federal Bureau of Investigation (FBI).

"Tell it to the FBI, Chief. You will be held in custody in the jail of the Federal Building in Nashville until the government finishes its investigation. If all goes well, you and your buddies could be on parole in ten years," said the Captain calmly.

The federal agents put the three police officers in their car and drove off.

Silverio and Antonio looked at the entire scene in shock. Apparently, the Captain had been warned by the Commandant of Camp Como about the problems Silverio and Antonio faced when they drove through Nashville.

The officer was prepared.
He had alerted his team and the FBI and got them ready.

In less than an hour, the Chief, Scarface, and the Giant were behind bars.

CHAPTER 86

FRANCESCA

The dark figure was three meters away.

It came closer.

The starlit sky revealed a silhouette, short and slim. It could be armed. Joe and Tom had never killed anyone, but now they were prepared to do so. They screwed silencers to their revolvers to keep any gunshot sounds from echoing across the bay and reaching enemy gun emplacements. Within minutes, they could face Italian and German soldiers and be arrested as spies. Joe thought about his necklace with the cyanide capsule. The thought of using it frightened him.

The person in the shadows was now a meter away. The brothers jumped up and pointed their pistols.

Their faces were hidden in the darkness, but the metal of their revolvers glowed in the lunar light.

"Who are you?" said Joe in Italian.

"Aristotle was here," said the figure from the shadows.

It was the voice of a woman. *"So was Plato,"* responded Joe.

The men were relieved. They put away their pistols. "Welcome to Salerno," she whispered as she emerged from the night to show her face. It was that of a young lady with blondish brown hair, large dark eyes, and lovely, delicate features.

"My name is Francesca. I am a partisan. I will accompany you to a small town near Nocera Inferiore because the Germans have set roadblocks everywhere and are patrolling the wooded areas with dogs. On your own, you could never make it," she explained. "Colonel Lukas sent me because I know how to maneuver through and over the mountain passes," she said. Some partisan leaders had fictitious names to protect their identity. Lukas was one of them. He organized the resistance in the region around Salerno and Naples. Joe and Tom memorized his profile: blond with greenish-grey eyes, athletic and muscular, medium height, and able to speak Italian, Swedish, and English. He was a natural leader, fearless and cunning. He had parents from Sweden and Italy, and he had grown up in London.

Francesca wore a checkered shirt, trousers, and a blue windbreaker, with a red scarf around her head. "We will take a route through the hills. It is longer, but safer. There are Germans everywhere. We have to be careful to avoid anyone seeing us." "How old are you?" asked Joe. Francesca laughed at the question. She looked like she was 16, with her baby face and quick smile that wrinkled the skin around her eyes when she laughed.

"I will be 26 next May, but I feel as if I am 60 years old, with all that has happened in this horrible war. But I can shoot and kill as good as any man," she said with determination, as they moved toward a tree-lined area adjacent to the dunes.

Before leaving the beach, they ripped apart some bushes and used them to sweep away their footprints as they approached the forest.

A path cut deep into the woodlands. It ascended high into the Apennine Mountains that crisscrossed Italy, north and south, east and west. The shrubs were thick with brambles and thorns, and they needed flashlights to find their way since the path often dissolved into obscurity. After 4 hours, they stopped on the side of a steep hill to watch the sun rise over the bay of Salerno. It was a magnificent sight.

Wild fig trees were scattered among oaks and poplars. Some

were filled with fruit. Francesca picked a few for the Americans to taste. It was marvelous. Tom thought of the figs of home. These were better.

As the light pushed away the shadows, the three travelers became conscious of the dangers around them. Military planes flew overhead. Explosions and machine-gun fire echoed in the distance. It was hard to understand where the sounds were coming from, as they moved into the peaks surrounding Salerno. Gradually, the tumult of war melted away as they climbed over a high hill and descended into a deep valley filled with farmhouses, animals, and streams. For a few fleeting moments, they felt secure amidst the beautiful countryside rich with grapevines and orchards.

They quietly raced past the inhabited areas to avoid detection.

As they came to a path parallel to the main road, they heard an ominous sound of barking dogs and voices shouting in German.

CHAPTER 87

THE GERMANS

$\mathbf{A}$ large flag flew over the building of the Italian Army headquarters in Salerno. A mariner passed through the entrance and walked to the first desk he found that had someone in uniform. He removed his hat. He wore a grey jacket with a white shirt buttoned at the neck. His clothes were worn and filled with patches. He carried with him the scent of the ocean. His hands were cut and cracked from pulling nets and casting lines, and his face was covered with a white beard.

A Sergeant, sitting at a desk stamping papers, looked up indifferently at the man from the sea. "What is it?" he asked the fisherman. "I saw a submarine last night," he said. The Sergeant jumped up. "What, a submarine, where, when?" he demanded. "Four miles west of the port, around 2 AM. It unloaded a rubber boat. Two men got in and rowed to shore. I watched them with my binoculars as they buried the raft and went up the beach. They met someone and disappeared into the woods," explained the seaman.

The Sergeant raised the phone. "Get me the Admiralty," he told the operator. "Yes, sir," responded a young lady. Within an hour, Italian military forces and the German High Command in Salerno knew an Allied sub had been off the coast and sent two men ashore.

"They are spies, and we must capture them before they unite with the partisans," demanded the German general to his counterpart in the Italian Army. "If we discover where they are going, they could bring us to the headquarters of the rebels," remarked an officer of the Gestapo. The SS was deeply involved in the Italian campaign after landing in Sicily. "We must follow them, but not stop them until we locate where the band of traitors are assembling," said the SS officer.

Italian PT boats, equipped with depth charges, went to find the submarine. German planes scoured the hills looking for hikers in the slopes surrounding Salerno. A contingent of German troops set out for the beach. They arrived 12 hours after Joe, Tom, and Francesca started their journey. Six teams of two men and a German Shepherd scoured the area for clues.

After two hours, the dog wildly burrowed deep into the sand not far from the water. As the animal dug, it tore into a grey sheet of rubber. "Look at this," yelled a soldier as he pulled out the raft. The German teams assembled and examined the boat. An officer came forward.

"American. This is what the fisherman saw last night. They dropped them off out there and they rowed here, buried the craft, met a partisan, and set out over the mountains," explained the German Lieutenant as he pointed toward the sea.

"Get the dogs to sniff and smell the inside of the boat. I want three teams in the woods and two on the roads. I will take a team that will head north about ten miles from here and move into the forest to see if we can find a trace of them that far away," he explained.

Without a comment or a question, the soldiers and their dogs headed off on their assignments to uncover the mystery of who landed on that remote shore, and why. Two weeks later, they would know the answer.

CHAPTER 88

THE LOVERS

Carlo waited anxiously at the bus stop.

It was across the street from Luigi's General Store. His heart beat rapidly as one vehicle after another stopped, unloaded, and picked up travelers and went on.

An hour passed, and he worried, asking himself, "Is she all right? Has something happened? Did she forget? Should I go into the store and ask Luigi if I can call her home? What if Carmela answers? What do I say?" He paced back and forth looking at his watch, glancing at the sky for rain, peering far down the street and searching for the next bus.

A bus turned the corner and headed his way. It moved slowly and stopped. Carlo watched as the passengers descended. The last person to leave was Helena.

"My love, I am sorry, but we were caught in traffic and . . ." she said, when Carlo lifted her off the ground with a warm embrace and kissed her. They lingered for minutes.

The world melted away.

The lovers were oblivious to the stares of passersby.

Finally, they collected themselves, held hands, and walked. Helena wore a blue outfit with a necklace and a cameo. It was her mother's. She was wearing high-heeled shoes, which brought her almost to Carlo's chin. He had on a grey jacket, black trousers, and an opened shirt.

"Sweetheart, I have a surprise for you," said Carlo as they crossed the street.

They passed the general store and went to the adjacent shop that Luigi planned to rent.

"Darling, this is our future," he said as he explained the plan to open a bakery after he went back to Italy, and they got married and returned to America.

"It is wonderful!" said Helena. "I can get a job teaching, so we have enough money to pay our bills. Wheeling is a good place to raise children. I am so happy!" said Helena with tears in her eyes.

She looked at Carlo and felt a sense of emotion and love that seemed natural and perfect.

He took her in his arms, and they kissed with the sensation that their lives were now one, forever.

CHAPTER 89

RETURNING HOME

The convoy moved slowly through towns and cities as it crossed one state line after another to reach the U.S. base in North Carolina where the caravan and its passengers would rest overnight. Silverio was in a reflective mood as he drove. He put together the pieces of his journey and thought about the meaning of it all.

"Antonio, before this trip, to me, America was work, family, and opportunity. Now, it means much more. When someone says 'America,' they think of New York or some other big city, and they draw conclusions, good or bad, about the entire country. Instead, the United States is more than a city, a job, or a bank account. This place is about people who care and are struggling for truth, and to try to do the right thing, even though it does not always work out that way.

"There are problems and failures, sure, but there is a constant battle for fairness and honesty. Good people do not always win in America, but they do not always lose, either. Amazing, how those bastards that arrested us in Nashville are behind bars, now! Justice was served! They had no right to treat us the way they did.

"I still cannot believe those Klansmen are now friends of that black pastor, but they are. Why? Because, for some strange reason, God uses man as his tool to right wrongs. The key is trust, compassion, and love.

"Bruno convinced the Italians not to join the escape. Why? Because the Americans cared about him and treated him as a human being.

"That is the secret of this marvelous land. As long as the U.S.

is magnanimous, it will always be great, and it will be the exception to all other nations and all other people, I believe.

"The strength of the United States is that they trust people like you and me. Do you understand, Antonio? They believe in us to help them for civil defense, to assist in the war effort, and now they relied on us to save lives in a prisoner of war camp. And we were not born here.

"Only in America can this happen! Only here can they have faith in a pair of immigrants to fight for the values this country is all about!

"God bless America!" Antonio's face beamed his enthusiastic agreement, and there were tears in his eyes, as he nodded many times, wordlessly, emotionally, gratefully — Yes! Yes! Yes!

CHAPTER 90 ━━━━━━━━━━━━━━━━━━━━━━━━

THE CHASE

Nocera Inferiore was 10 miles away. Francesca was a splendid guide. As soon as she heard the barking of the German dogs, she brought Joe and Tom back into a wooded area where they could be safe and still proceed on their journey. They climbed over steep hills and through valleys that glowed with the colors of autumn. The forests were filled with red, yellow, and golden colors. Trees were laden with chestnuts, almonds, and walnuts.

They heard a buzzing sound. The three travelers looked up.

A German plane was circling overhead. It looked like a giant falcon searching for prey.

"They are on to us," said Joe. "You are right," responded Francesca. "We have to be careful. They could be following us to see where the partisans are located. It means we have to change our route, but still get there as soon as possible," she said anxiously. The plane hovered over them for what seemed an eternity as they hid among the shrubs and bushes. They could not be seen, but all the Germans needed was a suspicion they were following a certain path, and if so they would pursue them with a vengeance.

"Last week the Nazis arrested two young men from our village. They took them off the street and accused them of being partisans. It was not true. After they tortured and beat them, they shot them in the public square in front of their parents, relatives, and friends.

"It was awful," explained Francesca tearfully. "I hate them and will fight them even if I have to die," she exclaimed with anger in her voice, as they marched vigorously ahead.

The sound of the barking hounds returned. This time, the animals and their masters were in the forest. Perhaps they were a mile or two away. The trio marched faster.

There was no place to hide.

Tom wondered if they would make it. They were up against formidable odds. He thought about his parents and Anna. "We are on the other side of the world," he wrote to her in his last letter, mailed from North Africa. "Everything is fine, and we are awaiting orders. Our training was splendid, and we are ready to do our duty. I am not worried. I feel strong and capable of facing any challenge," he wrote, just to calm her fears.

Tom was troubled and concerned about the unknown, and his ability to confront it.

"My love, all I do is think of you, night and day, and when I can return to your loving arms. I love you with all my heart, Your Tom."

Courtesy, Creative Commons CCD

The howling dogs seemed closer. "We may have to get ready to take on that team of mutts and their owners," said Joe, taking his pistol from his holster.

"I am not so sure," said Francesca. "Once we get over this mountain we are nearly home. We can hide there in many places, and they will never find us," she insisted.
Suddenly, an image emerged amidst the trees.

It was a large wooden cross with a statue of Jesus nailed to it.

They stopped. Each prayed for deliverance from the evil pursuing them.

"It is a good sign," said Francesca. "Follow me, and do not worry!" she exclaimed.

CHAPTER 91

DON LORENZO

Castellonorato, *Courtesy, Lazio Tourism*

A thousand meters above the sea stretched a small town on a peak close to the city of Formia on the western coast of Italy, facing the Pontine islands. Castellonorato was an ancient village built by a noble family to protect the inhabitants who lived along the hills and valleys of Lazio from barbarian invasions. Over the centuries, monasteries and convents were built as part of the ecclesiastical institutions of the town. One of the oldest churches was that of St. Catherine of Alexandria. It had several priests and nuns who came from various parts of Italy.

A young cleric had just been ordained and assigned to this parish of farmers, shopkeepers, and artisans.

The priest was ugly.

He had a wide, malformed nose and warts on his chin, cheeks, and forehead. His face and head were disproportionately wide and crowned with thinning hair. Thick eyeglasses gave him the appearance of being partially blind. He stuttered when he spoke, and he quickly became nervous at the slightest thing. Yet he was kind, honest, and, in his own way, courageous.

Don Lorenzo felt fortunate to be in a place close to Ponza, where he was born. He could see the island on a clear day from the church tower. He missed his parents and friends and felt this was his sacrifice as he devoted himself to God and to serving his flock in this hamlet in the mountains.

As the Germans swept up the Italian boot in late 1943, they rounded up Jews everywhere they could find them.

Those fortunate enough to escape were hidden throughout the country, particularly by Catholic priests and nuns. In a monastery in Salerno, a dozen Jewish families hid in the back of a church. There they were cared for by monks who brought them food and sheltered them. After the fall of Mussolini, things changed, and the Germans became more aggressive. By the time Italy capitulated in September 1943, German divisions occupied almost every major city in the country, including Salerno.

"Jews are no longer safe there," said an Italian partisan to Don Lorenzo. "How many are they?" he asked. "About 40. There are ten families. We have managed to provide false names and documents, but they can no longer stay in Salerno. The Nazis are breaking into every religious community. They have killed anyone they suspect is harboring Jews," he explained.

The young priest from the Island of Ponza was more concerned about how to feed 40 people than his own safety. "How will you get them here?" he asked. "Tonight we will move them out in four garbage trucks. They will be hidden under the refuse. Instead of going to the dump, we will take the back roads to get here. I expect we can make it before dawn," said the Italian patriot.

Don Lorenzo admired the young man, even if he was a Communist who professed being an atheist and an opponent of the Catholic Church.

The priest could not ask permission from the bishop or his pastor to help in the risky venture. The whole affair had to be top secret.

Don Lorenzo thought hard about it.

"What would Jesus do? Didn't he give up his life for us? He would take any risk to save these people. The Lord told us, *'There is no greater love than to lay down one's life for one's friends.'"*

The young cleric from Ponza was afraid, but he was ready to die to save his Jewish brothers and sisters.

Once he had the refugee Jews in the church, he would let the pastor know about it, and then he would deal with the consequences. "Bring them right away. I will get the crypt ready so we can hide them," he told the partisan. "Thank you, Don Lorenzo," he said as he left on a motorbike.

The priest watched him as he descended the steep roads leading to the valley below and wondered, "How many lives have I put in danger, including my own?"

CHAPTER 92

THE WELCOME

The further the convoy was from Tennessee and Mississippi, the better Silverio and Antonio felt. After five hours into their journey home, they felt that their odyssey was behind them. The two men had developed a special bond. Faced with adversity, they became brothers. Few challenges could match what they had gone through.

Both were changed. They were older, stronger, wiser, and not afraid.

They had grown spiritually and morally.

"That pastor had an effect on me," said Antonio. "You know, I am not that religious, but the way he forgave those men who tried to kill him and burn down his church was amazing. His response was to save their lives. This has to be the hand of God in all of this. It must be!" insisted Antonio.

"You're right, Antonio! It was amazing, yet the pastor acted like Christ would have acted. He did what Jesus would have done. He would have forgiven his enemies and healed their wounds. That black man showed me that there is a God. There must be, and He is in you and in me and in the pastor, and even in those Klansmen. He is in Bruno and in the Colonel at the Camp," responded Silverio.

"From now on, my compass in life has two sides. When I have to make an important decision, I will ask 'What would Lincoln do?' When I have to make a moral choice I will ask, 'What would Jesus do?' And I know I will find the right answer," he said.

At that moment, Silverio felt his body tremble.

He sensed the Holy Spirit had given him a life-changing revelation.

Thoughts of what they had gone through and of family and gratitude were with them as they approached Camp Le June in North Carolina. The base was new. It had been opened in May 1943 as a center to train Marines. As soon as the caravan entered the garrison, the military vehicles went to the barracks so that the soldiers could rest and recover before resuming their journey north the next morning.

Silverio and Antonio were instructed to pull up to the Commanding Officer's building. When they left the Cadillac, a highly decorated man in uniform came to greet them. "I am the Commandant. Welcome to our facility," he said with a strong handshake. He and the Captain of the convoy escorted Silverio and Antonio to a special dining hall.

When they entered, two hundred men and women rose and applauded.

'I guess they are clapping for the Captain of our convoy,' reasoned Silverio in his mind. Instead, the Commandant asked everyone to stay standing. He introduced his guests as, "Two citizens who risked their lives to prevent a POW escape at Camp Como in Mississippi. Thanks to their gallantry, no one was injured or killed. Please join me in giving them a warm welcome and showing them the gratitude of their nation." For a full five minutes, the guests in the dining hall delightedly clapped and celebrated the valor of the two longshoremen from New York.

CHAPTER 93 ━━━━━━━━━━━━━━━━━━

RETURN TO THE CAMP

Carlo and Helena sat in the back seat of the Buick. Antonietta was in the front. Luigi was taking him to the train station. He was returning to the camp in Alabama.

The couple held onto each other, afraid of losing what they had found: true love.

A hundred promises were made up to that moment. They pledged eternal love, to write each day, telephone when they could, and pray for their future life together. Carlo promised to return every other month.

Luigi purposely drove slowly.

He wanted Carlo and Helena to be together as long as possible.

Finally, they reached the station only minutes before Carlo's train was to depart. He hugged Luigi and Antonietta and thanked them for their affection, generosity, and hospitality. Helena followed him along the platform as he carried his suitcases filled with food and new clothing.

"Darling, do not worry," said Carlo. "I will return after the start of the New Year. Pray the War ends soon so we can be married."

All Helena could do was nod as Carlo boarded the train.

She was speechless.

She wept out of sadness.

The railcars moved.

Helena felt her stomach churn.

Steam rose from the entrails of the train covering the platform.

She waved a handkerchief and blew kisses to Carlo, who was hanging from a window, holding back his tears.
Helena watched as the train disappeared.

She was in shock.

A piece of her was gone. She felt bewildered and empty.

Slowly, she wandered back to the Buick and climbed in.

Antonietta understood what the young girl was feeling.

"All will be well, my child," she said calmly. "Be grateful that God gave you this gift of love. He will take care of both of you. Before you know it, all this tragedy will be over, and you and Carlo will live a life of love and peace. Luigi and I are looking forward to being the aunt and uncle of your children," she said with a broad smile.

Helena felt better. Antonietta's words comforted her. "Thank you for being so kind," she responded, drying her tears and lifting her head proudly.

"You are right. I am happy I found Carlo. We love each other. Nothing else matters," she said with determination.

CHAPTER 94 ━━━━━━━━━━━━━

THE PARTISANS

Courtesy, Gianluca Santangelo - Nocera Inferiore

$\mathbf{T}$he sun was setting over the mountains when the three travelers saw Nocera Inferiore.

The city spread from one end of the valley to the other, with low-lying buildings reaching into the hills. By zigzagging through forest paths and crossing streams, they evaded the teams of Germans and their bloodhounds. The trio stopped on a slope overlooking the town. Francesca flashed a mirror to capture the last few rays of sunlight and sent them toward a church tower in an adjacent town. A similar signal came from the turret. "It is okay to proceed," she said. They descended quickly.

Nocera Inferiore, *Courtesy, Italian National Archives*

It was almost dark when they reached the cathedral of Santa Maria. Francesca guided them to the rectory, which was the home of the priests. She knocked three times, waited, and then knocked again. It was the password.

The door opened slowly.

A short man in a black cassock and a white collar greeted them.

"Good evening, Don Roberto," said Francesca. The prelate's back was curved from age. His hair was white, and his face was filled with lines from years of listening to confessions and tending to his flock of farmers, merchants, and shopkeepers.

He comforted them when they were troubled, baptized and married their children, and sent them to heaven when they died.

Now he was tired. He knew the end was near.

His last act was to help the resistance defeat the Nazis. He saw them as the devil incarnate.

"No human being would kill children and murder defenseless people. Only criminals infused with the souls of demons could do such things," he believed.

He would fight to stop them, even if it cost him his life.

"Come in, my child," whispered Don Roberto, as he looked about to make sure no one could see them come into the church. Joe and Tom removed their hats and made the sign of the cross as they entered. Don Roberto nodded and smiled at them.

"Thank you, and God protect you, my sons," he said as he blessed them.

Francesca took the Americans into a large room filled with hanging religious outfits arrayed in open cabinets.

She pushed away the garments in one closet.

A short rope hung from the inside. She pulled it and a trapdoor opened to a dark staircase. All that could be seen was a thin, dim light below.

Joe took out his flashlight. They slowly went down the winding marble stairs and clutched the walls as they descended. The steps were worn and slippery. The staircase was clammy with humidity and smelled of the ages. At the bottom they found another door with a light shimmering along its sides. It was old, thick, and heavy. Francesca rapped the four measured password knocks. A tiny portal opened. A pair of eyes stared at them and looked them over. The heavy sound of a large bolt was heard. The door opened.

A tall young man with thick blond hair covering his head and forehead with long bangs welcomed them. His eyes were greenish brown. His frame was muscular and slim. He wore a black leather jacket with zippered pockets. He stared at the Americans. "Welcome to Italy!" he said in perfect English as he stretched out his hand to greet them. "Glad to be here," said Joe. "Smells like our father's wine cellar," mentioned Tom, as he sniffed the musty air. "This was the place where the friars crushed their grapes," responded Francesca. "Now it is where Colonel Lukas and the partisans gather to plan our attacks on the Nazis," she commented.

Two men in their twenties were standing around a table with a light hanging over it. A map of the entire area from Nocera to Salerno to Naples was laid out with roads, rail lines, bridges, and tunnels. Fausto and Paolo shook the hands of the Americans. One had a wound on his right arm bandaged with thick gauze. Tom stared at it.

"German mortar shell," said Paolo. "We hit a convoy of trucks carrying troops, killed as many as we could, and escaped into the hills. The Nazis shelled and machine- gunned the slope. I got hit with shrapnel in the upper arm. It tore my arm open to the bone. By the time we got to safety, I had lost half of the blood in my body. Francesca saved my life. She's a great doctor," he declared. "She speaks perfect English, when she wants to," said Lukas. "She studied in London to become a physician because there were so few female doctors in Italy. Francesca wanted to be among the first, and she is," he said with pride.

"Where did you learn your English?" asked Tom to Lukas. "I was born in London. My father, Andrew, is Swedish, and my mother is Italian. Dad is in Hungary now. He is a member of the Swedish Foreign Service and is granting visas to Jews so they can get out of the country before the Nazis arrest them."

The group surrounded the table with the charts. "Looks familiar," said Joe to Tom. "Sure does. We have studied this area in great detail," he declared to the three men and Francesca.

"Good, because over the next few days we will destroy every major piece of infrastructure the Germans can use to win this war," explained Colonel Lukas.

CHAPTER 95 ▬▬▬▬▬▬▬▬▬▬▬▬▬▬▬▬▬

THE NAZIS

Don Lorenzo could not sleep. It was 4 AM. He was anxious. He got up for a third time to climb the church belltower to view the roads under Castellonorato. An old oil lantern was his only illumination as he hiked up the steep wooden staircase.

It creaked under his feet. Some rungs were loose.

'One day, this will collapse. I hope I am not on it when it does,' thought the priest. Finally, out of breath, he reached the top of the belfry.

The town was asleep. He put on his binoculars.

He searched for vehicle lights streaming along the motorways in the valley, hundreds of meters below in the ancient city. In the distance, he saw something. Beams, like burning embers, popped in and out of the winding pathways.

He watched as they wound up the gravel lanes leading to Castellonorato.

He counted one truck and then another.

'Only two?' he thought.

'How is it possible? There must be more.'

He looked again.

Courtesy, Opel Blitz, 1944

The moon cast a yellow glow on the lorries. As one turned to climb into the main road, the priest saw something that made his heart sink.

They were open, greenish-grey trucks, filled with soldiers, with large black and white crosses painted on the sides of the vehicles.

'The Germans! Oh my God!' thought the young cleric.

He felt sick. Within minutes, they were in the square in front of the church.

Don Lorenzo watched from above in terror.

They stopped. It was still dark. An officer got out and looked about. He was slim and dressed in a tight uniform with tall, black boots. A luger was strapped to his belt. His only light was from the sky, which lit up the piazza, interspersed with the dark shadows of men and machines. He got back into the truck and proceeded to the center of town.

'They are going to occupy the city,' worried Don Lorenzo.

He was frightened.

'What happened to the convoy? Did the Nazis find them? If they get here, how will I hide them, with German's all over town?'

He was nauseous.

He looked, again, over the edge of the tower to the roads in the valley.

More vehicle lights.

Slowly, the trucks moved up the circular lanes leading to the cathedral.

The priest counted four.

"It is them," he said to himself. He ran down the stairs. A rung cracked under the weight of his foot, and gave way.

Don Lorenzo hung on to the balustrade, looking down the shaft of the steeple. He was terrified.

He almost fell into the hole. It was a 30-meter drop. Gradually, he calmed down.

He held onto the railing for dear life as he gingerly climbed down the rest of the staircase to the ground floor.

CHAPTER 96 ━━━━━━━━━━━━━━━━━

THE JEWS

Four trucks, with grey tarpaulins covering their cargo, steered into the church square. The drivers got out to greet Don Lorenzo, who had just made it down from the tower. He was out of breath as he nodded to them. He opened the church door. The drivers lifted the covers off the bulging mounds of refuse.

The smell of rotting rubbish filled the piazza.

Under the garbage was another cover. Empty wooden crates separated the garbage from its delicate cargo to provide air.

They pulled off the canvas.

Men, women, and children were huddled together.

They desperately took deep breaths of air, as if coming from under water.

The partisans helped them off the trucks. The passengers were exhausted, afraid, cold, and famished. They coughed to exhale the vapor of the decaying refuse. They were dressed in their best clothes, because they had little or no belongings with them. Each family had a small sack of undergarments and toiletries. All else was lost, including their homes and possessions.

Now, all they had left was their lives.

Don Lorenzo escorted them into the church. He was the only one who made the sign of the cross. He heard the men get into the vehicles, slam the doors, start the engines, and drive away. Forty-four humans were assembled before him. Thirty-two adults and twelve children.

They were shaking in fear and shock.

The youngsters clustered close to and clung to their parents.

"Mamma, I need to go to the bathroom," cried a four-year-old girl.

"We have to go, please," pleaded the mother. Don Lorenzo swallowed hard. The church had only one small restroom in the sacristy. It was a bowl and chain. He pulled out his pocket watch. It was a gift from his parents when he was ordained a priest. 4:30 AM.

The pastor and the nuns would be up in an hour.

"Okay, who needs to go?" he asked. Everyone raised their hands. "Follow me." He lined them up in front of the toilet. "Go quickly, we do not have much time," he said. As soon as they relieved themselves, they went back into the church. Forty-five minutes had passed.

Meanwhile, Don Lorenzo opened the crypt. It was a marble door in the center of the church. He used a special hook to lift it. A staircase led to a deep, dark chamber with stone coffins on each side holding the remains of noble families of the town. No one had been interred there for years, since it was now required to be buried in a cemetery. There was no light in the vault. The priest used his lantern to light the way as the Jews went into hiding in the bowels of the church. He gazed into their frightened eyes as he sealed the vault.

Fifteen minutes later, the pastor and nuns strolled into the cathedral to prepare for mass. They walked over the cover of the crypt as they took their places in the pews.

CHAPTER 97

THE AIRLIFT

"**T**hese won't do," said Joe to Colonel Lukas and his team, as he examined the arsenal the partisans had: five World War I Beretta semi-automatic pistols, two 1918 submachine guns, and three bolt-action service rifles dated 1891. "Look, you can't use these 1915 hand grenades. They could explode in your hand," he explained. "We will put together a list of equipment and ammunition, spare parts, and other provisions that we need. You must tell us if there is anything special you require, including medication," said Joe turning to Francesca. "Once we get the coordinates for the parachute drop, we will have everything we need to give the Germans a run for their money," explained Tom. Fausto and Paolo required a translation, since the Americans spoke with a heavy Neapolitan dialect interspersed with English phrases.

Joe and Tom had special radios in their backpacks. One was put into operation immediately, so they could transmit encrypted messages to the American communi-cation center in Sicily. A list was prepared of guns and ammunition, medical supplies, and K-rations needed by the partisans. It was conveyed to headquarters.

The next night, a lone plane flew from an aircraft carrier off the western coast of Italy toward Nocera Inferiore. It carried two half-ton containers of supplies to the designated location outside of town.

The sound of aircraft motors triggered enemy activity.

As soon as the plane crossed the sea and was over land, giant searchlights beamed into the clouds combing the night sky.

The plane with their supplies was spotted.

Suddenly, anti-aircraft guns fired hundreds of rounds of shells, filling the darkness with flaming white flashes.

Joe, Tom, and the partisans watched in horror as the plane tried to evade the gunfire. It was flying at 10,000 feet.

"Bring us to 20, 000," commanded the pilot to the navigator. The Italian anti-aircraft weapons were medium range and could not exceed 15,000 feet. German armaments reached from 25,000 to 50,000 feet, depending on the size of their guns. Joe and Tom could see where the artillery was in place. It was behind the beach, not far from where they landed.

"Let's take it out," said Joe to the partisans.

He and Tom had six hand grenades. "Only if it is necessary," demanded Colonel Lukas. "If we attack, it will tell the Nazis where we are.

"Within minutes, we would face a hundred troops," he whispered.

At 20,000 feet, the anti-aircraft flack evaporated into clouds of gunpowder far below the plane. "Once we have the coordinates in place, release the cargo, and then get us up to 30,000 feet and let's get out of here," commanded the pilot. The anti-aircraft fire continued fruitlessly for another 30 minutes as the plane jettisoned its load and flew away.

The team looked at the white parachutes gleaming in the moonlight as they descended to earth.

They rushed to reach them.

The partisans commandeered a coal truck to carry the freight and a winch to lift the shipment. Within minutes, they found the parachutes and their payload.

The boxes were amazingly heavy.

It took nearly an hour of hard work to get them into the vehicle, cover them with coal and canvas, and speed back to the church. The crates were opened behind the cathedral.

There were enough weapons, plastic explosives, and hand grenades to supply two dozen men. Pharmaceutics and canned goods were part of the parcel. Any trace of the parachutes and boxes were quickly disposed of.

The team now had the tools to inflict damage on the Nazis.

Partisan spies were all over Italy, feeding information to the Allies on German troop movements, gun emplacements, fortifications and supply depots, and the location of German camps.

Once the Italians put together the latest information and they were double-checked, Tom sat at the radio and fed the data into the system.

It was sent to Central Command in Palermo and simultaneously to North Africa.

Preparation for the invasion of Salerno was underway.

CHAPTER 98

DON ALFONSO

"You were not at mass this morning, Lorenzo," said the pastor. The young priest was summoned by the vicar to explain his whereabouts. Don Alfonso had been head of the cathedral for five years. He ruled his parish with an iron hand and demanded loyalty and obedience from his team of priests and nuns.

"I was indisposed, Don Alfonso," explained Lorenzo, nervously.

Perspiration covered his brow. He stood before his superior, wringing his hands and shaking all over. He felt faint and needed to go to the bathroom.

"What do you mean, 'indisposed?'" said the pastor, sharply.

"I was attending to an urgent matter that was beyond my control," he replied, quivering.

"Explain yourself, before I lose my temper," threatened Don Alfonso. The pastor was in his early sixties. His white hair and sallow complexion made him look much older.

Don Lorenzo did his best to pull himself together. He took a deep breath.

"As you know, the Germans are occupying Italy. They are also anti-Semitic and are rounding up Jews to send them to concentration camps. Rumors are that they will kill them," responded Don Lorenzo.

"What does that have to do with us?" demanded the pastor. "We are Christians, and we cannot allow these helpless people to be persecuted," said Don Lorenzo.

"Our Lord was a Jew," he insisted. His words cascaded from his mouth.

"Jesus would have done all he could to save them," he stated.

The pastor sat dumbfounded, not understanding anything.

"I am certain the Holy Father would agree that we should take every opportunity to help the Jews in this terrible situation. We received messages from the Vatican to do all possible to save the Chosen People from the Nazis. Even His Holiness is hiding them in the walls of Vatican City," maintained the young priest.

The pastor stared at Don Lorenzo with penetrating eyes. He comprehended that something grave was in the air.

Don Lorenzo spoke rapidly. "This morning I brought 44 Jews into the church and hid them in the crypt. Ten families: twelve children and thirty-two adults. They are there right now. We must feed and take care of them and hide them, so that the Germans do not find them," he said running out of breath.

The pastor was paralyzed.

"You did what? Jews in our church? Families, children? To be fed? We barely have food for ourselves? Are you mad?

"Do you realize what you have done? These monsters will find out and shoot us all!" cried the pastor, raising his voice to a fever pitch.

He covered his face with his hands.

He was distraught, worried, and angry, and he was afraid.

CHAPTER 99

THE CRYPT

"I could not in good conscience let these people die," exclaimed Don Lorenzo to the pastor. "We must find a way to protect them. They were sent to us by God," insisted the young prelate. The pastor wrung his hands. "Who else knows about this?" asked Don Alfonso. "No one," he answered. "All right. What is done is done. This must stay a secret, or we are all finished. I will inform Mother Superior. We need her sisters to help. I will get food and clothing. They cannot stay in the crypt. It is damp, dark, and has no ventilation.

"Tonight, I will arrange to house them in the wine cellar of the seminary down the road. Once the Nazis start searching house to house, they will discover them. We must act as soon as possible and must be careful to move them with utmost care," explained the pastor.

"I have an idea," said Don Lorenzo. "We can take the boys and put them in the seminary elementary school. The girls can go to the nun's school and live in the convent. The families can work in the fields, tending the olive trees and the grape vines," he said enthusiastically. "Good ideas for now, but we cannot keep them here for long. The Germans are insidious. They do not respect the rights of religious institutions or the right of sanctuary. Sooner or later, we will have to find another place that is more secure for them," reasoned the pastor.

The pastor went to see the head of the nuns while Don Lorenzo went to the crypt. He locked the church doors, so that no one could come in. Normally, the church was open all day and into the evening.

He could risk no one learning his secret.

He brought loaves of bread, water, and bottles of milk for the babies, and a large bucket to serve as a toilet.

The marble door of the crypt was heavy.

Don Lorenzo felt the muscles in his back pull as he lifted the portal.

Sunlight flowed in.

The priest saw the faces of 44 terrified people protect their eyes from the light as they huddled with their children.

CHAPTER 100

CARLO'S LETTER

Helena clutched the envelope and looked at Carlo's handwriting. It was clear and filled with circles and arcs.

She saw how carefully he wrote her name and address.

A week had passed since he left for Alabama. It seemed like years.

He was a prisoner again. His captivity now extended to her.

She was captured by his love, and frozen in place until they met again. She waited each day for a message, a call, or any sign from him.

It took seven long days before a letter arrived.

The postal mark showed that he mailed it the day he left her at the station. It traveled for a week to reach her.

She was frightened. 'Has he changed his mind? Did something unexpected happen? Is he well?' thought Helena as she pondered what was in the message.

'The letter in this envelope is like me, a hostage of love,' she mused.

Her life was filled with thoughts of him. His image was everywhere. She saw his face in the moon and stars, and she dreamed of his voice and still felt the sweetness of his lips, the warmth of his embrace.

Gently, she tore the paper. She pulled out the note. After a deep breath, she unfolded it and read:

My Darling Helena:

A moment ago, I was in your arms and now I am on a train back to prison. As you disappeared in the distance, my heart sank and I felt fear, loneliness, and the need to be near you, always.

Before we met, I was a man emptied by war and despair. I had no hope. The world was filled with darkness. Then I saw your face. You brought light, love, and optimism into my soul. The second I touched your hand, I felt my life transformed into something new and exciting, with dreams for tomorrow. You are my past, present, and future. You are my port in the storm.

I love you.

Our love has no limits or boundaries. We are together, no matter how far apart we may be. Our hearts and souls are united.

I love you more than my life and will do all I can to be with you.

I need you, because I love you.

As soon as I arrive at the camp, I will ask for permission to travel to you next month and every month.

I wish I could marry you now and show you all that is in my heart to make you happy and fulfilled.

Forever yours,

Carlo

Helena held the letter to her bosom. Tears ran down her cheeks. Emotion took control of her being.

She felt Carlo's love, like a warm breeze on a summer night.

It caressed her and made her feel secure and happy.

CHAPTER 101

NEW YORK

The giant portal of the George Washington Bridge welcomed them. A huge American flag hung in the viaduct and waved in the sun rising over Manhattan.

As they crossed the river, Silverio and Antonio gazed at their metropolis. Its tall buildings, boulevards and lush parks appeared like a great oasis of freedom compared to their journey through the southern states. Weeks had passed. It seemed like ages. The moment the Cadillac reached the other side of the river, they breathed sighs of relief and exhilaration. They were bound for home, so close.

The two Italian immigrants waved goodbye to the Captain in the lead vehicle of the convoy, and to the soldiers. A special bond existed with these men in uniform. They were together in their fight for liberty and honor. Silverio and Antonio would be loading ships with arms and protecting the homeland, while these valiant young men went off to war, risking their lives to defeat tyranny.

As the caravan turned to continue its trip to war, Silverio and Antonio paused to take off their hats in homage to these warriors they knew they would never see again.

Yankee Stadium, *Courtesy, New York City Historical Society*

Half an hour later they reached Yankee Stadium. It seemed like a monument to the American pastime of baseball, instead of just an arena for merely playing a game.

For Silverio and Antonio, it was a symbol of American liberty and meritocracy.

Poor boys could rise to become celebrated sports heroes, idolized by fans, and hailed by children, as their ideals of courage and determination.

Yet even these god-like figures were now in uniform, fighting for their country along with famous actors and people of every kind, from all walks of life.

Silverio recalled these words he had read in a book:

"Indeed, almost all Americans were now in agreement — capitalists, Communists, Democrats, Republicans, poor, rich, and middle class — that this was a people's war. By sure evidence, it was the most popular war the United States had ever fought. Never had a greater proportion of the country participated in a war: 18 million served in the armed forces, 10 million overseas, and 25 million workers gave of their pay envelope regularly for war bonds. It was a war against an enemy of *unspeakable evil. Hitler's Germany was extending totalitarianism, racism, militarism, and overt aggressive warfare beyond what an already cynical world had ever experienced.*"[1]

The two longshoremen from the Bronx were proud.

They had done their part for America and for Italy, far above and beyond the call of duty, and they were prepared to do more.

---

1   Howard Zinn, "World War II: A People's War?" June 9, 2009, https://libcom.org/history/world-war-ii-peoples-war-howard-zinn

CHAPTER 102 ━━━━━━━━━━━━━━━━━━━━━━━▶

PONZA

Famine, like a cloud, descended on the Island of Ponza.

There was no food.

Children and the old were the first to go.

Church bells no longer pealed to honor the dead.

So many were carried to the cemetery that the carillons ceased.

It was a continuous procession of suffering, as mothers buried their babies because they had no bread or milk.

They died in their arms.

Santa Lucia departing Ponza, July 24th, 1943, *Courtesy, Ponza Racconta*

Since the sinking of the ferry Santa Lucia in July 1943, the island was isolated. Food became scarce, and by September hunger swept the archipelago like a tempest. There was no grain, meat, coal, oil, cheese, or fresh fruit.

Fishing was perilous, as German and Allied aircraft sank anything afloat.

Farmers were frightened to till their land and be targets for enemy planes.

Ponza, 1943, *Courtesy, Ponza Racconta*

Italy was caught in a deadly vice.

As it capitulated, the Nazis occupied the country.

The Allies set out to rid the nation of the Germans and, in the process, Italians suffered from the onslaught of both sides.

Ponza, a rock in the Mediterranean, was no exception. The first to come were the Nazis.

Courtesy, German National Archives

Gina was 9. She was a lovely child, with black hair and large, brown eyes, and a jovial face filled with smiles and joy.

The day *they* arrived was locked in her mind like a memory shut in a safe, to be imprisoned forever.

It was dawn.

She was looking out her window at the gorgeous port of Ponza. All was calm.

Fishing boats were paralyzed in the harbor, unable to set sail, because to do so would mean facing sure destruction. Nothing moved. Sunlight shimmered across the bay and lit up the blue, white, and red colors of the vessels sleeping in the port.

Suddenly, she saw a speeding craft enter the marina and park at the wharf.

It seemed to come from nowhere.

A contingent of soldiers in greenish-grey uniforms leaped onto the waterfront, brandishing machine guns.

They marched like conquerors from the quay to the center of town.

Passersby stopped, frozen in fear, running to hide behind walls and doors. A group of Fascists came to greet them.

Fascists in Ponza, *Courtesy, Framenti Di Ponza*

Gina partially closed her window to avoid detection, as she watched the Germans occupy Ponza.

Her recollection was of sight and, most of all, sound. The noise of their boots bouncing off the ancient cobblestones of the island's main street sounded like explosions of terror.

The tremors covered the square and echoed off the buildings, homes, and stores, and crawled up the stairs like invisible plunderers, patrolling, searching, and determined to control and destroy. The little girl was frightened. Each time she heard the beat of the German boots, she and anyone else in sight fled like rabbits seeking shelter from hunters.

The Nazis seemed to her and the inhabitants of the island like giant predators who came to devour them and the little they had.

CHAPTER 103 ━━━━━━━━━━

DON GABRIELE

Don Gabriele lifted his binoculars to see the vessel approaching Ponza. He was standing on a cliff at Cala d'inferno, one of the highest peaks of the island with a 360 degree view. The sun was rising. He saw a boat rushing to the port at a high speed. It was filled with soldiers.

As they entered the harbor, he searched to see a flag.

"Is it Italian? Perhaps it is an Allied craft? Oh my God!" he realized. "It's the Nazis."

The German maritime flag, with the swastika in the center, flew above the ship. Chills ran up Don Gabriele's spine.

He rushed back to the church to sound the alarm. He rang the bells in the church.

"Get the word out to everyone on the island that the Germans are landing. They are to hide all their food and to stay indoors and not move. Avoid any contacts with the Fascists," he told a group of boys in the Church of the Assumption in the part of Ponza known as Le Forna. They darted to alert people.

The pastor prayed that his island would be spared further suffering. Its young men were in combat. Only women, children and the elderly were left behind to starve as the weight of the war grew heavier each day. Contact with the mainland was lost. Boats and ships had been sunk. Only a telegraph line existed. It was in the hands of the Fascists who patrolled and controlled every inch of the archipelago.

The priest was the pastor and patriarch of Ponza. He was over seventy, but looked much younger. He had boundless energy, was strong, handsome, and alert. His flock comprised fishermen, farmers, shopkeepers, and their families. Most were illiterate. He was their scribe, counselor, mediator, mentor, and guide, from birth to death. Don Gabriele was by far the most important and influential person on the island.

He knew the Nazis would find him and demand collaboration. He could handle the Fascists, since they had the flexibility of Italians. Several were from Ponza, and he knew them inside out. But the Germans were different. They were impossible to reason with. Don Gabriele had been a chaplain and medic in World War I. He remembered the brutality of the Austrians and how they took no prisoners and ravaged small towns and defenseless civilians.

The Nazis were worse.

All he could do was keep the population calm, avoid taking any risks, and plead with the Almighty that the Allies arrive soon.

CHAPTER 104

JACOB

It was not a tranquil night in Castellonorato.

The sun had disappeared rapidly into the sea.

A thick mist covered the mountains and valleys.

The sound of German trucks, motorcycles and armored cars snapped the chilly nocturnal air. The sounds cast a pall of terror in the darkness as a platoon of women, children, and men snaked their way across a square, onto a road, and through narrow streets to reach sanctuary from the cruelty and brutality of the Nazis.

It was two in the morning when Don Lorenzo woke the Jewish families.

"Not a sound," he said to them as they exited the crypt.

Youngsters, still asleep, were carried by their parents. The elderly could barely climb the stairs and were helped by the younger adults. It was a frightening scene. Don Lorenzo looked in all directions before moving 44 desperate souls to another safe haven. A few gas lanterns overlooking the plaza pierced the curtain of dusk as they slowly reached the door of the institute.

Don Lorenzo lifted the knocker and rapped it with force.

The sound bounced off the nearby buildings with an echo that woke the neighbors. The door opened quickly. In the darkness, the refugee Jews filed in to be sheltered in the cellar of the seminary. "Where are you going?" asked Jacob to Don Lorenzo. He was the patriarch and elder among the Jews. Jacob was their counselor and gave the families a sense of hope.

The Jews looked to Don Lorenzo as their protector and savior.

"I have to get back to the church and resume my normal duties to avoid anyone asking questions. Don Alfonso and the rector of the seminary will work with the Mother Superior of the convent to take care of the women and children. I will be back this evening with more food and warm clothing," he responded.

Jacob took Don Lorenzo's hand.

"You are a good man. Why are you doing this? You know they will kill you if they find out?" questioned Jacob.

The young priest looked into the old man's eyes. They were gentle, kind, and wise. "How could I not? I know you would have done it for me," responded Don Lorenzo. Jacob reflected. "Perhaps, but I am not sure I would have the courage," he admitted.

Don Lorenzo took Jacob's hand and held it with both of his in a gesture of love. He responded, reciting from the Book of Deuteronomy:

"There will always be poor people in the land. Therefore, I command you to be openhanded toward your fellow Israelites who are poor and needy in your land."

"And," he continued, "a Jew, 2000 years ago, taught us:

'There is no greater love than this, to lay down one's life for one's friends.'"

CHAPTER 105 ━━━━━━━━━━

COLONEL LUKAS'S PLAN

After the fall of Mussolini, King Victor Emanuel III sent emissaries to negotiate an armistice with the Allies.

The summer of 1943 found hundreds of thousands of Italian soldiers in a tragic situation. Politically and militarily, they were allied with the Germans and were fighting alongside them on battlefields from Africa to Greece and from Italy to Russia. The end of the Fascist regime signaled a change that the Italian high command was not prepared for, as the war intensified and the Allies began an all-out assault on the Axis powers.

Allied bombing of strategic locations from the north to the south of Italy began in mid-August 1943, after the conquest of Sicily. It forced the Germans to redeploy their forces to protect cities like Naples and Salerno, which were major ports for German vessels supplying men and material for the occupation of Italy.

"We have two objectives," explained Colonel Lukas to his team, which now included two Americans and five more young men. "First, we want to make it hard for the Germans to reach Salerno before the invasion. Second, after the invasion we want to stop them from retreating, so that they can be annihilated or captured. We have to disrupt their movements and blow up key arteries between Nocera and the invasion point. Tonight, we have to move out and take our arsenal with us. We will camp out in the hills and continue our operations from there, from now on."

The church where the partisans hid and met was no longer safe.

German troops occupied the town and were searching every home and building for traces of partisan activity.

At midnight, one week before the invasion of Salerno, Colonel Lukas and his band of heroes and heroines snuck out of the cathedral and wound their way into the countryside to reach a farmhouse that would be a safe haven.

Don Roberto blessed them, and he said a special prayer for this group of men and women that was ready to sacrifice all to liberate Italy from the Fascists and the Nazis.

Six hours later, German storm troopers burst into the church and dragged the priest from the altar while he was celebrating mass.

He was beaten, handcuffed, and carted off to Nazi headquarters.

CHAPTER 106 ▬▬▬▬▬▬▬▬▬▬▬▬▬▬▬▬▬▬▬

SISTER CRISTINA

Don Alfonso hesitated before knocking on the door of the priory.

He collected his thoughts. He was tense. Confronting the Mother Superior, also known as Sister Cristina, was a challenge. She was a difficult person to deal with. Sister Cristina was the Abbess and Head of the Order of nuns adjacent to the seminary, not far from the church of Don Lorenzo. She was a beautiful woman in her late forties, with a white and pink complexion and large penetrating eyes. She was not tall, but she always stood erect and straight, giving the impression of height, presence, and power. She was often impatient and did not suffer fools easily. She was a natural leader and looked the part. Sister Cristina was feared and loved.

Santa Cristina by Paolo Veronese

Her real name was a mystery. All that anyone knew was that she came from a prominent family in Rome whose father was a diplomat and whose mother was from the Island of Ponza. She had a splendid education and realized her vocation in elementary school.

As an adolescent, she felt females deserved the same rights as males. To prove their value, women were to be militant and change the world. Jesus, for her, was the ultimate activist. He challenged the established order and died for his principles. She would do the same. She would follow Him.

She was fascinated with the story of Santa Cristina, whose name she chose. The Saint was a third century martyr who faced unbelievable ordeals and incredible torture for her convictions. Yet she knew God was with her. Cristina sacrificed her life for the Lord and was a symbol for those determined to persevere at all costs.

As Mother Superior, Sister Cristina was Spartan in her ways. She was the first in the chapel at five thirty AM and the last to leave. In the evening, she led final prayers and inspected every room to assure each nun was in her cell, asleep. She followed the rules of her Order to the letter, and expected the same from her community of religious women. She was kind, compassionate, gentle—or strong, as the need arose.

Most of all, Sister Cristina was resilient. She was a strict disciplinarian and a tough administrator who ran a staff and organization of 50 nuns; a large team of gardeners, handymen and workers, to maintain the convent; a school and dormitory for three hundred girls; and a chapel and the living quarters for 200 people. It was a walled-in city block.

Built in the 15th century, the religious house grew to be an elementary and high school for girls from the rich and middle class. As Director of the Abbey, she also fed the poor and educated their children, took care of the homeless, and assisted wayward girls. She urged her nuns to heal the sick and elderly and to visit and comfort those in prison.

Don Alfonso found the courage to knock on the door of the cloister. A small nun in a white and black habit greeted him. "Good morning, Sister. I came to pay a courtesy call on Sister Cristina," he said, tripping over his tongue. "Good morning, Father. Do you have an appointment?" asked the little nun. "No, I do not. Please inform

Mother Superior that the matter is urgent," explained Don Alfonso as he removed his cap. "Please wait here," she said kindly. The waiting area was only a hard wooden chair surrounded by religious images on the walls. Thirty minutes passed. The priest paced back and forth mumbling to himself. An hour went by. "Sister Cristina will see you now," announced the small nun.

Don Alfonso was shown into a large, dim room with little furniture. The curtains were closed. The only light came from burning candles and a tiny window protected with iron bars. A lifelike statue of the Virgin Mary was at the entrance, followed by a cross with Jesus mounted on it. The images seemed to have an internal glow, as if the Holy Spirit resided in these walls. Mother Superior was at her desk. The flickering candlelight shone off of Sister Cristina's face and gave her an image of sanctity and strength. Her habit was carefully woven with fine cotton cloth and seemed tailor made. It fit her from head to toe, so the priest could not separate the person from the uniform. She was writing in her journal when Don Alfonso entered.

She did not get up to greet him. "What can I do for you, Father?" she asked, without raising her eyes to look at him. "Good morning, Mother Superior. How are you?" said the priest. "I am fine and quite busy," she replied abruptly. "It is a lovely day, is it not sister?" he responded shyly. "Did you come here to discuss the weather, Don Alfonso?" "No, no, you see Sister, we have uh, 'special guests' at the church," stuttered the priest. "Is the Holy Father in town?" questioned Sister Cristina sarcastically.

"I do not know how to explain this," he muttered. "Two nights ago, Don Lorenzo admitted ten Jewish families to hide in the cathedral. My first impression was shock, but now the damage is done," he explained. "We are doing the best we can under the circumstances. They are all now in the seminary under the care of Father Andrea. If the Germans find out, they will kill us all," he uttered, shaking. Sister Cristina stared at Don Alfonso. She reflected on what he said and weighed her words carefully before replying.

She rose. She raised her voice. "You call this 'damage?' Do you realize the Lord sent these unfortunate people to us? We must defend them against the Nazis, who are devils. They respect nothing and no one. They are criminals. Don Lorenzo is a hero. Rest assured, we will care for the women and female children. Send them to me immediately," she said with conviction.

CHAPTER 107

DON ROBERTO

Don Roberto was handcuffed and dragged from the altar by his feet. He was still wearing his garments while celebrating the mass. The priest was thrown into a truck and driven to Gestapo headquarters. His knees and back were badly injured when he was pushed and kicked into a dark cell in the basement of the building. The priest's face was filled with bruises.

He remained silent despite the continued questioning of his persecutors. After two days without food and water, he was brought into a chamber, stripped of his clothes, and strung up by his arms with coarse ropes. A soldier beat him with a wooden bat. The priest screamed throughout the ordeal. His head, arms, legs, back, and buttocks were covered with wounds. Afterwards, he was untied and taken to another room, where two men were waiting.

He was shackled to a chair. His face was covered with bleeding gashes. His mouth was taped. Nearly every inch of his body had been clubbed. Parts of his white hair were yanked out, exposing his scalp. A soldier wrenched the gag, ripping the skin from his lips and cheeks. The priest bent over in silence. The pain was excruciating.

The soldier snapped back Don Roberto's head. The bright light hanging in the room blinded him. "Open your eyes, Father," ordered the SS officer. He wore a black uniform with medals and gold decorations. Don Roberto slowly lifted his swollen eyelids. "It is time to talk, Father," insisted the German. "Witnesses swear that partisans entered your church. We searched the crypt and found boxes with English language inscriptions and a shortwave radio," he thundered.

"Your collar is no protection. For two days, you have said nothing. Two men have been arrested along with you. If you tell us where the partisans are, we will free them and spare their lives. Isn't that what you are supposed to do? Lay down your life for others?" he said mockingly.

Don Roberto looked at him. He smiled. "I have nothing to say," he stated weakly. Blood dripped from his mouth. The Nazi officer nodded to the soldier. He taped Don Roberto's mouth shut. He untied his left arm and released his hand. The priest looked at him with terror in his eyes. The soldier held his hand by the wrist and placed it on the table. Don Roberto nodded, "No, no." The Gestapo officer lifted a large hammer and pounded his hand until the bones were shattered like glass. The priest yelled in silent agony. Tears flowed from his eyes. The tape was once again yanked from his mouth. He wept uncontrollably.

"Tell us what we want, or we will do the same to your other hand," bellowed the Gestapo officer. "You will never hold a chalice again," he said. "Where are the partisans?" he screamed. Don Roberto looked at him. With the little strength left in his body, he spit saliva and blood into the face of the Gestapo chief. It ran over his mouth and cheeks and stained his uniform. He slapped, punched, and kicked the priest, and then nodded to the soldier.

He taped his mouth again and took Don Roberto's right hand and smashed it with the hammer many times, just as was done to the left hand. The cracking of bones echoed throughout the room.

CHAPTER 108

FATHER ANDREA

"**W**elcome, my children," said Father Andrea with a smile, as he helped each person enter the portal of the seminary.

He took special care with the old and the children.

"Blankets and cots are laid out in the basement for you to rest tonight. In the morning, we will take care of your other needs and make sure you are all fed. Please let us know of anything special you need, and we will do our best. Tomorrow, with the help of the good sisters, the women and female children will be transferred to the convent," he told them as they organized in the courtyard of the institute.

The Jews were speechless.

They were exhausted. Some were ill. Fortunately, the seminary was self-sufficient and had a doctor on the grounds.

Father Andrea was fifty-five. He had been rector for a decade. He was a Jesuit priest.

He grew up in an Italian family in Bolzano, in the North of Italy. His first language was German, and he was raised as a Lutheran. Growing up in a clan of brilliant attorneys made it natural for him to go into the study and practice of law.

By 28, he was considered one of the best lawyers in Bolzano.

A bright future was ahead of him, when a drive in the countryside altered the course of his life.

It was a lovely fall day. The hills and highlands around the city were gorgeous.

Courtesy, Fiat Motors

Motorways wound up and around peaks to reach little towns that seemed like nests perched on the tops of mountains.

Andrea drove to enjoy the fresh air and clear his mind as he reflected on a new case he was handling. He took an unpaved road in the woods. He could hear the birds chirp in the barren foliage.

It was a beautiful setting.

The air was clean. Heavy rain fell on the countryside for ten days. The forest smelled of wild mushrooms.

It also was scented of the damp ground, which had absorbed a dangerous amount of moisture that had loosened the roots of the woodlands.

Drivers were warned about rock and mudslides, as well as falling trees.

As Andrea turned a curve, he heard cracking wood.

Huge trees lined the road.
Suddenly, three fell from the edge of the forest onto his car.

The vehicle collapsed under the weight of the giant timbers. Heavy branches and trunks penetrated the car and fell directly on its driver.

Andrea quickly lost consciousness as the trees crushed his body.

He awoke three days later in a hospital.

He was covered in casts. His parents were at his bedside. "This man saved your life," his mother stated, presenting an elderly gentleman dressed in black with a white collar.

"It was God, my son, not me. I was in the thickets picking mushrooms when I heard the crash of trees. I ran in the direction of the sound and saw your vehicle under the weight of giant oaks. Fortunately, I had met three lumberjacks in the woods, and I went and found them again. They cut away the trees, and we brought you to the hospital," explained Father Marco.

Andrea could not speak. He wanted to say thank you, but he felt paralyzed by emotion and pain.

The doctors told his parents that he would never walk again.

His neck and several vertebrae were broken, in addition to his arms and legs.

It would take months to heal, and he would spend the rest of his life paralyzed from the waist down.

His family prepared for the worst. Andrea felt he was an invalid and would be confined to a wheelchair forever.

The young man fell into despair.

Father Marco was a Jesuit priest who came from Naples. He was always optimistic and of good cheer. He thought each person had a mission. If someone was saved from death, it was because God spared them for a calling. Andrea, the priest believed, had a special vocation.

The Lord rescued him, and the priest was his instrument. Father Marco helped the young man heal and find his true purpose in life.

"You will walk again, my son," insisted Father Marco.

"God is our shepherd. He protects his sheep. You will be well," he assured Andrea. The words of the priest gave the young man hope.

Each day they prayed together for healing and for guidance.

They read passages from the Bible and reflected on the words and thoughts. The Spiritual Exercises of St. Ignatius comforted Andrea with encouragement and faith in God.

They consisted of meditation, prayer, and self-awareness. The Jesuit assisted him with his physical therapy and watched as his body and soul were transformed.

A year passed. Andrea made a splendid recovery. His bones and bruises healed.

It was summer. The hospital was nestled in a valley close to Bolzano. It was cool and sunny when Father Marco rolled Andrea out on the lawn. "Today is a special one, my son," said the priest. "It is the day that you will rise from that chair. The Lord and I will help you," he insisted. "It is July 31st, the feast day of St. Ignatius of Loyola. He founded the Society of Jesus, the Order of Jesuits. He liberated men and women to think, free their souls, and devote themselves to God," explained the priest.

The young man felt the electrical energy in his body rush forward, as he listened to the prelate's words of encouragement.

Father Marco lifted him from the chair. Andrea held on to him as he stood up and planted his feet on the ground. Pain from his soles and heels shot up his legs as his weight pressed on his extremities. He perspired and trembled as he held himself upright. He was afraid to fall. The priest let go.

Andrea remained standing. He smiled and then laughed. A day later, he took his first step, and then another. Within six months, he was running.

In the next year, Andrea changed.

He gained a new faith in himself and God.

He converted to Catholicism and studied to be a Jesuit priest. Five years later, he was ordained.

His new mission had begun.

CHAPTER 109

EXECUTION

The town square was surrounded with people. German troops emptied the houses, stores, and buildings, and forced the population to gather around the piazza.

"What's going on?" asked an elderly man of a woman in her forties. "The Germans are up to something terrible," she responded, with fear in her eyes. A rudimentary gallows was being mounted in the piazza. It was built with logs and cut timber. Three nooses hung from a long beam, with chairs under them.

As more inhabitants of the village assembled in the square, a truck pulled up to Gestapo headquarters. A soldier went to Don Roberto's cell and unlocked it. The priest was lying on the floor, paralyzed from his wounds. He could no longer move his limbs. His hands were swollen to three times their size. They were red, black, and blue. His ribs were broken. The soldier drew him to his feet. The priest shouted in anguish. The pain was unbearable. He could not walk. The old man was dragged up the stairs of the building and literally tossed into the back of the truck like a rag doll.

Minutes later, two other prisoners in handcuffs were thrown into the truck next to Don Roberto. Their faces were covered with wounds from the torture inflicted by the Nazis. The vehicle drove to the piazza. While in captivity, the priest prayed. He did not ask the Almighty to save him from his suffering. Instead, he pleaded with God to forgive him for his sins and forgive his oppressors. He recited *The Lord's Prayer* continuously:

> *Our Father who art in heaven, hallowed be thy name. Thy kingdom come. Thy will be done, on earth as it is in heaven. Give us this day, our daily bread; and forgive us our trespasses, as we forgive those who trespass against us; and lead us not into temptation, but deliver us from evil. Amen.*

The priest knew he would be killed. His real concern was the fate of the two young men who would die with him. They were innocent and he could not defend them from the evil that would take their lives.

The three captives were hauled into the middle of the town square. Their arms and legs were tied. The crowd gazed in horror. They realized what was happening. They wanted to run away, but they were forced to witness the murder of individuals like them, to be killed without a trial or anyone to speak for them.

The Gestapo leader took out a piece of paper. He read it in Italian with a heavy accent:

> *These three terrorists have collaborated with partisans and are guilty of treason. They will be executed. This is a warning to all those who harbor enemies of the state. They will face the same punishment.*

The people were in shock. Don Roberto was surrounded by the two young men, who pleaded for mercy, their hearts pounding in fear. It was to no avail. Three German soldiers lifted each one and stood them up on the chairs. They placed the nooses around their necks. The two men cried and begged. Don Roberto recited a prayer: *Almighty Father, have mercy on us and forgive us our sins and bring us to everlasting life. Amen.*

The Gestapo leader nodded his head. The three chairs were kicked over simultaneously. The cords swiftly tightened around the throats of the three men as the weight of their bodies pulled each rope, snapped their necks, and strangled them. Don Roberto's last thought was not about God. He made peace with his Creator and was prepared to meet him. He was dying for a cause larger than himself. The words of a Tale of Two Cities by Charles Dickens were his final reflection:

> *It is a far, far better thing I do, than I have ever done; it is a far, far better rest I go to than I have ever known.*

Fascist Wartime Poster, "Germany is Truly YOUR FRIEND,"
Courtesy, Italian National Archives

In minutes, the men were dead. The bodies hung in silence. As the people left the square, they passed a Fascist poster that turned their stomach.

CHAPTER 110 ━━━━━━━━━━━━━━━━━━━━━━━

SISTER CHIARA

Sister Chiara, principal of the elementary, middle, and high school was summoned to the office of Mother Superior. The meeting worried her. She met with Sister Cristina once a week to report on the education of the children and of the novices studying to be nuns. It was rare they met for any other reason, except emergencies.

She began as an art history teacher and was assigned to lead the education of the institute at the young age of 38. Her intelligence, pleasant personality, and her skill as an administrator made her a natural choice. Sister Chiara was also an amazing artist. Before taking her vows of poverty, chastity, and obedience, she was an accomplished illustrator, cartoonist, and portrait painter.

By the age of 25, her work was in galleries and museums across Europe and in the United States. In Germany, her talent was celebrated. She was famous for her startling modernist qualities, like the impressionists, but surreal and spiritual. She specialized in watercolors, which gave her work a definitive characteristic, nearly three dimensional. Viewers felt her images and hues changed before their eyes, like a hallucination.

Her colors varied from light greens and blues to pinks and mixtures of orange, red, and purple and yellow, projecting an internal glow of the subject, similar to Caravaggio. She felt her skill was a gift from God, because it transmitted emotions and feelings. The commercial world of art did not interest her. To paint for money was abhorrent to this free spirit, who viewed art as an expression of God's love for humanity. She was concerned about the condition of the human soul, which she often projected in her work.

Teaching children the magic of art was giving the gift of creativity at the earliest age. Education, for Chiara, was shown in her paintings where the combination of drawing and color gave the viewer something new to ponder, analyze, and contain within themselves forever. Example was also paramount to her. She felt obliged to live an exemplary life as a model for others, especially the young.

As a woman, she possessed a Mediterranean look that easily attracted lovers. Long, jet black hair, large ebony eyes, a snow-white complexion with perfect features, and a sculptured figure made her a natural beauty. Her love affairs were difficult, since they took possession of her feelings and troubled her spirit.

One day, she received a revelation. She believed she heard the Lord's voice. He told her to devote herself to others through her talent and to elevate hearts to heaven by her example and charity. Sister Chiara left "the world," as she would often say, to worship her Creator.

After she took her vows, her art changed.

She painted images in a more spiritual context and no longer put them on the market. They were "pieces of her soul," for all to see.

After she became a nun, she felt liberated to paint from her essence while teaching, directing, and caring for others. The abbey was her refuge to change the world by changing others.

Her personal collection of paintings and graphics now rested in the cellar of the convent.

They were priceless.

CHAPTER 111

HIDING THE CHOSEN PEOPLE

"**S**ister Stefania, you will care for Sarah and Miriam. Make sure they have enough milk and cheese in their diet. Get our doctor to examine them immediately. Sister Paola, their children of four, six, eight and twelve must continue classes and be integrated with the other children," were the instructions of Sister Cristina. Sarah and Miriam were expecting. One was in her sixth month, and the other in her fourth. The Mother Superior took in the women and female children. The elderly received special care in the convent hospital.

"You must keep this information absolutely secret. You understand," said Sister Cristina to Giuseppe, who handled maintenance of the entire religious complex. He knew what was involved. The risk was enormous. "We need more fuel. It is getting cold and we have people to care for," she said rubbing her hands anxiously. "But Mother, the Germans pillaged and sacked the city and the countryside. There is no wood or coal. Their troops emptied the stores and warehouses and stole the livestock and food from the farms," explained Giuseppe, in despair, with his hat in hand.

"It is all a matter of money, unfortunately," said Sister Cristina with conviction. She took a box out of her desk and opened it with a long key. "Several rich families are helping. Here is a one thousand Lire," she said, counting the money and giving it to Giuseppe. "Use it to buy whatever you need on the black market. I know this is sinful, but God will forgive us under the circumstances. I want a strict accounting of all costs," she told Giuseppe as he took the Lire and left the room. Sister Cristina knew that part of the funds would go to pay off several people, including the Germans.

"Sister Chiara is here to see you," announced the little nun. "Mother Superior, good morning," said Sister Chiara. "God has sent us more children to educate," stated Sister Cristina as she looked out the window into the garden. "We have a difficult and dangerous mission.

Can I count on your support?" she asked. "Of course, Mother," responded Sister Chiara. Sister Cristina explained the situation.

"Twelve Jewish children must be included in the classes of the school. Their names and documents have been changed to show they are Catholics. No one is to know about this, except you and me. No questions are to be asked. They must be treated like all the others. Do you understand?" said the Mother Superior looking into the eyes of the nun. "Certainly, Mother," replied Sister Chiara. She left the room.

"The Germans will come looking for them. God help us when they do," said Sister Cristina to herself.

CHAPTER 112 ━━━━━━━━━━━

IL DUCE'S BRIDGE

$\mathbf{D}$arkness was their only protection.

Five figures in black, with pistols, machine guns, and sacks of explosives stole their way through a forest, crossed a stream, and reached a train line.

It was slightly past midnight.

"They butchered Don Roberto," whispered Francesca. Rays of moonlight lit her lovely face. Her cheeks and forehead were covered in charcoal.

"Those two young men were taken off the street. They knew nothing about us. The Nazis hung them like criminals," said Colonel Lukas angrily. "Do you think the priest talked?" asked Joe.

"That's why they killed him," responded Francesca. "He refused to tell them anything," she explained.

"I will get my hands on those Gestapo murderers, if it's the last thing I do!" exclaimed Tom.

They were 300 meters from a railroad bridge on the line between Nocera Inferiore and Salerno. It spanned a river and canyon for over 500 meters. It was a vital link for the advancement of German forces moving to Salerno.

And no guards protected the structure.

Italian Railroad Bridge, *Courtesy, Superba, Associazione Dopo Lavoro Ferroviario*

"Paolo, get the explosives ready," ordered Colonel Lukas. "Fausto, prepare the wires, tape, and detonators. Joe and Tom, what else do you need from our sack of toys?" Joe pulled out his flashlight. "We need the clocks, to time the charges. Are you sure the convoy will cross at dawn? We want as many railcars on the bridge as possible,"

Colonel Lukas looked at a piece of paper. It was written in code.

"Our sources say they must pass here by six thirty AM to meet the German contingent at eight o'clock that arrives from the port. Once the train reaches Salerno's main station, the troops and material will be loaded into trucks. The rendezvous point is Salerno city center square, so they can set up operations on the beach and in and around the port. They must cross this bridge, then, or they will be late. A nice thing about the Germans: they are precise, predictable, and always on time," responded the Colonel with a smile.

"An alternative would be for Tom and me to detonate on site when the convoy is above us," said Joe.

"That is suicide. You would not last five minutes. The surviving soldiers would hunt you down. You are too valuable to die on us now," responded the Colonel with sympathy."

Tom and Joe ran to the bridge. They had drawings of the causeway and the weight tolerances of the columns and pillars. With them were a dozen packs of dynamite assembled in what looked like cigar boxes. Each container had twelve sticks of explosive. The bridge had six columns on each side and an arch in the middle. Except for its upper deck, it was 90% steel.

Only a massive explosion, precisely prepared, could bring it down.

The saboteurs preferred to place the charges at the bottom of the girders, but it was impossible, since the overpass spanned a huge canyon and straddled a river.

The two men divided their labor, each taking six columns, six per side. They tied themselves to a lifeline and descended one story from the deck of the viaduct. Like monkeys, they climbed down and across the metal posts, taped their cigar boxes onto the columns, and ran wires connecting each. Clocks set to go off at six thirty AM the next day were attached to the detonators, in order to run electric impulses through the wires to set off the bombs.

Mistakes could not be tolerated.

Not tying a line properly or failing to set the time accurately could endanger the entire mission. They checked and double-checked their work. Their deadly devices were carefully hidden in the mesh of metal ribs and columns.

Three hours later, they were finished.

Joe and Tom ran back to the team, who waited anxiously in the dark a half mile from the conduit. The Americans were out of breath and perspiring heavily.

"How did it go?" asked the Colonel. "There is enough gun powder on that thing to blow up the Empire State Building," responded Joe. "If the timers and detonators work, it will collapse under the weight of the railcars when they are in the center of the overpass, and crash into the river," explained Tom.

"Good. Let's get out of here," said the Colonel as the group of partisans set out toward a mountain overlooking the valley.

They nicknamed the crossing, "Il Duce's Bridge."

CHAPTER 113 ━━━━━━━━━━━━━━━━━

SABOTAGE

As the Allies advanced up the Italian boot, the Germans moved more resources to the south. The offensive cost the Reich strategically, as men and material were transferred from the Western and Eastern fronts to the Italian counteroffensive. It left France and Germany exposed, and it diluted the Nazi campaign in Russia.

Among Hitler's miscalculations was the impact of the U.S. in the fight.

After the Japanese bombed Pearl Harbor in December of 1941, Hitler immediately declared war on the United States and attacked U.S. convoys shipping arms to England. The Nazi dictator was certain America would be overwhelmed with the struggle in the Pacific and would be unable to engage in the European offensive. He was wrong.

Courtesy, US National Archives

"Such was the economic might of the Americans that they could pour increasing resources into the conflict in both theatres of war. Germany produced 15,000 new combat aircraft in 1942, 26,000 in 1943, and 40,000 in 1944. In the U.S., the figures were 48,000, 86,000 and 114,000 respectively. Added to these were the aircraft produced in the Soviet Union – 37,000 in 1943, for example – and in the UK: 35,000 in 1943 and 47,000 in 1944.

Courtesy, US National Archives

"It was the same story with tanks, where 6,000 made in Germany each year had to face the same number produced annually in Britain and the Dominions, and three times as many in the Soviet Union.

Courtesy, US National Archives

"In 1943, the combined Allied production of machine guns exceeded 1 million, compared with Germany's 165,000. Nor did Germany's commandeering of the economies of other European countries do much to redress the balance. The Germans' ruthless requisitioning of fuel, industrial facilities, and labor from France and other countries reduced the economies of the subjugated parts of Europe to such a state they were unable – and, with their workers becoming ever more refractory, unwilling – to contribute significantly to German war production." [1] The Nazi's ran out of vital energy supplies to fuel their war machine. No matter how skillful German commanders were, they could not match the Allies in men and material.

Hitler sent his top generals to Italy. Field Marshall Rommel, the famed "Desert Fox," went to defend the North. Field Marshall Albert Kesselring assumed responsibility of the South. The German Tenth Army's Panzer Corps moved swiftly into position. Tens of thousands of troops and artillery travelled over Italian roads and railways to reinforce the South.

1   Richard J Evans, "Why Hitler's grand plan during the Second World War collapsed," The Guardian, Tue 8 Sep 2009, https://www.theguardian.com/world/2009/sep/08/hitler-germany-campaign-collapsed

Courtesy, German National Archives

Three days before the landing in Salerno, a brigade of German soldiers, tanks, and heavy artillery advanced on the railroad traveling through Nocera Inferiore toward Salerno. In the wee hours of the morning, the locomotive pulling the convoy of tanks, guns, and soldiers came to a sudden halt 100 miles from the bridge, destined to be destroyed at dawn.

Rail tracks were sabotaged by partisans. The engineer spotted the trap and stopped just in time. It took an hour to set the tracks in place and get the convoy moving. The rendezvous with "Il Duce's Bridge" was late.

Courtesy, National Archives

The Germans ordered the Italian locomotive driver to accelerate the train to be on time. As more coal went into the boiler, the engine picked up steam to reach 100 miles an hour. At 6:20 AM, the caravan turned a corner. A giant valley lay before it with a long steel conduit spanning the gap.

On a distant hill, Colonel Lukas and his team gazed with binoculars as the train neared the crossing. His heart beat wildly. Joe stared at his watch, calculating minutes and seconds. "They are too far away to be on the bridge when the blast happens," remarked Colonel Lukas.

"But all we need is for the lead train to go off the edge, and it will take the rest of it with it," insisted Tom.

The sun rose in the east and cast a yellow glow on the valley and lit up the rail lines and surrounding mountains.

The river glistened as its currents skated off rocks and shoals and licked the banks covered with trees and vegetation.

The locomotive and its carriages rocketed toward the viaduct seconds before the charges were scheduled to go off.

It seemed to pick up speed as it neared the bridge.

"10, 9, 8, 7...1," counted Joe as the train reached the mouth of the crossing. The minute handle hit 6:30 AM. The team held its breath.

30 seconds past.

At 6:30 AM the convoy was 50 meters from the entrance to the causeway.

It raced closer to the destination: 40, 30, 20 meters.

Suddenly, a roar ricocheted off the hills like the boom of cannon.

A dozen cases of dynamite detonated simultaneously along both sides of the structure. The massive explosion literally raised the bridge from its pillars and sent it crashing into the river.

The blast deafened passengers in the lead carriages.

Vibrations were felt to the last rail car. The wooden deck of the bridge splintered into millions of toothpicks as the steel edifice buckled, collapsed, and sank 200 meters into the gorge.

Italian Bridge blown up in WWII, *Courtesy, Hyper War Foundation*

The engineer pounded the brake pedal as he saw the train fly towards the abyss.

The screeching of the train's steel wheels echoed through the canyon.

German Military Train Wreck in WWII, *Courtesy, German National Archives*

As the locomotive and its wagons came to an abrupt halt, troops and equipment crashed in all directions.

Tanks and artillery snapped their cables that bound them to the platforms and tumbled from the carriages.

The coal wagon crushed into the steam engine. Troop coaches fell from the tracks. Cars derailed as the train stopped 10 meters from the edge of the fallen bridge.

Huge clouds of smoke and dust surged from the chasm. The Germans looked down the valley and saw the wreckage.

A moment later and they would have plummeted to their deaths.

CHAPTER 114 ━━━━━━━━━━━━━━━━━

NAZI PLUNDER

"During World War II, the Nazis plundered from occupied countries, items of incalculable value estimated in the hundreds of millions of dollars. Spearheaded by Reich Marshall Hermann Goering, the looting program quickly created the largest private art collection in the world, exceeding that amassed by the Metropolitan in New York, the British Museum in London, the Louvre in Paris, and the Tretiakov Gallery in Moscow. By the end of the war, the Nazis had stolen roughly one-fifth of the entire art treasures of the world." [1]

"From March 1941 to July 1944, 29 large shipments including 137 freight cars filled with 4,174 crates containing 21,903 art objects of all kinds went to Germany. Altogether, about 100,000 works were looted by the Nazis from Jews in France alone. The total number of

1   Kenneth D. Alford, Hermann Goering and the Nazi Art Collection: The Looting of Europe's Art Treasures and Their Dispersal After World War II, McFarland and Company, North Carolina, 2012, Introduction, https://www.amazon.com/Hermann-Goring-Nazi-Art-Collection/dp/0786468157

Hermann Goring receiving a Vermeer as a gift from Hitler, *Courtesy, Library of Congress*

works plundered has been estimated at around 650,000. It was the greatest art theft in history." [2]

As the German occupation of Italy advanced, orders came from Berlin to confiscate anything of value in cities and villages throughout the country.

"Sir, we received a message from the office of the Reich Minister about art in Castellonorato. The artist, one of the Reich Minister's favorites, is a nun. Her name is Sister Chiara. She runs the convent school near the cathedral. Her paintings are in museums in the Fatherland," explained the Lieutenant to the Captain of the Gestapo Corps stationed in the town.

"It appears The Reich Minister is decorating Carinhall, his country estate near Berlin. I was there. It is beautiful. He will be pleased when we send him some of her work," said the Gestapo Chief.

"Interesting. Today a spy reported the nuns hiding Jewish children," he said with a cynical smile.

"A visit to the convent is in order," commanded the Captain.

2   Alex Shoumatoff, The Devil and the Art Dealer, Vanity Fair, March 19th, 2014, https://www.vanity-fair.com/news/2014/04/degenerate-art-cornelius-gurlitt-munich-apartment

Soldiers from the Hermann Goering Division Outside of Palazzo Venezia in Rome, Former
Headquarters of Mussolini, with art stolen from the National Museum of Naples,
Courtesy, the Library of the National Museum of Naples

CHAPTER 115

HOME SWEET HOME

Grand Concourse in the Bronx, *Courtesy, New York Historical Society*

$\mathbf{T}$he roads of the city were a comfortable sight to Silverio and Antonio.

Five miles more.

They were exhausted, hungry, and unable to fathom all that had occurred. Their journey was like a series of hallucinations. The adventures were surreal, frightening, and inspiring.

Silverio thanked God that he and Antonio were alive.

Images of Mississippi, Tennessee, the camp, and the prisoners were still vivid. Silverio felt the pain of the handcuffs. He heard the growling wolves and saw flames from the fiery bombs of the Ku Klux Klan. His shoulder was sore from the bullet that had pierced his flesh as he tried to save a black man in a church.

Nightmares of the trip into the Deep South were part of him and would flash in his memory like lightning for the rest of his life.

When they reached the Grand Concourse, they were struck by how wide the boulevard was and the surrounding elegance.

It was called the Champs-Élysées of the Bronx. Store fronts were meticulously designed and decorated. Flowers were arranged along clean sidewalks and in front of beige brick buildings with tall, uniformed doormen. Ladies with cheeks covered with talcum powder and lipstick, wearing tailored dresses, strolled about with small dogs with brightly colored collars. It looked and smelled like the Big Apple. Shops selling everything from clothing to fruits and vegetables lined the streets along with dry cleaners, bakeries, and movie theatres. Shades of red, green, yellow, and purple were everywhere. The cacophony of car horns was music. People of all shapes and sizes and nationalities walked the streets. A sense of freedom was in the air.

Only a handful of people knew of their trip into the Deep South of America.

The story was top secret.

Neither the enemy nor other prisoners of war discovered the escape. The longshoremen invented tales about car problems, traffic, and weather that delayed them. The Mayor of New York and the head of their Union knew better. Nothing appeared in the press.

General Post Office at 149th Street in the South Bronx, *Courtesy, US Postal Service Archives*

From the Grand Concourse, they turned on East 149th Street and saw the magnificent General Post Office with its Art Deco lines and Depression era frescos. Silverio had sent hundreds of packages of food and clothing to his relatives in Italy from that building.

Two blocks more.

They reached Our Lady of Pity Church. They stopped. The cathedral stood in the middle of the street. Italian artisans had shaped its façade with slabs of cut marble and a huge, circular stained-glass window glistened in the sun and emitted beams of tinted light that seemed to shine on the onlookers like rays of grace from the Almighty.

The men took off their hats and made the sign of the cross.
They prayed.

"Antonio, each of us has a calling in life. We went to Mississippi for a reason. It was bigger than us. We saved lives. We saved souls. It was God's will. Thanks to Him, we survived," said Silverio.

As they continued toward home, they looked back at the house of worship with gratitude and nostalgia.

The Cadillac travelled down Morris Avenue. It was the main thoroughfare of Little Ponza. Men pushing carts of fruit and vegetables, white wagons laden with bottles of milk and jars of butter moved up and down the street delivering their goods.

Cars of all ages, shapes, sizes, and colors and small trucks and horse-drawn buggies drove past rows of ugly residential buildings.

Turn of the century, four- to eight-story tenements lodged forty families in tight apartments with shared bathrooms and without elevators.

The flats were freezing in the winter and boiling in the summer.

149th Street and Morris Avenue in the South Bronx, *Courtesy, New York Historical Society*

Ladies strolled the sidewalks and raised long dresses as they crossed streets filled with mud and water and horse droppings.

The Cadillac had traveled thousands of miles. It needed rest. So did its passengers.

One more block.

They turned on East 151st Street. The cobblestoned road seemed to welcome them. They parked in front of their building.

Silverio looked up at his apartment, which was on the second floor. It was not much, but it was home.

Home sweet home.

CHAPTER 116 ━━━━━━━━━━━━━━

DON LORENZO AND THE NAZIS

The canvas sack seemed incredibly heavy to the young priest. It was tied and knotted with a long, coarse rope.

Don Lorenzo pulled the cord around his arms and neck and lifted the bag off the ground.

He was not a strong man, and he suffered from spinal problems.

He threw the huge pack over his shoulder. He felt bursts of pain in his upper and lower back as the weight sank into his body. It was excruciating.

He had to reach the Seminary. They needed food.

The Germans imposed a curfew. No one was allowed out after 8 PM.

It was midnight. Don Lorenzo could be shot.

The town was asleep. He snaked around the angles of buildings, in the shadows, avoiding lights.

It was cold, yet he was perspiring under the heaviness of his bag. Moonbeams flashed along the damp streets, guiding him to his destination.

Four blocks to go.

Suddenly, he heard the thud of heavy footsteps and the clacking echo of jackboots, bouncing off the cobblestones.

As he turned a corner, a patrol of German soldiers marched down the road towards him.

They were giants.

Over six feet tall, their greyish-green uniforms and polished helmets gave them the look of titans from another planet. The men brandished long rifles with bayonets. Several held machine guns. Each had hand grenades, pistols, and stilettos fastened to their belts.

Their faces were expressionless and seemed to be without eyes. They looked like robots.

The priest could see the Seminary. It was only three blocks away.

Now it seemed like a journey of a thousand miles.

He ran under a doorway, breathing heavily. His heart palpitated.

He waited. He watched.

The ropes of the sack cut into his flesh. The pain was agonizing. "Do not make a sound," he thought. Don Lorenzo closed his eyes and prayed.

A screeching shriek came from the street. It was like a baby crying and screaming in the night.

The noise ripped across the black opening where the priest hid.

He trembled. "Halt!" ordered the officer leading the squad. Don Lorenzo's ears almost ruptured at the harsh vibration of the Nazi's command.

The patrol stopped in front of the entranceway where the priest stood in the shadows.

Fear overcame him. He trembled and felt his stomach and bowels churn.

His heart pounded as if it would burst from his body.

His only shelter was darkness. He heard the soldiers breathing heavily in the night air. He smelled their breath, tinged with beer and tobacco. Clouds of mouth vapor were everywhere.

A white cat squealed and leaped from a barrel. It ran past him towards the soldiers.

He almost fell from fright. He listened. The warriors laughed as the terrified animal vanished into an alleyway. The platoon continued its march and slowly disappeared into the fog and mist.

Five minutes went by. For the cleric, it was a lifetime. As soon as the Germans were out of sight and sound, he raced down the street. Exhausted, panting and frightened, he reached the Seminary. The old door was freshly painted, thick enamel green. It glistened in the moonlight. The huge, bronze knocker was shaped like a hand. He lifted and pounded it several times. The priest did not care if he woke the neighbors. He needed to get into the sanctuary.

Minutes passed. It seemed like hours. He knocked again and again. A pair of sleepy eyes with a lantern opened the peep portal. "What do you want?" asked the young seminarian. "I am Don Lorenzo. Open this door now," he insisted. "Who?" said the seminarian. "Open this door, you fool. I am a friend of the rector," demanded Don Lorenzo. The seminarian obeyed. "Where is your bathroom?" asked the priest. "It is the second door to the right," he responded. Don Lorenzo dropped the bag and raced to the toilet. He returned ten minutes later. "In this sack is food for your new guests," he told the seminarian. "Put it in a safe place. I need to sleep here tonight. Please give me a room," he said. Don Lorenzo was spent, but he had made it.

Yet he sensed his challenges had just begun.

CHAPTER 117 ▬▬▬▬▬▬▬▬▬▬▬▬▬▬▬▬▬

THE CARRIER PIGEONS

Courtesy, Atlas Oscura

A thousand years before Christ, Greeks settled in Southern Italy. With them came culture and learning. New cities rose in a wave of commercial, religious, and intellectual growth. Among the artists, ecclesiastics, and philosophers were a class of fighters skilled at making war.

Three thousand years later, modern-day freedom fighters gathered in a Greek hollow overlooking the city of Salerno. The grotto was cut into the side of a mountain. It was used for ancient rituals and burials. The cave was damp, dark, and clammy, yet was a perfect place to hide. The new inhabitants were patriots battling to rid Italy of Fascism and Nazism.

In the cavern were tons of explosives, ammunition, food, and supplies.

Cages of carrier pigeons were mounted outside the entrance.

"We failed to destroy the train," lamented Joe. He was disappointed. "Look, the bridge is gone, the carriages derailed. Most of the big guns, armored cars, and tanks were damaged," insisted Colonel Lukas.

"Consider it a success. It will take the Germans a week to recover," he said. "Two days more, and we can blow up the tunnel and the ammo dump. It will slow down the Nazi counteroffensive after the landing," he explained. "The German divisions from the south are moving into the hills over Salerno toward Naples with heavy and light artillery. Once we have a solid fix on their locations, we can radio it to central command so naval and air bombardment can support troops as they cross the hills to reach Naples," said Tom.

Courtesy, National Audubon Society

"In the meantime, the birds need to keep flying. Reports from our spies show where the Germans are moving next," noted Enrico, in charge of communications for the partisans. He pointed to his pigeons. A hundred black, white, and grey birds chirped and cooed and were nestled in cages filled with hay, water dishes, and seeds.

Each was a trained aviator ready to carry messages hundreds of miles and return to home. All they expected was shelter, safety from predators, and food.

"I will send out a dozen in the next hour. By tomorrow the pigeons will be back with fresh information, unless falcons snare them or hunters or Germans shoot them down," he stated.

"Tonight, we hit the tunnel and the petroleum and ammo installation. Both are five miles from the beach. The Nazis need petrol desperately. They cannot fight without fuel. It will be a dangerous mission. Some of us may not come back. Francesca, it is no place for a woman. Stay behind," demanded Colonel Lukas.

"No. The Germans will pay for what they did to Don Roberto. They are killing civilians in small towns everywhere. I am not afraid. I will do my part to stop them, no matter what," she countered.

CHAPTER 118

THE TUNNEL

$\mathbf{A}$ cheerful, whistling worker casually walked to a German blockade on the crossing from a small town to a railroad tunnel leading to Salerno. "Heil Hitler," he saluted. The German troops smiled, "Viva IL Duce." The Italian linesman was a familiar figure. He carried a sack filled with fresh-baked bread and pieces of cheese. The Nazis gladly accepted and gave him a pack of cigarettes. In his blue overalls, grey cap, black boots covered with coal dust, and ruddy complexion he looked like a caricature of someone who labored in railyards. He carried a kerosene lantern. Fastened to his belt was an oil can. His job was to change the tracks when trains were approaching so they could enter the underpass directly. Giacomo was the father of four children. He lived in the village next to the main station. Short, stout, and strong, he seemed younger than his 38 years.

Courtesy, German National Archives

A huge convoy was on its way from the North, filled with men and firepower to reinforce German defenses against an invasion. Colonel Lukas and his team calculated the movements of the train, the hourly intervals of the patrol guarding the intersection near the tunnel, and the time needed to do their deadly deed.

The squad controlling the crossing would pass to the night shift at 9 PM. The train was scheduled to reach the tunnel at 9:30 PM. It would take 30 minutes for troops to arrive and replace their comrades.

For half an hour the junction would be guarded by only one soldier. Two hundred yards from the passageway were the Colonel and four men and a woman hiding behind a clump of trees. Conditions were perfect for the saboteurs and their plan. Enough moonlight illuminated the target and its surroundings while the black of night shaded them like panthers stalking prey in the jungle.

Courtesy, Adelaide Abandoned Tunnels

Fallen leaves covered the ground and made a soft but slippery bed under their feet. Their binoculars were fixed on a long pole with a hook overlooking the crossing. Darkness prevented them from clearly seeing the sign they searched for. The pole was for a lantern to be hung so the train engineer would know the tracks were switched to drive through the tunnel. Giacomo climbed onto the pole to fasten the lantern. He carefully took one rung at a time and held on to keep his balance. It was 9 PM. He turned down the flame and turned it back up three times. It was the signal. The saboteurs saw it.

The German patrol began the changing of the guard. The partisans went into action. Slipping and sliding down the hill, they raced to the underpass entrance. It was 9:05 PM. Flashlights gave enough visibility to work. Each had a role. Fausto was outside as the lookout. He would signal with an owl hoot, once all was clear.

Joe and Tom set 12 sticks of wrapped dynamite along the middle walls of the shaft where the weight converged on huge stone blocks. Once the rocks were dislodged, the walls would cave in. At 9:15 PM, Francesca, Colonel Lukas, and Paolo unraveled a wheel of wires and ran them from the explosives to two boxes with detonation handles. At 9:25 PM they heard a train whistle. The convoy was half a mile from the tunnel, moving at rapid speed.

The German detachment reached the intersection. Fausto gave the signal. The saboteurs rushed out of the passageway. Joe and Tom each took a detonator box and hid on either side of the underpass while their comrades darted into the woods.

The locomotive roared into the passage at 9:33 PM.

The Americans pushed on the wooden levers with all their might. An electric impulse surged through the wire, ignited the sticks of dynamite, and set off a gigantic explosion just when the locomotive was in the middle of the tunnel.

Joe and Tom felt the ground rise under their feet as they dashed into the forest to join the others.

The blast was heard from one end of the valley to the other.

The train was lifted from its tracks like a toy and slammed into the buckling sides of the shaft as the mountain collapsed on top of it.

Tons of stone, steel, debris, and cement rained on the carriages as they crashed and piled onto one another.

CHAPTER 119 ━━━━━━━━━━━━

THE AMMUNITION DEPOT

$\mathbf{F}$or a radius of three miles, the ground shook like an earthquake from the explosion. Animals broke down fences and raced out of barns. Farmers and city dwellers heard the sounds and realized the war was closer.

Courtesy, Umatilla Army Depot

Not far from the main train station was a colorless warehouse with a sliding roof, covered with gravel, which went all the way down to the ground. The large, triangular, wooden structure was a shed for grain and hay. The Germans took it over to store fuel, ammo, and arms. A regiment of a thousand troops was housed nearby. It was surrounded by dirt roads covered in grey pebbles. Several makeshift army barracks were within walking distance of the building. Jeeps and armored cars with black crosses and swastikas were parked along the sides of the garrison.

"Captain, the tunnel was bombed just as the convoy entered it. We have a gigantic train wreck and hundreds of casualties. We need help!" was the desperate call from the Sergeant at the rail crossing to the officer in charge of the ammunition depot. It was the closest installation and had an ambulance, nurses, doctors, and heavy equipment.

"I will come personally and bring emergency assistance and also a patrol with dogs to search for the partisans who did this," responded the Captain angrily.

Overlooking the storage complex was Colonel Lukas and his team. Their faces were blackened with coal dust to avoid detection in the moonlight. After the tunnel assault, they rushed to a hill near the warehouse and set up a position where they could see what was happening without being detected. A strong, cold wind cleared the air and provided visibility. Nestled among trees and shrubs, the night gave them protection as they spied on the enemy with high powered binoculars. They watched as the Germans assembled hundreds of soldiers, a fleet of vehicles, spotlights, and trucks and headed for the site of the wreckage. A Lieutenant and a Sergeant were left in charge. Four sentries with machine guns and radios were sent to protect the perimeter of the storage area. The other troops were asleep in a nearby barracks.

Colonel Lukas signaled to Paolo and Fausto. The two men crawled silently through the woods and down the hill near the guards in back of the warehouse. Francesca, Colonel Lukas, and the Americans slithered like snakes among the trees to strike the front of the building once the sentries were disabled. Paolo and Fausto took out sets of razor-sharp steel wires fastened to wooden handles. Originally, they were used to cut wheels of parmigiana. Now, they were lethal weapons.

Within seconds, the partisans were behind the two sentries. In a flash, they wrapped the wires around the soldiers' throats and pulled the wires in one, powerful motion, slashing and crushing the larynx and severing arteries and veins, preventing the sentries from shouting or breathing. They were nearly decapitated. The soldiers fell to the ground, gasping for air, writhing and bleeding profusely. In minutes they were dead. The saboteurs took their machine guns and slung them over their shoulders. Two other sentinels were in front of the warehouse, marching back and forth. As soon as they reached the corners of the building, the freedom fighters, like tigers, sprang on them with their cheese cutters. Both soldiers fell. Paolo and Fausto hauled them out of sight while they were still thrashing, struggling to breathe, and dying.

The team assembled in front of the warehouse door. It was bolted from the inside, which meant there were others in the building to be dealt with. Colonel Lukas went to the door. He spoke in German. "New orders from headquarters. Open up," he commanded in a strong Teutonic tone. The bolt snapped. The portal was unlocked. The Colonel and his team rushed forward, pushed the door open, and darted into the depot. A Lieutenant and a Sergeant stood stunned as Paolo and Fausto pointed their machine guns at them. The Sergeant raised a rifle while the Lieutenant pulled out his Luger. Both fell in a hail of bullets. The volleys echoed off the walls of the warehouse and were heard in the barracks.

Throughout the building were rows of boxes stacked with bombs and bullets and barrels of fuel and gunpowder. A forklift was in the main aisle to mount and remove the material. Live cannon and tank shells were piled in pyramids along the walls. Open crates filled with grenades and mines lay in the center of the structure. The warehouse smelled of sulfur. "We do not have much time," said Joe. "All we can do is use the dynamite. Tom, set the fuses so we have two minutes to get out of here. Colonel, you and the others cover us outside if anyone shows up," yelled Joe as he and Tom went to work assembling stacks of explosives and blasting caps.

Within seconds, six packs of dynamite were taped together and ready to be used. Joe lit three fuses and Tom ignited another three. They tossed them into the arsenal of shells and bombs and ran out of the building to reach their comrades. Joe threw a hand grenade near the barrels of oil and gunpowder. As they raced from the depot, they heard the hissing of cords as they burned to reach the explosives.

The shots fired by the freedom fighters in the warehouse woke the men in the garrison. Soldiers ran out of the quarters in their underwear with automatic rifles. They spotted the partisans. Just as the team dashed into the thicket, hundreds of bullets showered upon them. Francesca and Paolo were hit. Joe and Tom grabbed their wounded comrades and carried them to safety. Troops raced from the barracks to the warehouse.

A squad was ordered into the woods to pursue the saboteurs when, suddenly, a deafening explosion in the depository blew out the walls, pounded the roof, and set off a gigantic blaze, igniting thousands of pieces of ordnance and drums of petrol. Bombs and bullets flew for miles in all directions. Shells, grenades, mines, and casks of gunpowder went off in intervals of seconds, creating a hellhole of destruction. Howling winds fanned the fire that reached the garrison. In minutes, the building and parked vehicles were ablaze. Red and yellow flames from the inferno lit the sky and could be seen for miles. The German warriors ran for cover. For hours they watched helplessly, as their shelter, personal effects, and instruments of war blew up and turned to ashes and piles of sweltering rubble.

CHAPTER 120 ━━━━━━━━━━

INVASION

Allied Troops landing on the Italian Mainland, September 3rd, 1943,
Courtesy, Italian National Archives

Forty-eight hours after the daring partisan assault on the tunnel and ammunition depot, the Allies landed on the Italian mainland. Thousands of British and American soldiers hit sandy beaches and occupied large and small ports and waterways laden with fishing vessels and military craft quickly sequestered and commandeered for the Allied cause. One city and town after another fell following the heavy coastal bombardment of Calabria and Puglia from U.S. and Royal Navy warships, as troops crossed the Strait of Messina in Sicily and made their way north up the peninsula. Ports and airstrips and captured Italian facilities in Sicily provided vital logistics for the landings. With them came tanks, vehicles, armored cars, and heavy and light artillery ready to rid the country of the Nazis. Hundreds of engineers and skilled logistics experts accompanied the invading forces to create improvised causeways, restore communications and utilities, and build roads over hills and mountains and through forests, valleys, and swamps.

As the Allied forces advanced, the Germans retreated, destroying infrastructure that could be used by the enemy. Bridges, aqueducts, dams, roads, and rail tracks were blown up. Electric, gas, telegraph, and water lines were severed, inflicting enormous hardship on Italians trapped in the raging warfare of the Nazis and the Allies. Food needed to feed German troops was stolen at gunpoint from farmers and shopkeepers. Warehouses were emptied of vital supplies like medications and canned goods, leaving villagers to starve. Inhabitants of towns were massacred to prevent them from aiding the Allies as the Germans moved north. An enemy regiment was left behind to slow down the movement of the American and Commonwealth forces until reinforcements arrived.

German Troops defending areas near Salerno,
Courtesy, German National Archives

General Kesselring realized the attack was not the key objective of the Allies. Salerno and Naples were the real targets and, in the end, Rome. Hitler refused to provide more troops. Dwindling supplies and declining morale forced Kesselring to reposition his defenses around Naples and Salerno in the hope assistance from the Eastern front would arrive. It did not.

Six days after the invasion, American and British soldiers arrived in Salerno. On September 9th, 1943, one day after Italy surrendered, 165,000 troops with the U.S. Fifth Army landed on a 35-mile front south of the city. President Franklin Roosevelt said of the Italian capitulation: "After years of war and suffering and degradation, the Italian people are at last coming to the day of liberation from their real enemies, the Nazis." [1]

General Clark refused naval bombardments before the landings to surprise the Germans and reduce collateral damage. Nazi artillery emplacements were untouched. The enemy was prepared for the attack. Resistance to the invasion was fierce. German guns rained death and destruction on U.S. and British troops as they hit the beaches. Losses were heavy. Allied casualties totaled 2000 killed, 7000 wounded and 3500 missing. German losses numbered 3500. Yet, in a matter of days, the landing sites were secured and the Fifth Army pressed forward toward Naples. Germans retreated, forming a new line of defense above Salerno.While the Allies marched northward, German forces moved swiftly to apprehend and disarm 3 million Italian soldiers and sailors across the peninsula and in theatres of war in Europe and North Africa. Some escaped. Most were captured and sent to labor camps in Germany. Others joined the resistance. Hundreds of thousands never returned home.

1   The American Presidency Project, http://presidency.proxied.lsit.ucsb.edu/ws/index.php?pid=16312

Italian soldiers in Captured by the Germans, 1943,
Courtesy, German National Archives

CHAPTER 121 ━━━━━━━━━━━━━━━━

THE EXPLOSION

Colonel Lukas and his team dashed from the German warehouse. As they climbed high into the tree-lined hills, they looked through the forest to see firework-like explosions flashing across the sky with a scorching red and pink glow. The building was pulverized. It disappeared into a pile of flaming rubble. Blazing rockets and thousands of white-hot bullets flew through the inferno. Sirens sounded as the Germans rapidly reorganized to deal with the disaster.

After hours of trekking, the freedom fighters reached a small stone house. It was in the woods, surrounded by tall oaks, cedars, and shrubs. The grey, white, and black granite blocks of the home, carved from the mountains, gave the dwelling a look of security. Candles were glowing in the windows like lanterns to lead the liberators to this sanctuary in the forest. Curls of grey smoke surged from the chimney. The smell of burning hickory pierced the night air. The door of the cottage was flung open to welcome them.

As the exhausted warriors entered, they saw an ancient kitchen with walls lined with blue and white ceramic tiles and a large table and benches cut from logs; a floor of oak boards oiled with a dark brown varnish; a black iron kettle hung in the fireplace, cooking over red embers, emitting the fragrance of a rich soup filled with vegetables and meat. On the table, a loaf of coarse bread with a knife was next to a plate of melting butter, a slice of cheese, a bottle of olive oil, and a plate of salt.

In the next room, the living room, on the mantelpiece sat two pewter candlesticks covered with wax, a collection of blackened clay pipes, and a jar of tobacco alongside a long box of matches. A sofa was near a window, covered with a red woolen cloth, sided by end tables with antique oil lanterns. Hooks in the walls held coats and sweaters. Near the sofa was a wooden door with a white ceramic knob. The rusty hinges squawked and creaked each time it was opened. It led to a little room with a 4-poster bed protected with an embroidered spread knitted by hand.

Francesca and Paolo were unconscious. They had lost a great deal of blood. She was shot through the shoulder. Paola was hit in the upper leg. Tourniquets stopped the bleeding. "Put her on the bed and him on the sofa," said Benedetto, who was the owner of the house. He was a farmer. He lived alone and tended a few animals, raised corn and vegetables, grew grapes, apples, and pears. A barn and corral were behind the house.

Benedetto's hands were rough and cracked from years of hard work, yet his heart was that of a lion. He was fearless. It showed in his penetrating black eyes, dark complexion, and deep lines in his face and forehead, and thinning grey hair around his temples. He looked like a prehistoric warrior.

His wife was dead. She was lost delivering their only son, Giovanni. He was a strong, handsome young man who idolized his father. He did not live to see adolescence. He was murdered by Fascist gangs for criticizing Mussolini. He was 12 years old. His body disappeared and no trial was held. Justice melted away under the dictatorship. Benedetto had nothing left except his pride, anger, and desire to rid his nation of those who brought it suffering, hate, and calamity.
"I was a medic in the Great War and know how to handle these kinds of wounds," said Benedetto. "I have all the medications and instruments I need. I can hide them here and in neighboring houses for a few weeks, but the Germans will come looking for you soon. You have to get out of here," he insisted to Colonel Lukas. "Once we reach the Fifth Army, we will be okay," explained Joe. "Most of the troops have moved off the coast and occupied Salerno and the neighboring towns. The OSS team set up a monitoring post on the beach, and we need to get there," affirmed Tom.

"Tomorrow, we will bypass the German lines and cut across the valley leading to the landing area, behind Nazi artillery. It will be dangerous, but it is our only hope to reach the Allies," said Colonel Lukas.

CHAPTER 122

TORTURE

His hands and feet were tied with thick wires. They cut into his flesh, gushing blood. His face was swollen, darkened, and lacerated from beatings. He was semi-conscious. Two SS soldiers in black uniforms, with red swastikas on their helmets, carried him to a small, dark room with a green conical light hanging from a rusty chain in the ceiling. It waved back and forth as gusts of air shot through the space when someone moved. Ghost-like shadows climbed the walls and crossed the ceiling as the light rocked back and forth.

His clothes had been ripped from his body, tearing open puss-filled wounds from his torso, arms, and legs. He screamed in agony. He was thrust into a hard, metal chair and tied down with ropes. His head was swimming with pain, lack of sleep, hunger, and thirst. He thought of his wife and children. He knew he would never see them again. His eyes were swollen shut like those of a boxer.

A bucket of salt water was thrown into his face to revive him and increase his anguish. The thick, saline solution covered his body and seeped into his sores. He felt he was on fire, with flames dancing on his skin. He yelled at the top of his lungs. A foul-smelling rag was pushed into his mouth to muffle his cries.

For three days, the man was held in a Gestapo prison. He was tortured and pounded with a wooden Billy club from his scalp to his toes. It took only a day for the Nazis to take control of Giacomo's dreams, turn them into nightmares, and make him feel like a zombie. The linesman was arrested immediately after the explosion in the railroad tunnel as the German convoy, laden with artillery and tanks, blew up and derailed on its way to Salerno. He was dragged from his small apartment adjacent to the station, minutes after the blast.

His wife and children stood horrified with terror as they watched this good and kind man shackled, clubbed, and savagely thrown into the back of a green military pick up, without recourse or explanation. Giacomo was taken to Gestapo headquarters. It was a three-story building with four cells, two small interrogation rooms, and a basement where prisoners were electrocuted, hung by razor wires, and beheaded, or, if fortunate, shot in the back of the head.

Courtesy, Holocaust Memorials,
National Socialist Documentation Center and Memorial Museum,
Gestapo Prison in the EL-DE-House

The jail was a gray, windowless, concrete box with a tiny hole for a latrine, no bed or chairs. It was sealed with a steel door, imported from the Fatherland and secured with German deadbolt locks, impossible to open or close without three oddly shaped keys turned clockwise and counterclockwise.

Giacomo was tossed onto the floor of his cell with his hands and feet tied. He slept out of fear and suffering. Pain was overcoming him, so he lay motionless, praying for sleep or death. In his reverie, he heard the explosion in the tunnel again, the barking of attack dogs, and the screeching, incomprehensible commands of the Gestapo, as they kicked open the door of his home.

Giacomo knew the risks of helping the partisans. He was frightened. He had a family. Without him, they might starve as the war dragged on into one deadly year after another. Yet, for this simple man who worked on the rails, fear was an excuse. It was a reason to retreat and let evil overcome good.

He thought of his wife and children. What example would he leave them? What part would he play to battle the demons that controlled his nation? What sacrifice would he give to struggle against a foe that seemed invincible? He would give his life. Yes, he would make the ultimate sacrifice. His life and his children's lives would have little value under a Nazi dictatorship. Better to die for a just cause than live as a coward.

Now came the final test. Giacomo knew the Germans would torture him into revealing his ties to the freedom fighters. Then they would kill him. He trembled at the thought and pleaded for strength. His real fear was not dying. It was giving in to the monsters.

"Wake him up," came the command. Two men stood over him. His body was fastened to a chair. The light was blinding as he peered through the blood in his eyes. "Slap him again," demanded the Gestapo colonel. The soldier pulled his hair and raised Giacomo's head to face the officer. "You still refuse to tell us where the partisans are who you helped destroy the tunnel?" said the Nazi. "Water, I need water!" cried Giacomo.

"Give him a sip," he said. The soldier put a metal cup to Giacomo's lips and poured water into his mouth. He swallowed it. "More, more please," he implored. "You can have all the water and food you want if you tell us where they are," insisted the Gestapo Colonel. "I do not know anything," responded Giacomo. "Perhaps I can refresh your memory," replied the officer.

The Nazi walked to a table in the corner of the room. He put on a set of rubber gloves. He picked up an iron plier. It had a spiral, spear-like device in its center. It was an old dental tool used to extract teeth. He placed it close to Giacomo's mouth. "I am a bit clumsy with this," he hissed. "No, please no!" implored Giacomo. His legs trembled as one soldier held him down and another pried open his mouth.

The Nazi plunged his weapon deep into Giacomo's gums...

CHAPTER 123 ━━━━━━━━━━━━━━━━

THE CONVENT

Sunrise over Castellonorato came late that morning. It was past 7 AM, but it was light enough for the Gestapo Captain and a platoon of soldiers to prepare themselves. The officer donned his new black uniform, pinned with commendations and medals awarded by the Fuhrer for his work in rounding up Jews and enemies of the state. The Captain was proud of his record of arrests, tortures, and executions.

His boots were shined and gleamed in the sun.

He placed a monocle over his right eye and put on a pair of black leather gloves.

Guns, explosives, a cargo truck, a jeep with a driver were all they needed. The soldiers and their weapons mounted the lorry while the officer, a sergeant, and a driver got into the vehicle. "Move out!" barked the Captain as the convoy followed his jeep.

Two miles away, the nuns at the convent finished their prayers and breakfast and began preparation for another day of school for their children.

Sister Chiara made the sign of the cross in front of a statue of Our Lady as she entered her office. The Jewish girls had new documents and names. Most were now familiar with the basics of Christianity, attended daily mass, and were studying catechisms. Mothers worked in the laundry and kitchen. A few fathers from the Seminary cared for the grounds and gardens. Four months had passed since they had arrived.

A feeling of safety spread across the community.

The Chosen People felt welcomed and secure.

Sister Chiara sat at her desk reviewing school papers, when she heard engines outside her window.

She looked through the glass protected with iron bars. Below her was the convent portal. It was a tall, heavy oak door, sealed with locks and a long, rectangular log fastened to iron clamps. It was hundreds of years old and had protected the cloister from intruders for centuries.

The Nazi caravan rushed to the entrance.

The screech of tires and the sound of jack boots echoed through the stone walls and across the courtyard.

The children and teachers in the classrooms heard the ominous sound.

They were terrified.

The German sergeant leaped from the jeep and banged on the abbey door with the butt of a rifle. "Open up!" he demanded as the troops dismounted, cocked their machine guns, and prepared to assault the nunnery.

Sister Chiara ran to the portal. "Open it," she told the custodian.

Within a minute, the door was unlocked and the German convoy entered the courtyard. Sister Chiara stood erect. She watched as the Germans took positions in the convent square. She looked fearlessly at the German officer.

"What is the meaning of this intrusion?" she said.

The Captain stared at her. "I have reason to believe you are sheltering Jews," he stated coldly.

"We are a sanctuary of peace, education, and love. You have no reason to be here," she insisted. By now, Sister Cristina arrived on the scene. She heard the Nazi.

"I am the prioress of this abbey," she told him. "We have no secrets. You are free to inspect our facilities and the school, if you wish," she said with conviction. "I will be glad to escort you and your soldiers," she remarked.

She dreaded the worst, but she realized she had no choice in the face of these devils who respected no one, including God.

They could search the convent at will. Perhaps she could exercise some control if she and Sister Chiara accompanied them.

"The Sergeant and I will come with you. In the meantime, our soldiers will investigate the buildings and the school," ordered the Captain.

A cold shiver went up the spine of Sister Cristina.

—

CHAPTER 124 ▬▬▬▬▬▬▬

THE BUNKERS

It would be their most dangerous mission.

Colonel Lukas, Joe, and Tom had to reach the Fifth Army beachhead. It was a three- mile journey from outside of Salerno to the coast where the Americans were settled, despite constant attack from remaining Nazi embankments overlooking the landing site.

Courtesy, US Army Center of Military History

The casements, machine gun nests, and bunkers were manned by two, three, or four German soldiers who were volunteers, left behind to slow the enemy's advance. Some had heavy artillery, but most had automatic weapons. The Allied bombings eliminated the anti-tank and anti-aircraft guns. Three Italian-built bunkers with machine guns still survived, blocking the road from the sea to Salerno.

The Americans called them "pill boxes."

Under cover of darkness, the freedom fighters began their trip. Backpacks were filled with explosives, grenades, and ammunition. Attack plans were in place. Faces were blackened with coal dust. Outfits were dark with hoods and skull caps.

The three men zigzagged through rubble, bomb craters, and forests, and finally reached a high hill looking out over the beach. Below was a U.S. military port being built for additional landings to support the troops. Aluminum sheds were under construction, along with the laying of steel roads for tanks and trucks.

Suddenly, machine-gun fire sliced through the night.

A hail of bullets rained on the shore as soldiers and a few other personnel ran for cover.

The whistling red lights of the shells and the piercing noise of the artillery revealed where the three bunkers were.

They were one hundred meters apart, dug deep into the hillside, in a circle above the sea.

Each pill box was a meter thick of cement and steel with a 180 degree opening, wide enough to fit the barrel of a machine gun and allow enough sunlight and air for the soldiers to see and breathe. The concrete cylinders were impenetrable to small arms fire. Only airborne "bunker busters" could disable them, or manually launching grenades and explosives into the casement to kill the combatants.

"You take the one on the left, Lukas," explained Tom. "Joe, you go after the one on the right, and I will hit the center." The curtain of darkness was cover for the freedom fighters, but also for their enemies.

A full moon was seeping through the clouds.

The partisans required precision. Light was needed the instant they were to penetrate the openings in the embankments. All they had were flashlights. It was a daring undertaking.

The German soldiers in the bunkers were prepared for anything. They were ready to die for the Fatherland. Within minutes, Joe, Tom, and Lukas were behind the pill boxes. Each had targeted a thick steel door.

Joe snaked up to the casement. His heart was pounding. It was cold, yet he was perspiring heavily. He laid on the ground to catch his breath. Thoughts passed through his mind.

'How many soldiers are in there? How old are they? What are their names? Do they have families? Is there some way to avoid killing anyone? Will they come out to attack me? Will I survive this?'

Joe knew there were no answers. In a few fleeting moments, he would know.

He put in ear plugs to deal with the pounding machine-gun fire spewing out of the mouth of the bunker. He saw three pieces of artillery. Each was manned. He placed a plastic charge on the lock of the door and set it to two minutes with a timer.

Like a panther, he crawled to the front of the pill box, where the guns were blazing. Fortunately, no Allied fire was coming from the shore. He assumed that at sunrise bombers would come to finish off the three remaining bunkers.

Joe waited in the moonlight. He counted down for the explosion...5, 4, 3, 2, 1. A light flashed as the charge went off. The three German soldiers were stunned by the blast. It blew out their ear drums as the boom echoed through their small chamber. The startled men scrambled to secure the door. Joe took two sticks of dynamite, lit the fuses, and threw them through the gun turret. They soundlessly landed in the middle of the bunker.

Joe ran as far away as possible, hit the ground, and covered his head and ears. A minute later he heard the blasts. Tongues of fire and chunks of shrapnel shot in all directions from the openings of the bunker as shells and ordinances detonated in explosions heard across the shore. The Germans were trapped. In seconds, they were torn to pieces and burned to death.

Joe stood on the sand near the bunker. He took a drink of water from his canteen. His hands trembled. Tears flowed from his eyes. In the span of weeks, he had killed many men. He felt awful. His stomach churned. He prayed for those whose lives he took and asked God to forgive him.

As Joe rested, two more explosions happened simultaneously, as Lukas and Tom set off charges that killed the enemy soldiers in the remaining pill boxes. From the beach, Allied troops heard the blasts and saw the light of the blazing casements.

When the sun rose, all was silent, as smoke and the stench of smoldering flesh emanated from the concrete tombs.

CHAPTER 125

THE POEM

The clanking noise of the train wheels kept him awake. Carlo wanted to sleep and dream of Helena during the long journey to West Virginia. It was his fourth trip, yet it seemed like his first. His heart pounded with passion. All he could think of was her. He could not resist Helena.

She was beautiful, innocent, pure, charming, funny, and full of life. With her, he was another person. His defenses fell. Love took over his mind and body. It paralyzed him with visions of this woman holding his heart in her hand.

The frequent stops of the train woke him from his reverie. Carlo gazed on the endless miles of farms with machines plowing fields and livestock feeding off stacks of hay harvested in the fall. The countryside was rich, alive, and green, gleaming with the glow of spring. Fruit trees were filled with blossoms. Blankets of wildflowers, with all the colors of rainbows, decorated roads and paths leading to hamlets and forests. Miles upon miles of corn and wheat fields stretched from the towns into the horizon.

'America is huge,' he thought. 'It is an endless river of opportunity filled with energy that seems like a tornado of prosperity that sweeps up anyone who ventures into its path." It was the place for him. He wanted to enjoy the American dream of a tranquil life and never again think of death and war. His world was Helena and the United States.

He kept her letters in a locked trunk next to his bed in the barracks. He took several with him. They were tucked in a jacket pocket, close to his heart. He memorized words and phrases Helena carefully etched into the paper with her glorious calligraphy.

"My life started when I met you," she wrote. "It began the second you touched me and almost ended the moment we kissed. I trembled as if struck by lightning when your lips met mine. In an instant, the past disappeared. The present is you, and the future is you and us." Carlo caressed the pages of the letters. He looked at the watermarks that dotted the lines and sentences. Helena's tears of love were sealed into each sheet of paper like pieces of her soul.

She gave him a book of poetry by Robert Frost. Carlo's English was good. He took lessons and practiced each day speaking with American soldiers in the camp and read newspapers and magazines. He understood the sentiments and emotions of the words. One poem reminded him of the time ahead:

> *The woods are lovely, dark, and deep,*
> *But I have promises to keep,*
> *And miles to go before I sleep,*
> *And miles to go before I sleep.*

He had to return to Italy and sort out his life. The war was still raging. It could take years. Yet he was not afraid. Carlo was on a new and exciting road, and it would be with the woman he adored, which was like another of the poems in the book:

> *I shall be telling this with a sigh*
> *Somewhere ages and ages hence:*
> *Two roads diverged in a wood, and I —*
> *I took the one less traveled by,*
> *And that has made all the difference.*

"Wheeling!" announced the train master. Carlo opened the window to see the platform. Hundreds of people were walking to and fro, waiting to meet someone or embark on a journey to war or peace. He searched for her. From a distance, he saw her hat, and then her face. Helena was radiant in a red dress and a short coat.

She wore the pin he gave her. It was an enameled dolphin he found in a jewelry store. The colors were sea blue, and light green, with a grey tail, tinged with black, that reminded him of her eyes and hair. The golden, cigar paper ring he gave her when he pledged eternal love was on her finger. She wore only lipstick and a touch of talcum powder on her cheeks and forehead. The scent of Carlo's perfume blended with her snow-white skin to emanate a fragrance of honey and orange blossoms.

Carlo leaped from the train and ran to her. They embraced.

Her tears streamed into their kiss and cemented their lives with the tide of love.

Together, they were one earthly bit of heaven, and they rejoiced in knowing it.

CHAPTER 126 ━━━━━━━━━━━━━

REACHING THE FIFTH ARMY

After destroying the bunkers, Joe, Tom, and Lukas waited in the chilly night for the sun to rise above the beach to make sure they could be seen. It was impossible to rest. Bombers flew overhead. Explosions from raids on Italian cities inflamed the darkness with red and orange lights, flashing over the hills hugging Salerno. It was an inferno. Firestorms seemed like giant furnaces belching flames and smoke as huge bombs pulverized civilian and Nazi locations. Thousands died and millions were homeless.

The three men had changed, emotionally and physically. They were stronger, self-assured, cunning, and wise. A metamorphosis transformed them into seasoned warriors. A year of combat, sabotage, and heroic resistance to evil altered their souls and bodies. Any doubts as to why they were fighting melted away in the horror of enemy atrocities.

Innocent men and women were tortured, murdered, and persecuted. Those brave enough to rise up against the forces of tyranny risked their lives and those of their loved ones to rid Italy of the arrogance, corruption, and cruelty of Nazism and Fascism. Thousands gave their lives for truth and justice.

Two days passed since the freedom fighters had slept. They were exhausted. As they descended the sandy dunes, Tom took a handkerchief and made a white flag and attached it to a long pole to make sure they were not fired upon as they approached the base. He waved it wildly. "Do not shoot. We are Americans," screamed Joe.

"Halt!" yelled a soldier with a machine gun. He was tall, powerfully built, with broad shoulders and sea-green eyes. Gold Sergeant stripes decorated the sleeves of his uniform and his helmet. The automatic weapon seemed like a toy in his huge hands. He released the safety to prepare to fire. The three men heard the click and stopped. 'After all we have been through, this stupid brute will probably kill us. Our own army doing what the Nazis couldn't do,' thought Joe. He was afraid

.

The giant soldier pointed his gun at them. They raised their hands and identified themselves. "We are assigned to the OSS!" screamed Joe. "Do not shoot," he shouted. "Drop your guns and gear!" demanded the Sergeant. They obeyed. Another soldier, a corporal, took their arms, backpacks, and ammunition. He frisked them. Joe and Tom had knives and grenades fastened to their legs. "Put your hands behind your back!" demanded the Sergeant, while the other soldier removed their weapons and handcuffed them.

For two hours, these "invisible men" explained to a Major and a Lieutenant who they were and what they did in a year of ferocious attacks on the Germans. The American officers of the Fifth Army were cautious. It took three days to verify Joe and Tom's story.

Meanwhile, the men were kept in a tent under guard. Finally, the handcuffs came off. They showered, shaved, got a change of clothes, and were well fed. "I want a full report on your day-by-day operations," insisted the Major. "Include logistics data on the condition of roads, bridges, and terrain, and your recommendations as to where the Germans will strike next and how."

Joe, Tom, and Lukas organized their thoughts and recorded every detail of their exploits. On a map that accompanied their report, they pinpointed Nazi installations and suggested heavy bombardments to destroy them. Joe handed a typed document, with three carbon copies, to the Major. It was ten pages. He, Tom, and Lukas spent three more days at the U.S. base on the beach being interrogated.

It was a startling story of clandestine activity that challenged the imagination of the battle-hardened officers. Here were tales of tunnels, roads, trains, and Nazi ammunition dumps blown up, attacks on convoys, incursions into German camps, and transmitting information to the Allies to help in the amphibious landing at Salerno.

Every fact was checked. After their report was fully verified, they were moved to Allied headquarters and called before the Commandant, who was the commanding officer. He was a Brigadier General.

"I want to congratulate you on your heroism," he said, as he shook each man's hand. "I am putting you in for battlefield promotions. Your Italian companion will receive a special commendation from me. I will send a letter to Marshall Badoglio, the Italian Prime Minister, recommending him and his colleagues for the Gold Medal," stated the commandant with pride.

The General came from the state of Washington. He graduated from West Point with highest honors. He was tall, bald, and slim, with a deep suntan from two years in North Africa. He and his men fought in Tunisia, Morocco, Algeria, and Libya, where Germany's most celebrated hero, General Erwin Rommel, the "Desert Fox," was defeated.

The Allies captured 300,000 Nazi and Italian soldiers in Africa, put them on ships, and sent them to prisoner of war camps in America. Before the Americans left North Africa, the General presided over the burial of thousands of soldiers in the sand near the city of Carthage, Tunisia. It was one of the first U.S. cemeteries of World War II. It would not be the last.

By the end of September 1943, Salerno was still filled with German sharpshooters, who made it impossible for the Allies to safely occupy it. Allied headquarters was set up in an abandoned seventeenth century palace outside of Salerno. It was in poor condition with a leaking roof and no indoor plumbing or running water. It was cold, drafty, and uncomfortable.

American electricians installed lighting. Water was carried in from portable tanks. Beds were brought in with plenty of warm blankets. Offices with typewriters and desks were organized. The rooms were cleaned to prepare for administrative use.

In the palace ballroom, the General assembled the Allied high command for a special presentation. Maps of Italy and the

Mediterranean were spread across a long rectangular table. A chart of the western coast of Italy was pinned to a wall for all to see. Twenty officers from the army, navy and marine corps of the U.S. and British forces sat around the table. No notes were permitted. The windows were shuttered.

Joe, Tom, and Lukas were invited as observers. They sat along a wall with peeling floral wallpaper. The ceiling was decorated with a magnificent fresco of angels and Saints. The plaster was loose. Pieces of the painting were missing. It was an ancient relic of wealth and leisure. Joe and Tom were in Army officer uniforms. Lukas wore a grey woolen suit, a white shirt and tie, and a pair of soft leather shoes. After years in the rough, it was difficult to appreciate the clothes of civilization. The men were clean shaven, with closely cropped hair cuts.

Before his presentation, the General introduced his guests as "three heroic colleagues who conducted dangerous missions that helped prepare for our invasion. Our next operation is to land on the western coast, and establish a beachhead at Anzio and Nettuno, move north, and capture Rome," he explained. "It will not be easy. The Germans are dug in and have shifted firepower from the South to the Center of Italy to stop our advance and protect the capital. Our goal is to take Rome by June.

"There are reports of U.S. troops killing German and Italian prisoners and civilians in Sicily. Those involved will face Court Martials. Officers are to order all units to respect the Geneva Conventions regarding enemy combatants who surrender. Prisoners are to be treated humanely. We will not conduct ourselves like the Nazis.

"The partisans in Italy, the Catholic Church, and the OSS are supplying important intelligence data concerning German troop movements and operations. The Vatican has informed us of thousands of Jews being arrested in Italy and sent to extermination camps all over Northern Europe. Some Jews have been sheltered in convents and monasteries in Nazi-occupied towns. Church officials have asked us to help move them to safe havens. If not, they will be captured and murdered," he explained.

Joe, Tom, and Lukas looked at each other. A day earlier, a partisan alerted them to a large group of Jews in the town of Castellonorato. The Nazis were close to discovering them.

A priest was the key contact.

His name was Don Lorenzo.

CHAPTER 127

GRAND THEFT

"I understand you are an artist," hissed the Nazi Captain to Sister Chiara. She was startled. "Before I entered the house of the Lord, I taught art and did some painting," she responded, blushing. "Your canvasses hang in museums," he said. "Field Marshall Goering is an admirer of your work," mentioned the Captain. "You are considered one of the greatest artists of the century." His tone was filled with false flattery. "The Field Marshall has collected art throughout the continent to exhibit to the world the wonders of European talent," he lied. "An admirable objective," responded Sister Chiara, without conviction. "Where is your work stored?" inquired the Nazi.

Sister Chiara gulped. She looked at her superior. The collection was considered a convent treasure, to be sold if the nunnery ever needed funds to survive. Sister Cristina nodded to her. Sister Chiara closed her eyes. "It is in the crypt of the convent," she replied. "Let me see it," he demanded. The two nuns escorted the Captain along a portico filled with arches, surrounded by flowers blooming in the late September sun. Red and pink roses climbed along columns and arbors. A bed of herbs and a large garden of vegetables was in the center.

The Nazi stared at the hanging tomatoes, eggplants, and squash, as they entered the convent by an old wooden door worn by use and needing painting and repair. "See that we seize all the food before we leave here," murmured the Captain to the Sergeant. The nuns overheard the whispered words.

Sister Cristina asked the custodian to join them. The curator was a small, middle-aged man with a thick grey mustache. He wore a red shirt with pink patches and suspenders that held up badly worn brown corduroy pants. His shoes were covered with stains, and his nails and hands were blackened from work in the garden and cementing stones in the medieval wall that surrounded the abbey. He smelled of perspiration. Thick lines covered his face and forehead.

The custodian's life was the convent. He did all types of jobs to help the nuns. In return, he lived in a modest room detached from the priory and received a small stipend and three meals a day. He carried a set of iron keys and a wooden box of tools with him wherever he went.

Sister Cristina pulled a steel latch and opened the portal. They walked slowly into the chapel. It was austere and dark. Twelve pews were in front of a small marble altar. A large crucifix with a statue of Christ nailed to it was above the tabernacle. An image of the Virgin Mary and the Baby Jesus was in the back of the church next to a statue of St. Anthony. A heavenly ray of rainbow-colored light gleamed on the crucifix. It glowed from a stained-glass window over the entrance.

The curator removed his hat. The two nuns and the custodian bowed, genuflected and made the sign of the cross in front of the altar. The Germans stood at attention and watched them with cold faces. A metal ring was encased in a stone slab before the altar. The custodian lit a kerosene lantern. The scent spread across the small church and mixed with the fragrance of incense that hung in the air from mass that morning.

The caretaker lifted the ring and the marble cover. A long stone stairway shone down into the darkness. He slowly led the group down the steps. Light from the lantern penetrated the shadows. The sepulcher lit up, casting silhouettes and reflections through the burial chamber. Six white granite tombs lay on two sides of the vault. They held the remains of noble men and women who donated their treasure to build the convent.

At the end of the mausoleum was a large tarpaulin. Wooden frames jutted out from the covering. "Remove the canvas," said Sister Cristina to the custodian. Slowly, he took it off. Streams of dust fell to the floor as the colors of the paintings drifted in the light.

The Nazi drew a flashlight from his leather belt and picked up a frame. He held the light close to the painting. He examined it carefully. It was a portrait of a young girl. The smooth strokes, soft hues, and vivid images reminded him of Renoir. He lifted another. It was a seascape with boats floating on waves that seemed to move. A self-portrait startled the Nazi for the depth of emotion captured in the eyes and mouth. He rummaged through several more paintings.

"Which one will you send to the Field Marshall?" asked Sister Chiara. The Nazi looked at her. His light blue eyes were those of a serpent. He turned to the custodian. "Bring them outside," he commanded. The group left the crypt as the curator carefully brought each painting into the sun, under the portico. The Lieutenant who led the unit to search the convent returned to talk to the Captain.

He spoke softly in his ear. "We checked the documents of the girls and women. All seemed in order. I interrogated ten of them. They said the right things, but were nervous. I am sure some are Jews," he reported. The Captain reflected for a moment on what to say next.

"We are certain you are hiding Jews," he asserted in a loud voice. "You know the penalty is death," he exclaimed. The Nazi paced back and forth. "I am considering arresting you, your teachers, and all of your students," he declared. He rubbed his hands.

The nuns gasped. "I assure you this is not the case," asserted Sister Cristina. "There are no Jews here. You have my word," she said with conviction.

"All right. I accept your word for now, but I will be back to look into this matter in more detail," he affirmed, gazing at the paintings.

"Which one would you like to take?" asked Sister Chiara.

Tears welled up in her eyes. She felt faint.

He stared at her.

"All of them," he declared.

CHAPTER 128

DON LORENZO'S NIGHTMARES

Another sleepless night. Nightmares plagued him. He saw visions of death and heard screams from suffering children and barking dogs. Don Lorenzo could not rest. He was exhausted. For three days, he tossed and turned, trying to find a solution. The Nazi's knew about the Jews. The nuns staved them off temporarily by the emptying of their food pantries and the stealing of Sister Chiara's paintings. The Germans would soon raid the convent and monastery.

Trucks were being commissioned to put the Jews onto trains bound for a place in Poland.

It was called Auschwitz.

"Get them out of Castellonorato," he repeated to himself. "But how and where?" He held an image in his hand of his patron Saint, San Silverio. The young priest pleaded for guidance. "Please help me carry this cross. We must save these people. Give me a solution. Help me, help me," he begged. He prayed for hours.

He laid on his small cot perspiring and praying. Suddenly, he sat up. An idea flashed before him. 'Ponza. Take them to the island. They will be safe there! But how to get them there? Who will help?' he thought. "A message to Don Gabriele," he said out loud with conviction. "I will send him a note."

Don Lorenzo wrote a long letter in Latin. It was three pages. He put it in an envelope and sealed it with red wax. It was a list of church items he claimed he needed for mass. The inventory was coded. Every word had key letters that spelled something when combined and translated.

Don Lorenzo went into the church courtyard. An old Vespa with fading paint and a torn leather seat was parked against a wall. It was a gift from his parents at ordination. He checked the gas gauge. It was near empty. 'Will it be enough for the eleven kilometers to Formia and back?' he pondered. The muffler had a hole in it that created an infernal noise, and the tires were worn.

Castellonorato was three hundred meters above sea level. Steep, snaking curves with slippery, narrow, unpaved roads wound their way down the mountainside toward the coast. Don Lorenzo was not a skilled driver. The priest rarely used the motorbike. Workers in and around the church drove it for chores. Now he needed it to get to Formia, as soon as possible.

He tucked the letter in his shoe. He got on the bike and made the sign of the cross. His lack of experience showed. He was unsteady and almost fell off. Gradually, he got his bearings and felt somewhat comfortable. He took ten minutes to prime the engine. It started after several attempts. Clouds of oil-filled, black smoke belched from the exhaust. He checked the brakes. They were soft and irregular.

Slowly, he rode out of the courtyard and onto the main road. He tried the brakes again. They held a bit. He reached the top of the motorway at the pinnacle of the peak above the valley leading to Formia. It was a lethal, eighty-degree incline that disappeared into tortuous turns and continued down a steep, winding, one-lane thoroughfare, surrounded by trees and overhanging cliffs that fell into a rocky valley.

He buttoned his black coat, pulled his woolen hat over his forehead, and put on a pair of dark goggles. The glass was scratched and hard to see through. Don Lorenzo revved up the engine, prayed the Our Father, and pressed the bike's gear into forward. He burst out like a cannonball. Cold wind shot up his trousers, freezing his legs as the priest came flying down the hill.

It was a roller-coaster ride. Within minutes, the handlebars of the motorcycle shook. The Vespa seemed to fall head-long down the mountainside. The brakes failed. Don Lorenzo fought to restrain the wobbling vehicle. Trucks and cars dashed by as he constantly zig-zagged in and out of the road, nearing the edge of the cliff on his right by inches. He was flying at 100 kilometers an hour and out of control. He was hunched over the handlebars as he skidded, slid, jumped, and finally slowed and stopped at the bottom of the mountain.

The priest pulled over on the grass, climbed off the bike, wiped his brow with a handkerchief, and listened to his heart beating like a roaring engine. He shook from his toes to his ears. He was numb. Don Lorenzo looked to the sky. "Thank you, my Lord," he said as he made the sign of the cross. 'I cannot linger here to rest,' he thought. He got on the motorcycle. He sped off at a reasonable speed. He kept close to the right side of the road. Ahead, a painted slab of wood with an arrow pointed to Formia.

As he completed a long curve, he saw a frightening sight. A German jeep blockaded the road. Two soldiers with machine guns and a Fascist stopped motorists to interrogate them. "Show me your papers," commanded the Italian to Don Lorenzo.

The priest fumbled over his documents and handed over his identification. "Where are you going?" he asked. "I am visiting the Bishop," stuttered Don Lorenzo, begging God to forgive his lie. "Get off the motorcycle," said the soldier. The Fascist frisked him. He looked at his shoes. One seemed to be taller than the other. "Take them off," he demanded. Don Lorenzo felt faint. His blood pressure fell. He felt his bladder bursting and his bowels moving. He started to untie his shoelaces when he heard screaming.

"I cannot wait here all day! I have an urgent delivery for the German General Staff!" yelled a trucker. The soldiers marched toward the lorry. The Fascist turned to Don Lorenzo. He gave him his papers. "Get out of here," he declared. The priest went around the roadblock and sped toward the town at a dizzying speed. In the city center was a yellow building with the Italian and Nazi flag flying in front of it. It was Fascist headquarters. Two armed guards in black uniforms were on both sides of the entrance. He walked in.

A huge photo of Mussolini and Hitler together hung on a wall in the foyer. Don Lorenzo looked at the images. 'They are the cause of our agony,' he thought. He wanted to spit at the photo, but he controlled

427

himself. He took off his hat. A young man in a Fascist Militia uniform sat at a desk monitoring access. "I am here to see Captain Massimo," said the priest as he handed him his papers. He examined them.

"This photo is old," the priest stated. "It was taken many years ago, when I was just ordained," answered Don Lorenzo. "Is the Captain expecting you?" he asked. "No, but we are friends," replied Don Lorenzo. "His office is the second one on the right," said the sentry.

Massimo was from Ponza. Don Lorenzo baptized him, gave him first communion, confirmation, and celebrated his marriage to a girl on the island. He was an officer in the Fascist Militia and loved Don Lorenzo, who was his spiritual guide and mentor. Massimo was a good man, but growing up in Fascist Italy distorted his ideas. He was a patriot and devoted to his country, but he was taught to love Il Duce more. Don Lorenzo knew Massimo was soul searching. His doubts about the course Italy was on worried him. The more he learned about the Germans, the more he distrusted and hated them.

The priest was shown into the Captain's office. Massimo was behind a stack of papers, stamping documents. He had a grey uniform decorated with medals and insignia, and he wore a hat with the Fascist symbol.

"Good morning," said Don Lorenzo. Massimo looked up. He leaped from his chair. He smiled and embraced the priest warmly. For ten minutes they chatted about family, friends, and the suffering of the war. Massimo was a realist, but he held firmly to the cause. "The Duce will return after we defeat the Allies," he insisted.

"Italy has already lost the war," replied Don Lorenzo. "The Nazi's are now our owners. Il Duce counts for nothing. We need to save our country and bring the fighting to an end. Everyone must examine their conscience and change before it is too late," asserted the priest.

Don Lorenzo saw Massimo reflect on these words. The young man knew the war was lost. "The Fascists and Nazis will be tried for war crimes. Those who help the Allied cause now will be pardoned. You owe it to your family and your country," whispered the priest. Don Lorenzo appealed to Massimo's sense of humanity and survival.

"What can I do for you?" asked Massimo.

"I need a favor. I know your Fascist patrol boat goes to Ponza after dark to carry food and supplies to your colleagues and their families on the island. I need to get a letter to Don Gabriele and for you to deliver it personally," he stated. The priest handed him the envelope. Massimo looked it over. "What is it?" he asked. "It is a list of items I need for our poor church. I know Don Gabriele had these before the war and perhaps he can help us," he said. "All right. I will take it tonight," responded Massimo.

He suspected Don Lorenzo was up to something, but he could deny nothing to this man without a good reason. He examined his conscience. He realized he lived in a mirage. Mussolini was an illusionist. People thought he had magical powers. Like a sorcerer, he created a story, chasing a vision that was a dream.

"You can rely on me," said Massimo to the priest.

Don Lorenzo shook his hand. He raced from the building, which he felt contained evil spirits. Two hours later, he was back in his church in Castellonorato.

For the first time in years, he was too tired to thank God for bringing him back alive.

CHAPTER 129

GIOVANNINA

Giovannina slipped out of her warm bed and tiptoed into the night. It was an hour before dawn in October 1943. She wore a grey, cotton scarf around her hair and neck, a woolen dress, a black coat, and oversized rubber boots. They were her brother's. He was dead. Five months passed since he drowned in the sinking of the ferry Santa Lucia, struck by Allied bombers.

The ship was on its way to the island of Ventotene from Ponza. Giovannina's brother left a wife and two boys. He was 33. His parents and the entire family were devastated. Such agony was repeated in the homes of millions of Italians as the ravages of war continued.

She was the fifth child in a family of seven sisters and four brothers born in Ponza. All were exceptionally strong and healthy. They came from a clan of mariners and merchants who lived a disciplined life of hard work, frugality, and wisdom. The men were sea captains, and the women, wives and mothers.

Giovannina was delicate, petite, and lady-like. Her wardrobe fitted the occasion. She could dress like an upper middleclass matron or wear simple attire to cook splendid meals or to go outdoors. She was beautiful, with light brown hair, brown eyes, white skin, and a clever smile. Her strength was in her intelligence, personality, courage, common sense, and the ability to do nearly anything. She could weave textiles, make garments, farm, hunt, and fish, as well as run a household as a wife and mother. Most of all she was resilient. She was not physically strong, but she often forced herself to do what seemed impossible.

She married a non-commissioned officer of the Italian Navy, who also came from the island. The war separated them. He was in Rome as an aide to the Italian Admiralty's Office of Intelligence. She was trapped in Ponza with their four small children because there was no longer any transport to and from the mainland. She lost ten kilos, and the children were skin and bones. Now, Giovannina was determined to save them before they died of hunger.

She rolled sheets of newspaper around her feet so she could fit into the boots. Her clothes hung loosely over her thin body. She lit a lantern. The smell of smoke from the burning oil filled the room as she gently opened the front door. It was her only light as she climbed carefully down steps cut into the stone, and over rocks toward the water surrounding the island. She heard the gentle sound of waves embracing the rocks. The scent of sea air seemed like a fragrance from the gods.

Giovannina glanced about as she moved. Fascists and Nazis were on the prowl for anyone attempting to fish in the dangerous waters of the island. No one dared venture into the sea. Italian mines floated not far from the coast of the island and the mainland. The Allies constantly flew fighter aircraft over Ponza. The Germans occupied the island. They stole animals, food, crops, and provisions to feed their troops. The people of this small rock in the Mediterranean were caught between the Americans and British fighting to liberate Italy, and the Nazis and the Fascists engaged in a civil war to defeat the Allies.

Giovannina was frightened. At any moment a plane or a German patrol boat could appear. She could be killed in an instant. Yet, it was better than dying a slow death of hunger. She was thirty-seven, but she felt like a lifetime had passed. She had starving youngsters and aging parents wasting away from lack of nutrition. If she did not return with food, they would die.

The night air was still and silent. She was eager to reach her destination. As she approached the shore, a dark creature flashed before her. A grey bat shot out of a cave like a bullet. The young woman almost fainted. She slowed to catch her breath and moved on. A small rowboat rested on the beach. She pushed it into the sea. Without a sound, she climbed into the tiny craft and paddled away. She covered the lantern to avoid detection. The water was like a lake. It was calm, yet only a few weeks earlier it was filled with blood, bodies, oil slicks, and debris from sunken ships and planes shot out of the sky. In a dark, cloud-filled night, the roaring sea swept away every trace of war in a storm packed with thundering winds and pouring rain that seemed to wash away all signs of conflict and suffering.

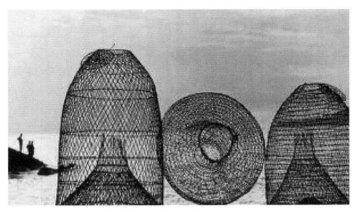

Fish Baskets, *Courtesy, Ponza Racconta*

Giovannina's hands were cracked and calloused from hoeing hard, dry soil to plant seeds and scratch out some crops for the spring and summer. Her skin broke out in bloody cuts as she rowed two hundred meters from the beach. The dimming light of a full moon guided her. She discovered the spot. She was directly above the fish basket. She knew where it was by the intersection of three points that came together in the sea. The view of the old fort, the rock shaped like a turtle, and the island of Palmarola were her markers.

She dropped a large, rusty iron hook over the boat and cast about the bottom searching for the trap. She found it. Rapidly, she pulled it up. It was the shape of a giant beehive, made with bamboo shoots, fastened with twine in a round rib cage, and a lid with a conical opening. Inside was bait hanging from a rope. The fish could enter, but not escape.

It was heavy. She sighed and took a deep breath. With all her strength, she hauled the trap into the boat. Giovannina's hands ached from pulling the coarse rope. She opened the basket and pulled out the fish and threw them into a bucket. An octopus and a moray eel, along with an assortment of small, colorful fish were part of her catch. The eel was dangerous. Its razor-sharp teeth could bite off a finger. She grabbed it by the back of the head and crushed it with a hammer and threw it in the pail.

Giovannina set out for another trap. It was two hundred meters away, under the crystal clear waters of Ponza. Moon glow rippled across the waves and lit up the sea. Floating near her was a small, green, metal object. At first, she thought it might be debris from a sunken ship, like a kitchen pot or some utensil. She stared at it in the shadows of the hour before dawn. The object was directly in front of her boat. She was about to hit it. Suddenly, she realized it was a mine. She screamed. The young woman swiftly steered away from it and paddled as hard as possible. Giovannina watched as the bomb floated by, only inches from her boat. After ten minutes, she stopped to catch her breath and calm down. 'Fear is the gift God gives to cowards' she thought.'I must go on.'

Thirty minutes later, she reached the trap, pulled it up and filled another bucket. She caught ten kilos. She was delighted. The sun was rising. Golden sparks of light flew over the waves.

Out of the blue, she heard a motor. It was a plane. It was brown with bright white markings and a frightening red mouth with sharp teeth, which gave it the appearance of a soaring carnivore.

Courtesy, British War Museum

A British Flying Tiger was circling the island. The aviator was waiting for dawn to better survey the area. Giovannina jumped under the canvas and lay still. She listened. The engine was like the sound of a huge wasp droning and hissing through the wind. The sea vibrated and the boat rocked as the plane dove to inspect the craft. The gushing air from the propellers nearly lifted the cover from her. She held it tightly. The pilot looked for movement in the tiny vessel. He was instructed to fire upon anything that ventured from the coast. The aircraft flew over the boat three times. Each passing struck Giovannina with terror. Finally, it went off towards the mainland.

The noise was gone. Giovaninna's heart trembled as she peeked through the cover. Sweat ran down her brow. She was breathing heavily. She opened her canteen and swallowed some water and poured it over her face. All was clear. She grabbed the oars and rowed wildly.

By the time she reached the beach, it was bright daylight. As she climbed along the cliff towards home, a bell tolled in the church. Another victim of starvation was dead. Each day, people perished from famine. Initially it was the very young and the very old. Now, starvation struck anyone. For a year, the island was cut off from food from the mainland. There was nothing left to eat.

Finally, Giovannina made it to the top. She was exhausted. It was early morning. A mist was rising over the hills and valleys of Ponza. She looked about. It seemed calm. Carrying two heavy pails filled with fish, covered with seaweed, she turned on the road toward her house.

Not far from her destination, a German soldier with a Fascist officer appeared. She froze. "Stop!" commanded the Fascist. Giovannina knew him. He was an islander and a distant relative. The two men walked to her. They stood erect to show power and authority.

The soldier pointed his rifle at her. "What do you have there?" demanded the Fascist. Giovannina was terrified and indignant. She was angry. "I have fish for my family. My children and parents are starving. I will bring this to them. You will have to shoot to stop me," she voiced with determination. "Calm down," insisted the Fascist. "Let us take a look at your catch," he stated with a smile. They removed the seaweed and examined the pails. "Nice. You are good at fishing," he exclaimed. She realized what they wanted and the position she was in.

Giovannina removed a boot, took out two sheets of newspaper and placed a kilo of fish in one sheet for the Fascist and another for the German. "That's better," he remarked. "Now get out of here," he demanded. The two men watched her as she sped away. Giovannina was furious. At least she was alive and could finally feed her family.

When she got to the house, her uncle, Don Gabriele, pastor of Ponza, was there. "God bless you, child. What abundance you bring into this home," he said as he looked at her catch. "You are amazing. Only someone with your courage could do this," he stated with admiration. Giovannina emptied the buckets into the sink and cleaned the fish. Some would be boiled and eaten quickly. The rest fried and pickled with salt and vinegar so they could last for days.

"Uncle, what do you hear from the continent?" she asked. Don Gabriele had a clandestine radio and was in contact with the mainland. "The Allies are moving rapidly up the boot. They took Salerno and Naples and are coming in our direction," he explained. "The Americans are feeding millions, while the Nazis steal all we have," he said. The pastor sat down. He was worried. "I got word from Don Lorenzo at Castellonorato. It was a message in code brought to me by a Massimo, the Fascist. Don Lorenzo is protecting Jews but the Germans have discovered them. He wants to bring them here," said the priest. Don Gabriele was distraught. He sat down and put his face in his hands. Then he looked to the sky.

"God help us. Give us the courage to save your children," he begged, with anxiety in his voice.

CHAPTER 130 ━━━━━━━━━

LETTERS TO SOFIA & ANNA

$\mathbf{F}$or a year, Joe and Tom fought side-by-side with Italian freedom fighters as invisible men, unable to communicate with the outside world. Finally, thanks to the Fifth Army, they wrote home:

My sweet Sofia:

I am well. I could not write until now. Thank God, I am safe and healthy. I am in Italy. Tom and I are with our comrades in arms and are in good health and well taken care of.

I miss you, your warm embrace, hearing your voice, and looking into your beautiful eyes, and saying, "I love you" to you.

I spend my nights dreaming of you and our time together. I kiss your photo before I sleep and kiss it again when I wake.

I do not know when we will see each other again.

We are fighting to end this war. It is terrible. The people of Italy are suffering. The Nazis are brutal with "hair on their hearts," as our parents would say in Italian. No one is spared.

We will defeat them and stop the killing.

Tom and I were promoted and awarded medals for our effort in the Italian campaign. It is a long road ahead before we rest. Please tell our parents we are OK and all will be well.

Pray for me.

I love you,

Your Joe

Dearest Anna:

I am fine, thinking of you and home.

It was impossible to write for the last year.

If eternity is endless time, then it is what I felt in not hearing your voice, or reading your letters.

I cannot call but can send you this short note before the mail goes out today. Joe and I are at the front in Italy. We saw danger and death and will see more before the war ends. Do not worry. We will make it.

No matter what happens, your love and prayers keep me alive.

The weeks and months will pass, and I know we will be together again. It is God's will.

War changes people. I have changed. I appreciate things like a warm bath, Mamma's cooking, sunshine, fresh air and peace, and the vision of your face. Today, I tasted an apple for the first time in a year. I held it in my hand like a gift. I smelled it. It was scented of sweet fruit and tasted like something the gods enjoy. I will never again take for granted the simple things of life.

Most of all, I will nurture our love. You are my garden of flowers. I will always treat you with affection, respect, and dignity.

Anna, you are my love and my life.

Give Mamma and Papa a kiss for me.

I adore you, Tom

CHAPTER 131 ━━━━━━━━━━━━━

THE GESTAPO

A parade of fears marched through his mind. Don Lorenzo paced back and forth in his room. It was small, painted light grey, with a tiny bed, a cross, a little table, and no window. It seemed like a cage. He felt like an animal. He was terrified. He knelt and prayed: "Oh Lord, help me carry this burden! Give me strength, wisdom, and courage!" he pleaded. Sweat poured down his brow. Finally, he composed himself and went to the chapel. At mass, he mumbled his prayers. His hands shook. He dropped a host while giving communion.

'How can I tell them?' he pondered. For months, the Chosen People were at peace. The convent and monastery were safe havens. The community was secure, well fed, clothed, and protected.

But it altered in a heartbeat.

Someone told the Gestapo. For a few pieces of silver, the informer put at risk the lives of innocent men and women. There was no time to lose. Don Lorenzo went to Father Andrea. He explained the situation. "Oh my God! What will we do?" asked the head of the monastery.

"I have an idea," replied Don Lorenzo. He told the Abbot his plan. "But we must act quickly. My sources say the Nazis will hit us the day after tomorrow. We have to get everyone ready now," he said nervously. "I will gather the elders," stated Father Andrea. In less than an hour, five men sat at a table in the abbey dining room. Three middle-aged Jews and two priests were assembled to talk.

Two clay jugs with wine and water were next to a plate of freshly baked bread and slices of cheese and a bowl of apples. The three Jews worked in the garden and did odd jobs in the church and sacristy. Their hands were dark, swollen, and calloused. Before their escape from the Germans, they were successful merchants with thriving shops, elegant apartments in fashionable city centers, and homes in the mountains and by the sea.

Their children went to public schools. Their relatives were doctors, lawyers, and dentists. Some were members of the Fascist Party. Veterans fought first with Garibaldi to unify Italy, and then for the King in World War I. For centuries, the Jews were model citizens who were known for hard work, patriotism, and love of education and tranquility. Italy was their home. They knew nowhere else.

With the stroke of a pen, their lives changed. In 1938, Mussolini targeted the Jews as enemies of the State. Properties, money, and wealth were confiscated by the Fascists. What was left was the fight for survival. Now, even that was in danger.

"The Gestapo knows you are here," said Don Lorenzo. He shuddered as the words fell from his mouth. Deep lines of worry cut into his forehead and face. "At any moment they will raid us and take everyone," he told them. The three Jews turned pale. "We have a way out," said Father Andrea.

"The Americans will help us," he declared.

"If they get here in time," muttered Don Lorenzo.

CHAPTER 132 ▬▬▬▬▬▬▬▬

ANZIO

Plans for the invasion of Anzio were underway. It was named, "Operation Shingle."

"Our attack force will be 40,000 troops, supported by twenty-four destroyers, five cruisers, 60 other ships, 238 landing craft, and 5,000 vehicles. We expect to reach a level of 70,000 men aided by 500 big guns and 200 tanks before the Operation is over. The Germans will reposition tens of thousands of troops from the North to deal with the landings that will open the roads to Rome," explained the Captain to a team of officers in the Fifth Army headquarters in Salerno. Joe, Tom, and Lukas were in the meeting.

Courtesy, Seabream Yacht Club

The officer pointed to a maritime map of Italy. "From the Island of Ponza to Anzio is 41 nautical miles. We must install radar on the island to monitor traffic, organize communications, and integrate our forces," the Captain emphasized.

"The Germans have occupied Ponza and control the coast from Civitavecchia to Sorrento and from Corsica to Sardinia. The waters between the mainland and the island are infested with sharks, and they are crawling with Nazi and Fascist patrols. German subs and ships get supplies and fresh water from Ponza. The island is a vital lifeline for the Axis powers," he declared.

"The mission to Ponza needs volunteers. It will be extremely dangerous," he stated seriously. 'If they manage to reach the island, they will not return,' he thought.

CHAPTER 133 ━━━━━━━━━

EMMA AND SAMUELE

"Samuele, get more potatoes. Go into the cave," demanded Emma. Her husband obeyed. He went up the steep steps that cut across the center of Ponza. They were made of basalt and were the last public works of the Bourbon kings of Naples for the Island of Ponza. The stairs were constructed in mid-eighteenth century. Some said that nothing else was done on the island since then.

Samuele climbed a hill and reached an old, wooden door with boards picked up in the sea and held together with rusty nails. A large black chain and a lock protected the opening. He brought the dead bolt from America. It was heavy and needed a special key. It opened to another door made of thick timbers and protected with a bigger lock.

An opening was cut into the mountain to create a huge cave. Greeks and Romans used it for wine. Inside the grotto were scores of sacks filled with flour, fava beans, lentils, and baskets of potatoes, carrots, beets, and dried fish. Bushels of apples and pears lined the sides of the cavern. Dried, red-hot peppers hung from cords in the ceiling.

It was a secret place and sealed like a safe to protect it from the famished people of Ponza who would do anything to eat. Emma and Samuele hoarded the food before it became scarce, knowing the islanders would starve.

They were rich, kind, and generous. At the turn of the twentieth century, they went to America. Samuele worked on the railroad in West Virginia. He began as a laborer. In a few years he was a boss managing gangs of Italian immigrants laying tracks, maintaining the rails, and constructing stations from the south to the north of the United States.

Samuele was a clever entrepreneur. He bought an abandoned coal mine and reopened it. He sold coal to be used in trains and homes. He supplied both the materials for the railroad and the workers. Emma ran a boarding house. Fifty Italians lived with them. She fed and housed the men while Samuele provided jobs. In the span of a dozen years, they made a fortune.

In 1923, they returned to the island. Emma wore a mink coat when she landed. Inside the lining was sowed fifty thousand dollars in US bank notes. Three huge trunks had false bottoms, filled with American gold coins. Samuele and Emma were in their mid-forties, and they were wealthy enough to retire on the island.

He invested ten thousand dollars to create the first station on Ponza to generate electricity. By the mid-1920s, the island had light, while most of Italy was in the dark. The electricity generator gave power for water pumps and light for surgeons and shopkeepers.

As the war dragged on, Emma and Samuele opened a soup kitchen in their house to feed the multitude of starving families. It was in the historic center of the island, overlooking the port. Each day, dozens of people lined up to eat or or take cooked food home.

Samuele had land where he raised fruits and vegetables. He safeguarded the site with armed guards. What he did not cultivate, he bought on the black market including flour, olive oil, and cheese.

He hated the Germans. They were cruel criminals, but he had to deal with them. He bribed the commander of the Nazi forces so he could feed the community and conduct his own affairs. Boxes of lobsters and loaves of bread and cheese graced the tables of the German officers on Ponza, thanks to Samuele, who also slipped them small sacks of gold coins. The Germans supplied barrels of diesel fuel to run the power station.

Samuele and Emma were U.S. citizens and spoke perfect English.

They prayed for the Americans to arrive. They had no idea what they would have to face before their prayers were answered.

CHAPTER 134 ━━━━━━━━━━━

THE RESCUE PLAN

T he freedom fighters volunteered for the mission to Ponza. "Sir, we have a plan. We can save the Jews of Castellonorato and install radar on Ponza. We are in touch with the priest who hid the men, women, and children in a monastery and convent. In less than forty-eight hours, they will be arrested by the Nazis. We can bring them to Ponza and set up the equipment for the landing. The priest is from the island. He will be our guide to getting us there and protecting the families," declared Tom.

The three men described each element of their strategy to the Captain, who was with members of the RAF. "It is a daring scheme. It might work. A British officer and three communications specialists have also volunteered. They are radar experts," he said. They were introduced to a Flying Officer of the Royal Air Force, Radar and Signals Unit. He was tall, blond, tanned, and strong with broad shoulders.

His men were smaller in size, but each had calloused hands from working with metal, wires and coils. The British team were veterans of the North African campaign. They had seen action in the sand and on the sea, and they were part of the UK contingent in the Salerno landing.

The Englishmen immediately struck up a friendship with the Yanks and the Italian. They spoke of their children and families and showed photos of newly born babies and sweethearts. The Americans talked about home and Mamma's cooking and the loves they left behind.

Lukas listened to the conversation. He had little to say. His thoughts were with the thousands of Italians starving and suffering from the enemy onslaught. In his heart was anger and revenge.

He swore to himself he would make the Gestapo and Fascists pay for their crimes, or die trying.

Courtesy, WWII Museum

That same day, the freedom fighters and their UK colleagues went to the beach. They stopped to watch an unbelievable scene.

Courtesy, WWII Museum

Huge ships laden with cargo and men stretched from the break water into the fog of the horizon. One by one, they reached the shore to unload massive materials to wage war and destruction. Standing in the surf, soldiers formed human chains from the vessels to the beach, unloading freight from the mouths of immense, ironclad landing craft.

Courtesy, WWII Museum

Streaming in the distance were the titans of the oceans — enormous battleships, massive aircraft carriers, and mammoth support vessels.

Courtesy, HM Navy

From the middle of the sea, they fired colossal projectiles, filled with TNT, to bombard Italian hamlets occupied by Nazi forces.

'If I can see them, so can the Germans,' thought Lukas. The enormity of the vista swept away any doubt as to the outcome of the vicious conflicts ahead.

The sand was muddy and blackened with oil stains. Giant craters from enemy artillery lay across the beach. The dead and wounded had been removed. Footprints were the only signs that scores of men had very recently scrambled to save the living and carry away fallen companions. The stench of burning petrol from exhaust pipes and smoldering gunpowder hung in the air. Men seemed like thousands of insects crawling across the seaboard. It was an astonishing sight.

Troops organized equipment and goods to be transported from convoys to shore. The soldiers were exhausted, yet they pushed on to fulfill their mission. They traveled hundreds of miles over stormy seas to land on an Italian coast under the deadly guns of German artillery. Hundreds were killed instantly. Some drowned. Survivors were fighting the Nazis or securing the beachhead.

Courtesy, WWII Museum

They unloaded ships, moved vehicles, operated earth-moving equipment, and laid wire mesh over the sand to create embarkation areas for tanks, trucks, and artillery.

Joe, Tom, Lukas, and the Englishmen were struck by how young the soldiers were. Most still did not shave. Some had accents from the American South. Others sounded like they came from the Northeast of the U.S. Each was united to liberate Italy, win the war, and go home.

Joe listened to one G.I. His voice resonated a New York accent: "Where are you from, kid?" he asked. "Brooklyn. Ocean Parkway. My family is from Sicily, like nearly all the Italians in our neighborhood," he stated as he lifted a crate onto a truck. They shook hands. "From the Bronx," said Joe. "How old are you?" "Turned 18 last year and was drafted. My birthday is next week," responded the boy from Brooklyn. The young man had no facial hair. "Haven't seen any action yet," he said. "Our battalion moves out tonight. We go north to clean the Nazis out of the small towns on the way to Rome. When this is over, I am going to Sicily to find my family," he explained. Joe looked at him and waved goodbye. 'God, please help this boy make it to his birthday and make it home safely,' he prayed silently. Joe wondered how many kids like this one from Brooklyn would see their families again.

Courtesy, WWII Museum

The beach was littered with tons of supplies from the landing. Military green tanks of fuel with the U.S. Army insignia and endless crates of wooden boxes with ammunition and food supplies were scattered across the sand next to jeeps, armored cars, and earth-moving equipment, trucks, and grey, rectangular boats that carried the soldiers to liberate Salerno. The landing craft lay across the shore as far as the eye could see. Large white numbers were painted on them. Rust and sea grime covered the hulls.The six men inspected the vessels. Many were severely damaged. The boats were made of thick plywood ribs covered with wood and steel. Bottoms of some of the craft smashed on shoals, minutes before hitting the beach. Bullet holes peppered the bow of many. Others were shattered and splintered from German artillery. Some were blown apart and filled with blood stains.

Finally, they found one. It was in good condition. The motor worked well. They loaded the craft with fuel tanks, radar equipment, bombs, ammunition, explosives, firearms, food, and supplies. The boat was large enough to hold the civilians. It had a 250 horsepower diesel engine and could travel at 12 knots per hour at full capacity. It would take 9 hours to reach a beach close to Formia that would be near to Castellonorato.

The Captain looked at the group of freedom fighters and British technicians. "If you depart in uniforms and are captured, the Germans will treat you as prisoners of war. They shoot all prisoners. I suggest you go in civilian clothes just in case you have to mix in with your passengers to save yourselves. Of course, if discovered you will be considered spies and shot after they torture you. Take your uniforms. You will need them on the island. Good luck," he said somberly, thinking he would never see them again.

A PT boat would accompany the landing craft to the shore of Ponza. The Captain of the vessel had orders to engage the enemy up to the point of embarkation of the civilians.

After that, the patriots and their passengers were on their own.

Liberation

CHAPTER 135

EMMA & THE SICILIAN

$\mathbf{E}$mma was a leader. She symbolized the strength, wisdom, and courage of women. The island was a microcosm of the world, in her mind. It was a battlefield. Good against evil, and the rights of women against men, were encapsulated on this rock in the water. She felt men were often irrational, vulgar, and supremely ignorant.

She hated illiteracy, coercion, injustice, and tyranny. Most of all, she despised Fascism and Nazism. Both promoted the image of women as inferior. Their place was in the home, not in the world. Women were limited in what they could learn, do, and achieve. It was bondage. They had no rights, except those given by nature.

When she came from America, she brought crates of items that seemed from outer space. A piano, a telephone, clocks and watches, household utensils, a toaster, and a device with a magnifying glass to make images move like motion pictures. People would gawk and look at her drying and curling her hair with a machine that ran on electricity. They sat outside her home and listened to the radio and music she played on a record player.

Emma was a partisan without a weapon. Her arms were wisdom and the ability to secretly help those combating for liberty. She supplied the freedom fighters with food, clothing, and money. She schemed plots to bring down the Fascists.

Emma longed for the coming of the Americans.

She knew they would free Italy and free Ponza.

She studied up to the third grade, which was the standard of education in that era. But Emma was different. She was curious, inquisitive, intelligent, and a voracious reader.

As a young girl, she loved poetry and read the classics, recited Dante and Shakespeare, and hungered for books about geography and the world. Magazines and newspapers filled her house in America and her apartment on the island. She wrote splendid Italian and beautiful English, and she spoke both languages with articulation and care.

Courtesy, Wikipedia Commons

Her sister, Matilda, invited her to speak to the girls of the school. One hundred and sixty-five children assembled in a large classroom. The room was decorated with maps of the world. The flag of Italy was prominently displayed. On the left side of a crucifix was a photo of King Victor Emanuel III. He was without a hat or crown. On the right was an image of Mussolini wearing Fascist insignia. The face was proud, serious, and confident.

Courtesy, Istituto Luce and Italian National Archives

The children at the school were in white uniforms with blue collars. They were lively, lovely, and filled with energy and smiles.

All were enrolled in the Fascist movement. In the back of the room was a figure of Il Duce on horseback. The students learned the doctrine of the Party when they left the cradle and had to practice it in their daily lives.

They were taught to be the eyes and ears of Mussolini, and to defend the homeland by spying on their loved ones and reporting all to the Party.

Democracy and freedom, they were told, were the enemies of the people. It made them weak and passive.

As Emma entered, a short, dark man in the uniform of a Fascist officer stood in the back. He looked like a thin block of grey marble. He was erect, with eyes focused on the image of Il Duce. Emma knew him well. He was the head of the Party on the island. He was from Palermo. He was known as "The Sicilian." He was feared, despised, and revered. His face was eternally tanned, with sallow cheeks, black hair, a pencil thin mustache, large ears, thick eyebrows, and menacing eyes that seemed like bullets ready to be fired from a gun.

He never smiled.

The Sicilian hated Emma and her husband. He envied their position and power. He was frustrated. He could not control them. Emma and Samuele were the most famous couple on Ponza. He called them "The Americans." They were U.S. citizens and refused to join the Party. He once falsely accused them of listening to Radio London, which was prohibited.

They were wealthy, influential, and generous. Their family controlled the fishing fleet, the church, the municipality, and the schools. The teachers, doctors, lawyers, and notaries were members of their clan. They were untouchable.

The Sicilian considered them traitors.

The children rose when Emma and her sister entered the room. Matilda introduced her. Emma was elegant. She wore a grey suit with a gold pin, shaped and colored in the form of a peacock. She had a wrist-watch, purchased in a store on Fifth Avenue in New York. Her hair was pulled back in a bun to show her beautiful face, sculptured nose, and green eyes. Her complexion radiated health and vigor.

She was gorgeous and lady-like.

From a corner of the room, The Sicilian stared at her. Fire, hate, and anger were in his eyes.

Emma gazed at him, defiantly.

She looked at the girls and asked them a question: "Tell me, what is it that no one can take from you?" The children were confused by the question. Also, they were careful to speak. Someone in uniform was there. Anything said could be dangerous.

"It is education," said Emma. "No one can steal what you learn. No one can take your diploma or degree. It is yours forever. Learning will make you strong, independent, and free. Yes, someday you will be free to take on any role you wish," she insisted.

"What do you want to be when you grow up?" she asked the girls. A few would talk. They raised their hands. "I want to be a sea captain like my father," responded a pupil with curly, light brown hair and a lovely smile. "I want to be a doctor, like the one who saved my mother's life," replied another child. "When I grow up, I want to go to Rome and work in the government," remarked a student with black hair and long pigtails that hung from her shoulders.

'These dreams will never happen,' thought Emma as she peered at the beautiful faces filled with innocence. 'Each will conform to be what others want. They will not use the talents God gave them,' she said to herself.

"What would you like me to talk about?" she asked. One courageous child raised her hand. "Please tell us about America," she inquired. Emma weighed her words. The United States was an enemy of the regime.

"America is a big country. Many times the size of Italy. It is called 'The New World' because it is filled with opportunities. To be everything you want to be is not easy. But there, you have the right to try. Anyone can get a good education. Anyone is free to choose where they live and how they want to live. Anyone can choose who will govern them.

To succeed, people must study and work. Both things are available in America. Women work in all fields and can study. I learned to read, write, and speak English in a public school. I had a refrigerator, a washing machine, a Victrola to listen to music, a radio, and a curling iron for my hair, a telephone, and electric lights. I had nice clothes and good food because I worked, earned my own money, and was free to do so. It was because of education. Never forget how precious it is for you to be in school and to learn. God bless you," she said as she ended her remarks. The children gave polite applause.

Emma looked at The Sicilian. His face was filled with rage.

He took his thumb and ran it across his throat from left to right.

As Emma walked out, he whispered, "Someday, I will kill you."

CHAPTER 136 ━━━━━━━

FRANCESCA'S RESILIENCE

Her wounds ached. The bleeding had just stopped. Scars from the bullets that pierced her body looked like third degree burns. She disregarded the pain in her shoulder and leg. Francesca had a job to do.

After fighting alongside Colonel Lukas, she joined a new brigade of partisans. They moved to the south, near Naples, and attacked the Germans relentlessly. Many patriots died and were hurt in fighting, but she was spared for a higher mission. Her skills as a doctor and linguist were important and vital to the cause of liberation.

Courtesy, US Air Force and Wikipedia Commons

The team lived in an abandoned farm. It was in a basin at the foot of Mt. Vesuvius. There were no roads. Only mule trails could reach the area. Smoke, dust, and the smell of gas tinged the morning air. Francesca walked out of the barn under the shadow of the world's most dangerous volcano.

Each day the sky grew dimmer with grey and black clouds and ashes that seemed to naturally rain on the villages in the valleys surrounding the mountain. The earth was dark and stony, with layers of volcanic ash deposited over centuries onto the soil. It was rich and fertile and produced wonderful grapes and wine.

Francesca gazed at the sky. She heard the roar of engines mixed in with bursts of short, volcanic eruptions. She watched as American warplanes flew over and around the spewing smoke from the center of the peak. The aircraft looked like giant moths fascinated by the dark and deadly flames rising from the bowels of the earth.

Spellbound, they circled the ridges and dipped in close to the dome to photo the emerging magma. It was red, black, and boiling. The pilots were mesmerized. The spectacle was fascinating, poisonous, and deadly. Once they awoke from their trance, they resumed their mission to drop lethal explosives on the Nazi occupied towns in Campania.

The inhabitants who lived on the farm near Vesuvius died under Allied bombings. No signs of life could be found. Animals were slaughtered and crops harvested before they ripened. In the barn, Francesca set aside a corner for a makeshift hospital, where she nursed the wounds of her comrades.

It was carpeted with decaying hay and smelled of dried horse and cow manure. Rusted tools hung on the walls. Wheels from abandoned tractors lay in and about the shelter. The roof leaked and brown bats flew from the attic at night, hunting for insects in the dark. The men slept on the dirt floor with only coats to keep them warm. Francesca had a blanket and a cover. Washing and bathing was out of the question.

No medication, sedatives or pain-killing drugs were available. Bandages were torn from old linens donated by women and men committed to the cause. Wounds were cauterized with red hot irons to disinfect them. Scars from the burns lasted forever, as did the memory of the pain. If the injuries were not treated immediately, the patients would die of infection. Her equipment was a set of surgical instruments and some salt.

Francesca carefully wrapped the bandage around the torso of a soldier. He had been shot with a small caliber rifle. The bullet stuck in a rib after tearing several arteries and veins. She removed a long, small piece of lead from the bone, stopped the bleeding, and disinfected the cut with a mixture of salt and water. He was lucky. She saved his life. He would survive.

"Thank you. But why did you do it?" he asked. Francesca understood and spoke German. She looked at him. "I expect you would do the same for me," she responded coldly, as she got up from her patient's side. He stared at her, knowing well that under the same circumstances, she would have been executed instead of healed. The compassion of this young woman moved him.

He was a German officer. He was captured by the partisans when they attacked a convoy of two trucks carrying troops. All but two of the enemy combatants were killed in the fighting. He and a driver were the only survivors. His name was Hans, he came from Bavaria, and he was thirty-three. He grew up as a "Hitler Youth" and was told he was part of the Master Race destined to rule the world. Now, he and thousands of other German soldiers were humiliated by defeat and the devastation of the Allied advance.

The Master Race was no more. He realized the fallacy of Nazism. He hoped to live long enough to make amends for his sins and those of his people. His humanity had been sparked in his soul by the medical care he received.

The other German was an eighteen-year-old private who drove one truck. He miraculously escaped injury in the ambush.

The partisans planned to question the Germans. After getting what they needed, they would take them into the forest, have them dig graves, and shoot them. The Nazis and Fascists showed no pity for those who resisted them. Partisans and patriots were summarily executed. They would do the same.

Francesca did not agree.

She argued vehemently with her comrades. "We have to stop the killing. We cannot be like them. We are struggling for a new world. It must replace this one with civility, compassion, and democracy. If we treat our enemies like the Fascists and Nazis treat us, we cannot claim a higher ground based on honesty, ethics, and freedom," she insisted. "What example will we give those who rule Italy after the war? What message do we represent to the next generation?" she said with passion in her voice.

Francesca read from a pamphlet. It was U.S. propaganda, translated into Italian and dropped by the thousands across the country. It was about establishing a republic with fair elections, political parties, and a free press. The United States promised to rebuild Italy and give it liberty, after the defeat of the enemy.

In the booklet was the story of an American patriot. His name was Patrick Henry. He gave a speech a year before the thirteen colonies declared independence from Britain. It was March 23rd, 1775, at a convention in St. John's Church in Richmond, Virginia. They debated whether to resist the growing cruelty and tyranny of the Crown. Francesca read a passage from the pamphlet to her comrades:

> As he spoke, Henry held his wrists together as though they were manacled and raised them toward the heavens. "Forbid it, Almighty God! I know not what course others may take; but as for me, give me liberty" – Henry burst from his imaginary chains and grasped an ivory letter opener – "or give me death!" As he uttered these final words, he plunged the letter opener toward his chest, mimicking a knife blow to the heart.

The men were speechless. "In addition to everything else, I need them and the two trucks," exclaimed Francesca. She received a message from Colonel Lukas to join the partisan team in Castellonorato. She did not know the details, but agreed. She would do anything to fight the Nazis and end the war.

"All right," said the head of the brigade. "We will turn them over to you and Paolo for your mission. Be careful. They will stab you in the back.

Nazis and Fascists can never be trusted. The only good ones are dead ones," he said, with darkness in his voice.

CHAPTER 137

RUTH AND SARAH

"Mamma, why do we have to leave," asked Sarah? "I love it here. We are happy. My classmates are my friends, and the nuns are gentle and kind," she said, crying. Ruth could not explain the situation to her ten year old. How could she describe the terror of being arrested, persecuted, and murdered because they were Jews?

"We have no choice, my dear," she said, sadly. "The Germans will come and take us to a concentration camp and kill us. I cannot tell you why they hate us and want to hurt us so much. All I know is that we must go before it is too late," she explained.

Endless thoughts and fears ran through her mind. It was not enough for them to have lost all they had. Homes, clothes, wealth, possessions, heirlooms, and traditions, all vanished. Worst of all were stolen memories and hope. Family, friends, the past and future evaporated the instant they were forced to escape and leave a lifetime behind. Life now was a silent, slow motion film that was, in reality, a nightmare of dread.

Her anchor was her little girl, her husband, and faith in humanity. She believed in the brave people who rescued them. False identity papers, lessons in Catholiscm, baptisms, and sacraments were shields to protect from the Nazis. Robbed of their identity, names and way of life was the price for survival. Ruth and other Jewish families prepared for another escape, filled with pain, boredom, and torment.

Don Lorenzo explained the plan to Sister Cristina and Father Andrea. The Mother Superior and the Abbot were incredulous. Partisans, Americans, fleeing across the sea to an island seemed like science fiction. The only reality was danger. The Nazis were on their way. Families were allowed a small sack with underwear. Children could take a toy.

By midnight, they were ready. The Jews huddled together in the dining room of the monastery. As soon as the sun disappeared, the women and children left the convent to join their men and boys. For fleeting moments, families were reunited and given a chance to express love.

Don Lorenzo took his watch from his pocket. They were late. "Where are they?" he thought. Another hour passed. The trucks should have been here by now. Informers told him the Gestapo would attack at 4 AM. 'Three hours, we have time,' he said to himself. 'No, we do not. What if they lied? The Nazis could come any second,' the priest considered. 'Show no fear or everyone will be frightened,' he reasoned.

Suddenly, noises echoed outside the monastery. Motors, wheels, skidding, and stopping. "Who is it?" fretted Don Lorenzo.

He gazed from the window and saw a horrible sight. Eagles and swastikas.

"The Gestapo."

Don Lorenzo fainted.

Courtesy, German Army Archives

CHAPTER 138

ESCAPE FROM CASTELONORATO

It was past eleven when they started the trip. They were late. It was a struggle to find petrol for the vehicles. She got into one of the two German troop trucks and began the journey to the small town overlooking the port of Formia. The German lieutenant was her driver. Paolo and the other German soldier were in the other truck. Francesca and Paolo fought alongside Lukas and the Americans and gave their blood for a cause they felt was bigger than themselves. Now they faced almost certain death or almost certain salvation.

Francesca reflected. Her twenty-ninth birthday was next month. She felt sixty. Age accelerated inside and outside of her as she suffered the stress and anxiety of fighting for the liberation of her land. She was older. Lines in her face and strands of grey hair were proof. Her blondish brown curls were disheveled and her eyes were bloodshot from weeks of little sleep.

She wondered if she would reach a third decade of life. At times, she felt she had lived enough. The horror of war weighed on her soul. Yet she was optimistic. She had dreams. She believed in a better world and would die for it. She felt people were good, including her enemies.

Before embarking on her mission to Castellonorato, she talked to the German officer and soldier. "I need your help to save the lives of innocent people. They are Jews. I am not asking you to betray Germany. I am asking you to be a human being. If you help me, I promise to turn you over to the Allies, who will treat you well," she explained.

"How do we know the Allies will listen to you?" asked the officer. "Two members of American intelligence will lead the mission. They swear to give you letters of introduction to the Fifth Army. Once I hand over the civilians to them, I will accompany you to headquarters and will personally vouch for you," Francesca said with conviction.

The men thought: 'Germany was losing the war, and it was just a matter of time. We have seen the atrocities of our own Nazis and are appalled. Our sacrificing for the Fatherland should not include murdering babies.' The German Lieutenant said, "We will join you but will not kill our countrymen." "If all goes as expected and you do your part, there should be no bloodshed," answered Francesca in a positive manner.

It was a hope and a prayer.

CHAPTER 139

RAFFAELE

Samuele banged on the door of the rectory. Don Gabriele was sound asleep. He dreamed of his time as a medic in World War I on the Austrian front. It was a nightmare. The echoes of guns and explosions sent beads of perspiration down his face. He was restless. The noise of banging on his door seemed like shots from a rifle. He leaped from his bed. The priest stumbled over his nightgown and took off his nightcap. It was cold. He rubbed his eyes and opened the door.

"The Americans left Salerno an hour ago," said Samuele, excitedly. Don Gabriele lit up. "They land on Vindicio Beach at dawn. Two trucks will pick up the people and go to the coast. We have enough food in the cave to feed them for a month. The doctor promises to take care of the pregnant women and anyone who is sick. Raffaele and Emilia will keep us supplied with all the vegetables and dried fruit we need. They have a cow and two goats for milk for the children," explained Samuele.

"Good," said Don Gabriele. "Come in and let's put on some coffee," said the priest. He was anxious. Emma was Don Gabriele's older sister. They were close. Samuele and Emma made an interesting couple. She was down to earth and practical. Samuele was a handsome, good-hearted dreamer and ladies' man, and he enjoyed his wine. Generosity and altruism kept them together. They loved people. They were childless, but thought of adopting. Italy was filled with millions of orphans.

Raffaele was a cousin. He lived on the rural side of Ponza. He was nicknamed King of the Plains. He had the most land, and much of it was flat and good for raising corn and grain. He worked in America for a quarter of a century. His gardens had irrigation systems from the New World.

He had generators that were made in New York, and they produced electricity to pump water and to provide illumination and energy to run motors. His wife, Emilia, was tough and fearless and willing to help others in need. Of their three children, two were in America. Raffaele was a proud U.S. citizen. He spoke good English.

But he and his wife knew the risks involved in helping rescue these unfortunate people.

If discovered, they would be hung.

CHAPTER 140 ▬▬▬▬▬▬▬▬▬▬▬

ENCOUNTER ON THE HIGH SEAS

Piloting the landing craft was difficult. Tom could not control the rudder. The boat was not made for choppy waters. It was flat-bottomed and bounced like a cork in the sea. The engine was strong enough to propel it forward. It was a slow, agonizing trip. Joe and Tom barely kept up with the PT boat. Lukas and the Englishmen rested like tranquil passengers.

The vessel led them through a circular route beyond the range of German coastal cannons. It was dark. Only a half moon provided light. The salt spray from the sea was cold. The team shivered from chill. In the distance were Allied convoys steaming toward the southern Italian coast. Tom and Joe felt safe.

An hour into the journey, matters changed. An enemy patrol vessel burst from the shore with glaring spotlights. It aimed directly for the landing craft. The Captain of the PT boat saw it. He made a right full rudder. He crossed in front of Joe and Tom's boat. The waves covered the bow and doused the men.

As soon as the German cruiser was in range, the Captain of the PT attacked with a thirty-seven millimeter cannon and two twenty millimeter guns. The volleys missed the German ship, which turned and zigzagged to avoid being hit. It aimed at the PT boat. Two shells splashed in front of the landing craft and exploded. Joe and Tom felt the sea lift them high into the air. Their boat hit the water like falling from a tall building. Joe felt a sharp pain in his back as he was thrown from one side of the boat to the other.

The German ship was coming to ram the landing craft. It was a minute away from slicing into it when a huge explosion stopped it.

The PT boat fired its heavy guns just as the Nazi ship turned broadside.

The shells penetrated the center of the vessel.

The magazine was hit.

It ignited a store of torpedoes.

The ship burst into an enormous ball of smoke and flames. The eruption in the bowels of the vessel blasted it open, detonated the fuel tanks, and touched off an inferno. It sank in seconds. The Captain and crew of the U.S. Navy ship watched from the bow as the German vessel disintegrated and disappeared.

A seaman made the sign of the cross and prayed for the souls of his enemies.

The freedom fighters felt the heat of the flames as they rapidly steered away from the blazing wreckage and the fire burning on the surface of the water.

The American boat searched for survivors.

There were none.

CHAPTER 141 ━━━━━━━━━━━━━━━━━━━━━━

FRANCESCA & THE GERMAN LIEUTENANT

Francesca held her Beretta tightly. It was in her left trouser pocket. She believed the German Lieutenant's promise, but she was not taking any chances. She trusted no one. Sometimes not even herself. The slightest sense of betrayal, and she would shoot him. She was in an enemy vehicle, sitting next to a German officer.

The scene was frightening, surreal, and astonishing.

Courtesy, Wikipedia Commons and US Air Force Archives

From Nola, near Naples, they turned their trucks north by northwest and took the road along the coast to Formia. It was a path of unbelievable destruction. After the liberation of Naples in September 1943, the Nazis regrouped and occupied nearly every town in the region of Campania.

For each German killed by the resistance, the Nazis took vengeance by executing ten to one hundred Italians.

Courtesy, Wikimedia Commons and the Archives of the Royal Air Force

To rid the territory of the enemy, the Allies carpet-bombed the area, wiping out entire villages, ports, roads, and bridges.

Francesca felt sick and scared, but could not show it. She sensed she was teetering over a deadly chasm. On one side were the Nazis fighting to keep control of Italian soil, while on the other side were the Americans and British feverishly destroying everything in their path to eradicate any trace of German rule.

At any moment, she sensed she could be killed by the Allies for being a suspected collaborator or tortured and executed by the Nazis for being a spy.

The three-hour trip to Castellonorato was anguish for Francesca.

On the outskirts of Formia, they ran into a German roadblock. An armored car, a jeep, and two motorcycles controlled all movement in and around the district. Francesca steeled herself. Her muscles tightened in her arms and legs.

"Halt!" yelled a soldier. He was dressed in a crisp green uniform with a helmet, boots, and a rifle. The two trucks stopped. Francesca froze. The Lieutenant showed his identification. Francesca listened carefully to what he said to the soldier. "We have orders to reach Castellonorato tonight. The Italians are translators and members of the Fascist Party." He gave the guard Francesca's and Paolo's false documents.

The soldier looked closely at her. He walked over to Paolo's truck. He stared at him. Paolo avoided eye contact. The German thought for a moment. He recognized that face.

"Get out," he ordered. Francesca hid her pistol under the seat as she opened the door of the truck. Another soldier came. He frisked her first. No incivility was involved. The fact she was a woman made no difference as he moved his hands in all directions over her body. She felt naked and defenseless. The same was done to Paolo.

The guard wanted to call the command post at Castellonorato to verify the story. It was 3 AM. Waking an officer at that hour was risky. Everything checked out, even if he suspected he knew Paolo from somewhere. Paolo's face was on a Gestapo poster. He was suspected of being a partisan.

A bounty was on his head.

The guard miraculously waved them through. The journey continued.

They were sixty long minutes from the monastery.

CHAPTER 142

THE ROSARIES

Sister Cristina held a child in her arms. Sister Chiara hugged one mother after another. The two nuns and the staff of the convent and the monastery bid farewell to the Chosen People that God sent them to shelter. Clothes for the children were knitted by the nuns to warm them on their journey over the sea. Small bags of food and toiletries were given.

Sister Cristina gave the adults and older children special gifts. "These rosaries were made from scented wood. They will protect you. When the war is over, return to us. This will always be your home," she said. Tears poured down her cheeks. She was barely able to speak.

As they gathered to leave, Don Lorenzo became frightened. Two trucks with Nazi insignias arrived. He did not know what to do. He was speechless.

Francesca took out her pistol and jumped from her vehicle. "Paolo, keep your eye on them," she said, referring to the Germans. She ran to the door of the monastery. She knocked forcefully. Don Lorenzo slowly opened. He peered at the young lady, who seemed like a little girl in men's clothing. He was weak with shock.

"I am Francesca. We are here to take everyone to the beach. We need to leave immediately," she insisted. Two soldiers in German uniforms descended from the trucks. The priest looked at Francesca. He was gripped with fear. He pointed at the men. "There is no time to explain. We must get everyone out now," she demanded.

Don Lorenzo waved to the families to march out and get into the vehicles. Suddenly, the adults stopped. "German trucks," exclaimed an elderly man. "You are safe," insisted Francesca. "I am an Italian patriot. We seized them from the Germans. The soldiers with us are aiding us in your escape. Trust me, all will be well," she explained.

They had no choice.

Don Lorenzo lifted himself into the back of the truck.
Everyone followed.

Minutes later they were racing down the hill towards the beach.

CHAPTER 143 ━━━━━━━━━━

THE LIFE LINE

"Tie it to the ring," commanded the seaman to Joe. He obeyed and tightly fastened the cord to the front of the boat. Joe finally understood why he spent hours in OSS training learning how to knot ropes. A long, thick line stretched from the landing craft to the rear of the PT boat. The Captain insisted they tow the vessel to the beach to avoid more enemy attacks. "I cannot risk the safety of my men for this mission," he asserted.

The landing craft jumped as the PT boat pulled it abruptly. The Captain increased speed until they passed thirty knots. Joe and Tom, Lukas, and their English comrades were soaked as water washed over and into their ship. They shut off the engine to conserve fuel. The craft bounced over the waves at high speed. It trembled. Tom was afraid it might crack the keel or damage the hull. The boat was taking in water. The men took turns to bail it out.

Courtesy, Ponza Racconta and Lazio Tourism Authority

The sea grew deeper and farther from the coast as their boat moved faster.

The moon was full.

It looked like a bright balloon hanging in the sky, guiding them to destiny. The men fixed their eyes on the ball of light. They could almost touch it. The water sparkled with tones of silver and gold. High shadows appeared in the distance. Land. Twinkling lights emerged from the shore. Fifty miles to go.

Courtesy, Lazio Tourist Office

The coast grew closer. In the distance they saw the silhouette of an ancient tower standing on a peak to protect the shore. Light seemed to emerge from it and bath the water with a white glow.

The Captain of the PT boat had a nautical map of Italy. Vindicio beach was the landing point. Thirty miles more.

The Navy ship accelerated and then stopped abruptly, ten miles from the beach. The Captain flashed a light to salute the freedom fighters. He gave orders to drop the line.

The umbilical cord was severed.

Protection gone.

Their Guardian Angel vanished in a torrent of surf.

Tom started the engine.

He turned toward the coast.

Courtesy, Ponza Racconta

Suddenly, the moon dimmed. Clouds rushed in from nowhere and blanketed the sky. Winds grew. The boat seemed to be picked up, pushed and pulled by invisible hands. A blast lit the night and shook the men to their heels. Lightning and thunder flashed along the shore. Droplets of rain poured on the travelers. The sea grew stronger. Waves rose to a menacing height.

Five miles to go.

'Now what?' said Tom to himself as he steered the vessel over rolling breakers that increased in size and strength by the second. More bolts of lightning and crackling rumbles of thunder covered the coast with an ominous radiance.

The men looked at their captain as he valiantly steered. His right arm and elbow ached from managing the rudder. More water flowed into the boat. White caps surged higher and brightened the black sea as rays of lightning flared across them. The boat bounced violently in and out of the surging waves.

Tom lost control. 'We will not make it,' he thought.

He heard the ribs of the boat groan as the sea pummeled the fragile vessel. It could snap at any second.

Tom's fears grew.

The engine stalled.

It stopped.

CHAPTER 144 ━━━━━━━━━━━━━━━━━━━━

NAZI PURSUIT

The odor of the exhaust fumes from Francesca and Paolo's trucks was in the air of the monastery courtyard when the Nazis arrived. Rubber skid marks were still warm.

Three large German vans, two jeeps, and an armored car stopped abruptly in front of the cloister. A tall, muscular soldier banged on the main door. "Open up!" he shouted.

Father Andrea was expecting them. He made the sign of the cross. He took his time to leave his room and walked slowly down the stairs, crossed the garden, and unlocked the portal.

The Nazis rushed into the courtyard with their vehicles. Eight warriors charged into the buildings, kicking open doors with rifle butts. They screamed for everyone to get out of bed. The students, teachers, workers, monks, and nuns descended into the center of the abbey. It was four AM.

The Gestapo officer was in his best black uniform. He wore a monocle, leather gloves, highly shined boots, and medals from the Fuhrer in recognition of his efforts to rid the Reich of its enemies. The decorations were symbols of evil to the nuns and monks who stared at him as they opened the doors to their sanctuary.

On his last visit, the Nazi recorded the names and identification numbers of children and adults suspected of being Jews. Preparations were made for the arrest and transfer of them all and their protectors to Auschwitz. The German soldiers searched the buildings and grounds. There was no sign of those they were looking for.

"Where are they?!" yelled the Gestapo chief. Sister Cristina and Father Andrea were silent. A soldier ran up to the SS officer. He saluted, "Heil Hitler! Sir, two trucks just left here filled with civilians. They are heading for the coast," he exclaimed. The Nazi leader turned crimson with rage. His monocle fell from his eye.

He raised his right hand and made a fist. He waved it at Sister Cristina and Father Andrea. "You will pay for this! I promise you!" he threatened, clenching his teeth.

"After them!" he ordered. The Germans leaped into their vehicles, stormed out of the courtyard, and raced down the hills at top speed in pursuit of Francesca and Paolo.

It was raining. The roads were poorly paved and slippery. "Go faster!" ordered Francesca to the German lieutenant. "The road is wet and my night vision is poor," he responded. Francesca looked at her watch. The rendezvous on the beach was in thirty-three minutes, if all went well. At the speed they were going, it would take an hour. She did not realize the Gestapo was in hot pursuit and only minutes away from reaching them.

She took out her pistol and put the gun next to the German's temple. "I said to go faster, and *I mean it*," she stated with determination. She cocked the trigger. The lieutenant pressed the accelerator.

He doubled the speed.

The passengers were jolted with fear as the truck made sharp turns, nearly falling off the edge of the cliffs surrounding the motorway.

Children cried.

After they maneuvered the last steep curve, Francesca saw the coast. She heard the sea howling and watched it glimmer as bolts of lightning and thunder shattered the night air.

She worried. 'Can the boat make it in this weather? How can I protect these people? Will the Nazis capture us? Is this our last day of life?' she asked herself.

CHAPTER 145 ━━━━━━━━━━━━━━━━

PERILOUS VOYAGE

Rain pelted the craft. The wind raised it up and slammed it deep into the surf. The men felt they were in a Jack in the Box. Tom struggled to turn on the motor. He pulled and pushed the choke. He tried several times, and nothing happened. On the sixth attempt, the engine roared. He pressed the gear forward and went into top speed.

He prayed, "God, please get us to the beach safely and on time."

A delay was certain death.

He looked at his watch as the downpour drenched his helmet, face, and hands and seeped into his clothes. He was cold. Fifty minutes to landing. They were late.

Suddenly, the wind changed. Tom felt a gust shove the stern. The craft moved forward faster. It sailed over the waves. It seemed to glide. He turned the rudder a hard right toward the shore. Sea gulls flew over the ship.

They were not far from land. Then something extraordinary happened. The lightning and rain stopped. The sea calmed like a lake, while puffs of air pushed the boat.

Tom smiled at his comrades. They would make it.

Courtesy, Wikipedia Commons

Fog descended on the sea. It started near the vessel and, like three vast arms, spread from the water to the coast as the first hints of daylight twinkled in the sky. The men in the boat could not believe their eyes. Visibility was enough to see land, yet the mist was a heavenly shield. Dawn was hours away, but a luminous path of light led the freedom fighters to the coast.

It was miraculous.

The sand on the beach was beige and yellow. It seemed like a soft bed waiting for them to rest as the craft gently landed on the shore.

"Joe, make sure the machine gun has ammunition. Load all rifles and pistols. Get grenades ready," he ordered.

CHAPTER 146 ━━━━━━━━━━━━━━━━━━━

DANGEROUS DETOUR

Francesca was desperate. She looked in the rearview mirror beyond Paolo's truck. In the distance, she saw flashing lights. A convoy of Nazi vehicles was following at high speed. They were three miles away and gaining on them. She was too nervous to pray or think.

Unexpectedly, a tractor, pulling bales of hay cut into the road, two hundred meters in front. The German slammed on the breaks. Francesca jumped out. She drew her gun and raced to the vehicle. The driver was an old man. He wore a cap, had a white beard and a black coat.

He took off his hat when he saw Francesca. He nodded as she spoke. She was agitated. She pointed, moved her hands, and told the farmer what to do. She hugged him and ran back to the truck.

"Get moving," she commanded. The lieutenant drove past the farm vehicles. Paolo did the same.

The beach was twenty minutes away.

The Nazis accelerated. They found the trucks. It was a matter of minutes before they overtook the partisans and the Jews. The German convoy descended the last hill.

They saw the vehicles approach the beach.

The farmer looked in the distance.

The Nazis were racing toward him.

Calmly, he turned the tractor and parked it across the road.

He drew a long metal hook from the cart and pulled the bales of hay off.

They tumbled along the motorway.

He went to the tractor and opened the hood.

He removed the distributor cap.

The old man made the sign of the cross, said a prayer, and vanished into the forest.

CHAPTER 147 ━━━━━━━━━━━━━━━━━━━

HITTING THE BEACH

The team jumped into the water and waded to the shore.

The two trucks stopped just above the dunes overlooking the beach.

Tom and Joe opened the bow of the vessel. Francesca and Paolo helped everyone carefully get off the vehicles. They led them to the boat. Don Lorenzo was in a daze. He got into the craft and sat down.

Tom poured gallons of fuel into the motor while his comrades loaded the families onto the boat. In minutes, the vessel was packed. "Get in," Joe said to Francesca. She had no choice. She, Paolo, and the Germans got on board. Joe and Lukas sealed the bow.

Tom started the engine. A stream of black smoke surged from the exhaust.

The craft was dangerously overloaded. Fifty people were huddled in a vessel built for forty. Tom put the gears into reverse.

The boat did not move.

It was stuck on the sand.

Joe, Lukas, and the Brits leaped off. The five men pushed the vessel with all their strength while Tom shifted the engine to its highest speed.

The boat nudged. They pushed harder. It moved into the water and sailed.

The five patriots struggled to get into the ship. The male passengers grabbed their arms and helped pull them aboard.

They it made seconds before the vessel reached deep water.

Tom turned the craft toward Ponza.

The fog was dense and seemed impenetrable.

The boat maneuvered into the mist.

CHAPTER 148 ■■■■■■■■■■■■■■■■■■■■■■■■■■■■

THE MIRACLE

The SS Captain was the first to see the blockade. He held on to the dashboard. "Stop or we will crash!" he yelled to his driver. The jeep slammed into the bales of hay, twisted abruptly, and landed on the side of the road overlooking the gorge. One truck smashed the tractor and pushed it over the cliff. The second one collided with the cart. The other vehicles stopped just short of a collision.

Little damage was done, but time was lost.

The Gestapo officer was startled, furious, but resolute. He was unwavering. He brushed the straw from his uniform and hat, and got out of the car. He pointed to the debris. "Get it off the road immediately!" he ordered the soldiers. In minutes, the motorway was clear.

The mad race continued.

The convoy crossed the coastal highway and sped to the shore. The beach was ahead. The SS Captain saw the trucks. He was delighted. 'Now we have them,' he thought. The caravan stopped on the dunes near the vehicles. The troops leaped onto the sand and cocked the triggers of their machine guns. The officer ran ahead. He pulled out his Luger.

The two German trucks were parked above the shore.

They were empty.

The soldiers searched the area.

The Nazi stared at the sea. His lips and mouth twisted in frustration.

He saw the ship. It was out of range of his weapons.

The vessel filled with Jews was sailing toward the horizon.

He held his gun at his side.

He watched the boat fade into the fog.

CHAPTER 149

SHARKS AND FASCISTS

As they left the shore, they saw the masts of ships sunk in the shallow water. Each was a story of war. Boxes, bottles, shoes, hats, and clothes floated as symbols of lives lost and dreams denied. No one spoke as they watched the wreckage pass and disappear.

The children snuggled close to their parents. The boat was crowded. There was no space between people. Everyone was huddled together as if they were one person on a journey of life or death.

Two hours into the trip and all was calm. The sea was silent. The sun rose like a friend, bringing warmth to the passengers and crew. The fog evaporated. The silhouette of the Pontine Islands and Ponza lay ahead. The air smelled rich with scents of salt and algae. The water was turquoise and light green.

A sound surfaced. It echoed over the waves. A ship engine. Tom recalled the words of the Captain: "The waters between the mainland and the island are infested with sharks and crawling with Nazi and Fascist patrols." He alerted his comrades. Joe pulled out his binoculars. He searched the sea for three hundred and sixty degrees. Two miles south, a trail of smoke blackened the sky. A patrol boat was steaming in their direction.

The men knew what to do. Rifles, machine guns, and grenades were prepared. Tom turned to Francesca. "Tell them a vessel is sailing toward us. Everyone must put their heads down and stay under the edge of the boat." Francesca explained what was happening. Alarm, fear, and crying was heard in voices and whispers.

Don Lorenzo made the sign of the cross and prayed for these souls he was protecting.

"God be merciful," he prayed out loud, fervently.

"Spare us and deliver us all from evil."

Courtesy, of the Naval Archives of Italy

The ship rushed toward the craft. It was one hundred meters away. Four men were on board, flanked by torpedoes, machine guns, and heavy artillery. The freedom fighters took aim.

Flying from the boat were two flags: the Fascist banner and the Swastika:

CHAPTER 150 ━━━━━━━━━━

ARRIVAL

Beach of Chiaia di Luna, Ponza, Courtesy, Ponza Racconta

Don Gabriele went first. He entered the tunnel leading to Chiaia di Luna. He carried an oil lantern. Emma, Samuele, Raffaele, and Emilia followed. He wore his priestly tunic, collar, and a round hat. He was dressed in black, as were the others. Nearly everyone on the island was in mourning. Families faced death from conflict or famine.

Don Gabriele recalled the Great War. In World War I, he was a medic and chaplain. He saved lives and souls. He had assumed a struggle so bitter, senseless, and terrible could never happen again. It was the "war to end wars." It was not. It was the war that started another war.

Incredible pain did not end arrogance and pride. The desire to dominate, profit from, and control others was greater than man's hunger for peace. Love, altruism, reason, education, freedom, and the search for harmony were the solution. It demanded courage, good sense, and a commitment to peace. Perhaps his world was an illusion, Don Gabriele said to himself. 'It was better to fight for a heaven on earth than just wait to reach it in the next world,' he thought as he walked through the tunnel.

Courtesy, Ponza Racconta and Fragmenti di Ponza

The passageway was two thousand years old. The Romans built it to move people and cargo to the harbor on the other side of the island. Winds determined which haven was used. When it was impossible to reach the main port because of the weather, they could land on Chiaia di Luna.

The walls were chiseled out of stone and lined with bricks in a pattern that looked like the spine of a fish. Holes were carved to carry light and air into the tunnel. It was an example of the genius of the ancient world.

As they set foot on the beach, the islanders marveled at its splendor. It truly looked different, spectacular, enchanting, and magnificent.

The rising sun was sweeping away shadows of darkness that covered the grey, yellow, and white hues of the rock surrounding the sand. A perfect semicircular cove emerged with crystal clear water bathing a shoreline of fine pebbles and seaweed. Light glistened from the sea and sent rays from the sun to unite the coast with the wall of colored stone.

It was a panorama of beauty only God could create with his eternally mystical mind. For centuries, travelers had sat on the beach in awe, watching the tides rise and fall in a hypnotic voyage across time and space.

Don Gabriele and his party rested and waited.

"They should have been here by now," exclaimed the priest. He was worried. "Someone may see us if we linger," he said. "Let's hide in my cave," replied Samuele. He unlocked a door that opened to a huge cavern. Samuele's grandfather used dynamite to open the mountain and create a shelter for his fishing fleet. It was sixty meters long and ten meters wide. Four boats rested on wooden blocks in the back of the cavern. Each had oars and fish baskets. Lining the walls were tools, anchors, and large iron hooks designed to pull nets and traps from the sea bed.

Don Gabriele paced back and forth. He was afraid. Secrets on Ponza did not exist. Families were related. News, plots, and rumors floated from one person to another like molecules of air. Don Gabriele dreaded the Fascists.

Some abandoned the party when Mussolini fell from power. Others joined the partisans and the Allies. As soon as Il Duce formed a new regime in the North, many continued the struggle beside him and the Germans. It created a civil war. It was hard to know who was on which side.

The priest took out his rosary. He prayed as he waited. "Lord help us," he repeated to himself.

Emma was the first to hear the sound. A motor. She ran out of the cave. The others followed. A mile from the shore she saw a grey military craft steaming toward the beach. Behind it was another boat.

Don Gabriele took out his binoculars. He looked carefully at the approaching vessel. "Oh no!" he screamed. He dropped the glasses and collapsed.

His worst fears were realized.

Waving from the ship was a Swastika on a flag and a Fascist flag.

CHAPTER 151

ESCORT

The Captain of the vessel wore the Fascist insignia. He was an officer. His men were in black and grey uniforms. They reported to him. He was their leader, friend, confidant, and father figure.

For years, they worked with pride to follow the words, principles, and philosophy of Benito Mussolini. "Country, family and God, believe, obey, and fight" were the slogans that became part of them.

Then came Hitler, the war, and the Nazi occupation. German betrayal, lies, and atrocities shocked them.

The Fascist patrol ship came within twenty meters of the landing craft. The Captain lifted a loudspeaker to his lips. "Stop your boat! We will not harm you!" he said.

"It is a trick," said Tom to his comrades. "When I give the order, open fire, and make sure you shoot through the heart," he commanded.

Don Lorenzo recognized the voice. He looked at the Fascist ship. It was Massimo. "Stop," he yelled to Tom. "Hold your fire. He is a friend," insisted the priest.

"What do you want?" asked Francesca to the Fascist leader. "We will get you safely to Ponza," said Massimo. "My comrades and I will help the Allied cause," he stated with conviction. Francesca explained to Tom and his men. A conversation ensued.

"What happens if we run into the Germans and Fascists on Ponza?" asked Tom. "We will handle them," responded Massimo. "Trust me," he said. "He is sincere," affirmed Don Lorenzo. Tom gazed at his comrades. Joe, Lukas, and the Englishmen nodded. He looked at the startled faces of his passengers. They felt confused, frightened, and powerless.

Tom was concerned about the Allies. At any moment, his boat filled with refugees could be attacked by U.S. or British planes. They needed to get to the island fast.

"Okay," said Tom. The Fascist crew tied a line to the craft. Tom shut off the engine. They were towed at high speed. Two hours later, they saw the peaks and slopes of Ponza. It was green and lush, with thousands of terraces filled with vines, fruits, and vegetables. Homes were bright white and gleamed like wedding cakes across a grand, contouring vista of hills and valleys. The colors were amazing. Endless shades of yellow and red were knitted into the volcanic rock of the island, creating a mosaic of colors, shapes, and figures.

"Chiaia di Luna is up ahead!" shouted Don Lorenzo. A grand bay appeared. It was a perfect crescent. It seemed to open arms of safety to these strangers trapped in the violence and insanity of war.

The Fascist boat anchored. Tom started the engine and sailed to the beach.

Don Gabriele got up from the sand. "Uncle, it is me, Lorenzo!" yelled the priest, waving to Don Gabriele, who was his mentor and close relative.

The pastor was in shock as he welcomed the Chosen People to the Island of Ponza.

CHAPTER 152

CARLO'S FEARS MELT AWAY

Courtesy, Wikipedia Commons and the American Red Cross

A red cross was on the right of the envelope. On the left were Italian postage stamps. Luigi read it to his wife and to Carlo, Helena, and Gabriela:

> *My Dear Son: I hope you and your family are well.*
>
> *We are not.*
>
> *The war has taken our home, our friends, family, and town. We lost everything. We are living in the hills with my sister. The pastor of the parish told us we could write via the Red Cross. All we have is our health and our hope that our children are safe.*

Carlo wrote from America. The letter took three months to find us. The important thing is that he is fine and comes home soon and helps us to rebuild our lives. We are old and tired and need someone to take care of us.

Thank you for the package of coffee and clothes. Most of all, thank you for the money. It meant so much to us. I am saving every dollar for when Carlo returns.

Boxes of food and clothing from America are reaching thousands of people. Everyone is waiting for them to liberate our valley.

God willing, the war will end soon, and we will be together again.

With all my love, Mamma

Luigi put the letter down. Carlo was speechless. Helena held his hand. He rose from his chair and paced back and forth in the room.

He had arrived the night before from the camp. He was given a five-day pass. The Commandant took a liking to Carlo. He was a splendid baker, worked hard, got along with everyone, and was a model to his fellow inmates. He was trusted. The Americans saw a person who was honest, dedicated to his craft, and was respectful. He was given frequent leave to see his family. He always returned to the camp on time, without the slightest problem.

Carlo felt welcomed by the Americans. He and his comrades were treated well. The food was excellent. They worked and were paid for it, they were allowed to play soccer, they read books and newspapers in Italian, they listened to the radio, and they were allowed to see movies. He never felt he was in prison until that letter arrived from his mother.

"What can I do?" he said to his family. "I am a prisoner. I will be sent home when the war is over. What will I find? Misery, destruction, and our parents who need my help to survive. What about me and Helena? How long will it take for us to be married and return here? Can I abandon our parents?" He desperately asked all these questions, knowing there were few answers.

"Listen," said Luigi. "America will win this war. It will take time, and we have to be realistic. Yes, you will return home. You will do all you can to help our parents. I will send you money. Helena will come as soon as permitted. You will get married and return here. We will immediately file papers to bring our parents to America and all of our relatives who want to come. All you can do is your best. The rest, leave it up to God," responded Luigi.

"You have me," said Helena. Carlo looked at her. Tears welled up in his eyes. He was overwhelmed with love.

She embraced him.

Carlo's fears melted away in the arms of the girl he loved with all his heart.

CHAPTER 153 ▬▬▬▬▬▬

THE INFORMER

Behind a bush overlooking the beach of Chiaia di Luna was a man with a telescope. He viewed the scene and mentally recorded details of who, what, when, and where. He closed his device and hid it in his jacket. Like a wild animal, he ran to the center of the port of Ponza. It was a mile away. He dashed up the steps of the two-hundred-year-old building that seemed to dominate the city. A flag with a Swastika flew over the roof. He knocked on the door of Nazi headquarters. It opened to a small office, with a young soldier standing next to a middle-aged officer smoking a cigarette. Telegraph and radio equipment were in a corner.

Courtesy, Wikipedia Commons and the Encyclopedia Britannica

Machine guns, rifles, and explosives were in a green metal trunk under a photo of Hitler that hung on the wall facing the door. It was the first thing anyone saw as they entered.

The countenance was fearsome, with hair parted over the forehead, dark features, the brush-like mustache, large, blazing, domineering eyes, bulging from the contours of a brooding, fanatical face that peered into one's soul. The gaze was penetrating and hypnotic. The image bathed the room with a setting of cruelty, fear, and evil.

A chill went down the spine of the man with the telescope each time he saw that photo.

He took off his hat. He was expected.

"Heil Hitler!" he saluted with a limp arm. He spoke rapidly. "Sir, it was about fifty people. They just got off a boat with an American star and white numbers on it at Chiaia di Luna. It was accompanied by a Fascist patrol launch. I saw Don Gabriele and others from the island help them. I will give you their names. I felt it was important to report this to you," said the small man to the German officer. The informant was a worker employed by the Nazis to spy on the population of Ponza.

He was promised gold. And he was despised by his fellow Italians.

He even looked the part of a traitor: His facial features includes short, disheveled hair; a face pockmarked with small holes; a brown and grey beard; squinting eyes, constantly shifting; and a large round nose. He did not wash or shave. He always wore the same shabby brown jacket, black trousers, and a tattered woolen hat. He had a name, but everyone on Ponza Island knew him as "The Spy." He would pop up like a fox looking for prey. No one trusted him. Even the Germans were disgusted to be in his presence, but they needed him.

"Don Gabriele," mused the German officer. "I should have put him in chains long ago. He is related to the American immigrants. They are all waiting for the Allies, but they do not know the Fuhrer has a secret weapon that will destroy New York," he declared, speaking to The Spy and his aide. "They are smuggling political enemies to hide them on the island. Before I arrest them, I need to know when and where the next Allied landing will happen. We will not be taken by surprise again," insisted the Nazi. "I cannot trust the Fascists anymore," he sneered.

The German troops on Ponza numbered merely twelve. Nine were in the port, and three were in the rural part of the island known as Le Forna. Their role was to command and control Ponza, and to perform reconnaissance and communication for headquarters. Coded messages on Allied movements of ships and planes were sent directly to German headquarters in Italy. The contingent was too small to fight, but large enough to keep order on the island.

'As soon as I find out what I need to know, I will kill them all,' said the Nazi officer to himself.

CHAPTER 154 ▬▬▬▬▬▬▬▬▬▬▬▬▬

THE CAVES

Courtesy, Ponza Racconta

"You wait here," said Don Gabriele to the freedom fighters. "It is safe for now," he said as he went off with Don Lorenzo to care for the refugees. It was a cave not far from Chiaia di Luna near another beach known as Il Core. They hauled boxes of equipment, firearms, bombs, and bullets and cans of food into the cavern.

The landing craft was towed into Samuele's cave. He removed the doors to make space. He had an ingenious device he brought from America. It was a winch, with a powerful wire and mechanism with a handle. Logs were placed under the boat like wheels. It was difficult and required enormous strength to prepare the task, but then one man could pull and store a vessel weighing thousands of kilos. The choice was to hide the landing craft or sink it. Either decision was dangerous.

In the cave where the combatants rested, were barrels and bottles of wine piled deep in the heart of the grotto. The terraces produced some of the finest grapes on the island. The vines were showered by the sun and sea air, and the soil was rich with minerals. Roots went deep into the ground to search for sustenance. The fruit was golden yellow or blueish black or blood red. The wine was softly dry with a mild taste of salt. It was unique in all the Mediterranean area.

Flavors of wine were magnified by the taste of fish and lobster from the vibrant waters of Ponza. Food cooked by the islanders was simple and wholesome, blessed with traditions of preparation that reached back to the Phoenicians. The terraces and sea provided nearly all they needed to survive, until the war came, which brought with it famine, heartbreak, and fear. Now, the first flickers of liberation appeared.

The warriors were tired.

Weeks of anxiety, peril, and action had sapped their strength.

And the hardest part was still ahead for them.

While the priests and islanders protected the families, the warriors had a job to do. The communications system had to be installed before the Anzio landings. It would take time to find a location, wire in electricity, and secure an area for operations.

Worst of all, it had to be done under the noses of the Nazis.

CHAPTER 155 ━━━━━━━━━

MUSSOLINI PRISONER IN PONZA

Ponza - Panorama dal Parco della Rimembranza

Courtesy, Ponza Racconta

After helping the freedom fighters hide the landing craft, Massimo and his comrades sailed to the other side of the island. They entered the port of Ponza. Fishing and cargo ships were docked and silent. Trade and commerce was paralyzed. No one entered or exited the harbor. A dock was marked for the Fascists. The captain and crew parked the boat, left the keys in the ignition, and disembarked.

He and his comrades stopped for a moment in their walk. They looked to the left at a familiar figure high above the port. It was the Fascist symbol, a giant concrete centurion guarding the island.

The beach at Santa Maria in Ponza, where Mussolini was held in the building on the left, Pensione Silvia, *Courtesy, Ponza Racconta*

On July 28, 1943, another Fascist gazed at the same image. Benito Mussolini was arrested and brought in exile to Ponza, the place where he had imprisoned hundreds of political opponents. In poetic justice, his enemies watched as he was paraded by, put in a jail, and then taken to a villa and kept under house arrest. It was the eve of his sixtieth birthday.

In his diary on the island he wrote, philosophically, "Everything that happened had to happen… blood, the infallible voice of blood, tells me my star has fallen, forever."

Hotel Campo Imperatore, 1943, *Courtesy, Wikipedia Commons*

Marshall Pietro Badoglio, the new Prime Minister of Italy, decided to constantly move the nation's former dictator to avoid a German rescue.

Eleven days after arriving in Ponza, Mussolini was taken to the Island of Maddalena near Sardinia, and then, on August 26th, he was moved to the ski resort, Hotel Campo del Imperatore, on the snow-covered Gran Sasso in the Apennine Mountains, two thousand nine hundred meters above sea level. The former dictator was guarded by two hundred carabinieri.

It was impenetrable — or so they thought.

German glider landing on Gran Sasso Mountain, September 12th, 1943, with
carrier plane in background, *Courtesy, German National Archives (Bundesarchive photo)*

Hitler's spies traced the movements of Il Duce. On September 12th,
1943, the pages of history and the fate of Mussolini were rewritten.

German Paratroopers landing near Hotel Campo Imperatore to rescue Benito Mussolini,
September 12th, 1943, *Courtesy, German National Archives (Bundesarchive photo)*

In a daring adventure, Nazi paratroopers in gliders launched from planes flying above the mountains, landed in front of the hotel where Mussolini was imprisoned. Aided by a General of the Carabinieri, they liberated Il Duce without firing a shot. Forty-seven days after being arrested by the King, Il Duce was free.

Mussolini Leaving Hotel Campo Imperatore

After his rescue, he was taken to Hitler, who convinced him to organize a new government in the North of Italy and continue to fight the Allies.

It ignited a civil war.

Massimo thought about how his own fate had changed. A year earlier, he was greeted by throngs of people asking favors and flattering him for his power and success. Now, no one came close. The Islanders avoided him and his colleagues, as if they were lepers.

The Fascists went from the owners of Italy to a gang of criminals who brought the nation to ruin.

Before, they were adored, feared, and trusted. Now they were loathed. They governed with an iron hand for twenty years and boasted the regime would last centuries. Instead, within months, their power melted like ice in the sun.

Massimo and his comrades saluted the Germans patrolling the island. They needed to keep appearances up for the sake of safety.

Massimo reached his family home. It was a simple house with a garden and gooseberry and fig trees. The chickens, geese, goats, and rabbits were gone. No vegetables were growing. Food was scarce even for the families of Fascists.

He opened the portal with his key. His mother, Assunta, heard the door. She was in the kitchen, wearing a woolen shawl to keep warm. There was no firewood or coal. She knew the footsteps of her only son. She rushed to him. "My boy!" she said, kissing his face and hugging him. Massimo held onto Assunta just as he did as a child. His father was dead, a Carabinieri killed in an Allied bombing on the mainland. Assunta had no one else but Massimo left to her.

He took off his hat and introduced his companions. Assunta said, "I do not have any coffee or sugar. I have some chicory. I used that for coffee. It is very bitter, but it's all I have" She took out a small slice of dried bread and put it on the table. She was starving.

Massimo and his comrades had leather luggage with the Fascist emblem. Inside were pieces of cheese, pasta, canned food, salami, cigarettes, olive oil, and coffee. It was taken from vendors on the black market. They were arrested and locked in prison. Their ill-gotten goods were distributed to the Fascists and Gestapo.

Assunta hugged the pasta and cheese. She asked no questions and set about preparing a meal.

Massimo showed his friends to their rooms. In his room, he removed his uniform, hat, boots, and medals. He took his Fascist ID card and put it on the pile of clothes. He brought them to his mother. "Mamma, please burn this. All of it," he told her. His colleagues did the same. In a few hours, their years spent growing up as members of the Fascist regime went up in smoke.

They kept their weapons.

The next move was to join the resistance before being caught and shot.

CHAPTER 156 ━━━━━━━━━━━━━━━━━━━━━━

SAVE THE REFUGEES

The operation to save the refugees was difficult and dangerous.

The risk was execution.

Don Gabriele and Don Lorenzo knew this. They entrusted the refugees to ten courageous families on the island.

Emma, Samuele, Raffaele, and Emilia provided food. It was one incentive to the islanders to care for these unfortunate people, but not the most important. The other was a sense of Christian charity and humanity. The war created suffering for all. Anything to relieve agony was an opportunity and a good work by the many kind, brave, and generous inhabitants of the island. They would share the little they had with others.

Samuele spent a fortune bribing the Germans and black marketers. He kept the soup kitchen going while feeding the families protecting the Jews. No one knew the origin of these outcasts from the mainland. They were homeless and in need of a place to live until the end of the war.

Most inhabitants of Ponza had little education, and many could not read or write. They spoke a dialect of Neapolitan. Sometimes it flashed back to what was spoken on the Island of Ischia following the earthquake of 1883, when survivors migrated to Ponza. For many emigres, who spoke proper Italian, it was incomprehensible.

The islanders were fascinated and respectful of their cultured guests. They came from cities they knew existed, but which they had never seen. Some played musical instruments like the piano and violin. They talked about history, geography, and were fluent in foreign languages.

In contrast, life for the people on Ponza was mainly a house, a garden, and the sea. For generations their families lived, loved, and died in a few square kilometers of land on an island.

These strangers changed their lives forever.

CHAPTER 157

THE BEAUTY OF PONZA

A cave near the rectory was their hiding place. Don Gabriele arranged for the freedom fighters to be concealed not far from the Church of the Assumption in the island. It was a beautiful chapel, built stone by stone with the help of parishioners who literally carried sand, pebbles, and limestone to mix with cement, and rocks from all parts of the island to create their church. Joe and Tom's parents were born not far from the lovely sanctuary. As children, Maria and Enzo hauled bricks and blocks to construct the house of worship. They were baptized and married in that house of God.

Courtesy, Ponza Racconta

For a few fleeting moments, Joe and Tom left their hiding place. The sun was rising leisurely above the island. Light gave color and life to the earth and the sea as it constantly foamed, rose, and descended, covering the coast in a magnificent world of shimmering turquoise, stretching from the outer banks of Ponza to the beaches of Palmarola. The two soldiers from America were enthralled by the visions of beauty.

Courtesy, Ponza Racconta

The green of the vegetation was not a normal color. It had shades from light to dark, mixed with yellow and blue. A multitude of herbs, plants, and grasses lived side-by- side, climbing on the terraces and rocks of Ponza.

It seemed the island hosted microclimates, where bright red, wildflowers blossomed in one corner, but could not grow in another, creating worlds within worlds of animation. The terraces scaled hills and settled into valleys, filled with soundly sleeping vines waiting to awake to the warmth and nourishment of the spring.

Courtesy, Ponza Racconta

The young Americans were fascinated with all the paths, houses, walls, and roofs painted white. "She looks like a bride," said Tom as he gazed at a cluster of homes with domes to catch rain. All was neat, orderly, clean, and immaculately bright.

A red cat sat calmly on a wall in front of a blue door, watching birds flutter in the trees.

It was magic.

As boys, Joe and Tom often wondered why immigrants from Ponza suffered so much nostalgia. Now they knew.

Each day, as they grew up in Little Ponza back in New York, they heard stories of life on the island. Tales of fishing, hunting, exploring, and living by the sea, as if Ponza was the universe, filled with stars, planets, and galaxies. It was alpha and omega. It was the beginning and the end. Memories were filled with flavors of food, shellfish, the scent of fresh baked bread and pizza, and the fables of the giant tuna that got away. Ponza was romantic, exciting, and adventurous.

It was also very poor.

Courtesy, Ponza Racconta

Islanders turned a dry and desolate rock in the water into a dreamlike land of struggle, survival, and human achievement.

Life was hard in heaven.

It was a paradise of beauty mixed with the violent scenery of ancient volcanoes that painted abstract figures into stone that glittered in the glow of the sea, with hues that changed as the minutes and moments marched through the day.

The view of the Mediterranean and its distinctive perfume captured these two young men who had grown up on the noisy and smelly streets of the Bronx. They wondered why anyone would leave such a glorious pearl in the sea.

They were home.

Ponza was the birthplace of their parents. It was in their blood.

It was their secret.

No one knew the Americans were descendants of the island.

It would be revealed at the right moment.

First, they had a life-threatening job to do.

CHAPTER 158 ━━━━━━━━

PARTISANS FIGHT

"I do not trust Massimo and his men," whispered Flavio to Francesca. He was the leader of the partisans on Ponza. He was short and stocky, with jet black hair, fiery eyes, large nose and lips, and a muscular body. A thick black beard tried to cover a jagged scar that ran from his ear to his chin, dividing his face like a rough road on a map. His hands were hairy and dark with cracked nails. Oil and gunpowder stains were on his clothes and trousers.

The Nazis and Fascists were searching for him and his small band of loyalists. They were accused of aiding the enemy and sinking a German patrol boat in Ponza's port. A bounty was on their heads. Each night they darted from one safe house to another.

"Don Lorenzo swears by him," murmured Lukas. "He and his men saved our lives. They got us to the island. The Americans and British came here to protect the refugees and install a communications system for the next invasion. Let's test Massimo and his team to see if they will really help us," suggested Francesca. "We need their assistance," insisted Paolo. "A communications system has to be set up on the island. The Germans are everywhere. Massimo and his men can help us deal with them," said Paolo.

Flavio walked over to Massimo, who was six inches taller than him. Massimo was handsome, clean shaven, with closely cut hair, manicured nails, and a deep tan. His men seemed carbon copies of their leader.

"Your monsters imprisoned my father," sneered Flavio. "Why? What was his crime? He was just a school teacher who refused to join the Fascist Party. We had a shortwave radio in our house. He was accused of listening to the BBC. Without a trial, he was locked in a prison on Ventotene for five years. He died in jail. It destroyed my life and my mother's!" he yelled.

"You see this gift on my face?" said Flavio as he pointed to his scar. "I was twelve years old. I would not give the Roman salute. A Fascist took a razor and slashed my face as an example to others. I nearly bled to death. One of my classmates was shot and killed by a Fascist when he refused to share his grapes with him. So tell me, why I should accept you as a brother in our cause to rid your people and the Nazis from the earth?" demanded the partisan leader.

"I am sorry for what happened to you and your family. I made many mistakes. I believed in ideals. I was raised thinking our country could be great and strong and proud. I was wrong. When I discovered what the Germans were doing, I was horrified. I wanted no part in the atrocities they were committing against our people.

"I am no longer a Fascist. I am an Italian and am from Ponza, like you. I will fight to end any trace of this regime and the Nazis. I swear this to you on the heart of my mother! My men will do the same. We are ready to die for liberty!" declared Massimo. He was impassioned. Sweat poured down his forehead. His lips trembled with emotion.

Flavio stared at him. The pupils of his eyes looked like arrows. "If I get the slightest hint of betrayal, I will shoot you like a dog," he said with bitterness in his voice.

"I would rather die with a bullet in my head than live like a criminal," asserted Massimo.

Flavio nodded.

They shook hands.

CHAPTER 159 ━━━━━━━━━━━━━━━

INTERCEPTING GERMAN CODES

One of Flavio's men guarded the German Lieutenant and soldier who participated in bringing the families to Ponza. The partisan was the youngest of the group. He was seventeen, medium height, with curly brown hair and big brown eyes. His rifle looked like a cannon in his short arms. He had a small pistol in his belt and a hunting knife fastened to his lower leg.

The boy came from the rural part of the island and could barely read or write. He knew one thing; He was fighting to end tyranny and for a better country. He would die for it.

He had hurt no one in his life.

The prisoners were held in a remote cave. The partisan was ordered to shoot if they tried to escape. Francesca, Lukas, and Paolo came to see them. She brought cigarettes, bread and cheese, and a jug of wine and several bottles of water.

She carried a stack of papers in a briefcase. The messages were in German. They were coded. Flavio seized them from the German patrol boat before he sunk it with a stick of dynamite.

The officer knew the codes. "Tell me what they say," she demanded. She held her hand on her pistol. He looked at her. "I promised I would help you and the Allies as long as what I do does not take German lives," he responded. "The information in these messages could be fatal," he said.

"It could also help end this war," she insisted. She shoved the papers in front of him and gave him a pad and a pencil. He studied each page and took notes.

"If what you give me is accurate, I will fulfill my first promise. As soon as the Allies land on Ponza, I will turn you over to them and you will have letters from my American comrades to see that you are treated well and fairly.

"If I discover you have lied, I give you a second promise. I will return and shoot you and your companion," she said calmly and coldly. The German stared at her.

He knew she was the type to fulfill either promise.

The documents were copies of short telegrams sent from German headquarters on Ponza to the Nazi high command. It was information that patrols and communica-tions teams garnered from surveilling the sea between Ponza and the mainland.

Francesca could only distinguish the dates. All the messages were sent in the last ten days. The Nazi officer wrote slowly. He examined each message carefully. He handed his notes to Francesca.

She read them several times.

"Damn it," she said, stomping her foot.

She and her companions raced out of the cave.

She had to reach Joe and Tom immediately.

It was a matter of life or death.

CHAPTER 160

CARING FOR THE REFUGEES

Don Gabriele and Don Lorenzo were quiet. They did not visit the homes where the refugees were hiding. It was too dangerous. The Germans constantly patrolled one end of the island to the other. The greatest fear was the sound of Nazi boots pounding the pavement. It sent chills and terror.

"We may have enough for two months," said Samuele to Raffaele. The two men took stock of what they had and what they needed. Each family received a loaf of bread a week, eight eggs, three kilos of potatoes, three kilos of vegetables, and a kilo of flour. Milk was only for small children and babies.

It was not enough. But it was all they had to prevent starvation.

"God will help us," said Don Gabriele to Samuele and Raffaele.

"I hope He knows how to bake bread," quipped Samuele, who was not a very religious man. Don Gabriele raised his eyebrows but stayed silent.

"The families are getting along well. I know that in most cases they have a hard time communicating because of the dialect, but they get by," said Raffaele. "I brought books from the school to each home that has children. Also, I managed to get some for the adults to read," explained Raffaele.

Samuele opened a telegram he received that morning. He had a telegraph system in his office at the power station. Enough dollars kept the Nazis away.

He held it in his hand and sat down. "I just learned that the black market boat was seized this morning by the Germans. They had our flour, potatoes, and eggs," he said in despair.

"Our food will not last another thirty days!" he cried.

CHAPTER 161

GERMAN PLANS TO THWART THE INVASION

"The Nazis know about the invasion," she said. "They got it from intercepting Allied messages and matched the information from data supplied by spies. According to them, the next landing will be either Gaeta, near Formia, or Anzio," she said. Francesca was troubled and worried.

"One message said the beaches at Anzio were too shallow to handle landing craft. Another said Gaeta was more likely, but the roads to Rome were better from Anzio," she explained. "The Germans are searching for definitive information as to which location it will be and when," asserted Francesca.

"Plans are underway to move troops and heavy artillery to either or both areas by the end of January," she explained. "Unless we alert headquarters in time, our soldiers could fall into a trap," she declared.

It was almost Christmas. If the intelligence was accurate, the Allies had less than a month to execute their plans.

While Francesca was talking with Joe and Tom, the British team was assembling boxes of communications equipment. Radios, wires, antennae, and sets of electrical and mechanical devices were being prepared. Samuele provided long cable lines. Raffaele brought an American electric motor. The gear was heavy and bulky. The freedom fighters had no vehicles to help them. Everything had to be carried by hand. They needed manpower.

Courtesy, Ponza Racconta

"Samuele found an ideal location because it faces Anzio," said Tom. "It has a house, where we can set up our equipment and mount the antennae. He will run electric wires to the building so we have energy.

"The site is perfect for the transmission of signals to the fleet to prepare for the landing. It is on high ground, so we can reach headquarters in Salerno," explained Tom.

"We have one problem," interjected Joe.

"Three Germans live in the house next door."

CHAPTER 162

OPERATION SHINGLE

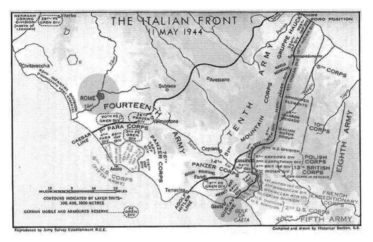

Courtesy, Wikipedia Commons and US Army Archives

It was code named *Operation Shingle*. After the successful incursions in Sicily and Salerno, the Germans quickly redeployed resources to control the vital arteries leading to Rome. The Allied High Command planned another amphibious operation to land further up the Italian coast behind the German Gustav Line, positioned along the Valley of Garigliano River in the center of Italy, cutting off movement from the North and the South to Rome. The Nazis set up installations to prevent the Allied advance, which was named *The Winter Line*.

Operation Shingle would force the enemy to draw troops from Cassino, opening the way to the Italian capital.

It was a brilliant idea, but tremendously risky.

Military commanders argued against it. Without sufficient resources, another offensive could be disastrous. Assault ships were already being positioned for the invasion of Normandy.

Operation Shingle had to be executed under utmost secrecy.

Winston Churchill agreed and ordered it done. The Allied command consented.

The towns of Anzio and Nettuno were targeted. They were thirty miles south of Rome. General Clark insisted that two divisions be positioned for the invasion force. It was December 1943 — five days before Christmas Eve.

Courtesy, Wikipedia Commons

It was freezing cold on Ponza that night. A wild, frigid wind soared from the north and blanketed the island. Buckets of rain and hail pelted every inch of the archipelago. Lightning and thunder blasted through the sky and covered the horizon with a blazing radiance.

It was bone-chilling cold, and perilous to move on the icy roads and paths or to climb terraces with torrents of water surging in every direction. Gales howled like sirens.

The freedom fighters had no choice. The telecom center had to be up and running in forty-eight hours. Vital messages needed to reach the Fifth Army before it was too late to change the invasion plans.

It was 2 AM.

Thirteen men and a woman set out on a glacial winter night to attack a German installation. Six carried the communications gear. The others were armed with machine guns, grenades, automatic rifles, and revolvers with long silencers. It took an hour to crawl in the dark to reach their destination.

Massimo knew the terrain well. He was the guide. Under the shadow of a small house, the freedom fighters stopped to catch their breath.

"Tom, you and the Brits wait here. The rest of us go for the Nazi house. No gunfire, if we can avoid it. It would attract attention. If possible, we take them alive," commanded Joe. "If not, I will take them out," he said pointing to his pistol with the silencer.

Joe looked at the chimney. He thought for a moment, 'Perhaps if I climb on the roof, I can drop a couple of grenades like Christmas presents for them,' he mused for a moment. The idea disappeared from his thoughts.

Inside the small, one-room structure were three German soldiers. They were in their early twenties and had never traveled outside of their homeland. Two were blond with blue eyes, and one had black hair and dark eyes. All three came from small, peaceful farms in Bavaria.

Rifles and machine guns stood in one corner of the room. Three belts with Lugers and ammunition were on a chair. Uniforms were hanging in a closet. The house had a tiny stove and was burning coal and wood to keep the room warm. Muddy boots were drying nearby. Helmets, coats, and hats hung on a wall. Books and magazines were on a chair near the beds.

They were sleeping. Ponza had been an ideal assignment for them. No action was required. It was safe and quiet. But they yearned to go home. The soldiers slept soundly and dreamed as their shelter was silently surrounded by enemy forces.

Two windows were on the back of the house and two on the sides. The door was an old wooden portal with a deadbolt, locked from the inside. Massimo brought a thick oak log that he and

Paolo would use as a battering ram. Joe was ready with his pistol. Francesca cocked the trigger on her machine gun. The others went to the back and stood at the windows to prevent an escape.

Everyone waited for Joe to give the signal.

Joe looked at Massimo.

"It has to be on the first attempt. If not, I will kill them," he whispered.

CHAPTER 163

GENEROSITY

"What is it like in a city?" Concetta asked Rachel. The Jewish woman and her family of four lived with Concetta and her husband, Claudio, and their three children. The two women became friends. No questions were asked about faith, politics, the past, or the future. All that mattered was the present and survival.

Rachel and her family were filled with gratitude. They could not find words to express thanks for the courage and generosity of these humble people. Small acts of kindness, gestures, and a growing friendship bonded the families into one. Rachel helped wash clothes and clean. The children became like brothers and sisters sharing books, stories, and dreams of tomorrow. The little food they had was shared equally.

Her husband assisted Claudio to till the terraces behind the house and prepare the vines for the spring. He did other chores. No sewers were on the island. Each night he helped Claudio fill and carry buckets of human waste, deposited as fertilizer under the grape plants and into the gardens. Malodorous puffs of air often reminded the family where it was.

Rachel's husband was a teacher. He lost his job in 1938 when Mussolini's Anti-Jewish laws went into effect. The children were expelled from school. They survived thanks to families and gentile friends who tutored them and sustained the family. When the Germans occupied their city, they escaped. Everything was left behind.

"Our town was peaceful. We rode bikes to shop and work. What we needed was in walking distance of our house. Bakeries, food stores, and markets were nearby. The children walked to school. There was no crime.

"The people in our building were friends and neighbors. We helped take care of each other's children and shared our food and recipes. Together we went to the mountains to ski in the winter and to the shore for vacations in the summer. Life was tranquil and good," said Rachel with sadness.

Then came the Nazis, and everything changed.

CHAPTER 164 ━━━━━━━━━━━━━━━━━━━━━━━━━━━▶

DELIVERANCE

Massimo reflected for seconds. It was his moment of deliverance. He had to show loyalty. He held the log tightly. "Put all your weight into it when we hit the door," he murmured to his comrades.

Joe nodded.

Massimo felt the force of five strong men unite behind him. He rammed the lock. The door broke in pieces and swung open as the deadbolt snapped. Francesca turned on a flashlight and barked orders in German.

The three soldiers leaped out of bed in their long underwear. One searched for a weapon. Massimo dropped the log and jumped on him. He slammed his revolver on the back of the German's head. The soldier fell over, unconscious.

"Do not move!" yelled Francesca. "Put your hands on your head," she commanded. The soldiers obeyed. They were shocked and afraid. Paolo handcuffed them. Massimo lifted the soldier he had disabled, put him on a bed, and shackled him. "You are prisoners of war. If you behave, you will survive. If not, you will be shot," she said emphatically.

Joe signaled to Tom and the others. They raced to the house next door. It was abandoned. An electrical wire ran from a pole to the roof and down a wall. A bulb hung in the room. It had a black switch. Tom turned it on. The room lit up like daylight. The shutters and windows were sealed.

The team carried the equipment into the house. The experts surveyed the inside and outside. The British officer took out a piece of paper. He drew a design and map of where and how all would be installed and placed in proper position. He opened crates, taking out cables, transmitters, multiplexers, combiners, grounding equipment, and radio frequency devices.

Positioning the antenna mast was the most delicate problem. He brought a spare one just in case. His men fastened the cable to a corner and ran it up to the ceiling. The wall was thick and hard to penetrate. "We have to get the wires to the roof so we can mount the antenna," said the English officer. "Run them out the window for now," suggested a colleague.

All night long, the freedom fighters installed the communications equipment. The rain and the wind made it difficult and dangerous. Several times, Tom and his English colleague nearly slid off the roof. Finally, the antenna was in place.

Time was running out.

As dawn broke, the British officer felt it was the moment to test the radios. Everyone was tense.

He put on his headset.

He turned on the switch.

Silence.

No signal.

CHAPTER 165 ━━━━━━━━━━━━━━━━━━━━━━━━━━━

RADAR

The German High Command knew another invasion was underway. They did not know when and where. Information arrived daily to German Commander, Field Marshall Kesselring in his headquarters in Monte Soratte, a town on a mountain ten kilometers from Rome. Data went to his forces along the Garigliano valley and to Berlin.

Kesselring's experience with Sicily and Salerno tempered his strategy. A landing could not be prevented. A counteroffensive could be mounted if two vital factors were available: time and intelligence. Without them, resources could not be redeployed. Kesselring waited for reinforcements from the Eastern Front to drive the Allies from Italy. He believed he could win the Italian campaign.

Courtesy, German National Archives and Wikipedia Commons

Information from Ponza was vital. Movements of Allied shipping were picked up by radar systems and sent via telegraph and radio transmission.

Courtesy, Ponza Racconta

From the cemetery in Ponza, the Germans could see the Mediterranean from three hundred and sixty degrees. Vessels steaming to the coast and aircraft from all directions showed up on radar. Visually, a set of binoculars gave essential details.

Soon they expected to see an armada of Allied warships. They would report it to Kesselring.

The band of freedom fighters on the island knew about the Germans' plan.

And they were ready to die to make sure it did not happen.

CHAPTER 166 ━━━━━━━━━━━━━━━━━━

THE RADIO

Tom tried again. The radio did not work. He needed patience to solve the problem. It was a luxury. Time was running out. The radio was heavy and bulky. He had to examine the insides. He turned it around in frustration. He removed the back cover and searched for the problem. The tubes were in place. Outlets and inlets were mounted properly.

'The wires — look at the wires,' he said to himself. He examined the attachment of the two electrical wires twisted around metal probes. They were loose and frayed. He removed them. He cut away a piece of the cable and pulled out a fresh portion of copper that was longer. He twisted it around the probes.

He turned the dial. Lights went on in the radio. Tom was elated. A loud, fuzzy sound came out that was indistinguishable. He turned the dial to the proper frequency. Static and crackling noise emitted.

It was the antenna. 'Oh, my God,' he thought. Back to the roof. Installing the antenna was perilous. The roof was old and weak, and the clay shingles were fragile and slick. Now they had to reinstall it.

The British officer climbed along an outer wall of the house. His colleagues gave him a boost. The wind was still strong. Heavy rain and hail poured down. A thick layer of ice covered the shingles. Many were broken and out of place. It was slippery and dangerous to crawl along the gable. He wondered how much weight it could sustain. He heard the roof creaking and moaning under him. He imagined it breaking and falling through. The ceiling was six meters from the ground. It was certain death.

He made it to the chimney. He grabbed it and pulled himself up. The antenna was fastened to it. The gale had turned the antenna in the wrong direction. He reinforced the mast by tying another pole alongside it on the smokestack. The freezing water and ice pelted his face and froze his hands. His clothes were soaked and seemed like a layer of ice on his body. He was losing traction. Several bricks came loose.

Shingles moved under his feet as he stood up. He held onto the chimney. Two bricks popped out and fell. He looked down. It was a twenty-meter drop into a hollow filled with jagged stones. He gripped the flue. His life depended on it.

Tom was at the radio, with a window open near him. "Tell me what happens when you turn the dial," the British officer yelled down to Tom. As he repositioned the antenna, audible echoes came from the radio. Some were in German. Others in French. Finally, he found the channel to transmit to the Fifth Army. "Got it," yelled Tom.

The British officer was cold, dizzy, and exhausted. He was frightened. A false move, and he would fall from the roof and slide into a deadly gorge.

He could not hold on. He was losing consciousness. His hands were slipping from the chimney.

Suddenly, he heard a noise. It jolted him. Something was being put up against the roof. The rim of a ladder appeared next to him. Joe climbed up and grabbed his hand. The two men slowly went down.

"Where did you find that?" asked the Brit of Joe, while pointing to the ladder. "It was outside the house next door. The Germans think of everything," he responded with a smile.

CHAPTER 167

MESSAGES

"**N**azis expect landing to be Anzio or Gaeta. They do not know dates, but they are searching for information," was the message the British officer on Ponza sent to the Fifth Army. The memo was encrypted in a Native American language. The Germans had difficulty breaking the code. The Nazis were certain their messages were safe. The German Enigma machines assured extraordinary, infinite-letter combinations that no one could decipher unless they also had an Enigma machine.

The Allies did have an Enigma machine for decoding, but the Nazis didn't realize that.

A colonel in charge of communications of the Fifth Army sat down with a specialist. He handed him a typed memo. "Send this to all units," he ordered. It read, "OS off until spring. Stop mobilization."

"It should go encoded," he told him. "Sir, if I send the message in that form, it could be picked up by the enemy," he explained. "Send it as I have instructed. That's an order, Sergeant," he commanded. "Yes sir," he replied. He put on his earphones, typed it over a telegraph machine, and it went out.

That same day, a copy came into German headquarters on Ponza. "They cancelled the invasion," said the Nazi officer to his team. He turned to his communications expert. "Transmit the Allied telegram to Field Marshall Kesselring. Mark it 'Eyes Only.' Sign it with my name and rank," he insisted.

'I will get a promotion for this,' he thought to himself, with a broad smile.

With Operation Shingle canceled, the Germans knew the Allies would conduct another massive assault to weaken and annihilate them. Through double agents, the American and British intelligence services got information to the Nazis of the next attack: the Gustav Line, along the Garigliano River. The Allies would hit it in mid-February. The German focus of attention was no longer on another coastal invasion.

Forces moved from the Eastern front and the German homeland to protect the Gustav Line and repel the invaders. It left the cities of Germany exposed to ferocious Allied bombing.

The Allied plan was working.

The freedom fighters celebrated Christmas and New Year's in a damp cave in Ponza. They feasted on dry figs, canned anchovies, and crackers. Local wine was somewhat bitter and salty. The occasion was memorable. They were alive. Many comrades were dead or critically wounded. The war was still a long and bitter duel between two ways of life: democracy and dictatorship. The patriots realized this as they toasted a free Italy and the heroism of those struggling for liberty.

Joe and Tom had their own radios as direct lines to OSS Operations in Salerno. They spent days receiving and transmitting encrypted conversations.

By January 12th, the situation reached a critical stage.

It demanded urgent action.

The new British communications center was big enough for a meeting of the freedom fighters. The German prisoners were in a cave guarded by a group of partisans.

It was past midnight during the second week of January. "We must take the German headquarters," said Joe, solemnly. "Why?" asked Flavio. "Is it not better to wait until the island is occupied by the Allies? We have set up the telecom equipment. All we have to do is hide and wait," he declared.

"The situation is grave," asserted Joe. He explained why and what the plan was.

It was bold, dangerous, and fraught with flaws, everyone agreed.

But there was no other choice.

.

CHAPTER 168

THE AMERICANS ARE COMING

The German commander was angry and frustrated. 'Three of my soldiers held by the rebels somewhere on this God-forsaken rock, and I cannot do anything about it,' thought the officer. His spies said they were in a grotto guarded by the partisans. Rescuing them risked a showdown with the freedom fighters. It was not worth it. His captured colleagues were prisoners of war.

His priority was information to the High Command. 'The invasion is still on, he said to himself. 'Why would the Allies send unencrypted messages? It was obvious: to send false information and trap us,' he believed.

The Spy knocked on the commander's door. The Nazi occupation was ending. He wanted his money. He was shown in. "Your excellency," he said in a whisper, taking off his hat. "I am here to receive what you promised," he asserted. The officer looked at him in disgust. He pulled out a stack of wrapped bank notes. They were Wehrmacht military currency. He tossed them to the The Spy. "What is this?" he said in bewilderment. "Where is my gold? You promised me gold!" he insisted, turning blood red. "There is no gold, you fool!" responded the German. "There never was any gold! Do you think I would waste gold on the likes of you? Get out of here before I have you shot!" he yelled, smirking. The Spy put the money in his pocket and slid out the door. In a matter of days the currency would be worthless.

The beginning of the end was near.

On the night of January 19th, a division of British troops quietly advanced toward German installations on the Garigliano. At 2100 hours (11PM), a red ball flew up into the sky. It was the signal to attack. Volleys of shells shot out of big and small guns aimed at the German lines. It was a ferocious battle.

Reinforcements flowed from all directions to bolster the Nazi forces.

American Soldiers land on the Beach at Chiaia di Luna Ponza, January 1944,
Courtesy, Ponza Racconta

On the same day, a dozen American landing craft reached the beach of Chiaia di Luna, unloading hundreds of soldiers. It was a practice run to prepare for the assault on Anzio.

Courtesy, US Naval History and Heritage Command

The next morning, a huge fleet of warships and troop carriers steamed from Naples, crossing Capri and Ponza, bound for Anzio.

The invasion was on.

CHAPTER 169 ━━━━━━━━━━━━━━━━━━━━━

NAZI COMMAND

Courtesy, Ponza Racconta

J oe led his team to the port of Ponza. By now he knew the island like the back of his hand. It was before dawn. It took two hours to surreptitiously walk from Le Forna to the harbor over a torturous path that crossed terraces and ravines. It was made more for mules than men
.

The patriots stopped for a second to see the views of the port and the adjacent town of Santa Maria. The setting seemed perfectly picturesque and peaceful.

But it was not perfect in any way. Boiling under the surface were the flames of war.

It was 6 AM on the morning of January 19th. The band of brothers reached the oldest part of Ponza. It was deserted. War had paralyzed movement, commerce, and trade. Fear swept the people of the streets. Like panthers, the partisans ran in and out of doorways until they reached the road leading to the Nazi command center and the cemetery.

The band divided into three groups: One went toward the radar station, another to the telegraph poles, and the third to the residence of the German commander, behind their headquarters.

In the office were three messages prepared for Field Marshall Kesselring. "Invasion of Anzio is proceeding," read the first message. "Allied troops landed in Ponza conducting maneuvers for invasion of Anzio," was the second telegram. "Fleet of Allied warships, supply carriers, and troop vessels spotted coming from the South and bound for the coast. They are one day away from leading the invasion force to Anzio," explained the third telegram. His colleague, the radar operator, joined him to send messages about Allied air and sea movements.

At 6:30 AM, four partisans reached the poles carrying telegraph lines. Two guarded the area with machine guns as a colleague climbed the pole.

At precisely 6:35 AM, a group of freedom fighters got to the German radar installation and lookout point in the cemetery of Ponza.

At 6:40 AM, Joe led his team to the home of the Nazi commandant. Next to his house was the apartment that formerly housed the Fascist political prisoners. A garrison of German soldiers slept there.

At 7 AM, the telegraph officer went to the office. He opened the door of German headquarters. Next to his machine were the three messages prepared by the commander for immediate transmission.

He picked up the first one and sent it.

CHAPTER 170

CAPTURED

"You are too late!" said the Nazi Commanding Officer. "My men are informing headquarters of the invasion, as we speak," he smiled wryly. "Get your clothes on," commanded Joe, pointing a machine gun at him. The officer was handcuffed. As he marched out of his room, he saw his soldiers being taken away in shackles.

Joe pressed his pistol with the silencer into the lower back of the German. They reached the door of his office. It was locked from the inside by the telegraph and radar operators. "Tell them it's you. A false move and I will kill you and them," whispered Joe. His comrades were behind him, ready to break into the building. The officer obeyed. The lock clicked, and Joe kicked open the door. "Do not move, or you are dead!" he screamed. The two men stood up petrified. In seconds they were manacled.

Moments earlier, the telegraph specialist typed the lines of the first message. Something was wrong. The clicks for the Morse Code were silent. The machine was dead.

The radar technician could not operate his equipment.

Joe's colleagues had severed the wires seconds before the telegrams were to go out.

CHAPTER 171

OCCUPATION OF PONZA

The boys from the Bronx and their brave militia of patriots took over the Island of Ponza and overpowered the German command, without firing a shot.

Joe and Tom, as the senior officers of their militia of patriots, were the titular commanders of the occupation forces on the island. In a solemn ceremony, the partisans joined the Allies to bring down the Nazi flag that flew over the island. They raised the flag of Italy. It was a beautiful sight as the red, green, and white colors flew against the blue skies of the island.

"Are you and the English going to fly your flags over our country?" someone asked Joe. "After all, we are a conquered nation and a colony," he said. "Italy is free. The people will elect who they want to govern them. All we want is a small piece of ground to bury our dead and go home," responded Joe.

On the morning of January 21st. they asked the priests to help assemble the citizens of Ponza into the town square in front of city hall. Over a thousand people came. Joe and Tom were groomed and wore Army dress uniforms with their Lieutenant Colonel insignia. Lined up next to them were their companions. The Englishmen, the partisans, and the former Fascists stood by the Americans with weapons swung over their shoulders.

It was an amazing sight.

Joe introduced everyone. He complimented his comrades and those who helped rid the island of the Nazis. He spoke in the dialect of Ponza. It was his first language. The islanders listened. They were confused, surprised, and delighted.

"The blood in my veins and that of my brother's is your blood. We are your children born in America. Thanks to you, we exist. We came to free you from slavery and famine. Soon, American ships will arrive and bring food for your families. The nightmare of war is over. God bless Ponza and a free Italy!" he declared.

The crowd roared with applause and praise. The freedom fighters were surrounded by citizens expressing gratitude, with tears of joy.

The priests hugged everyone. Samuele and Emma were there as interpreters and intermediaries. Raffaele came over to Joe and Tom. "Boys, come with me," he said.

They returned to Le Forna. It was covered with thousands of terraces, trees, and white domed houses. They walked down a long path and headed for the sea. Above the shore was a large house with a magnificent courtyard.

Below the house were an endless line of manicured terraces filled with vines and fig trees. "There he is," said Raffaele. He pointed to an elderly man pruning plants. The two American soldiers marched down a white-washed path toward the farmer. Several people were working the ground and tilling the soil. They saw the two men in uniform approach and became frightened.

It was the first time they saw American soldiers.

Joe and Tom stopped and stared.

In the distance was the man they were longing to meet.

CHAPTER 172 ━━━━━━━━━━━━━━━━━━━━

TOMMASO

Tommaso was a simple farmer and fisherman. He was in his sixties and in decent health, save for a weakening heart and declining eyesight. He was short and balding, with white hair and a ruddy complexion. His brown eyes smiled easily, frequently creating lines and creases along his face. He was hardworking, honest, and good hearted, but sad. He was alone. His wife had died two years earlier.

All his children were in America. He missed his youngest child most. She was his favorite. Her name was Maria. She married the boy next door, Enzo. He took her to the New World. Tommaso knew he would never see her again.

Twenty-five years passed. She had two boys. The oldest was Giuseppe, named after Enzo's father, and the youngest, Tommaso, after him. He loved them from a distance. He never saw a photo. All he knew was they were men fighting for America in Europe. He often wondered where they could be. Were they wounded or dead? He felt powerless, and his heart suffered from nostalgia. He prayed God would allow him to see his grandsons before he died.

That day in January was chilly but sunny. It was perfect to prune grape vines and fig trees. He loved his terraces and gardens. Along the stones he planted flowers of all sorts. Raffaele gave him seeds from America of blossoms that lived all year round. He was admiring a pink azalea when he heard footsteps. He looked up. His distance vision was poor. The figures were blurry.

Tommaso thought he saw men in greenish-brown uniforms. "Germans? Italians?" he wondered. He twisted and turned his head to see a little clearer as they came closer. "What do they want with me?" he thought, apprehensively.

They were three meters away. The men stopped. He stared. They had a strange outfit with shining eagles, medals, and decorations. Their faces were somewhat familiar. He did not know if he should be afraid or curious. They came closer.

"Grandpa!" said Joe, as he removed his hat. His brother was right behind him. Tommaso dropped his tools. His mouth opened. His eyes watered. His throat blocked. He could barely breathe. He was speechless. His heart pounded. He was out of breath as he cried. He gazed at his grandsons.

"My boys, my boys!" he cried.

Tommaso opened his arms. Joe and Tom ran to him.

The old man's tears covered their faces and hair. He held them tightly, as if to never let them go. They sensed the fragrance of the soil and sea in his skin.

It was their skin.

They found the man they had long dreamed of.

CHAPTER 173 ▅▅▅▅▅▅▅▅▅▅▅▅▅

FLYING FORTRESSES

It was 2 AM on the morning of January 22nd, 1944.

Ponza slept.

The evening before, word had raced around the island.

The Germans were gone. They were free. Peace was near.

The islanders rested on a quiet night.

Then all hell broke loose.

Explosions filled the night air. They echoed across the sea and thundered over the island as if Flying Fortresses were dropping gigantic bombs on Ponza. Everyone rose from their beds. Should they run or hide? No one knew what to do.

Don Gabriele and Don Lorenzo heard the blasts echoing off the terraces and homes of the island. Ponza trembled as the ground vibrated. 'An earthquake,' was their first thought.

They raced out of the church. Plaster fell from ceilings and walls. From a cliff, the priests saw a breathtaking sight.

In the sea, between Ponza and Anzio, were an endless array of colossal shadows bounding in the waves. They looked like floating dragons spewing fire. Each minute, red and white flames shot out of the mouth of the sea monsters, propelling scorching missiles toward the mainland.

The deadly light soared into the clouds and stars. It was blinding. The priests covered their eyes in fear and panic.

Eruptions, like blasts from volcanoes, filled the coastline with flames that reached high into the night sky. They were seen fifty miles away.

An armada of three hundred and seventy-four warships of the U.S. and British navies with mammoth guns were bombarding German installations on the coast near Anzio. The salvos were a torrent of bombs that pulverized the town and the area for a radius of miles. They continued until dawn. Vessels stretched from Ponza to the mainland in an endless carpet of ships. Then came the planes.

RAF bomber flying over the Apennines to strike German installations before the Anzio landing, January 22nd, 1944, *Courtesy, Royal Air Force Second World War II Official Collection*

At sunrise, Royal Air Force squadrons attacked German forces and sought to pinpoint assaults on areas occupied by the Nazis.

Troops and equipment come ashore on the U.S. Fifth Army beachhead near Anzio, 22 January 1944. *Courtesy, US Naval History and Heritage Command*

By the end of the day, two thousand three hundred vehicles and one hundred and fifty thousand soldiers, ready to break through enemy lines, landed on the beaches of Anzio, along with one thousand five hundred pieces of artillery.

Two thousand seven hundred aircraft participated in the invasion.

The Germans were stunned.

CHAPTER 174 ━━━━━━━━━━━━━━

DEBRA'S NIGHTMARE

Her cries turned into screams. She tossed in bed and pulled the covers over her head like a shield. She saw visions. She heard sounds. It could be felt, sensed, and touched. The nightmare was real.

It was October 1943 again. The Nazis raided the Ghetto in Rome to round up the Jews.

In her shadowy dream, she listened as the engines of the German trucks roared into the square under her building. They seemed like winds of a hurricane about to engulf her home.

Boots banging on the pavement, barking dogs, and the rushing, running, racing of giants pounding on doors, yelling untranslatable phrases. They resonated in Debra's mind like a blasting loudspeaker. She saw and heard it, again and again.

It was a movie speeding through her mind like a tornado.

She could feel the strong hand of her mother taking her from the apartment as they ran to the roof. The building was attached to another. Her father held her as they leaped across. The family held hands. Dashing over another roof and another. They reached a shed on top of a building with a garden of trees and bushes. The door was rusted and opened. They snuck in. It was cold and pitch black. They had no coats.

It was freezing, with winds sweeping from the north that seemed to carry the Nazis to the four corners of Italy to arrest innocents like Debra and her family and send them to extermination camps.

"Mamma, mamma!" she shrieked.

Ester leaped from her bed. It was dark on Ponza.

Debra slept in a room next to the courtyard. The little girl was sweating, crying, and rolling in the sheets, as if possessed by a demon. Ester grabbed her.

She hugged her. "It is all right, my darling," she said, gently.

She held her daughter as though she would never let her go.

"They are gone. They will never return," she repeated, with hope in her heart.

CHAPTER 175 ━━━━━━━━━━━━━

FOOD FOR THE ISLAND

Four weeks after the invasion, a large vessel with an American flag steamed toward Ponza. The weather was stormy. It rained. The sea held the liberty ship in its hand. It was pushed, pulled, and lifted from one high wave to another. The wind tossed it like a cork. The risk of sinking in the cold waters of the Mediterranean was high.

The vessel was dangerously full. Sacks of flour, canned goods, and tons of bread, rice, dried fruits, powdered milk, and vegetables were stowed in the heart of the ship. It was on an emergency mission.

"There it is, Tom," said Joe. "Samuele, we need ten men to unload the ship. I will supervise the distribution of food, and you and Emma can organize the families to come and get their rations," stated Joe. He and his brother were once again in regular Army combat uniforms.

Courtesy, US Navy Archives and US National Archives

Three hours after being sighted, the ship sailed into the port of Ponza. Scores of people were gathering to greet and welcome them.

Courtesy, Marshall Plan Foundation

Women with children and the elderly came by the hundreds, finally. Faces were full of desperation, anger, anticipation, and fear.

Courtesy, National World War II Museum

Others were tired, confused, and ill. Malnutrition weakened small bodies. Mothers sacrificed for their children and gave the last morsel from their mouth to them. Food was the symbol of life when all seemed lost. For years the youngest ones, and what was left of their families, did not smile. No laughter, only the pangs of hunger. Fatigue, thirst, atrophy of muscles, and an inability to move came with the thoughts that nothing was worth living for. Hope, the anchor of life, seemed gone forever.

Then the ship landed.

The rain stopped. Skilled mariners from Ponza grabbed the vessel's lines. The Captain saluted his colleagues and waved to the people, who were patiently waiting and praying.

Cranes lifted pallets stacked with rice, flour, and all forms of food and fresh drinking water. American troops helped unload the vital cargo to feed the people of Ponza.

Courtesy, Italian Archives, Marshall Foundation and British Archives

A center was organized to house the supplies and distribute provisions in an orderly fashion. Soldiers were present to keep order. Distribution began with loaves of bread. Hundreds of boxes were carried into the building. Pieces were packed in wicker baskets for rapid distribution.

A five-year-old girl dashed to the front of the line. "May I have two pieces?" she asked. "One is for me and the other is for my mother. She is too weak to even stand up," she explained, with tears in her eyes. A man handed her two small, round loaves. She ran to the back of the line where her mother was sitting on a box. The woman was dehydrated and exhausted from walking across the island to reach the port. The fragrance of the bread changed her. She held it to her nose and face. She took a small bite. Her mouth hurt from the texture. It was the first time she had tasted bread in two years. The little girl looked at her mother as she ate her piece. She smiled. It was the first in twenty-four long months of starvation.

Courtesy, US Army Archives

As the food was given, children and old people surrounded Joe and Tom and their colleagues. An elderly lady, in her eighties, went up to Joe. She hugged him and kissed his cheeks.

"God bless you and protect you!" she cried.

At that moment, Joe felt that the fighting, suffering, and sacrifices were all worth it.

CHAPTER 176

FLAVIA

Stories thrived on the island.

Flavia was a teenager. She was from Rome and was Giovannina's oldest daughter. On the second day of distributing food, she went to the port, hoping to receive something to take home.

When her turn came, an American soldier asked, "Do you know Sammy's wife?" Flavia did not miss a beat. "I am his wife," she said with conviction. She was his niece. "Here, tell him this is from the Captain," he told her. She was handed two giant loves of white bread. They were long and rectangular and wrapped in thick, brown paper. 'The fragrance is something to die for,' she thought. The bread had a perfume of toasted almonds.

She was hungry. Flavia had not tasted bread for two years. She opened the parcel. Out came a golden-brown loaf that seemed it was baked for the gods. She bit into it. It was delicious. She had eaten nothing so good. By the time she reached home, half a loaf was gone. She walked in the house smiling, satisfied, and filled with happiness. For the rest of her life, she searched for that taste again, but never found it.

Gina, Flavia's sister, recalled the taste of raw potatoes. She was twelve. She was starving. She snuck into her grandfather's garden and dug deeply. She found a potato. It was covered with dirt. After she brushed it off, she bit into it. It tasted of soil and was hard and almost flavorless. She ate it all. That night, she had a tummy ache that lasted two long days. Gina never forgot the incident of the potatoes or the time she needed slippers.

The homes in Ponza were cold in the winter. The floors were frigid. Gina had no slippers. She took some straw and knitted a pair. It was work. It took two months. At the end, she created a nice set which, unfortunately, were both left feet.

Gina's aunt, Matilda, was a teacher. She played the piano. Emma, her sister, brought a group of American soldiers to Matilda's house for a meal and a concert. They were officers. She was nervous. She had never played in public before. Now she was asked to do so in front of strangers.

Emma introduced her. During the presentation, Matilda farted. It was loud. "How could you do that?" said Emma angrily to her sister. "Do not worry. They are Americans and do not understand those things," she said with confidence.

Emma received more packages of food from the Americans than any other person on the island. Bags and bars of chocolate were given to her. She put everything in a trunk. It was locked with an old, rusted key. Her nieces, Gina and Flavia, made another key. As soon as Emma left the house, they would sneak in and go to the trunk.

Samuele seemed to always be asleep at those moments.

In reality, he was not.

He watched the girls from a corner of his eye as they opened the trunk, plucked a few bars of chocolate, and ran away.

He smiled and always made believe he knew nothing.

One day, Emma realized that lots of chocolate was missing. "Do you know anything about this?" she asked Samuele.

"I think we have mice," he responded.

CHAPTER 177

MY SOLDIER

A glowing sun accompanied the distribution of food. It continued for days. It lit up the white streets and plazas of the island. A feeling of bliss, life, liberty, and happiness filled the air. Most of all, a sense of hope and a return to normalcy seemed to flow across each corner and angle.

Fascism, politics, and the war had created animosity and separated people who at one time loved each other. Now, with the liberation, all was changing. Fear was fading away. Families who had not spoken to each other for decades were reunited.

A sense was spread that tomorrow would be better.

Courtesy, US Army Archives, US National Archives

"Do you speak English?" said the little girl. She was perched on Emma's white balcony in the center of Ponza. It was a beautiful sight. She wore a white ribbon and a calico dress. Her hair was the color of copper. Her eyes were large and shined like black diamonds. She was gorgeous. She smiled to captivate anyone who saw her. It was a look of love, mischief, joy, and life.

American soldiers who delivered food to the island were strolling along the historic streets. Their boots were muddy from the wet roads after a night of pouring rain. A dozen of them gathered round to watch a colleague pick up the little girl and speak to her. He was an officer.

The soldier was tall with light brown hair, blue eyes, and a lean, muscular body. His face was dotted with tiny freckles that surrounded a warm, engaging smile of bright white teeth. He was handsome and distinct, and he had the air of a gentleman.

Maria was three years old. She was lively, alert, and intelligent. She was the smallest daughter of Emma's sister, Giovannina. The American was a major. He and his men had seen action throughout Italy, including the landings in Sicily, Salerno, and Anzio. Now he was in Ponza. He was struck by the little girl. She reminded him of his niece at home in America. They were the same age.

Emma taught Maria enough words of English to welcome the service men to the island. "Thank you for coming," she said to him. He cried. He took out a box of rations. His hands shook as he gave her two bars of chocolate and crackers. She kissed him on the cheek. "Where is your mommy?" asked the soldier. Maria took his hand and brought him to Emma and Giovannina. "Mamma, this is my soldier," she said proudly.

"Where are you from?" asked Emma. "Bronx, New York," he replied. "My sister Lucia lives in the Bronx," responded Giovannina. Questions and answers, and it was discovered the young man knew this family from Ponza that had settled in America. "Come for lunch today," said Giovannina. Maria jumped for joy upon hearing that her soldier would be with them for lunch that day. "Thank you," he said.

Three hours later, he returned.

He had showered, shaved, and wore his dress uniform. He carried a heavy sack and a large wooden box. On the side was written, "From the People of the United States of America." The soldier presented a fifty-pound sack of flour. In the box was a bag of rice, cans of powdered milk, dried carrots and turnips, peas, meat, and tuna fish, and three packages of spaghetti and a tin of olive oil, two rectangular loaves of bread, and boxes of crackers and bars of chocolate.

The coup de grace was a chicken. It was plucked, clean, and ready to cook.

"This is for Maria," said the Major. He took from his coat a parcel, wrapped in green paper with a yellow ribbon. Maria opened it slowly. She wanted to save the paper and put the ribbon in her hair. She leaped up and down when she saw the gift.

It was a lovely rag doll with a polka dot dress, red buttons for eyes, with blond, woolen hair and a pink stitched smile. Maria kissed it and pressed it to her face.

"I love it. Thank you," she said to her soldier.

She hugged him and wanted to never let him go.

The family gathered for a feast. Samuele, Emma, Giovannina, her children, and the American soldier sat around a long table. It was filled with smiles, joy, laughter, and food.

Samuele asked everyone to hold hands. Maria quickly took the hand of her soldier and held it tightly. It was warm and soft.

"Almighty God, thank you for the gift of love and the beginning of a new life for all of us because of the bravery and sacrifice of men and women who came from afar to free us. Bless this food as a sign of unending friendship among our families, our country, and our liberators. God bless them, and bless us all," he prayed.

It was an unforgettable meal.

Maria taught her soldier how to twirl spaghetti.

She loved the dried carrots and turnips, and she ate them like candy. It was a taste she never forgot.

For months, the American soldier visited the little girl with the ribbon in her hair.

She was more than a daughter. She was a companion.

Maria gave him a feeling of comfort and hope. She took him everywhere. He was, "my soldier."

She was proud and happy.

The little girl held his hand and brought him across the island to see the churches, the sea, and the magnificent views from the hills and valleys.

He fell in love with Ponza and with Maria.

Then he had to leave.

He put the little girl on his knee and said, "My darling, I have to go away. I am a soldier and must do my job," he said.

His voice cracked with emotion.

His heart beat like a drum.

"Why do you have to go?" she asked. Tears poured from her eyes. "Do not leave me!" she pleaded.

"I have to fight to end the war and bring your father back to you," he told her.

Maria looked deeply into his eyes. She clutched his hand. She kissed it. She caressed his cheeks and embraced him.

She cried. He cried.

They walked to the ship. His new-found family was with him. He hugged Emma and Samuele.

He promised to write and return to Ponza.

He picked up Maria. "Please do not go," she said, with tears streaming down her face. "I will be back. I promise you, Maria, I will be back and bring you the biggest and best doll you have ever seen," he said.

He could not hold back his feelings.

"Do not leave me!" the little girl screamed. "I will never see you again!" she yelled. Her soldier embraced her, kissed her, and gave her to her mother.

"Goodbye, sweetheart," were his last words as he walked onto the ship.

Maria and her soldier waved to each other until the vessel disappeared into the horizon.

She was heartbroken. She clutched her doll as she watched the boat fade away.

For the young man, the months with Maria were the best of his life.

He carried her memory into battle and into the next world.

He died five days later.

CHAPTER 178 ━━━━━━━━━━━━━━━━━━━━━━━

LST 349

German and Allied causalities exceeded 50,000 killed and wounded from the invasion of Anzio. Nearly 5,000 German prisoners of war were captured.[1] The cities of Anzio and nearby Nettuno were a pile of rubble. Countless civilians died in the bombings and enemy offensive.

A month after the attack, the Allies started the complex transfer of the prisoners to Naples, to board ships bound for the United States, where they would be interned in POW camps.

---

1   https://www.navsource.org/archives/10/16/160349.htm

German Prisoners of War after the Anzio Invasion, January 1944,
Courtesy, IWM and US Army Archives

It was a logistics nightmare.

American and Allied officers had little experience in Mediterranean navigation. Charts were often incorrect and hid dangers that only skilled Italian mariners knew.

Winds changed abruptly, and weather conditions were difficult to predict, particularly in the winter.

The coast was a floating field of Axis mines. Nazi aircraft attacked almost anything that moved, by land or sea. German U-Boats patrolled the waters like wolves in search of prey.

On an early evening in late February, a special form of craft set off from Anzio, bound for Naples.

The vessel had a number. It had no name, as if it did not deserve a namesake or to be honored and remembered. It was a utility vehicle, used to land troops during the invasion.

It was expendable, like the men and women it carried into harm's way.

Now it held a cargo of former enemies bound for safe internment in America.

LST 349 anchored off the coast of Italy, 1944,
Courtesy, US Naval Archives.

LST 349 was launched on February 7th, 1942, at the U.S. Naval Shipyard in Norfolk, Virginia. The greyish-black paint was still wet, as it was dragged across the Atlantic to load troops, artillery, and materials for the invasions of North Africa and the Middle East.[1]

By the time it reached Italy, the ship and its crew had won three medals for heroism.

Few would call it a traditional "man of war."

It was a huge, rectangular box with a flat bottom, designed to be a container. The vessel was one hundred meters long and ten meters wide, built to carry "tanks, wheeled and tracked vehicles, artillery, construction equipment and supplies. A ramp, cranes, and an elevator allowed vehicles access to the tank deck from the main level of the ship. Additional capacity included sectional pontoons carried on each side amidships, to either build Rhino Barges or use as causeways. Attached to the bow ramp, the causeways would enable payloads to be delivered ashore from deeper water or where a beachhead would not allow the vessel to land." [2]

LST 349 traveled at 12 knots with an endurance of 24,000 miles with its two, 900 horsepower General Motors engines. Twin 40mm guns, four single 40mm cannons, and twelve 20mm guns ran along both sides and the center of the ship. [3]

1   https://www.navsource.org/archives/10/16/160349.htm

2   https://www.navsource.org/archives/10/16/160349.htm

3   Ibid. navsources archives

Crew of LST 349, *Courtesy, US Naval Archives*

The crew consisted of nine officers and one hundred twenty enlisted men. The vessel could transport 150 passengers plus heavy military equipment.

LST 349 was made for intercostal beach landings and carrying supplies.

It was not suited for long trips in stormy seas.

A year and 18 days into its life, LST 349 sailed towards Naples. It carried 51 German and 3 Italian prisoners of war plus 25 vehicles and Allied passengers.

It was February 25th, 1944. [1]

The wind bellowed, and the sea soared and fell in massive waves that covered the craft, as a storm rose over the western Mediterranean. The ship headed for the sanctuary of the nearest land.

It reached Ponza in the evening.

The crew quickly glimpsed the sun slipping beneath the cloud-filled horizon as gusts lifted, tossed, and turned the vessel like a cork in a typhoon.

The captain cautiously steered the swaying ship toward the bay of Cala dell'Acqua.

It was treacherous.

At 7 PM, he dropped anchor near the shore in the shadow of an ancient Papal fortress. The captain maneuvered the vessel to make sure the anchor hooked onto a stone.
It was dark. All lights on board were out in fear of German submarines. The sea was calmer near the coast of the island, but still agitated.

---

1   https://www.ponzaracconta.it/2015/02/23/storia-di-un-naufragio/

The torturous rocking of the boat created panic among the seasick passengers. Rest was impossible. They prayed that by dawn the tempest would subside.

It did not.

At 5:30 AM, a massive hurricane engulfed the vessel. Explosions of freezing rain drenched the ship. Visibility was gone, as clouds of mist rose from the sea.

The boat was thrown in the waves. It twisted and rolled, and nearly capsized.

The sea was a cold, boiling inferno.

The officer on duty ordered the engine room to start the motors.

It was too late.

Within seconds, the vessel slammed against the rocks.

Chains, securing vehicles and equipment, shattered like bands of rubber. Jeeps collided and bounced off the sides of the ship in thunderous crashes that shook the vessel from stem to stern.

Suddenly, the anchor snapped.

The boat lurched forward. It climbed ten meters above the waves and fell like a roller coaster, tumbling into the sea.

LST 349 was at the mercy of the elements.

The captain ordered an emergency fuselage of cannon fire to alert the people of the island.

A sailor ran toward a 40 mm gun while pulling on a life vest. Cold rain pelted his face and froze his hands.

Thick, salty surf covered him, drawing him to the sea like a magnet. Slipping and sliding on the tilting deck, he reached the gun port. No time to put on gloves, a helmet, earmuffs, or goggles.

He turned the wheel rapidly to direct the barrel to the sky above the Mediterranean.

He pulled the trigger.

The blasts blew out his ear drums.

The retort from the cannon pounded his chest and face as he fired ten volleys into the darkness. The young man rushed down the ladder from the gun port and fell to the deck below as waves of water dragged him toward the abyss.

He held on to ropes and wires as he lifted the hatch and scrambled back into the bowels of the boat as water flooded the compartments.

In the bridge, the captain tied the tiller to keep the rudder from turning wildly. Rain and fog covered the cabin. He ordered his officers to deal with the emergency.

Radio contact was gone.

There was only one choice left: abandon ship, or die in a watery grave.

CHAPTER 179 ━━━━━━━━━━━━━━━━━━━━━━━━━━━▶

HEROISM

$\mathbf{T}$he roar of the cannon circled the island. People rose from their beds. Some feared Ponza was being shelled by enemy warships.

Others realized a tragedy was in the making.

LST 349, February 26th, 1944,
Courtesy, US Naval Archives and Ponza Racconta

LST 349 was tossed against the rocks like a plaything.

The sound of cracking and breaking steel thundered through blazes of lightning and a vast downpour of rain.

Men and women flocked to the hills overlooking Cala dell'Acqua to view the unfolding disaster. Several grabbed ropes and ran along the side of the mountain toward the sea.

An islander banged on the door of the house where the English communications specialists slept. He pleaded for help. The officer in charge organized his team to carry lanterns, cords, and winches. The group raced down a two hundred meter ridge as the sun rose over the Mediterranean. [1]

---

1   http://www.combattentiliberazione.it/sbarcodianzio/fred-goddard-english-version

Halfway, they stopped. The men saw a terrifying scene.

A long black ship was being hurled against the mountainside. The sea seemed like a colossal hand flinging the boat onto the granite slopes as if it were a toy.

The captain sounded the boat's whistle to alert the crew to muster stations. Through the noise of the raging sea, he yelled into a megaphone and ordered all to abandon ship. Lifeboats were untied.

The hatches opened. Water rushed into the boat as prisoners and sailors climbed to the deck.

Sailors and valiant people from Ponza saving passengers from LST349, February 26th, 1944, *Courtesy, US Naval Archives and Ponza Racconta*

Crew members flung rigging and nets to the shore with steel hooks. Once they were fastened, they were tied to the vessel as a lifeline.

Each time the sea drove the boat to the rocks, was a chance to leap to safety, sink into the water, or be crushed by the steel hull of the ship.

The smallest miscalculation was deadly.

The British officer rushed his team to the site.

He was born in Lancashire in World War I. He graduated from Kings College London with a degree in science and joined the Royal Air Force before England declared war against Nazi Germany. [1] He reached the rank of Flying Officer before his thirtieth birthday.

He was a pilot, a skilled communications expert. and an excellent swimmer.

Courageous men and women from the island helped the American crew. Ropes were thrown and tied to the vessel. Prisoners and passengers leaped to safety while the sea continued to rage.

Some were thrown into the surf by the heavy winds.

A few reached nearby rocks. Others were swallowed by the waves. Several officers, prisoners, and crew members jumped into a lifeboat. In minutes, it capsized and vanished.

---

1   https://kingscollections.org/warmemorials/kings-college/memorials/goddard-fred

Passengers from LST 349 seeking safety, *Courtesy, Ponza Racconta*

The Englishmen reached the vessel. They pulled men ashore.

Suddenly, several German prisoners were swept from the deck.

The British officer dived. He swam through the icy breakers. He rescued several men and dragged them to nearby rocks. He dived again and again, saving many lives.

Bitter cold and exhaustion overcame him as he disappeared into the depths of the sea. [2]

In the rescue effort, an explosion rocked the vessel. The boiler room burst. The eruption and the crashing of the ship against the shore, cut the hull in half.

The stern sank.

Thanks to the heroism of the men and women of Ponza and the Allied crew, one hundred and five Americans and forty-five German prisoners were saved. [3]

Bodies were found for weeks after LST 349 was sunk, including that of the British officer.

Survivors suffered shock and trauma. Many were cared for by families near the site of the shipwreck.

One family took in five seamen and nursed them back to health. They shared the little food and clothing they had. A sailor left a souvenir: a gold medal with a Madonna. On the back was written: *Mary conceived without sin; pray for us with recourse to thee.*

In the days following the tragedy, the bodies of officers, crewmen, and German prisoners were recovered as the sea carried them to the shores of Ponza.

---

2   http://www.combattentiliberazione.it/sbarcodianzio/fred-goddard-english-version

3   Ibid.

The first to be found was that of the second in command, swept into the waves while attempting to save lives. The Commander arranged for his interment in the cemetery on the island.

The burial ground was built on the ruins of an ancient imperial villa. It was at the entrance of the port on a high hill and seemed cut into the greyish-white stone. It was filled with tall mausoleums overlooking the harbor, like fashionable homes of the wealthy positioned to enjoy a magnificent view of the Mediterranean.

Samuele had a family tomb, filled with relatives of all ages, who died in the early part of the twentieth century. Several crypts held the remains of children who fell under the plague of the Spanish Influenza in 1918.
Near the family vault was the burial place of a young lady.

Her coffin was sealed in a wall along the stairs of the cemetery leading to the sea. Her memory was wrapped in that cold box of limestone, but her unforgettable story was one of lost love.

It was as profound as the tale of Romeo and Juliet, and as powerful as the saga of Anthony and Cleopatra.

Faraglioni di Lucia Rosa, *Courtesy, Ponza Racconta*

She was eighteen, and she lived in the early years of the nineteenth century. Her name was Lucia Rosa.

She resided with her parents and a large family of brothers and sisters. They tilled the land and fished, like nearly all the inhabitants of Ponza, and were considered prosperous, when compared to others.

Lucia Rosa was an obedient and religious girl who learned the arts and crafts of a homemaker, wife, and mother. She dreamed of having her own family and devoting herself to a special man.

Suddenly, it happened.
Love came like a bolt of lightning.

It was passionate and uncontrollable.

She met Antonio on a road leading to the port. He was twenty-one, lean, tanned with fine features, black hair, and coal-colored eyes.

His natural beauty shone like a ray of sunlight.

His poverty was also clear. He was a subsistence farmer with ragged clothes, who tilled the land of an owner. Yet, his eyes were filled with ambition and pride and, most of all, love for Lucia Rosa.

He was kind, sweet, and warm.

His love was filled with caring.

Antonio pleaded with Lucia Rosa's father for her hand in marriage. He refused. He prohibited his daughter from ever seeing him again.

The lovers could not resist each other.

Clandestine meetings happened until their secret was discovered.

She was beaten and punished.

Her father forced her into an engagement with a man she detested.

The announcement of the betrothal was to be on May 31st, the feast of the Visitation of the Virgin Mary.

Early that morning, Lucia Rosa told her family she would pick flowers for the ceremony to be held that night. She left her home and walked down the curved and crooked paths in the island, overlooking a string of jagged rocks that seemed to sleep in the sea.

She wore a grey woolen dress, decorated with pink hearts. As she descended along the side of the mountain, she picked violets and honeysuckle. Her hands and face were scented with the sweet perfume of wildflowers. Her ebony hair blew in the wind and covered her face, as she neared a cliff overhanging the bay.

Lucia Rosa reached the edge of the precipice and stopped.

She looked down.

It was a hundred-meter drop into the sea.

Yellow flowers decorated the perimeter of the mountain along with wild fig trees, brimming with pink blossoms and buzzing bees.

CHAPTER 180 ━━━━━━━━━━━━━━━━━━━━━━━━

BURIAL

Samuele touched the white slab on the sepulcher of Lucia Rosa as they passed along the stairs with the coffin of the American sailor.

The white slab read, *"Here lies a young girl who gave her life so that love could live."*

The descent toward the sea was long and difficult for the pall bearers.

The weather was gloomy. Strong winds circled the cemetery. Thick black clouds dumped heavy rain on the men in uniform carrying remains toward their resting place.

A small plot of land was the burial place of the men and women whose bodies were strewn on the rocks and beaches of Ponza.

It was a scenic spot with a broad view of the Mediterranean.

The pastor presided over the burial. He prayed as the coffin was lowered:

> *Even though I walk through the valley of the shadow of death, I will fear no evil, for you are with me; your rod and your staff, they comfort me. Psalm 23:4*

Samuele was asked by the Captain to say a few words.

> *Today we laid to rest a hero. He and his companions were bringing former adversaries to freedom. They gave their lives to save those of their enemies. They did not see them as rivals, but as comrades.*
>
> *As Jesus said, "There is no greater love than to lay down one's life for a friend." John 15:12-13*

CHAPTER 181 ━━━━━━━━━━━━━━━━━━━━━━━

FREEDOM

Within weeks, excitement returned to the island. Other ships came to bring food. They were guided by heroic men from Ponza and the Allies.

Hunger was gone. There was the right to be free and happy. Citizens could walk the streets, shop, and work and speak openly. Men went fishing and hunting. Curfews did not exist. Friends and relatives could talk, unite, and think without fear. The oppression of Fascism and Nazism was fading into the past. A bright future was ahead.

The war was not over, but for the people of Ponza, the final curtain was near.

The British team built a helicopter pad next to the communications unit. It was already known as The English Camp (Campo Inglese) from the visit of British Admiral Napier in the 18th century. The Englishmen stayed on the island to begin transport to and from the coast and build up the communications facilities.

For years, the bells on the churches had been silent. They pealed only for death. The moment the Nazis left, Don Gabriele rang the bells in all three churches. The chimes were heard far and wide. Their music resonated through the hills and valleys and reached the ears of fishermen pulling their nets and fish baskets.

The German soldiers were put in a boat for transfer to the Fifth Army's prisoner of war operations in Naples. Two had letters from Joe. Fascists accused of crimes were arrested, to be tried in Italian courts.

Emma watched as The Spy was handcuffed and paraded to the ship bound for Naples. He passed her on the road. He stared at Emma "We will be back!" he screamed "And I will kill you!" he cried. She spit in his face.

God and liberty came to Ponza.

The freedom fighters knew their job on the island was over. They had to move on to new adventures.

A day before they separated, Joe and Tom and the partisans held a party to commemorate their time together. It was a moment of pleasure and nostalgia. They gathered in a restaurant in the port and ate fresh fish caught that day and drank wine saved for years in barrels below the ground. The comrades recalled their battles, triumphs, and tragedies, and spoke of the time ahead with optimism and wonder.

The world changed.

Italy changed.

They changed.

The following day, an Allied boat came. The partisans boarded. They went to the mainland. The Italians joined groups in the North and continued the battle to rid the nation of the Nazis and Fascists.

Joe and Tom had to leave.

It was hard, but it was inevitable.

CHAPTER 182

THE TAILOR

There was a tailor on the island. The two boys from the Bronx went to him. They brought measurements and sizes. In less than two days, they had a suitcase filled with clothes.

Tommaso was expecting them for their last dinner. He was a good cook. Thanks to the food Joe and Tom brought, he prepared pasta, cooked meat, and potatoes. He opened a bottle of wine made by his grandfather. It was in honor of his "boys."

The scent of tomato sauce filled the air. For Joe and Tom, it was the perfume of their mother. "Grandpa, we have a gift for you," said Tom. The old man looked puzzled. 'The greatest gift was to be with my grandsons,' he thought. They gave him the suitcase. It was leather, with his initials on it.

He had never had a suitcase and had trouble flipping open the locks. Finally, he managed. He opened it. Inside were shirts of various colors, two sweaters, two trousers, and two suits. "Put this on Grandpa," said Joe. It was a long-sleeved cotton shirt with stripes. "Let us see if the jackets fit," insisted Joe. Tommaso put on the shirt and the jacket. He looked splendid. He hugged and kissed his boys. "You did not have to do this," he said with humility. "Nothing is greater than seeing both of you," he stated.

Tom took out another box. It was filled with small cigars. The old man was overcome with love and emotion. He was without words. In another package was a shaving brush, razor and soap, and a fine Italian after shave. They gave him an envelope with fifty American dollars.

They sat down to eat. Each morsel was special. It was special because Tom and Joe were with their grandfather. Their mother, Maria, had told them stories of his fishing and farming and kindness. The men from America understood. Tommaso thought first of others, then of himself.

When his neighbors were not stealing the food from his garden, he was harvesting it and sharing it with them. He was there to help them repair homes and plow terraces. His satisfaction was to see the children of those who lived near him grow into good human beings, like his children.

Tommaso opened a drawer in an old wooden cabinet in the kitchen. It was filled with memorabilia. He took out two photos. Both were of Tommaso. One was him fishing and another in his First World War uniform. He gave one to each. "Please do not forget me, my sons," he said, with tears streaming down his face. "From this moment on, I will pray for your safe return home to the arms of your mother," he declared.

Joe and Tom were speechless. They were filled with love for this man who a few weeks earlier was unknown to them.

"Grandpa, we have to go," said Joe. They embraced him and kissed his cheeks. The old man was weak with emotion. He hugged his boys and bid them farewell, as they walked away from his home down a path and on the road to the port.

They promised to return.

He wondered if he would be alive to welcome them the next time his heroes returned to Ponza.

CHAPTER 183 ━━━━━━━━━━━━━━━

OFF TO WAR

Joe and Tom were packed. Two cotton sacks with U.S. Army insignias were filled with clothes and souvenirs from Ponza: seashells, a fishing kit, and postcards, but mainly knitted socks and hats. Before they departed, they went to see Don Gabriele and Don Lorenzo. The two priests resided in the rectory in the church in Le Forna.

"We came to say goodbye," said Joe. Don Gabriele put his hand on Joe and Tom's shoulders. "Two men who have done so much for so many," he stated. Don Lorenzo said, "You are brave. God protects his champions."

"Will you give us your blessing?" asked Tom. The soldiers knelt before the priests.

"Almighty Father, accompany your sons, Joseph and Thomas, as they continue their journey of struggle to liberate the world from evil. Be at their side. Comfort them in moments of crisis. Give them courage. Let them be strong and merciful in the fulfillment of their duties. If they lose their lives, take them into your kingdom and keep them at your side for eternity," prayed Don Gabriele. He made the sign of the cross over them.

Don Lorenzo took out two rosaries. Each had a small glass chamber with an artifact. "This is a relic of San Silverio," he described. "Keep these with you at all times and pray with them in your hands," explained Don Lorenzo as he blessed them. They hugged each other and left.

Joe and Tom visited several families hosting the refugees. All were well. At one home, one woman they saved took their hands in hers. She looked them in the eyes. "You did not have to do what you did for us, but you did. You did not have to risk your lives for us, but you did. You made choices. I thank God for the good and courageous hearts he gave you. I promise you will always be in my thoughts, for the rest of my life," she said, as they embraced and departed.

It was getting dark. Electric lights and oil lanterns went on in the port. A huge crowd was waiting. Joe and Tom were hailed and praised as they boarded the vessels. Samuele, Emma, Raffaele, Emilia, and others were there to say farewell. All eyes were wet with tears.

As the ship pulled away, a flock of white doves flew over it.

The people pulled out handkerchiefs.

It seemed like a moving carpet of white banners of peace to illuminate the island as the sun went down.

They waved wildly to honor the boys from the Bronx as their ship slowly vanished into the sea and darkness.

CHAPTER 184 ━━━━━━━━━━━━━━━━━━━

JEWISH BRIGADE

Jewish Brigade, Courtesy, Imperial War Museum

While Joe and Tom were fighting in Italy, in a desert in Egypt five thousand determined young men marched and trained with visions of fighting to bring down a common enemy, Nazism. It was July 1944. The summer offensive began. Jewish youth, mainly from Palestine, formed a brigade of freedom fighters to combat the forces of evil. They were under the command of Jewish officers of Her Majesty's Army.

They carried the Zionist flag, wore British uniforms, and swung Allied arms over their shoulders in proud defiance of anti-Semitism and the horror of Nazi atrocities. They fought, died, and were wounded alongside the Allies in Greece and North Africa.

By March of 1945, they were on the ground in Italy and engaged the Germans until the Nazis surrendered in May 1945. Members of the Brigade liberated Holocaust survivors and helped many move to Palestine. They were heroes.

Michael Evenari was one of the freedom fighters. He recorded his memoirs during the final days in Italy, as the war came to a close:

"During this period, I spent some time in a Roman military hospital with a broken kneecap. One day, when I had a chance to get out for a few hours, I decided to visit the Vatican at a time when, by chance, Pope Pius XII happened to be giving an audience to soldiers from the Allied forces. He gave a short speech, and then walked along the first row of the audience where I, heavily bandaged, had been given a place.

"As he passed by, people knelt down and kissed the fisherman's ring. As non-Catholics, two of us, a British officer standing next to me and myself, remained standing. The Pope stopped and asked me in English: 'Where are you from, my son?'

On the spur of the moment, wanting to show off my Latin, I answered: 'Terrae sanctae civis sum Judaeus. Tibi gratias ago nomine populi Judaei quia salvabas vitam Judaeorum tam multorum' (I am a Jew from the Holy Land. In the name of the Jewish people, I thank you for saving the lives of so many Jews).

Although after the war, the Pope was sharply attacked for his passive attitude towards Hitler's regime, we came across many Jewish families, who had been sheltered in monasteries and saved from the Germans at the Pope's order.

Slightly taken aback, the Pope looked at me and asked in Hebrew: 'Then you speak Hebrew. Let me bless you.' He spread his hands out over my head in the manner of the priests of the Jerusalem Temple, and then recited the priestly blessing in Hebrew: 'The Lord bless thee and keep thee." [1]

1   Evenari M. (1989) With the Jewish Brigade in Italy. In: The Awakening Desert, Springer, Berlin, Heidelberg.

CHAPTER 185 ━━━━━━━━━━━━━━━━━━━━━━━━━

OSS STRATEGY

The winter of 1944 was brutal. February was the worst month. Snow and freezing rain fell on soldiers of the Fifth Army as they advanced toward the German lines in the Center and North of Italy. Troops had to walk through icy mud and sleep in frozen foxholes without blankets and only raincoats to protect them. They were plagued with illness, and bombs, bullets, and an endless array of enemy traps.

German troops occupied the high ground in hills and valleys throughout the heart of the peninsula. They controlled the movement of partisans and Allied forces with their snipers, machine guns, mines, and artillery attacks.

"We need intelligence on Nazi emplacements in key areas. They hold strategic locations and control the arteries to Rome," the OSS commander explained to Joe and Tom. They arrived in Allied headquarters near Salerno with visions of Ponza still in their minds. The situation on the mainland was critical and more dangerous than ever.

"We are bogged down. Until we can use overwhelming air and firepower, we will be at the mercy of the Nazis," he said. The officer pointed to a place on a map. A mountain rose five hundred meters over a town in a valley. Below the peak were winding roads leading to the capital of Italy. It was one hundred and thirty kilometers southeast of Rome.

Built deep on top of the mountain was a huge, ancient monastery.

"We must find out if the Germans are in the abbey," demanded the intelligence chief. "Enemy gunners are in place along sides of the mountain. Three attempts to take the monastery failed. German machine guns killed and wounded many of our troops and forced us into retreat. They control the high ground. We have to break through so we can move over the roads to reach the Gustav Line defenses and knock them out. If we discover the enemy has occupied the abbey, we will have to bomb it and blow up the entire mountain," he said with reluctance.

Courtesy, Italian National Archives and Republic of Ireland National Archives

The Allies did not want to destroy the monastery, which was a world-renowned treasure of medieval art.

"What do you want us to do?" asked Joe.

"Climb up to the abbey and find out if the Germans are inside," he responded. "It is suicide," said Tom, anxiously. "If you use the skills you learned in camp, you will make it and return," said the commander, confidently.

"What is the name of the place?" asked Joe."

"Monte Cassino," he replied.

CHAPTER 186 ━━━━━━━━━━━━━━━━━━━━━

THE CALL

She sat in the telephone booth, anxiously waiting for the phone to ring.

'Is he in a lot of pain?' she wondered. 'Who is taking care of him?' she asked herself. 'Are the nurses pretty in the infirmary?' she pondered with a jealous air.

Helena was in a drugstore. It had a wooden telephone cubicle, lined with glass and a small seat inside, under the pay phone. People walked in and out of the shop wondering when the young lady would leave the compartment so they could make a call. She sat for nearly an hour. "Are you going to sit there all day?" inquired one annoyed customer. Helena smiled and did not respond.

He walked away in search of another place.

Helena wore a short-brimmed hat with white gloves and a blue dress trimmed with lace along the collar. She had no makeup. She did not need it. Her complexion was smooth with rosy red cheeks. Her eyelashes were long and dark. She looked like a princess.

She spoke with Carlo the day before, but it seemed like years ago.

Time had a different meaning for lovers.

It was too long to wait when they were apart, and too short when they were together.

Carlo hurt his back picking up a sack of flour. He was bedridden. Fortunately, a public phone was in his barracks. It was thirty meters away. He painfully limped to reach it, but he could not stand up for more than a few minutes. There was no chair or seat nearby.

He called her every day.

The phone rang once. She grabbed it. "Sweetheart," she said in a low, sensual voice. "How are you, my love? Are you in pain, my darling?" she asked passionately.

"I love you," responded Carlo. His voice was deep and manly.

"The pain shoots from my lower back down my right leg," he said. He could barely stand up. He held onto the phone apparatus as if it were a crutch.

"Did they give you something?" inquired Helena, sweetly.

Carlo recalled the cute Army nurse with the blonde hair and blue eyes who took care of him.

It was not her looks he remembered, but the size of the needle she held in her tiny hand. "This will sting a bit," she said. It was the latest painkiller used for soldiers in battle. The drug was a cocktail of morphine and other products meant to temporarily reduce the anguish of war wounds.

Carlo looked at the needle. He swore it was the same used by veterinarians in Italy to inject horses with vaccines. It seemed thick, long, and exceedingly painful.

The nurse thrust it into a vial of yellow fluid. She pulled on the hypodermic as it sucked medication into the glass chamber. She pushed it to eject air. It was ready.

Carlo slowly pulled down his trousers. It was a torment to make the slightest effort. "Do not move," she said. The nurse felt the muscle and found the thickest part. She quickly plunged the needle into the meaty backside of his buttocks and injected the thick liquid. It took forty-five excruciating seconds.

"Owwww!" screamed Carlo, loudly. He jumped at the sudden pain. It felt like an animal with sharp teeth was taking a big bite out of his rear end. She pulled out the needle. The nurse applied alcohol with a cotton swab to the puncture. A few drops of blood appeared.

"You should feel better soon," she explained smiling. "Thank you," responded Carlo. He was not sure what hurt more, the injection or his back? He was perspiring and tired.

'He is a good-looking man,' she thought. The nurse was from an Irish family and seemed naturally attracted to tall, dark, and handsome men from the Mediterranean. "The doctor prescribed an injection a day," she told him. "Please be here tomorrow at the same time," said the nurse as Carlo limped out the door of the camp hospital.

"I felt better after the pain killer took effect, my love," Carlo told Helena. "It wore off in three hours, and now I cannot move again," he explained.

"I am so sorry sweetheart. I wish it was me and not you," said Helena. She sincerely meant it.

She loved this man so much she would willingly take on his agony.

"I will write you, darling," he said. "I cannot stand at this phone any longer, my love," exclaimed Carlo.

"Goodbye, my sweetheart," whispered Helena.

Carlo returned to his bunk. He held on to anything and everything as he hobbled into the barracks. He staggered and sat down. The bed was a slim mattress with a thick string of metal ribbons holding it up. It hurt to lay down. He took a pencil and piece of paper from under the bed and wrote:

My sweet and lovely Helena:

A second ago I heard you. Your voice is the song angels sing. You are the echo of heaven, my love. I can still hear you.

I miss you so much.

The thought of you soothes me and relieves my pain. Before I sleep, I think of your warm arms embracing me and the scent of your perfume. When I awake, my first thought is of you.

One kiss is all I need to survive and continue until we meet again. Then, you will fill my arms and my heart the way you fill my dreams.

I love you,

Your Carlo

CHAPTER 187 ━━━━━━━━━━━━━

ORDERS

It was an order.

Joe and Tom did not volunteer for the mission.

Chances of their return were slim.

They were expendable.

It was the first week of February.

Thousands of soldiers died trying to reach the monastery.

It was hopeless.

They would be two more, they thought, as they began their journey into the inferno.

Tom stopped in the library to get a book about the monastery. He found a poem that he read to Joe from Henry Wadsworth Longfellow entitled "Monte Cassino:"

> *From the high window I beheld the scene*
> *On which Saint Benedict so oft had gazed;*
> *The mountains and the valley in the sheen*
> *Of the bright sun, and stood as one amazed.*
> *Gray mists were rolling, rising, vanishing;*
> *The woodlands glistened with their jeweled crowns;*
> *Far off the mellow bells began to ring*
> *For matins in the half-awakened towns.*
> *The conflict of the Present and the Past,*
> *The ideal and the actual in our life,*
> *As on a field of battle held me fast,*
> *Where this world and the next world were at strife.*
> *For, as the valley from its sleep awoke,*

I saw the iron horses of the steam
Toss to the morning air their plumes of smoke,
And woke as one awaketh from a dream.

Tom reread the last line, and he wondered when his nightmare would end.

CHAPTER 188 ━━━━━━━━━━━━━━━

MONTE CASSINO

It was nightfall. They were in black. The boys from the Bronx were experienced commandos, decked out in uniforms filled with pockets of ammunition, explosives, pistols, and knives. Each had a grappling hook and a rope and a bulletproof vest.

If one of them died, the other was to carry out the mission. They were to scale a mountain with thousands of enemy troops lodged in it. Their goal: intelligence.

The weather was awful. Snow was on the ground. Mud and rain and water flowed rapidly down the side of the peak. It flooded paths and made climbing nearly impossible.

The freedom fighters were left in a safe area one mile from the German line. They had to cross it and scale Monte Cassino and get into the abbey.

It had been attempted several times. No one ever returned.

By Christmas 1944, the Germans built an endless network of machine gun and artillery positions along the area leading from the valley to the monastery. It was a circular beehive of death surrounding most of the mountain.

German General Fridolin von Senger and the Abbot of Monte Cassino,
Courtesy, German Federal Archives

The Nazi General in charge of operations established a close relationship with the Abbot of the monastery.

German soldiers unloading treasures from the monastery of Monte Cassino into Palazzo Venezia in Rome, November 1943, *Courtesy, German Federal Archives*

He arranged for the most valuable documents and artifacts to be trucked to Rome for safekeeping. Berlin publicly acknowledged the regime's respect for Italian cultural heritage as part of their propaganda.

It deified Nazi atrocities.

Small villages on the way to Monte Cassino were uprooted by the Germans to construct defensive locations. The inhabitants were thrown out of their homes and turned into slave laborers to create barricades and shelters. Hundreds of men, women, and children who were not murdered, actually died of exposure, living in freezing caves along the road to the monastery.

Allied troops, trying to cross the ravine or take the mountain, were sitting ducks. German outposts saw everything and anything that moved. A hail of gunfire cut down two thousand soldiers in forty-eight hours when they attempted to take the embankments.

It was called "Death Valley."

Crossing it was impossible.

As long as the Germans held the high ground, they controlled the road to Rome.

General Mark Clark, head of the Fifth Army, did not want to destroy the monastery. He argued against it. He did not believe Germans were in the abbey. He said that if it were destroyed, it would be a perfect ruin for the Germans to occupy and use as an artillery outpost and communications center and be even more difficult to take.

The British disagreed.

The OSS wanted to prove there were no Germans in the building. They insisted it would be useless, pointless, and tragic to bomb it.

The Vatican sealed a pact with both sides not to use religious sites for combat and to respect holy places like Monte Cassino, which was built by St. Benedict in 529. It was one of the most historic places on earth. Monks for centuries copied sacred manuscripts and preserved them for posterity within the walls of the abbey.

Monte Cassino was holy ground for the religious and cultural community of the world.

The Germans sought to compel the enemy to destroy the monastery. The plan was to turn public opinion and the Catholic Church against the Allies. Clark knew this. But he needed reliable intelligence to convince his superior, British General Bernard Alexander, to prevent the bombing of the abbey.

The American high command saw it as the senseless destruction of an historic site and the needless killing of innocent civilians sheltered in the abbey.

And they argued it was a waste of vital air power needed for the invasion of Normandy.

CHAPTER 189 ▬▬▬▬▬▬▬▬▬▬▬▬▬▬▬▬▬▬▬▬▬▬▬▬

DO NOT ENGAGE THE ENEMY

"I want to go home," said Tom to Joe. "Me, too," responded his brother. They were breathing heavily and filled with fear. They made the sign of the cross. Joe grabbed his rosary beads and said a prayer.

The pair snuck across the enemy line like cats. They had memorized a map of the mountain. According to them, only one path was not controlled by the Germans. It was on the southeast side and did not face the valley. It had no strategic importance.

"You are not to engage the enemy," said their Commander, as Joe and Tom started their journey. "If you attack or are discovered, you are finished. Capture is out of the question. Do you understand?" The brothers nodded in agreement.

They could not defend themselves.

Under their shirts was a thin chain around their throat. A cyanide capsule was attached. Joe felt his deadly necklace. He imagined it to be the poisonous snake that bit Cleopatra.

It was 3 AM. Most of the enemy were asleep, except for sentries and lookouts.

Darkness was their shield.

Sunrise was four hours away.

The commandos ascended. The monastery was five hundred meters above the ground. To reach it, they had to scale two miles of twisting terrain filled with rocks, boulders, bushes, goat trails, cactus, and Germans.

The enemy was everywhere. Caves dug high into the hills along the mountain were natural positions of attack.

One hour into their climb, the rain stopped. The moon cut its way out of the clouds and shone on them.

It seemed like a heavenly light.

They were halfway there. The sky lit up the monastery. It was high above them. The journey seemed too easy. No sense of the enemy anywhere.

Silently they scaled a cliff and made it to the top. They rested on the flat ground. The abbey was in the distance. Slowly, they rose from the clammy surface of the rock.

Instinctively, they sensed something.

Twenty meters away was a moving shadow.

A soldier in a raincoat with a rifle stood guarding the path.

Joe and Tom heard snoring.

Beyond the guard was a grotto with a team of German soldiers, sleeping.

The barrel of a long gun nosed out of the cave. It was a key enemy position.

The commandos hit the ground. The sentry heard a noise and walked toward the cliff. He came within a meter of Joe.

'Sneak up behind him, cover his mouth, cut his throat, and throw him into the ravine,' he thought. 'Bad idea,' he said to himself. 'Better to wait.'

They had two choices: kill the soldier and risk detection, or turn back and look for another path. The second option made more sense.

The soldier turned and returned to the cave.

Climbing down the cliff was more dangerous than going up. Joe went first. He leaped and settled on a ridge. Tom jumped. He landed on the edge and was falling off. Joe grabbed him and pulled him to safety. It was a narrow escape.

They circled around to the east side of the peak. The walls of the monastery were high above them. Step by step, inch by inch, they crawled, walked, and ran to reach the summit.

Out of nowhere, something large and black raced toward them. The commandos hit the ground and took out their pistols. It came closer. Joe removed the safety from his revolver. He screwed on the silencer. It came within two meters of Joe. A light from the sky flashed on it.

It was a goat.

The freedom fighters took deep breaths and continued toward the abbey.

The monastery complex was huge.

The walls were five meters high, three meters thick. A road leading to the building was five miles long on a twisting incline leading to the valley. German vehicles and artillery were lined along the way.

Joe loosened his rope. He threw the hook high to reach the edge. It missed and fell. It crashed on the rocks. The commandos looked about to see if the noise woke anyone. After three attempts, the hook grabbed a side of the wall. They pulled themselves up and over and slid down into the courtyard.

It was empty. It was dark.

Moonlight guided them.

"You take the outside. I'll go in," Joe said to Tom. It was 5 AM. The monks were at mass. Joe searched for an open door. He found one and went inside. He hugged the wall and listened. Oil lanterns led down a corridor. A chorus of men were chanting at the end of the hallway. Joe pulled out his pistol. He reached a door. Light was coming from the sides and the opening. It was a chapel.

Joe slowly opened the portal. Three men in brown tunics with white ropes and sandals were facing the altar. A priest was celebrating the mass. The monks were singing a Gregorian chant.

Joe hid in the shadows. The mass finished a few minutes later. He emerged. He walked to one monk and stood behind him. He tapped him on the shoulder. The friar turned, startled and stunned. Joe put his finger to his lips. "Father, I will not hurt you. I am an American soldier. All I want is information. Are there any Germans in the monastery?" he whispered. The monk nodded no. "Who else is here beside you and your colleagues?" he asked. "Three hundred people from the town are in the basement seeking refuge," he responded. "Do the Germans have any guns or soldiers stationed on the abbey grounds?" he inquired. "The only emplacement is fifty meters from the outer wall," he replied. "Bring me to the basement," said Joe. The monk obeyed.

Below the monastery was a huge chamber that ran under the building with thick columns. Hundreds of women, children, and old people were huddled on the floor sleeping. The room was cold and smelled of unwashed bodies. Joe surveilled the area and walked among the slumbering refugees.

"Thank you," he said to the monk and ran out of the building. Tom was entering the courtyard. "No Germans inside, but right below are dozens of gun units. One is within throwing distance of the wall," Joe explained to Tom.

They had the information they needed.

Now, they had to get back.

Liberation

CHAPTER 190 ━━━━━━━━━━━━━━━━━━━

GENERAL ALEXANDER

British and American press reported German artillery positions and observation facilities inside the monastery perimeter.

Lieutenant General Ira Eaker, Commander of the Mediterranean Allied Air Forces, along with two other officers, flew over the abbey in a small plane. They described seeing clotheslines with German uniforms in the courtyard and machine-gun emplacements almost adjacent to the monastery walls. [1]

A radio antenna was also spotted in the monastery complex.

General Bernard Freyberg, head of the Monte Cassino operation and Commander of the New Zealand forces and his team believed destruction of the abbey was a military necessity.

If it was not occupied immediately, it would be, once a major assault was launched.

German troops would take shelter in the abbey. Undamaged, it would be a splendid position for a counterattack.

Destroyed, the monastery would be a pile of rubble and a death trap to soldiers seeking refuge in the debris, was the view of the New Zealanders. [2]

Clark continued to disagree. Pressure from Winston Churchill to act forced the Allies to decide.

It was now up to General Alexander.

1   Hapgood, David; Richardson, David (2002) [1984]. *Monte Cassino: The Story of the Most Controversial Battle of World War II* (reprint Ed.). Cambridge Mass.: Da Capo, pp158-161

2   *Majdalany, Fred (1957). Cassino: Portrait of a Battle.* London: Longmans, Green. pp121-122

CHAPTER 191 ━━━━━━━━━━━━

INTO THE LINE OF FIRE

The commandos had an hour.

Daylight would arrive in less than sixty minutes.

They had to race down the mountain, cross the German lines in the valley, and make it to Allied territory.

They took the same route back that they had taken coming in.

Sliding, running, and jumping along the rugged hillside in the dark, they risked serious injury. They could fracture a leg or break their necks.

They stopped at the place they found the German sentry. No one was in sight. It could be a changing of the guard, they thought.

It was faster going down than going up, but equally perilous.

Forty-five minutes into the journey, the first glimmer of sunlight appeared on the horizon. Joe and Tom saw the road below. Once they crossed it, it was a clear run to reach the Allied line of defense.

Out of nowhere came a huge ray of light.

They were horrified.

A German searchlight was combing the area. They kept still and followed the beam as it moved in a semicircular pattern seeking anything that moved.

Joe and Tom ran as soon as the light changed direction.

They went down a steep slope and landed on a flat embankment.

The road was just ahead.

Joe stepped forward and felt a thin cable snap in front of his foot.

It was a trap.

The Germans planted trip wires to alert them.

Suddenly, streams of light flashed. Machine guns fired from all directions. Joe and Tom hit the ground. A storm of flaming bullets flew over their heads. They felt the fiery heat of the projectiles on their cheeks.

They were pinned down.

The Germans kept firing without seeing a target. "In three minutes, they will reload," whispered Joe to Tom. "It will take another three to fasten the ammunition belt to the guns," he murmured.

He looked at his watch.

He hoped it was not running fast or slow.

One, two, three minutes passed.

They got up and ran toward the road. A barrage of gun fire showered around them.

A bullet hit Tom.

He fell, screamed, and grabbed his right calf. Joe lifted his brother and tossed him over his shoulder. Another round of sizzling shots bounced off the ground and stones. Tom shrieked. He was hit again. Scorching lead ricocheted and shattered on the rocks.

Joe felt like he was hit with a baseball bat in the stomach.

The clothes and skin along his belly were burning.

He continued to run.

He turned a corner. They were out of range of enemy fire. He kept moving, faster and faster.

Tom was bleeding and crying with pain. Joe did not feel the weight of his brother on his back.

All he thought of was sprinting one hundred meters more.

He made it. An Allied patrol was waiting for them. Joe placed Tom gently into a jeep. His brother was almost unconscious.

Blood was streaming from his legs.

Joe felt a boiling sensation in his abdomen. He placed his hand under his trousers.

It was filled with blood.

CHAPTER 192

CANDLES

Anna and Sofia lit one each. A hundred flaming lights glowed in the chapel. They were for a son or daughter at war. A special place in the church was set aside for candles dedicated to loved ones fighting in Europe or the Pacific.

The young ladies made the sign of the cross and meditated. "Please bring him home," pleaded Sofia to the Lord. "Keep him safe," asked Anna. Letters from Joe and Tom were in their purses, protected like jewels.

Sofia wore a red dress, little make up, and her hair was tied in a bun like the women working in factories. She and Anna had a "Victory Garden" of fruits and vegetables they raised on a vacant lot in the neighborhood. They shared the crops with the parishioners at the end of Sunday mass. Anna sang in the choir each morning. She had on a white outfit with a heart-shaped pin. It was a gift from Tom.

Sofia and Anna were like sisters. They shared thoughts, fears, dreams, and questions. Where are they? When will they return? How are they? Many uncertainties crossed the minds of these beautiful, wonderful, and loving women. For Maria and Enzo, they were the daughters they longed for. In the small Italian neighborhood, they were angels.

Comfort, strength, and optimism was what they brought to families captured in the fear of conflict. They baked cakes and muffins for husbands and wives waiting for news from the front. Hours were spent listening to mothers talk about their children and waiting for letters.

Prayers were said at every mass for those suffering the ravages of war. The Church collected and sent hundreds of care packages to refugees in Italian towns. People who were unknown, were in the thoughts and hearts of strangers in America. Food, clothing, and anything to comfort them was enclosed in those boxes. Letters were written by students to children in refugee camps to show love and friendship.

Three times a week, the pastor of Our Lady of Pity Church held a prayer vigil for the safety of those from the parish in uniform.

Father Francis, the pastor, climbed the pulpit. "This evening" he began, "we thank God for the progress our troops are making in Europe. They are not fighting as conquerors, but as peacemakers. We say special prayers for the souls of all those who have lost their lives in this terrible conflict. Our hope is their sacrifice will end the bloodshed and bring peace, respect, and freedom to the world. We pray our men and women will be home soon and our Almighty Father keeps them safe until they return."

Anna and Sofia held hands as they recited the Our Father. The pastor asked a special invocation to God for the entire community:

Oh Lord, preserve from harm the members of our village in the Army, Navy, Coast Guard, and Marines. Even in war, help them be merciful, kind and caring, and to respect life and liberty.

Give strength to the families, friends, and relatives of our members in the military and relieve their concerns and anxiety. Help our men and women in combat deal with daily challenges and preserve them from violence and suffering.

Lord, please help all nations work together for lasting peace, tranquility, and harmony. Creator of mankind and the universe, we understand the price of liberty we must pay.

Please bless our freedom fighters with courage, hope, and strength. Be compassionate and healing of their souls and bodies and shield them from darkness and bring them to the light of your love and our love. Amen.

CHAPTER 193 ━━━━━━━━━━━━━━━━━━━━━━━━━

HIT

There was no time to put Tom and Joe on stretchers. They were driven to the field hospital and carried to a large green tent. It was a makeshift facility with a red cross painted on it.

Tom was unconscious. Half of the blood in his body was gone. A bullet pierced his right calf and severed an artery. Another sunk deep into his left leg. He was put on an operating table. Doctors rushed to save his life. Two nurses sedated him with ether, attach intravenous bottles containing fluids and blood, and monitored his heart rate and vital signs.

His clothes were cut away, exposing his wounds. They were deep. Bullets had to be removed and damage repaired.

It was a race against time. He was dying.

On the operating table, Tom went into cardiac arrest. His heart stopped.

A doctor pumped his chest while his colleagues controlled the bleeding and pulled the lead from his body.

In the throes of death, Tom had visions. He saw a long path of light. At the end of it was a lake and a park filled with trees and a group of people. They were wrapped in a mist as they came towards him. He recognized faces of boyhood friends who perished on the battlefield, and relatives who had passed away. They smiled and reached out. He took their hands. He felt peace. Pain, anxiety, and worry were gone. An experience of lightness and happiness lifted him.

Tom sensed he was hovering high above the operating table. He saw his body covered in blood and physicians dressed in white with gloves, masks, and instruments, feverishly working. In those fleeting seconds, Tom felt secure. The hands he held were warm and welcoming.

Abruptly, something changed. He returned to earth. The weight of the world seemed to fall on him. He felt helpless and heavy. Sorrow, anguish, and anxiety replaced peace and tranquility.

His heart beat again.

Tom was alive.

CHAPTER 194 ━━━━━━━━━━━━━━━━━━

ON THE EDGE OF DEATH

Joe was awake. His lower extremities ached. He was trembling and weary. A doctor examined his wound. Fragments of shells seared and punctured his abdomen and wedged in his muscle tissue. They were not lethal, but they had to be removed. The wound was medicated and disinfected.

"Doctor, how is my brother?" asked Joe. "We removed the bullets, but he desperately needs another transfusion. We are out of his blood type," explained the physician. "Take mine. We are both B minus," insisted Joe. "Hold on," responded the doctor. "You went through a severe trauma. If I take your blood now, you could go into shock and die," he explained.

"Doctor, let's not waste any time. Take it now," insisted Joe. The physician consulted his colleagues. Tom's condition was grave. Joe's operation could wait a few hours, but his brother could fall into an irreversible coma, any moment.

The prognosis was poor.

Joe was shivering and weak. It was a risky procedure. The lives of two men were on the line.

War is hell.

Joe was wheeled into the intensive care unit. Tom's face was deathly pale and covered with an oxygen mask. He was unconscious. Both legs were bandaged.

The doctor literally ran a tube from one man to the other. "I want you to keep squeezing this ball until I tell you to stop," said the Doctor. It was the same rubber ball he and Tom played with in the Bronx. Joe smiled and squeezed it. He watched as his blood flowed into the body of his brother.

It took two hours.

The Doctor removed the tube and disinfected Joe and Tom's arms. "We have done everything we can. If he wakes up in the next three days, he will survive. If not, he will be a vegetable or will die," noted the physician. "I want you to rest. Tonight we will take those fragments from your gut."

Joe could not walk. The pain was atrocious. He was helped back to his bed. He shared the tent with a hundred other soldiers. Many were wounded with arms and legs missing. Others were blind in one or both eyes. Most were deafened from bomb blasts and explosions.

The worst wounds were within. Souls and minds were damaged for a cause in a distant land, for a people they did not know and could not speak with. These warriors knew their sacrifice was for freedom and to protect their homeland from the onslaught of tyranny. Now they lay in a cold tent, with painful memories and bodies never to be the same.

Some would not return home.

Survivors had a new sense of courage and would be forever fearless.

More tents were going up to heal the thousands of men who tried to scale Monte Cassino. There were not enough doctors or nurses to care for them. Medication was scarce. The facilities were freezing and damp, and disturbed by the noise of war. Explosions and bombers prevented the patients from resting, and at any moment Nazi aircraft could attack the hospitals.

Joe wanted to sleep. He felt nauseated. His head was spinning.

A hand grabbed his shoulder and stirred him. It was the Commander of the OSS. The officer was in combat clothes with a helmet and pistol on his belt.

Joe tried to get up but could not. He was groggy, filled with pain, and his vision blurred. "What did you find out?" asked the officer. Joe slurred his words, but they were clear enough. "Sir, no Germans are in the monastery. No gun emplacements on the grounds. Artillery within walking distance of the walls. Machine gun nests right below the building and circling the mountain," he reported. "Good work," said the officer. "How do you feel?" he inquired. "Tired but OK. Worried about my brother," responded Joe, wearily.

"I will make sure you are both taken care of," he said as he shook Joe's hand and departed.

Joe fell into a deep sleep.

Five hours later, parts of the metal were removed from his body.

CHAPTER 195 ━━━━━━━━━━━━━━━━━━━━━━━━

COMA

Tom was comatose. He lay motionless.

Three days had passed since the transfusion.

Joe sat next to him all day and night. He prayed with his rosary. He held his brother's hand and spoke to him.

"You remember when Pop caught us smoking?" recalled Joe. "We were behind the shed. We lit up and began to cough. It was awful. Pop heard us. He saw we were smoking and grabbed us by the ears. 'So you want to smoke? Okay. Smoke this,' he said. He put those two big cigars in our mouths. We puffed on them and turned green. It was terrible. Since then, we have never touched a cigarette," laughed Joe, hoping against hope that his brother could hear him.

"And what about the fish? We went on the stinking boat outside of Sheepsheads Bay in Brooklyn. Everyone laughed at us because we were only kids and had two bamboo sticks as fishing rods, no reels, and a ton of tackle. No one caught anything. Then, just before the end of the trip, we brought in two huge whiting and won the pot. It was a hundred bucks. They went crazy. I still remember my fish. It must have weighed twenty pounds," said Joe.

"Mine was bigger," whispered Tom.

He opened his eyes and turned to his brother.

Joe cried loudly.

He hugged Tom and did not want to let him go.

His brother was alive.

CHAPTER 196 ━━━━━━━━━━━━━━━━━━━━━━━

DESTRUCTION

Tom awoke in the wee hours of the morning of February 15, 1944. He was unconscious for three days. A surge of blood in his veins revived him and healed his wounds.

Joe was bandaged below the waist. The doctors removed only a few pieces of lead. Several fragments were in so deep that field hospital surgery could be dangerous. The shrapnel hurt. Joe was in constant pain.

Bombing of the abbey of Monte Cassino, February 15th, 1944,
Courtesy, Archives of the US Air Force

"Can I have some water?" asked Tom. Joe brought him a glass and a straw. As he drank, the glass vibrated. The ground under the tent shook.

Overhead, gigantic Flying Fortresses dropped bombs on the abbey. "What's happening?" asked Tom. "The Brits overruled Clark. They are bombing the monastery. Yesterday they dropped leaflets to warn the friars of the attack. It will take a lot of blood to get the Germans out of the mountain," said Joe, sadly.

One hundred and forty-two B-17s, forty-seven B-25s, and 40 Martin B-26s released one thousand, one hundred and fifty tons of TNT and incendiary bombs on the abbey. In hours, it was a pile of rubble. During the bombing, artillery barrages pounded the mountain, seeking to destroy Nazi fortifications. In the afternoon, another fifty-nine bombers wreaked more destruction.

The Abbey of Monte Cassino after the bombing,
Courtesy, Italian National Archives

When the smoke cleared, key German positions remained untouched. Later, it was discovered that British intelligence had improperly translated intercepted Nazi messages, interpreting them as having troops in the abbey when there were none.

Following the raids, a ground attack was hampered by foul weather. Two hundred and forty civilians sheltered in the abbey were killed.

Few Germans died. Wild winds blew bombs in various directions. Allied and German troops were killed in random explosions. Several hit the compound where General Clark was working and went off only meters from his trailer.

After the bombing, Nazi paratroopers occupied the ruins and used it as an observation and fortress, compounding the difficulties for the Allies.

In subsequent assaults, the Allies lost fifty thousand troops and the Germans twenty thousand before Monte Cassino was finally captured.

CHAPTER 197 ▬▬▬▬▬▬▬▬▬▬▬▬▬▬

IT IS NOT OVER

By early March 1944, Tom's wounds were almost healed. He was able to walk, but not run. Joe faced a chronic soreness in his abdomen, which was manageable with pain killers. His ability to move was limited to walking. The brothers assumed their time as operatives was over. The next phase of their clandestine career was a desk or a ship home. They were wrong.

"Men, you will receive Purple Hearts and commendations for bravery, over and above the call of duty," said the Commander of the OSS to the brothers. "Thank you, sir," responded Joe. "You have demonstrated courage, skill, and ability to organize partisans and carry out complex and dangerous missions. I am proud of you," he stated. His words had meaning. Joe and Tom felt honored.

"Your next assignment is Rome," he said with a smile. He made it sound like it was a travel destination and not another deadly mission. Joe and Tom were shocked.

"We will continue to attack the Germans on the Gustav Line until we break them at Monte Cassino. Then the road to Rome will open, and we will push the Nazis further north. The Germans have occupied Rome since last September. We need to weaken their defenses and distract them while we prepare the assault on the city.

"Your job will be to set up a communications center to monitor their movements and organize partisans for sabotage and work with the Vatican. You leave today for Naples to get supplies and prepare all you need for Rome," he explained. "A colleague in Naples will brief you on the situation in the capital and your contacts. It is complicated. Good luck," he said. Joe and Tom saluted as the officer walked away.

A host of feelings surged through the minds and bodies of the freedom fighters. Surprise, anger, excitement, and worry welled up inside. Another murderous assignment. It was not fair. Two years of death and destruction was enough. Physically and mentally, they were tired. Up to now they had escaped death. Good fortune and God saved them. Had their luck run out? Had the Almighty abandoned them?

Questions rose as they looked at their bulletproof vests. The protective gear was filled with holes from German machine-gun fire. Black and blue marks covered their backs from the pounding of the slugs. They nearly died on Monte Cassino.

Was death waiting for them in the Eternal City?

CHAPTER 198

PETER

The three-hour trip to Naples was not easy. A nineteen-year-old Private was their driver. He was seventeen when he lied about his age to enlist in the Army. Peter was from a family in Brooklyn that came from a small town near Palermo. He landed in the first wave of the invasion of Italy and survived. His Sicilian was good enough to help him talk Italian soldiers into surrendering without a fight. Peter was jovial and filled with good humor and optimism. His youth and outlook were refreshing to the battled-hardened veterans he was escorting to Naples.

It was sunrise. Theirs was the only jeep on the road.

"Sir, my mother makes the best eggplant parmigiana in the world," said Peter as he took sharp turns. "Twice a month she makes cannoli. There is a store near our house that sells the best ricotta in New York. It is perfect for her cannoli," he explained. "Sir, you and your families are invited to Sunday lunch at our house when we go home," he declared happily.

He took a photo from his pocket. "Isn't she the most beautiful girl you have ever seen?" he asserted, filled with joy. It was a snapshot of a dark-haired girl with large eyes and heart shaped lips. She was lovely. "Veronica's family comes from a town near Benevento. We went to grammar school and high school together. As soon as I get back, we are going to be married," said the young man from Brooklyn.

He was filled with dreams and love. He sang songs for his sweetheart as he drove past shattered farmhouses, decaying animals, and homeless families on the road to Naples.

Joe and Tom looked at the faces of the people lining the road. They were desperate, exhausted, and hopeless. A woman held the hand of her little girl. Her world was attached to her. The little she possessed was in a sack on her back. Everything she owned was there. Her clothes were in rags and her body shrunk and dissipated by hunger. She looked at them. Her eyes spoke about despair, compassion, and charity.

Joe and Tom wanted to help. They were powerless and impotent.

All they could do is fight to end the war.

For an hour, Peter talked about home and how much he missed his family and the routine of daily life in the Big Apple. "I have a job lined up on the waterfront when I go back," he said. "My father got me into the union, even though I was underage," he laughed. He was happy and carefree. "I got a driver's license at 16. It was false, but you know New York. You can get anything you want as long as you pay for it," he said jovially.

Halfway into the journey they heard a roar. A fighter plane approached from the German lines. It was a Stuka. "Get off the road," yelled Joe. "Head for those trees," he commanded. Peter turned abruptly. The jeep bounced over bushes and stones.

The Stuka dove toward the highway. It shot at the refugees. They hit the ground. It turned toward the jeep and raced to catch it before it entered the forest.

It opened fire.

A volley of high caliber bullets followed them and surrounded the vehicle. Some pierced the front end. The jeep was hit. The spare tire and rear were struck. They made it to a small forest and drove in among a clump of poplars and oaks.

Joe leaped out. "Get under it," he ordered Peter and Tom, who quickly jumped beneath the vehicle.

Joe spent days in OSS training with a forty-five caliber Thompson submachine gun. It was an incredibly lethal weapon, originally used by American gangsters in the 1930s. It had a range of one hundred and fifty meters. It weighed five kilos and could release over seven hundred projectiles a minute. The caliber and consistency of the bullets made it perfect to pierce aircraft metal.

Joe became a skilled sniper and sharpshooter with a highly automatic weapon. It required precision, strength, and determination. It was difficult to manage a firearm which by nature fired sporadically. Joe described it as controlling an anti-aircraft gun on the pitched deck of a ship in a storm. Now he had his chance to use his talent.

He took his Thompson from the back seat and attached the ammunition drum. He hid behind a large pine. The fighter was circling like a falcon looking for its target. It dashed down close to their hiding place. Joe saw the face of the pilot.

He was determined. He wore goggles with thick black rims and a brown leather outfit.

The plane dived toward the edge of the forest. It swooped down within one hundred meters of its target.

The German flyer knew the jeep was in the nearby trees. He pressed the button on his weapon. A deafening fusillade of fiery shells and smoke chopped into the woodland, cutting branches and leaves and digging deep into the trunks and soil.

Joe aimed his Thompson at the underbelly of the plane just as the pilot turned upward from his target. He fired. The gun shook as he pumped hundreds of rounds into the sky. Dozens hit the plane. Three punctured the pilot's chamber. One entered under his feet.

He was hit.

The aviator screamed. A bullet sliced into his leg. It seared the leather of his trousers and burned into his calf. He was bleeding and in agony. He shrieked with pain. He gained enough altitude to put the aircraft on autopilot while he applied a tourniquet.

He was furious. His features flushed red with rage.

He turned toward the forest.

Joe knew he had struck the airplane. He assumed the pilot was wise enough to go back to his base.

He was not.

Peter and Tom came out of the woodland to join Joe. Suddenly, the shadow of an aircraft was seen overhead.

He was back.

The plane looked like a giant eagle. It dived in their direction. The three men scrambled to take cover.

A rapid barrage of machine-gun fire stormed at them. Peter was hit. Tom pulled him to the ground.

Joe grabbed his Thompson and ran out of the trees just as the plane steered upward. He fired at the left wing. Flames shot out of the engine and black smoke engulfed the aircraft.

The fuel chamber was hit and burned.

The airman was frantic. He headed for the German lines. Joe watched as he crossed high over the road. Fiery sparks jumped across the fuselage. Thick black smoke gushed out of the sides. It began to nosedive. It sounded like a siren as it fell.

The plane plunged into a grove of trees and exploded into a firestorm.

CHAPTER 199 ▬▬▬▬▬▬▬▬▬▬▬▬▬▬▬▬

NAPLES

A bullet had entered Peter's left shoulder and went through. He was gushing blood and crying. It felt like his body was on fire. Tom applied pressure to the wound and stopped the bleeding. The young soldier was frightened. "You will be okay," said Tom.

Joe drove. As he left the forest and got onto the highway, he saw carnage. He was devastated. Bodies were strewn everywhere. In the distance was the tail end of the German plane burning. Joe knew his enemy was dying in flames. His feelings were mixed. Hate mingled with sorrow. The pilot died doing his job, just the way Joe could die doing his.

But scores of innocent civilians were killed. Cries for help came from both sides of the road where the dead were entangled with the living.

Joe stopped. He saw the woman with the little girl. He ran to her.

She was wounded. A bullet was in her arm. Her daughter was bleeding from shrapnel in her legs. Joe placed them in the jeep. He found a little boy of eight with blond hair and blue eyes. He was hemorrhaging from his chest. Joe placed him in the front seat. He tried to take as many wounded as he could.

Within minutes, the jeep was filled with eight people.

Joe raced the engine and got moving.

Two hours later, they reached Naples. The city was destroyed. "Allied bombing had flattened industrial Naples into a mass of rubble and twisted girders. More systematically, the Germans, too, had taken their toll. They destroyed or removed all transportation facilities, blasted communications installations, knocked out water and power systems, and broken open sewer mains. They demolished bridges, mined buildings, fired stockpiles of coal, burned hotels and university buildings, looted the city, ripped up the port, shattered the railroads, and choked the harbor with sunken ships and the wreckage of port installations." [1]

Joe made it to the Fifth Army field hospital. He and Tom asked the doctors to care for the civilians. Peter was taken to a special unit where other soldiers were being assisted. Thousands of noncombatants were being cared for by the Allies as the war entered its final year.

Joe thought about the senseless slaughter of innocents. He wanted to cry, but he knew it would do no good. He was not allowed. He was a man, a soldier, a warrior. Tears, feelings, and emotions were forbidden on the battlefield.

He had a job to do.

End the bloodshed, even if it meant losing his life.

---

1   Martin Blumenson, United States Army in World War II, The Mediterranean Theater of Operations, Salerno to Cassino, Center of Military History, United States Army, Washington, DC. 1993, p. 166.

CHAPTER 200 ━━━━━━━━━━━━━━━━━━━━━━

MARGHERITA

She refused to let go of his hand. He had saved her life and that of her little girl. Her arm was medicated and bandaged. Margherita was thirty-five. Her child, Alba, was six. Mother and daughter were laying side-by-side in an American hospital in Naples. Alba slept quietly. Her legs were covered in gauze.

Their home, near Monte Cassino, was destroyed by Allied bombings. All was lost except their lives. Her husband was in a Nazi slave labor camp somewhere in Europe. Her parents were murdered by the German flyer. Their bodies, along with hundreds of others, lay unburied on the highway from Cassino to Naples.

She had no one except her little girl.

Joe stayed with her throughout the night.

He wiped the perspiration from her forehead and made sure she had water and food. Margherita felt secure and safe in the presence of this Italian-American soldier who spoke her dialect.

He held her hand.

He brought Alba chocolate and cookies and fresh milk. He found a ceramic doll in the rubble on a street in Naples and gave it to her. She was delighted and for the first time in months, smiled.

"God bless you," said Margherita. "You saved our lives. I will always be indebted to you and will pray for you always," she said. "Thank you. I will need your prayers," said Joe as he bid farewell. He kissed Alba and hugged her.

As he walked out of the hospital, he wondered what would happen to them.

He said a short prayer for the mother and child.

The little boy with the chest wounds did not make it. He was the one loss of the eight civilians.

It was a senseless tragedy.

Joe and Tom had an appointment with the OSS head of operations. He was to brief them and help prepare them for their mission in Rome.

CHAPTER 201 ━━━━━━━━━━━━━━━━━━━━━━━━

GENERAL CLARK

General Clark, General Alexander, and their colleagues waited and watched with binoculars from a hilltop three miles from the city of Cassino. It was the early morning of March 15th.

While Joe and Tom were in Naples, the Allies executed the third major attack on the monastery and the town of Cassino, at the crossroads leading to Rome.

Five hundred and fourteen fortresses, three hundred fighter bombers, and two hundred eighty aircraft released tons of explosives on the hillside and the village. Hundreds of artillery pieces fired over two hundred thousand rounds and twelve hundred tons of shells.

Two thousand civilians died, which was ten percent of the prewar population.

The massive bombardment was a failure. It made the subsequent assault more difficult for Allied troops.

Thousands of soldiers moved over the cratered, impassable terrain to find German positions intact.

More air attacks did little to help the Indian and New Zealand fighters make progress. A week after the massive bombings, General Clark called an end to the assault.

After four thousand casualties, the mountain, the city, and the valley rested in German hands.

Enemy soldiers, guns, and fortifications emerged from the rubble like ghosts.

The Germans remained in firm control of the center of Italy, spanning from sea to sea.

The Gustav Line of fortifications was created using Italy's natural barriers to defend the Nazi position on the peninsula. The topography and geology provided obstacles besides mountainous areas like Monte Cassino.

The Allies encountered ancient swamps filled with mud that bogged down tanks and heavy equipment, forcing troops to move on foot over hills, crossing streams and rivers, scaling slippery banks of clay, preventing soldiers from taking adequate cover from enemy snipers and attacks.

It was hopeless and deadly.

General Alexander ordered a halt to all incursions.

Three hundred and sixty-five thousand highly trained, battle hardened, dedicated, and enthusiastic German soldiers were amassed along the Gustav Line.

They came from a different background than the Allies. The ten nations that fought at Monte Cassino were from nonmilitary societies. Armies were hastily raised in the face of Nazi and Japanese aggression with little or no experience in war.

German troops were inculcated with a mission to bring the Fatherland back to greatness. Service in the military was honorable and necessary. Hitler nurtured the culture that German forces in World War I were betrayed by politicians. The present conflict was to correct the injustices of the past and save Europe from the tidal wave of Bolshevism.

Monte Cassino saw some of the bloodiest battles in history. The Germans had the psychological and physical advantage, while the Allies had overwhelming human and material resources.

The dilemma was that intense bombing and artillery barrages did not soften Nazi defenses.

German soldiers were in bunkers, basements, and caves, wore earplugs to protect their hearing from the sound of bomb blasts, and prepared weapons and plans against Allied incursions during bombing missions. Position, strategic logistics support, fire power, and determination gave them advantages to hold the line and exhaust the Allied efforts to break through.

After three bloody attempts to take Cassino, the Allies had to decide what to do next before the Germans mounted a counterattack to defeat them.

CHAPTER 202 ━━━━━━━━━━━━━━━━━━

GENERAL CLARK

Naples was dismal. It was a city of bombed out buildings, dust, and disease. People were begging in the streets as the Allies organized food distribution and care for the homeless. Two weeks passed, and Joe and Tom were waiting for orders and plans for Rome.

OSS headquarters was in the basement of an old palace where the Fifth Army set up operations. The room was windowless and smelled of secrecy and intrigue.

A young Army officer, fresh from Washington, conducted the briefing. He was tall, handsome, articulate, and a graduate of an Ivy League University. His hands were clean and manicured, and he was meticulously dressed and well groomed. He had a thick Boston accent. He had never held a rifle or a pistol. His strength was reading, writing, and analysis. He was a journalist by training and came from a wealthy family from Massachusetts. He was recruited by the OSS because he could think on his feet, solve problems, and express himself well.

Next to him was an Italian in civilian clothes. He was introduced as "Boris." He was thirty-eight, medium height, light brown hair, grey eyes and an olive complexion, with broad shoulders and muscular arms. He was a chain smoker. A cigarette dangled from his mouth. He wore a black leather coat and black trousers with a black shirt. Something bulged from his chest. Tom assumed it was a handgun, probably a semi-automatic Colt 45. Millions were manufactured in Norway before the war.

Thousands ended up in the German and Italian armies.

Boris was an operative.

His real name was Vittorio. His father was from Torino and his mother from Reggio Calabria. He grew up in Rome, where his mother taught elementary school and his father worked in a bank. He studied at the University of Rome and finished his degree in finance when the war broke out. He was recruited as an officer and was sent to "conquer" Greece. He and the bulk of the Italian forces laid down their arms after Italy surrendered to the Allies.

He escaped capture by the Germans and found his way back to Rome and joined the freedom fighters.

He had a year of experience in sabotage and killing.

People being rounded up to be killed in the Ardeatine Caves, March 1944, *Courtesy, Republic of Italy National Archives and the Museum of the Fosse Ardeatine*

"Two days ago," began the OSS officer, "a team of partisans set off a bomb in the center of Rome, killing twenty-eight Germans and two civilians. The next day, the Nazis declared that ten Italians would be killed for each German, unless the saboteurs gave up. The information we have is not clear, but our sources tell us that three hundred and thirty-five people were killed in the reprisal. Some were Jews. Many were taken off the street, and others came from the Nazi prison at Via Tasso. Students, teenage boys, doctors, lawyers, workers, shopkeepers, and even a priest was in the group. We think the killing was done outside of Rome in a place called the Ardeatine Caves. The order was for three hundred and thirty. The additional five were shot to eliminate a witness. Nazi officers personally killed each person and then dynamited the hole to seal it. Three of our operatives were among those murdered by the SS. We know they were tortured. The Gestapo pull out teeth and nails. We assume they gave information," he explained dryly.

"It means," he went on, "our communications center was compromised. We need to reorganize and set up a new place so we can track Nazi movements in and out of Rome," he said. Joe and Tom were angry and shaken about the latest German atrocity. They knew what fate was in store for them if captured.

"The equipment and a backup system is ready. Boris will be your guide. He will turn you over to our main contact in Rome. Her name is Sheila," he stated.

CHAPTER 203 ━━━━━━

GOING HOME

"So, you got your ticket home, kid," Tom said to Peter with a smile. His shoulder was wrapped in bandages. Part of it was in a cast. His arm was bruised and discolored.

"The bullet severed a tendon and shattered my collar bone. Looks like my chance at a pro career in baseball or tennis is over," responded Peter, laughing. "The offer to have dinner with us after the war is still open, sir," he said. "Tell Mamma to get the cannoli ready," replied Joe.

The three men hugged and bid farewell.

Tom and Joe visited the Italian civilians in the hospital. They brought gifts to each one.

"I want you to have this," said Joe to Margherita.

It was an envelope with one hundred dollars.

She opened it.

She was astonished. "No, I cannot accept your money," she declared. Joe said, "You will need this for Alba, once you leave here. I hope it helps."

She hugged him and kissed his cheeks.

Tears streamed down her face.

"You be a good girl and take care of Mamma," said Joe to Alba. She nodded and stared at him.

"Who is going to take care of you?" she responded, hugging her doll.

"God will protect me, and you, too," he said. He picked her up and kissed her.

The boys from the Bronx left the hospital with heavy hearts, knowing they would see none of them again.

CHAPTER 204 ━━━━━━━━━━━━━━━━━━━━━━━━

FLIGHT TO ROME

Joe, Tom, and Boris mounted the plane. It was the only way to reach Rome. The roads were in the hands of the Nazis.

It was one in the morning, Wednesday, March 29th, 1944. Spring was on the calendar but winter was in the air. It was cold.

The aircraft was a medium-sized troop carrier designed for parachute drops behind enemy lines. The OSS officer said the Germans rarely shot at small planes, to avoid showing where gun emplacements were located. At least, this was the conventional view.

Joe noticed bullet holes in the fuselage as they got in.

Tom recalled his first and only jump. The fear and pressure was still in his mind and, most of all, in his stomach. He was nervous and anxious as they strapped themselves into the side of the aircraft.

Joe saw this. His brother was pale and restless. Once the propellers started, the plane shook violently. Tom quickly became nauseated. It taxied and bounced along the runway for thirty minutes. The pilot raced the motor.

The noise was deafening as the airplane lifted off the ground and shot into the night sky like an arrow. It climbed in a vertical pattern for forty-five minutes and leveled off.

Tom thought he would die.

Joe, Tom, and Boris were the only passengers.

Boris as silent. He had not uttered a word since the briefing.

As they crossed German territory, they saw fires and lights. Towns were burning as the Nazis consolidated their position along the

Gustav Line. Villages were flattened. It was an awful sight. From the ground, a searchlight appeared. It reached into the sky. The plane flew into it.

Instantly, cannons roared. Anti-aircraft batteries fired torrents of missiles exploding with blinding lights around and in front of the aircraft. The hull trembled with each blast. The pilot pulled back on the wheel and took the plane into the clouds. The airliner shook as it reached higher altitudes. The volley of missiles slowly ended.

But no one felt safe.

Two hours later, they flew over Rome. The city was enveloped in darkness. Nothing could be seen except enemy skylights searching the heavens. The pilot was skillful enough to avoid being detected.

St. Peter's and the Vatican were invisible. The churches, monuments, and ruins of the Eternal City slept.

The copilot came out. "This is where you get off," he told them. "We are over the newest section of Rome. It is called EUR. Mussolini built it to be the new capital. The Nazis have few patrols in the area. They are in the center because it is safe from Allied bombings. EUR is four miles from downtown," he explained. "We are at eight hundred feet. All you have to do is jump, wait ten seconds and pull your ring," he described. "I will dump your gear after you are out, so you will find it nearby. I will make sure I do not drop it on you," he said giggling.

Tom did not appreciate the joke. He was perspiring heavily. The German attack on the plane added to his anxiety.

Boris was like a figure out of a wax museum, emotionless and cold. "Stay with me," said Joe to Tom. "I will jump first and you right behind me. When I yell pull, we both yank the ring at the same time," he explained. Tom's mouth was dry. His legs were weak. He was feeling faint.

Boris noticed Tom's apprehension.

The copilot opened the door. Wind rushed into the cabin, pushing and pulling everyone and everything. Straps, ropes, and gear went flying around the plane.

Joe saluted the pilot. He looked back at his brother. Tom nodded. Joe looked out. It was pitch black. Nothing could be seen. For all he knew, he could be jumping right into the hands of the Nazis, he thought.

He made the sign of the cross and leaped into the night.
He disappeared.

Tom limped to the door. Boris was behind him.

Tom hesitated. He held onto the plane. The Italian pushed him. Tom tumbled uncontrollably into the sky, tossing and turning. The plane vanished. Seconds later, he heard "Pull," and he jerked the ring. The chute flew out of his back. It yanked him high towards the stars and carried him into a cloud. He kept his eyes closed. He stopped climbing and descended rapidly. Currents of cold air froze his face.

He thought he saw the outline of a parachute below.

He was groggy and numb with fear.

The star-filled night guided him. Square and round objects and buildings seemed fast asleep along black thoroughfares.

The wind turned him in one direction and then another. He had no control.

As he fell, he perceived something strange rising in his direction. It looked like a mammoth, marble rocket mounted in the center of a square. It rose high above the ground. At first he was mesmerized. Then terror flew up his spine.

It was a gigantic obelisk.

He was about to crash into it.

CHAPTER 205 ━━━━━━━━━━━━━━━━━━━━

THE JUMP

Joe hit the ground. It was hard. His abdomen ached. He could feel the stabs of the metal shards in his muscles.

He fell into a wide cobblestone piazza surrounded with marble columns. He grabbed his parachute and rolled it up. He saw a large garbage bin and stuffed it into it. "What luck," he thought. "It is better to be lucky than smart," he said to himself.

He looked at the sky. He searched for Tom. He saw a parachute turning and twisting as blustery gusts lifted it toward a tapering stone spire, at least fifty meters in height.

Joe ran to it.

Tom saw the point of an obelisk. If his parachute landed on it, he was finished. He would be stuck. To be released, he would have to cut his cords. The fall would kill him. If he crashed into the pillar, he risked serious injury.

He was rushing toward it like a bullet. For an instant, Tom saw a vision. He was a little boy, holding the hand of his mother. They were at the novena of San Silverio in Our Lady of Pity Church. Maria took Tom up to the statue. "Thomas," she said. "Someday you will need help. Ask him, and he will reach out to you," she explained. The little boy stared at the face of the patron Saint of Ponza. That moment flashed in Tom's mind as he plunged through the night. "San Silverio, help me," he prayed. "Please save me!" he cried into the darkness.

The parachute continued to fall. Unexpectedly, it spun and twirled in different directions. A flurry of freezing air brought his chute within inches of the column. Tom hung in space watching as the parachute slid alongside the gigantic block of marble.

He descended slowly to the ground. He did not know if he should laugh or cry. Tom lay face down on the cold stone ground. He was breathing heavily. He thought his heart was about to break out of his body. "Thank you," he prayed.

Joe ran over to him. He put his arms around his brother. Tom looked at him and smiled. "Here's another nice mess you got me into," he said, quoting Stan Laurel to Oliver Hardy.

Boris landed shortly after Tom. He saw where his comrades were. He disposed of his chute and ran to them. "Are you all right?" he asked. "Okay," responded Joe. "The van is nearby. I will get it, pick you up, and get the gear," explained Boris. Joe gave him a nickname: The Bulldog.

In minutes, Boris circled the block and picked up Tom and Joe. Three large boxes lay on the road. There was no traffic. They loaded the crates and drove. They turned a corner with headlights off.

"Where are we going?" asked Joe. "We are heading for a place along the Tiber River," Boris replied.

A back road through sleeping neighborhoods and past ruins brought them near the synagogue. It was closed by the Nazis when they raided the ghetto.

Beyond the Jewish Quarter was the road leading to the Vatican and the river. Boris saw a vehicle moving two blocks in front. It was a German three-wheeled motorbike. Boris raced into a lot next to the basilica of Sant'Andrea della Valle.

A door separated the driver's side from the rear of the van. The three men scrambled through it and hid in the shadows among the crates. Joe took out his pistol and attached the silencer.

The motorbike pulled into the area.

The soldiers got out of the vehicle.

A horseless coach, two cars, and the van were parked. They took out flashlights. One German inspected the coach and cars. The other went to the van.

'I can jump out and shoot them,' Joe said to himself.

He knew the idea was a nonstarter. His mind was running wild as the soldier flashed his light in the van. He searched in, under, and around the vehicle. He saw nothing. He went to the rear and tried to open the door. It was locked. Tom jumped at the sound of the twisting handle.

Joe cocked the trigger of his gun.

The soldier signaled to his colleague.

They got onto the cycle and left.

CHAPTER 206 ▬▬▬▬▬▬▬▬▬▬▬▬▬▬▬▬▬▬▬

BORIS

Boris was a Roman. He spent most of his life in the city. He knew it well and where Nazi roadblocks and Fascist outposts were.

In less than an hour, they reached a street along the river. The embankment was ten meters above the road. Boris guided them to a stone stairway leading to the Tiber. A green, rectangular houseboat was docked. It was twenty meters long and three meters wide. It was made of long planks of oak and pine.

The vessel was moored with four anchors, two on each side, to keep it in place in the face of currents and winds. It was old and seemed abandoned. No other boats were in the area. Movement on the river stopped once the Germans occupied Rome.

The three men jumped onboard.

The Bulldog opened the door with a key.

Inside was a cabin with a small window, two tables, four chairs, and two bunk beds. All was in order and relatively clean.

"Why is this a good place for a communications center"? asked Tom. "Look out the window," responded The Bulldog.

On the other side of the river were a host of government buildings. One stood out. Its lights were on.

"What do you see?" he asked. "A classic style edifice with giant anchors on both sides of the entrance," replied Tom. "It is the Ministry of Naval Affairs. The Germans occupied it as soon as Italy surrendered. Cable traffic originates and ends in those walls," explained Boris. "From here, you can intercept messages as well as send them to our stations in the South," he noted.

"I will bring you food every two days. If you need to reach me, you will find me at this address near the Spanish Steps. The code is three knocks, and the password is Churchill. It is the same here. We are printing leaflets and newspapers to support the Allied cause," explained Boris. The three men shook hands. Boris departed.

It was 4 AM. Tom and Joe were spent.

They laid on the bunks and tried to sleep.

Courtesy, Carlotta Di Felice and Isabella Raffa

Minutes later, a woman walked briskly toward the hideout of the freedom fighters on the Tiber. It was still dark.

A pistol was in her purse.

She wore sunglasses and a hood to hide her face, and a black coat and shoes with rubber soles so she could move quickly and quietly. She made sure no one saw her.

She was one meter and sixty-five centimeters in height but seemed much taller with heels. She was statuesque, with an hourglass body and a round bosom. She looked lush and fertile, filled with the treasures nature gives women. Her eyes were black, large, round, and richly intelligent. Her hair was ebony and shined with a luster as if it were brushed by the Goddess of Light.

One feature stood out. Her nose was slightly curved at the bridge, like Scheherazade of the Arabian Nights. Her beauty was natural, elegant, and captivating.

She was a *femme fatale*. She attracted men like moths to a flame.

She worked for the Gestapo.

CHAPTER 207 ━━━━━━━━━━━━━━━━━━━━━━━

RITA

SS Headquarters in Rome, 1944, Via Tasso 145,
Courtesy, Museo delle Fosse Ardeatine and Republic of Italy Archives

She was hired in 1939. She was nineteen. The German government needed local, bilingual specialists to organize their Office of Cultural Affairs in Rome.

Her father was someone they trusted. He was a high-level official of the Fascist Party. Mussolini sent him to work in London and then to the Italian Embassy in Berlin. There she learned perfect English and German. She studied French and Spanish. She was a natural linguist. She was beautiful and intelligent. Her dream was to teach languages.

The new office was on Via Tasso, an obscure street in the San Giovanni section of the capital. It was part of the Diplomatic Mission of the Third Reich. From its inception, it was a center of intelligence and spying on the Fascist regime of Benito Mussolini, Adolf Hitler's closest ally.

With the Nazi occupation of Rome, it became Gestapo headquarters. She was assigned to the office of the number two in command of the SS in the Eternal City. She became his personal secretary.

The Nazis trusted no one.

Her sobriety, cold aloofness, and quiet and efficient work ethic gave her an Arian quality. She was a talented actress who pretended loyalty to the Reich and Fascist Italy. A few SS officials suspected something. She was followed regularly. Her apartment was searched frequently. As a routine, she was frisked randomly at least twice a week. Nothing was found.

To her superiors, she was beyond reproach.

They were wrong.

Her name was Rita.

The partisans knew her as *Sheila*.

CHAPTER 208 ━━━━━━━━━━━━━

SHEILA

Joe tried to sleep. His mind was weary, but his body was not. The flight over Nazi territory, the anti-aircraft fire, the jump from the plane, and the race to Rome filled his veins with adrenaline. He turned and tossed on the bed when he heard a sound. He leaped, stood up, and took his revolver from under the pillow.

Tom was awake.

The boards of the boat outside the door creaked.

"You expecting visitors?" Tom whispered sleepily. Joe put his finger to his lips. He walked quietly to the portal. It was dark. Tom got up from the bunk.

Three knocks on the door. "Churchill," said the visitor. It was a woman's voice. Joe opened. A ghost-like image in black stood before him.

"May I come in?" said the apparition. Her face was hidden. Joe opened the door. He looked outside before he closed it.

He pointed the pistol.

Courtesy, Carlotta Di Felice and Isabella Raffa

She removed her hood. The most beautiful creature he ever saw emerged. "Who are you?" he asked. "Sheila," she replied. Joe put down his weapon.

"Welcome to Rome," she said in the Queen's English. Her voice was divine. It was deep, tender, and musical. Her eyes were magic. She looked into theirs and saw men of might and courage. They saw determination and cunning.

Tom pulled a chair from the table. She sat like a princess. Joe offered a cigarette. She declined. "We have work to do," she explained. "Not far from here is a hospital on an island. The doctors are our allies. Jews are hidden as patients, and several Jewish doctors have been saved as part of the staff," she explained.

"In the basement, we can set up a radio transmitter. The doctors will report Nazi activity and troop movements," Sheila said.

"When do you want to do this?" asked Tom.

"Now," she responded.

CHAPTER 209

"THE DEVIL"

"We must crush the resistance immediately," said the leader of the Gestapo in Rome. He was boiling with rage. His face was red and his eyes filled with fury.

As Chief of the Security Police and Security Service, his role was to run an elaborate and ruthless intelligence service, round up Jews, imprison dissidents, and destroy patriots opposed to the occupation. He was a Lieutenant Colonel, decorated by the Fuhrer and selected by Hitler.

The Romans called him "The Devil."

The Gestapo leader was of medium height, with a smooth, pink complexion, closely cropped, brushed-back brown hair, and clear eyes that were cold.

He blushed frequently, sometimes in anger and other times with the cunning of a fox and savagery of a wolf. He never smiled.

The Devil had no sense of humor, compassion, or empathy, and he never used the word "mercy." He loved his work and was an example to his henchmen of brutality and cold-blooded determination.

The most powerful man in Rome could snuff out a life or liberate a person with the snap of a finger.

He was a consummate liar and murderer. In September 1943, he demanded fifty-eight kilos of gold from the Jewish community in Rome. In exchange, he swore not to expel any of them. A few weeks later, he rounded up a thousand people from the Ghetto and sent them to Auschwitz. His plan was to deport the entire population of ten thousand. Fortunately, most escaped and were protected by the Church and rebels fighting the Nazis.

The Devil spoke Italian with a piercing Teutonic accent. When he interrogated prisoners, his strident voice conveyed horror and fear.

Torture and murder were a natural extension of his mission to glorify the Third Reich in its quest to dominate the world. His job was to exterminate those who refused to accept Nazi rule.

Guerillas were disrupting German operations. They were dealt with by an iron hand.

Ordinary people suffering from the famine and persecution of the occupation found the courage to protest or speak about their plight. Thousands of innocents were killed by Fascist militia and German troops. They tortured, shot, or hung anyone suspected of being an enemy sympathizer or who was overheard whispering a few words of dissent.

Information was reported quickly to the Fascists and the SS. The Gestapo raided homes and dragged men and women to the killing fields outside of Rome or murdered them in the basement of Via Tasso.

Partisans and political prisoners were interned in Regina Coeli prison before execution. Hundreds of men and women were taken from the jail or picked up on the street and shot in the Ardeatine Caves. The Fuhrer wanted the "world to tremble" after the killing of German soldiers in Rome. The reprisal was the result.

It was organized and executed by The Devil.

More atrocities were to come.

Neighborhoods suspected of hiding partisans were surrounded and sieged by the SS. Men and teenage boys were arrested and sent to slave labor camps in Germany. Most never returned.

In one instance, women protested to the authorities about the reduction of bread rations.

Liberation

A group of them was taken to the periphery of the city and shot.

Acts like these became commonplace in the Eternal City under the reign of the Nazis.

CHAPTER 210 ━━━━━━━━━━━━━━━━━━━━

"THE BEAST"

On a bright, spring day in early April, the most feared man in Rome called for a meeting of key officials. In the office of the Gestapo Chief were the Director of the Fascist movement, the head of Special Fascist Police Unit in Rome, the Director of Regina Coeli prison, the German officer in charge of the SS police squads, the Ambassador of the German Embassy to the Holy See, and a double agent close to the OSS.

"Berlin reports that a massive Allied invasion will take place somewhere on the coast of France. A new attack on the Gustav Line will happen soon. The rebels know where and when. Each one is to be interrogated and tortured until they talk. Then, they are to be immediately executed," he insisted.

The Italians obeyed. They worked with the SS to pay informers and organize spies and agents who posed as members of the resistance.

Fascists joined forces with the Gestapo out of loyalty to the regime or cowardice and fear. Others collaborated to enjoy power. Some were inherently cruel and sadistic with criminal minds like those of the Gestapo.

A Fascist fanatic, known to Romans as "The Beast," led a special task force to hunt down insurgents and find deportees for the Germans. He was given a free hand by the leader of the Gestapo. His "gang" became synonymous with violence and brutality. The Beast created prisons and torture chambers. Hundreds of men and women fell under his cruelty and viciousness.

It was said even Mussolini feared him.

"Bring in wives and children for questioning. Tell these bastards that if they do not talk, we will kill their family," The Devil ordered.

"The Church is involved. The Pope himself is hiding Jews. Allied soldiers escaped from our prisons. They are hidden by the Catholics. Enemies of the state who fled concentration camps are protected by the Vatican. There are American, English, and French priests in the Holy See who are intelligence officers for the Allies," he screamed. "Find these spies and arrest them," he commanded. "As soon as I get orders, I will capture the Pope myself!" he shouted.

At any moment, he could wipe Vatican City off the face of the earth. It was neutral and defenseless and surrounded by the German Army. The Holy See depended on Fascist Italy for its livelihood. Electricity, water, utilities, and food came from Rome.

"Portrait of a boarding school class in which a Jewish boy was hidden. Class photograph of students at the San Leone Magno Fratelli Maristi boarding school in Rome. Pictured in the top row at the far right is Zigmund Krauthamer, a Jewish child who was being hidden at the school. Rome, Italy, 1943–44." [1] *Courtesy, US Holocaust Memorial Museum*

---

1   US Holocaust Memorial Museum. https://encyclopedia.ushmm.org/ content/en/photo/portrait-of-a-boarding-school-class-in-which-a-jewish-boy-was-hidden?parent=en%2F580

"Hit every church, school, monastery, convent and hospital and search them. Jews and partisans are being sheltered by the Catholics. Arrest all the religious involved. Posters and placards are to be distributed all over the city. We will increase rewards for information for the apprehension of resistance fighters and Jews. For every German killed, we will shoot ten Italians, as ordered by the Fuhrer. Make sure this is clear and these directives are carried out," he demanded.

The Eternal City was hostage to the Nazis.

German soldiers and Fascist officials organized, controlled, terrorized, and persecuted the population of Rome.

Information about The Devil's plans leaked out of Via Tasso.

The source was Sheila.

CHAPTER 211 ━━━━━━━━━━━━━━━━━━━━━━━━━━━

THE HOSPITAL

By early April, another radio was installed in the crypt of the hospital. Tom trained a nurse and a team of doctors to use it. Messages were sent to partisan units and the Allies on Nazi activities in Rome, including information on escaping prisoners and data in intercepted German telegrams.

Resistance fighters and Allied soldiers hid in the clinic. Meetings were held with informers. Attacks arranged on Nazi warehouses, garages, telephone switchboards, trucks, railway convoys, and even the German Military Tribunal at Via Veneto. A network of rebels spread throughout the city, despite Nazi reprisals. It included diverse political groups and people from all walks of life.

To deal with the growing unrest, the Germans moved arms and supplies into Rome by rail. Joe and Tom planned a daring attack on a supply train bound for the Ostiense station. The key player was a Lieutenant in the Rome police. He was an OSS operative.

"These should fit you," he said to the boys from the Bronx. They were police uniforms.

His name was Fabio. His family came from Calabria and settled in Rome in the 1920s. His father worked as a laborer to reclaim the Pontine Marshes and build EUR, which were two major projects of the regime.

As a boy, Fabio despised the coercion, haughtiness, and lies of Fascism. He went along quietly, waiting for the time to resist. He rose quickly in the ranks of the police. Fabio was honest, patriotic, and obedient, up to a point. He refused to participate in the arrests of Jews or civilians who had not committed a crime. He suffered watching the Nazis and Fascists terrorize innocent people. His superiors consented. Many hated the regime as much as he did, but they felt powerless.

He was strong, tall, and fearless.

"The train arrives at 4 AM from Milano. It is carrying tanks, artillery guns, explosives, ammunition, and food for the troops. The station is heavily guarded," he explained.

Tom and Joe were impressive in their uniforms. Fabio cut their hair so it fit properly in the hat. False IDs made them members of the Rome police force.

At 1 AM, Fabio arrived at the houseboat on the Tiber in a police car. Joe and Tom loaded a box of dynamite into the trunk.

The train from Milano would pass through the village of Pomezia. It was an hour drive from the capital. The town was heavily bombed during the invasion of Anzio. The Nazis rebuilt the rail link, which was a vital supply line from the north.

Fabio drove quickly through the city until he reached EUR. A German soldier with a parked jeep waved for him to stop. He was in his early twenties with blond hair and blue eyes. He wore combat gear and a heavy green coat. A rifle was swung over his shoulder. Rome was his first assignment.

"Your papers," he commanded. The policemen showed their ID. He used a flashlight to look at each one to match the documents with the faces. He examined the back seat. "Open the trunk," he insisted. Joe's blood pressure rose. He put his hand on his pistol.

Fabio took out a letter. He showed it to the soldier. The young man read it carefully. He returned it to Fabio and saluted. "Heil Hitler," he said. "Viva IL Duce," replied Fabio. He waved them through.

After a few minutes, Joe asked, "What was in the letter?" Fabio smiled. "The second in command at Gestapo Headquarters gave me a special pass saying that I was on a secret mission for the SS and was not to be delayed," he said.

"Sheila," thought Joe.

CHAPTER 212

THE MONSTER

Nazi headquarters at Via Tasso was originally the German Embassy Cultural Center in Rome. The building was transformed in January 1944 by the new head of the Gestapo. Fourteen large and small prison cells were created. Several special rooms were designed as torture chambers. Windows and openings were sealed so no one could look in or hear the screams.

Rita was promoted because of her skills and trust. She was personal secretary to the second in command of the Gestapo. He was ambitious and handsome and relished carrying out orders and giving them. He was cold, quick, cruel, and vengeful. He was known as "The Monster." His boss was The Devil.

Her office was on the first floor. It housed the admin section and communications center. She translated from Italian to German and vice versa. Letters, directives, messages from Berlin and Rome were prepared and sent by her. She was an expert in shorthand. The Nazi penchant for accuracy required taking minutes and recording conversations. Rita was in meetings and was the official translator between the Germans and Italians.

She reported for work at 8 AM and left at 9 PM. She preferred to walk home but was often escorted by an SS driver. The people of Rome considered her the worst of collaborators.

Her father was sent to the Russian front along with two hundred and thirty-five thousand soldiers. Half of them never returned. Her father was among the dead or missing.

Rita hated Fascism from when she was a child. Violence, militarism, arrogance, cruelty, and the subjugation of women were the hallmarks of Fascist Italy.

When the war broke out, she was determined to fight, even if it meant living and working in a den of vipers.

CHAPTER 213 ▬▬▬▬▬▬▬▬

RAID ON THE HOSPITAL

The chief physician recognized Sheila's voice. "They are coming tonight at 6 PM. Orders are to arrest anyone suspected of being a Jew or a fugitive. You will be taken in for questioning. You and your staff will be arrested and tortured." She hung up.

The hospital was run by a Catholic religious order that dated to the XVI century. It was on an island in the Tiber. Two thousand years earlier, the Romans organized a sanatorium to care for and isolate lepers and victims of the plague. The clinic was built on the ruins of that ancient facility.

The chief physician studied medicine in Bologna and the United States. He knew America well. When he looked at the calendar for that day, he noticed it was April 13th, the birthday of Thomas Jefferson, third President of the United States and writer of the Declaration of Independence. The doctor revered Jefferson and the sense of freedom and liberty he represented.

The doctor spoke impeccable German, English, and French. He was named chief physician after ten years of practice at the hospital. He was a devout Christian and respected people of all faiths and nationalities.

The doctor hired all the Jewish physicians, nurses, and caregivers he could save. The "patients" were Jews and refugees hunted by the Nazis. There were over a hundred. In the basement was the radio center set up by Joe and Tom. Ten American soldiers hid in the crypt.

At 6 PM, a car with a driver and an officer of the SS and a truck with a dozen German troops drove into the courtyard of the hospital. The soldiers immediately descended and stood at attention with machine guns and rifles, as the SS officer emerged from the German limousine.

He wore grey combat gear and a pirate's patch over his right eye, which he lost in battle.

The chief physician heard the noise and left his office to meet the SS leader. The doctor was wearing a tunic and face mask, surgical hat, and gloves. He looked like a deep-sea diver.

"To what do I owe the honor of this visit?" he said to the Nazi. "You are sheltering enemies of the state. We will search your premises. Once we find them, we will arrest them, you, and your staff for high crimes," the SS officer said in harsh and menacing tones. The doctor looked surprised and astonished.

Then he smiled.

"Your Excellency, we have nothing to hide and no one to hide. You are free to search. For your visit, may I suggest you and your men put on protective masks, gloves, and special clothing, which I will be happy to make available to you?" explained the doctor. "What for?" demanded the Nazi. He was irritated and angry at this delay.

"I am so sorry," said the doctor, calmly. "I thought you were aware that our hospital is a special place that cares for patients with highly communicable diseases. It has been this way for centuries. The Italian campaign in Ethiopia returned personnel with exotic ailments that are quite contagious. African tick bite fever, African sleeping sickness, and amoebic meningitis are particularly painful and deadly, and we have a group of patients with these illnesses. I am afraid they will not recover. One rare disease attacks the eyeballs and creates blindness as the parasite eats the optic nerve. Several patients have this. Many have viral hemorrhagic fevers with constant coughing that creates deadly particles in the air and makes the illness spread quickly," he said with excruciating detail.

"Please forgive the explanation Your Excellency. Let us not delay. I will escort you to the changing room," he stated. "I do not need your protective clothing," said the Nazi. "Arian blood is the most powerful on earth," he insisted.

"As you wish. Please follow me," said the doctor serenely. As they entered the hospital, the Nazi was struck by a terrible stink. It was the stench of decaying bodies. His eyes bulged. "What is that disgusting odor?" he demanded. "As you know, several of the illnesses I explained destroy muscle tissue, which becomes gangrenous and putrefies quickly. I am afraid we will need to do more amputations tonight," he said, shaking his head.

Nurses, doctors, and hospital staff wore the same outfit as the chief physician. They went about their business as if nothing were happening.

The doctor and his German guest walked down a corridor and, besides the smell of decomposing flesh, was that of excrement. The SS officer covered his mouth with a handkerchief. "You see, Your Excellency, several terrible sicknesses affect intestinal fortitude. The sphincter, sometimes, is eaten by a nasty parasite. It results in uncontrollable bowel movements. I must say, too many of our patients have this," he explained with composure.

They entered a large white room. It was filled with fifty people. Wild coughing and agonizing moaning was going on. "Our patients with African viral meningitis are constantly coughing. It is very painful to their lungs and throats. I have lost a nurse to this disease, and I am afraid I may have a doctor infected as well. Your Excellency, would you like to speak to them? I am sure they would be as honored by your visit as I am," he said with a broad smile.

The Nazi turned and marched out of the room, down the corridor, and out of the hospital. The chief physician followed him. "Your Excellency, would you like to examine our basement where we keep the corpses and do our autopsies?" he asked. "We have a very interesting sewage system down there where we dispose of human waste. It is quite fascinating," said the doctor.

"No, thank you," responded the Nazi, emphatically.

The SS officer signaled to the soldiers to return to the truck. "If you or any colleagues need any special attention, Your Excellency, I will personally be glad to arrange their internment in our facility," said the doctor.

"This hospital is off limits to all German personnel!" screamed the Nazi as he entered his vehicle.

The caravan started their engines and drove off. The doctor stood and watched as they left. Once they were gone, he removed his hat and mask.

He walked back into the hospital. The staff was gathered to greet him. "Thank God! We made it," he said, sighing. There was not a dry eye in the room.

The doctor signaled to two porters. They came up to him. "You can now arrange to bury those bodies and clean up the shit," he ordered.

CHAPTER 214 ━━━━━━━━━━━━━━━━━━━━━━━

THE TRAIN

They drove to the outer edge of Rome. The area was in ruins. The train was due to pass the village in an hour.

Tom bundled thirty sticks of dynamite with blasting caps in three packs. Each was wired to a battery-operated detonator with a wooden handle. Tom double-checked to make sure it functioned properly and the explosive was in good order.

He attached two of the packages to the rails. The third one was placed in the track. Tom ran the wires over the rails and into a ravine. It was a distance of twenty meters. The three men hid, with the detonator between them. The police car was behind a clump of trees within walking distance of the railroad.

Thirty minutes went by.

'The train should be passing the spot any second,' thought Tom. His hands were perspiring as he clutched the handle of the device.

"I feel a drop of water," said Joe. "What?" exclaimed Tom? It started to rain heavily. "Oh no!" he yelled. Tom ran to the tracks with three sacks under his arm. If the dynamite became wet, it would be useless.

A train whistle sounded. It was nearing the station. Tom saw the train in the distance. It was moving at a high speed. He re-bundled the first pack to protect it from the rain.

The train was getting closer.

He did the same to the package in the middle.

By the time he reached the third bundle, the light of the locomotive was shining on him.

He rolled off the track just as the train was about to strike him.

Tom ran to the detonator. Joe and Fabio ducked and put earplugs on. The locomotive passed. Three flatbed cars filled with artillery guns and tanks raced to the spot. Tom pressed the handle down as hard as he could.

He felt the vibration of the electric charge shoot from the detonator box through the wires. He jumped into the ravine next to his brother and Fabio.

A light flashed and a tremendous blast sounded across the flat land and over the farms for fifty miles. The explosion was heard in the far outskirts of Rome.

The explosion lifted the crashing cars and plunged them into the embankments, tearing up the tracks and destroying the artillery into a pile of twisted metal.

The box cars, filled with provisions, catapulted into each other in a spectacular pile up spilling thousands of broken crates and bales onto the rails.

The blast touched off fires along the tracks as the goods burned.

German troops appeared, searching the area for the culprits.

In the distance, an Italian police car headed for Rome.

CHAPTER 215 ━━━━━━━━━

RITA'S NIGHTMARES

Rita faced recurring nightmares. In her dreams, she felt vipers crawling up her legs and down her back and ravenous wolves growling at her. She saw saliva drip from their tongues. It was real. She heard the snarling animals and sensed the slithering serpents circle her body and reach her throat.

She woke screaming, sweating, and panting. It was reality.

She was surrounded by wild beasts.

She was immensely courageous, brilliant, and played parts like a professional actress. Her coolness and bravery, she knew, had its limits. She feared cracking and breaking the next time she heard men and women shriek in the Via Tasso torture chambers.

It was the ninth of May, her twenty-fifth birthday. She felt she would not see another. Her worst fears were being discovered. The Nazis tore fingernails out, cut off limbs, toes, and tongues, and ran electric shocks through bodies.

Death was better.

She carried a small pill box in her bra. It had three cyanide capsules. Rita was tempted to take one. "Just a bite, a burning sting in the throat, a crushing feeling in the chest, and in minutes it will be over," she thought. No. It was the coward's way out. Her mission was not accomplished. Lives were to be saved. Freedom needed to return to humanity. To do so, the Nazis must be destroyed.

They provided her a small apartment within walking distance of Via Tasso. She suspected it was taken from a Jewish family. She felt their presence. She often wondered who they were, what they were like, and if they were still alive. She prayed for them each day.

Her family home in Trastevere was closed since the death of her mother. She died of a broken heart when her husband went to the front. Rita loved her father. He was kind and caring, but she hated the philosophy he represented.

CHAPTER 216 ━━━━━━━━━━━━━━━━━━━━━━━━━━━━

JOURNEY TO ROME

$\mathbf{A}$fter the liberation of the island, boats moved sporadically from Ponza to the mainland. It was May 1944. The war raged. People were still dying and suffering throughout Italy. The nation was in ruins.

Giovannina had not seen her husband in over a year. When they separated, he had the family ration cards, which permitted quotas of bread and food. When Italy capitulated, he no longer had a role. His position in the Italian Navy disappeared. He was sent home to their small apartment in Rome. As the war deepened, it became impossible to travel or communicate. Mail was suspended.

The young woman was trapped on the island, with no way to feed her four children, except by courage and tenacity. She managed with the bravery only a mother could exhibit in time of need. She was wise, fearless, and determined.

She wanted to be with the man who was the father of her children.

Love propelled her to the Eternal City.

Giovannina lost forty pounds in a year and suffered physically and emotionally from the ravages of the conflict. At thirty-six, she went into menopause. She looked like she was sixty.

She was in mourning for losing her brother, the murder of her nephew at the hands of the Nazis in a German concentration camp, and the death of relatives and friends. Hundreds of bodies were carried by the sea to the shores of the island. Giovannina went to the cemetery every day to search for a familiar face. She never found one.

Her brothers were at war. No one knew where they were or if they would return home.

She had no news from her husband in over a year.

She waited days for the first boat to come to Ponza. It was bound for Naples. She was alone, dressed in black, without a penny in her pocket. All she could afford was the passage.

It took eight hours to reach Naples. The trip was filled with fear. The Germans bombed or shot at anything that moved. The Allies battled to overcome Nazi defense positions on land and sea.

It was a clash of titans.

Amazing women like Giovannina were caught in the crossfire of a senseless and cruel war.

The masts of sunken ships littered the horizon. Debris of all sorts drifted among the waves. Some of these floating remains saved islanders from famine.

Entering the port was heartbreaking. One of the most beautiful harbors on earth was destroyed. The wharfs were crushed under the force of Allied bombing. Capsized boats and vessels of all sorts were like wooden and steel cadavers imprisoned in underwater graves.

Naples was a city of rubble. Beggars lined the port waiting for the Americans to distribute countless tons of food to feed the hundreds of thousands of Neapolitans dying of hunger.

CHAPTER 217 ━━━━━━━━━━━━━━━

THE MONSTER'S SECRETARY

It was 6:30 AM. She walked to the office. Rita wore a grey outfit and a matching hat with a white shirt. Her deep red lipstick accentuated her heart-shaped mouth. As always, she was elegant, lovely; and attractive.

Heads turned as she strolled.

It was raining hard. Her feet were wet and uncomfortable. She needed a new pair of shoes, she thought. Stores were closed. Rita continued to wear the shoes and clothes of her mother. She thought of her constantly.

Despite her anxiety and turmoil, she transformed herself into the Secretary of The Monster. Her demeanor was professional, alert, and quiet.

At the entrance of Gestapo headquarters, she was waved in. Rita did not have to wear her ID or be stopped and frisked. She was known, respected, and, by too many, feared.

Her desk was clean and orderly. The early morning telegrams were stacked neatly in a pile on the right. Letters and messages to be prepared were on the left, each with a strict deadline.

Her boss, The Monster, was waiting for her outside his office.

"Good morning, sir," she said. "I will prepare your coffee in a moment," she stated, as she organized herself. "That is not necessary," he replied. "Today is a special day. I have arranged a little something for you," he said, sweetly. He opened his office door and on the conference table was a silver tray with coffee, milk, and croissants. "It is your birthday, and we will celebrate," he declared.

He took her by the hand and brought her into the room. She froze at his touch. It felt cold and clammy. He pulled out a chair, and she sat down. He poured coffee into a cup. "Sugar, milk?" he asked. "No, thank you. I prefer it black," she responded, with a false smile.

A day earlier, she had arranged for his wife and children to return to Germany. The Allies were not far away. The rats were jumping off the ship, she thought.

He sat next to her. His eyes rolled over her body. She became tense and felt naked. "Sir, thank you so much, but I have a great deal of work to do," she said nervously. Rita tried to rise from the chair. He grabbed her shoulder and sat her down. "We have worked together for years. It is time for you to call me by my first name," he said. Honey seemed to drip from his tongue. Rita felt sick. She remained silent.

He rose from his chair and circled behind her. He put his hands on her face. "You are so lovely," he said. His mouth opened with desire.

She pushed his hands away. "Please, do not touch me," she said emphatically. He was not pleased. Rita assumed he would pull out his Luger and shoot her. No one would ask questions as they took her body from the building and dumped it into an unmarked grave.

"You misunderstand me," he said, coyly. He realized he needed a different approach to seduce her. "Tonight we are hosting the Deputy Defense Minister from Berlin at my house. I would be honored if you were my hostess for the evening," he stated calmly. "Of course, sir. I am at your service," she responded.

"Good. A car will pick you up at 6 PM. This is a little gift. Wear it with pride. You are now a member of the Party." He gave her a small black jewelry box.

She opened it.

It was a pin with a red Swastika.

"Thank you," she replied.

As soon as he went into his office, Rita ran to the bathroom and threw up.

CHAPTER 218 ▬▬▬▬▬▬▬▬▬▬▬▬▬▬

THE COAL TRUCK

The sun was setting when Giovannina arrived. She got off the ferry and ran to a long line of trucks. Cargo brought in from America was loaded into the vehicles. Some were bound for the front, but most were on their way to help people throughout the South survive.

To heat the homes of Italians, the United States brought in ships filled with coal and oil and wood.

"Are you going to Rome?" she asked one truck driver after another. Ten said no. Finally, one said yes. "I have no space in the cab of the truck," he said. Three people were crowded inside. "I will travel with the coal," said Giovannina, with resolve. She climbed on the pile. It was dirty, dusty, and wet, and horribly uncomfortable.

The truck bounced and coiled through the demolished roads of Naples for two hours before reaching what was left of the highway leading to Rome. Thousands of refugees walked along the motorway, among burned-out tanks, military vehicles, and artillery.

The driver tried to avoid the holes in the road created by bombs and bullets. He turned from one side to another, tossing Giovannina over the black stones like a cork in the sea. It was terrible. Her back, legs and arms were bruised and ached. Her mouth, lungs, and nose filled with dust. She coughed and cried and held on for dear life. Several times, the truck made a sharp turn and she almost fell off.

'I wonder how he is,' she thought. 'Is he well? Will he recognize me? Is he alone?' These questions ran through her mind.

The young woman prayed constantly during her agonizing journey. After five hours, the truck stopped at a warehouse ten miles from Rome. Giovannina and the others got off. It was past midnight.

The building was an American military facility. The U.S. Army was stocking supplies for the liberation of Rome.

The Germans still occupied the capital. The truck driver spoke a little English. He explained to an American soldier the plight of Giovannina. The soldier had a jeep. He drove her as close to Rome as possible. They stopped at the only rail line still carrying trains to Rome. He bid her farewell as she waited for the train. It took an hour.

The train arrived in Termini station at two AM. No buses or trams were operating. The Nazis imposed a curfew. No one was allowed on the streets after 9 PM.

She hid in one doorway after another to avoid detection by the Germans. She walked through the city and crossed a bridge leading to the Vatican. St. Peters was black and silent. Church bells had ceased during the Nazi occupation.

It seemed to Giovannina that even the Lord was in mourning.

At 4 AM she reached the street of her home. It was peaceful, filled with trees and flowers, an oasis that seemed far from reality. She could barely walk to the door of her apartment. Her feet hurt and her body felt like it would fall to pieces.

She knocked. No one answered. She knocked again. "Who is it?" It was the voice of a man. "It is me, Giovannina," she responded. "Giovannina?" he said. "It is impossible. Who are you?" he yelled. "Giovannina," she repeated with tears. "Please open the door." He cracked open the portal and peeked at her. He could not make out who she was.

She looked like an old woman, dressed in black and filthy. "It is me," she said timidly. She knew he did not recognize her. Her voice was almost gone. He looked into her eyes.

"Oh my God!" he screamed. He grabbed her, pulled her into the house and embraced her. He kissed her again and again. The dust blackened his cheeks and lips.

He held his darling wife, swearing he would die before he ever let her go.

Love conquered war.

CHAPTER 219 ━━━━━━━━━

NAZI RECEPTION

Rita waited for the car. The rain was incessant. She wore a grey raincoat. She had an umbrella with her to protect her long, shimmering hair, black, low-cut evening dress, and high heels. The young woman pinched her cheeks to give herself color. A dash of French perfume around her pearl necklace was the finishing touch. She was stunning.

The limo arrived at six sharp. She got in. The Monster was in a tuxedo with medals and decorations. "You look marvelous," he said as he took her hand. She wore long white gloves so she could avoid the feel of his touch.

Rita pinned the Swastika over her heart. It seemed to weigh on her chest, burn, and affect her breathing. 'Stay composed. Pull yourself together,' she said to herself. The slightest mistake could reveal her true identity.

It took minutes to arrive at his flat. The apartment was in the center of Rome. It was furnished with seventeenth century furniture and paintings. Frescos were on the ceilings, and the walls were decorated with flying angels and cupids with bows and arrows. The balcony overlooked the Pantheon.

A caterer prepared drinks, champagne, and finger food.

The guests arrived on time. The Deputy Minister was in a white military outfit. He was tall and handsome and well-fed, with a large stomach. He stood erect as if a long pole was in his back. A red sash and a string of medals was on his chest. His black hair was greased and brushed back on the sides and over his head. The Nazi smelled of sandalwood. Other Germans came to the reception, including the Ambassador to the Holy See.

The Devil wore his dress uniform. He kissed her hand and stared at her. His eyes were cold. He had much on his mind.

Rita worked six years with the Nazis and still could not stomach their presence.

The Monster introduced her as "an exquisite example of Italian beauty." She blushed and stood next to him. A waiter passed around champagne. They raised glasses. "To the Fuhrer and victory," said the Deputy Minister.

The Nazis formed a circle and chatted. Rita made believe she was busy with the food and beverages while she listened.

"Calais. It will be Calais at the end of June," insisted the Deputy Minister. "The Fuhrer and the High Command are convinced of this. Fortifications are going up as we speak. The Air Force will sink every ship and boat before they hit the beach," he said jovially. "We will drive them into the sea. They will be so bloodied that they will sue for peace," he said arrogantly.

"Kesselring knows they will hit the Line at the end of this month with all they have. He will be ready. He has repelled two attacks. The third will be decisive." he said. "Will reinforcements arrive from the East?" asked The Devil. The Deputy Minister glared at him. "There is nothing left in the East," he responded.

Rita listened intently. She mentally recorded details, names, places, and times.

"What if we have to evacuate Rome?" asked The Monster.

"I will send the signal to destroy documents. Most valuable ones should be shipped to Berlin now," responded the Deputy Minister.

"What do we do with our Italian employees?" asked The Devil. He already knew the response, but he wanted it in an order. "Some have been with us for years and know our secrets," he said. "Kill them all, and kill their families. They are all spies," replied the official from

Berlin. "The Allies say they will try us for war crimes, if we lose. The less witnesses we have the better," he noted. "Make sure there are no prisoners around to talk," he added.

Rita was stunned, but not surprised.

CHAPTER 220 ━━━━━━━━━━━━━━━━━━━━━━━━━━━

CRAZY HORSE

The Monster accompanied her home after the reception. "May I come up and have a drink?" he asked, holding her hand tightly. "I am so sorry, but I have a headache and do not feel well," lied Rita. She let go of his hand and opened the door of the car and walked out. "Perhaps some other time. Good night," she said. He made an unpleasant face, slammed the door, and drove off.

It stopped raining. Rita watched as the German limo disappeared. It was past midnight. No one was on the street. Partisans set up two pay phone booths around the corner of her building. She ran to one and dropped in tokens.

It rang once, twice. Someone answered, "Crazy Horse." Rita responded, "Geronimo."

"They believe the Allied invasion of Europe will be at Calais. They claim fortifications are being built and the Air Force is ready to strike. They expect the assault at the end of June. Attack on the Gustav Line is expected at the end of this month. They are planning the evacuation of Rome, if need be. They will kill all prisoners and Italian employees." She hung up the phone.

Rita looked about and went to her building. She was consumed with dread and exhaustion. Her room was on the fourth floor. She felt her heart ache with each step. It took twelve long minutes to reach the door. Rita looked at it. A recurring fear was someone was in there waiting to kill her.

She turned the key. The sound echoed in the dark hall and down the staircase. Rita opened the door. Her hand reached for the light as if it was a switch for salvation. The darkness disappeared. Rita looked around. She was safe, for now.

As she removed her clothes, she thought. She knew she could not hold back his advances forever.

He would kill her, whether or not she gave him her body.

'When will the Allies come?' she thought. 'If they do not arrive soon, many will die, including me.'

CHAPTER 221

RAIDS ON THE ETERNAL CITY

For six weeks, Joe and Tom and the courageous insurgents conducted raids and disrupted enemy operations in and around the Eternal City. Dressed as police officers, they sabotaged Nazi outposts and facilities. They benefited from inside information that came from Gestapo headquarters.

Sheila was their angel.

The Devil, The Monster, and The Beast continued their evil onslaught. Searches were made of churches, convents, and monasteries. Jews and refugees were found and sent to concentration camps. Suspected spies and sympathizers were tortured and murdered.

Rita gathered and sent information vital to the Allies. She created safe havens to protect Jews and those the Nazis and their henchmen had on their list for elimination. She knew who they were and when they were to be apprehended.

But she could not save everyone.

It hurt her deeply each time they arrested and killed someone she felt could not be protected.

Two days after her birthday, the Allies staged their third assault on Monte Cassino and the valley below it.

It was one AM.

Sixteen hundred pieces of artillery rained fire on the entire front stretching from the town of Cassino to the hilltop. After the bombing and shelling, twenty-five divisions attacked German strongholds in one of the toughest and bloodiest battles of the war. After two days, the Gustav Line was broken and the Allies secured higher ground.

Three days later, the Line was penetrated at several points. The Germans lost forty percent of their combat strength and were encircled at Cassino. They began a retreat to the north while the Allies pursued them in desperate rearguard actions. Polish forces attacked Monte Cassino in ferocious clashes that drove the Germans from the citadel.

On May 19th, the fighters flew the Polish flag over the ruins of the abbey.

American Soldiers Marching Along Highway 6 towards Rome,
Courtesy, US National Archives

General Clark and the Fifth Army captured one town after another and opened the Anzio corridor leading to Rome.

CHAPTER 222 ━━━━━━━━━━━━━━━━━━━━━━━━━━

HER FATHER

Rita arrived at her apartment past midnight. Her mind and body were drained of energy. She needed to rest but could not.

She found a letter in her mailbox. It was from the Ministry of Defense. She opened it, ominously. Dark thoughts came to her as she tore open the envelope and read:

> *This is to inform you that your father died on the Russian front. He is buried near the town of Tambov Oblast.*
>
> *He was a hero who gave his life for Italy. He will never be forgotten.*
>
> *Enclosed is the only item found on his body, a letter to you.*

Rita was paralyzed.

In another envelope were three handwritten pages, dated months earlier. She recognized her father's handwriting, even though it was jagged and irregular. She imagined the anxiety in his veins as he wrote his last words.

> *Dearest Rita, I am in a freezing hole in a Russian prison camp. Thousands of Italian soldiers are scattered over this territory, suffering and near death.*
>
> *I have typhus and am dying of hunger, thirst, and frostbite. It is the first chance I have had to write. It is also my last.*
>
> *My days are numbered.*
>
> *I hope you receive this letter someday.*
>
> *My life was devoted to Fascism and its principles of pride in being Italian, promoting ethical and disciplined behavior and devotion to the nation and self-sacrifice.*
>
> *I believed dictatorship was efficient and progressive. I was wrong.*

I believed our leaders were great, honest, and willing to die for our country. I was wrong.

Instead, I found corruption, dishonesty, arrogance, incompetence, treachery, stupidity, and, most of all, cruelty.

I changed when the racial laws were decreed in 1938 and our Jewish brethren were persecuted, an injustice that will live as a dark moment in our history.

Mussolini lied to us. He said we were prepared for war.

We were not.

He said it would end quickly. It did not.

He declared war against America, a country we had no argument with. He sent our best and brightest men to die on the plains of Russia, with summer clothing, no boots, and World War I arms.

Deception and idiocy overshadowed the progress made by Fascism to build new cities, towns, and infrastructure, to drain the marshes, expand agriculture and industry, and to create new schools and universities.

All that is under the rubble of Allied bombs.

Millions of our people are homeless, injured, or dead from a senseless war started by a madman, who Il Duce embraced as his partner and friend.

We "conquered" a poor, downtrodden nation, Ethiopia, and called it an empire. It was an atrocity, as was our involvement in the Spanish Civil War. We fought alongside Hitler, the epitome of evil.

I am ashamed and pray God and you forgive me.

I pursued an ideology in good faith and discovered it was false.

I was told to die for tyranny.

My body will do so, but my spirit will not.

Rita, my most wonderful daughter, I hope you remember our moments of love and affection together. You are my angel and the most important thing I achieved.

I loved your mother with my soul and will die with my love for you in my heart.

Fight for truth and freedom, my darling. It is all that is worth dying for.

God bless you,

Your loving father.

CHAPTER 223 ━━━━━━━━━━━━━━━━━━━━━━━▶

RUSSIAN FRONT

$\mathbf{T}$he fiery blasts along the Gustav Line were seen and heard in a radius of fifty kilometers.

An eighteen-year-old girl from Ponza was studying in a Catholic boarding school in Gaeta when the bombing started. Flavia jumped out of bed. She thought the convent was exploding. The walls shook and the ground trembled. It felt like the earth would open up and devour her. It went on throughout the night. She could not sleep.

Flavia went to her collection of books. They were her friends. She needed someone to hold and protect her as the booming guns rained havoc and terror not far from where she lived.

Sifting through one volume after another, she came upon a math primer she had used three years earlier. A note tumbled out. She never saw it before. The young girl picked it up, increased the flame in the oil lantern, and read.

> *Dearest and Sweetest Flavia:*
>
> *For a year I have tutored you in mathematics. I am not sure you learned anything from me, but I learned much from you.*
>
> *I discovered a beautiful girl with a quick smile and a lively personality, who is eternally optimistic, honest, and serene.*
>
> *It was love at first sight. How could I not adore you? I love you and always will,*
>
> *Yours, Alfredo*

Flavia was shocked. Alfredo fell in love with her while he was helping her struggle through Geometry and Algebra. She was studying in Ponza. Her aunt, Giovannina, suggested her mother, Matilda, consult with Don Lorenzo, who was in Castellonorato, for a math teacher.

He sent Alfredo, who was three years older than Flavia. Alfredo had been an altar boy, a model student, and came from a splendid family. He was slim, handsome, with perfect features. He had a well-crafted nose, oval lips, and pink cheeks. Alfredo was always well-dressed and smiled warmly and easily. His fragrance was of freshly picked lemons.

Flavia was blossoming into a goddess-like beauty. Her body was sculpted like an hourglass. She radiated health and warmth with a bright smile of perfect teeth, fine features, and large dark eyes and black hair, pulled back in a bun, like her mother's.

The family had a strong tradition of education, especially for women. It was felt they were the strength and force in a family and were the compass to guide it, as men fought in the jungle of survival to feed their loved ones. Flavia's sister was studying in Rome to be a teacher. She would follow the same course at Gaeta.

Alfredo tutored her for a week in Ponza. They fell in love. He proposed marriage. Then the war came, and he was called to fight. He sent letters filled with tenderness and affection. She collected and saved each one. Flavia wrote every day. Those pieces of paper were Alfredo's lifeline as he went into Hell.

He was sent to the Russian Front. For a year, there was no news and no mail.

The Red Army set out to punish the invaders. Italian and German soldiers, captured or wounded, were humiliated and usually tortured and shot.

The Italians had summer clothes in the arctic air of the Soviet Union. It was terrible. Hunger added to the misery of freezing to death.

Alfredo and his companions hid in a barn as the Russians pursued them. His best friend, Giorgio, collapsed in excruciating pain, trembling and gnashing his teeth.

"Alfredo, shoot me," he demanded. "If you are my friend, kill me and stop my suffering," he screamed as he thrashed in agony on the hay covered ground of the barn.

Alfredo took out his pistol. His hand trembled. He pointed at Giorgio's head. "Shoot, please shoot," pleaded Giorgio.

He could not. Alfredo put away his weapon and hugged his friend. Giorgio died of hunger and cold a few days later.

Alfredo was injured when an exploding shell removed a piece of his left arm and damaged his elbow. He could never move it again.

He was saved by a family of farmers. They took him in and nursed him back to health. He walked, mounted trucks, and finally trains to get back to Italy. It took six long, horrible months.

In the spring of 1944, he escaped and reached Italy.

In the frigid land of the commissars, Alfredo clung to his love for Flavia. She was his anchor and North Star, pointing toward a life of happiness together. In his mind he wrote letters that could never be mailed and thoughts that stayed with him as he fought to survive and go home.

Shortly after returning, Flavia and Alfredo were married.

Love sustained them throughout the inferno.

CHAPTER 224 ━━━━━━━━━━━━━━━━━━━━━━━

NAZI MEETING

Friday, June 2st.

She wore perpetual black, as if in mourning. It was, she thought, the right shade for how she felt.

When Rita arrived at her office, The Devil, The Monster, and The Beast and their entourage of villains were gathered in the main conference room, not far from her desk.

Shouting and disbelief could be heard through the door. "Kesselring is a traitor! He should have died fighting! Instead, he is retreating to the North to save himself and his army!" screamed The Devil. "He is going to declare Rome an open city and abandon us! Troops are to evacuate as soon as possible! We have no one to defend us!" declared The Monster. "The Allies are on their way! It will take a week for them to fight through the towns on the road from Anzio before they reach the outer walls!" yelled the Beast.

The meeting went on for an hour.

The Monster rushed out of the room. He was perspiring and agitated. He ran to Rita's desk. "Organize departments to collect all documents! They are to be burned immediately!" he ordered. "Yes, sir," she responded.

A huge green safe was in a corner of The Monster's office. He turned the dial back and forth, apprehensively. After several attempts, the door opened. He opened it and pulled out a stack of papers and envelopes sealed with wax. They were wrapped in ribbons and cords. In the safe were thousands of dollars in various currencies and bars of gold and silver. Passports, official travel credentials, and a box of jewelry and gold coins were in the back, hidden from view. He piled the treasure into a suitcase.

He handed Rita the records. "Burn these immediately!" he told her. They were accounts of Nazi arrests, executions, and deportations, and registers of trains and transport to Auschwitz and other sites. Films and photos of victims were in another box. He gave it to her.

As soon as he left the room, she opened a locked drawer at the bottom of her desk. Archives of telegrams, messages, registers of conversations, decrees from Berlin, and letters were sealed in brown envelopes. A list of Nazi spies in Italy was in a special file named "Cassandra." The Cassandra package was thick and detailed. She added it to the papers to destroy. She put everything into a cardboard box, including The Monster's files.

Rita carried a written directive throughout the building. In five hours, piles of files were amassed in every office.

The building had a furnace in the basement and wood burning stoves on each floor. Uniformed SS personnel were entrusted with destroying traces of Nazi atrocities. Unclassified papers were strewn over the floor and tossed into trash cans.

Streams of black and grey smoke flowed out of the stoves and into the five chimneys in the roof as the incriminating documents went up in flames.

Rita carried her carton to the cellar. An Italian was in the basement. His name was Diego. His blue outfit was filled with coal dust, and his face was blackened. He had a shovel in his hands.

He was one of the eighteen full-time Italian workers who served the Nazis. His job was to stoke the furnace to make sure it functioned properly and there was hot water and heat in the building. He did odd jobs and repairs.

Plumbers, electricians, carpenters, and mechanics and waiters served the Nazis day and night. Few had choices. If they refused to work, they were targeted for persecution and considered collaborators with the enemy. They were paid in German occupation currency, which was worthless.

Rita brought the box to the boiler. "Diego, open the furnace," she said. He took a crowbar and jammed it into a latch on the furnace door. He pulled on it. Inside was a roaring fire.

Rita ripped the red pin with the Swastika from her dress and threw it to the floor.

She stepped on it and crushed it with all the strength in her body.

Then she tossed it into the flames.

"Close it," she said. He shut the door. "Get a sack," she demanded. He gave her a bag that originally contained imported coffee. She took the papers out of the box and put the files, photos, and films into the sack and knotted it.

"Bury it under the pile of coal in the corner," she told him. He obeyed. Rita watched anxiously as he shoveled the coal over the sack until it disappeared.

He looked confused. "The rats are abandoning the ship. The Nazis plan to kill the Italian workers and their families. Get the word out. Everyone and their wives and children are to disappear right away," she insisted.

"Do you understand?" she asked. He was in shock.

She shook him.

"They are going to shoot you and your children! Tell everyone and get out of here!" she screamed.

He nodded nervously and ran off.

CHAPTER 225 ━━━━━━━━━━━━━━━━━━━━━━━━━━━

THE IRISH MONSIGNOR

Joe, Tom, Sheila, and an Irish Monsignor in the Vatican worked together in the closing days of the Nazi occupation, when the Germans wanted to exterminate all those they considered enemies. Sheila provided inside information on Gestapo plans, while the Americans and the priest acted to save many lives.

Several thousand Allied soldiers were imprisoned in Italian jails. They were harshly treated. Some died in captivity. The Monsignor visited them. He struggled to help the soldiers escape and protect them in the Eternal City. It was a death-defying enterprise.

Guards and prison officials were bribed or threatened. Getaways were planned and organized with cars and vans in episodes that rivaled the most famous of prison escapes.

The priest prepared a network of safe havens, helped by clerics, anti-Fascists, and diplomats who sheltered POWs, refugees, and Jews. Apartments were rented. Religious houses served as secret sanctuaries throughout the Eternal City. The Vatican official arranged for false papers and passes. He continuously escorted Jews and escaped prisoners of war to convents and monasteries.

Five thousand Jews were hidden by the Church, assisted by the Monsignor and his friends. Three thousand were concealed in Castel Gandolfo, the town of the Pope's summer residence. Several hundred became members of the Palatine Guard, and fifteen hundred were secreted in convents, monasteries, and seminaries. Nearly four thousand were cared for in private apartments, many arranged by the Monsignor. [1]

The boys from the Bronx kept people moving from one place to another. Dressed in their police disguises, they brought the exiles to secure locations under the nose of German troops.

---

[1]   "The Scarlet Pimpernel of the Vatican," http://sites.rootsweb.com/~irlker/scarlet.html

The Gestapo discovered the network through paid informers. The Monsignor was their target. The Devil knew his name and where he was. He offered a thirty thousand Lire bounty on his head. He was determined to kidnap and kill him.

The priest's only protection was the Pope.

The Gestapo leader protested a violation of the Vatican's neutral status because of "rogue" religious people who were supporting the enemy and hiding criminals of the regime.

A white line was drawn across St. Peter's Square. It divided Vatican City from Italy. Crossing the line gave the Nazis authority to arrest anyone. Troops were posted to watch and control entrance and exit from the zone of neutrality.

The Devil waited for his moment to strike.

Once he seized the Monsignor, he had the pretext to attack the Holy See and capture the Holy Father himself.

CHAPTER 226 ━━━━━━━━━━━━━

BURN THE DOCUMENTS

Saturday, June 3rd, 1944.

The lights were on all night at Via Tasso. Staff worked to destroy traces of terror inflicted by the Nazis.

Rita did not leave her office. She did her part to burn documents. The effort continued into Saturday.

Heinrich Himmler, Courtesy, German Federal Archives

The Devil called a special meeting of the team. The Monster was at his side.

The conference room was paneled in wood, with a large Austrian oak table, a red flag with a Swastika in the corner, and a picture of Hitler in uniform. Next to the Fuhrer was a smiling photo of Heirich Himmler, head of the SS, and mastermind of the Holocaust.

The image showed him amused as he read a report, probably about the latest mass murders and liquidations.

Twenty uniformed and civilian Germans assembled around the table. Assassins and torturers stood side by side with clerks and communications officers, drivers, and intelligence and logistics experts as a gang of terror rarely known in recorded history.

"Full evacuation will be required in the next two days. Trucks, cars, and vans are being prepared as we speak. The Allies are not far from the capital. We are assured safe passage to the limits of the city, and then we will travel north to join the Army. There is no guarantee the Allies will spare us," he said. "I convey the gratitude of the Fuhrer for your dedication and sacrifice. Heil Hitler!" he said loudly.

All saluted and left the room, except The Monster and the chief aide to The Devil.

He turned to his assistant. "Assemble all Italian employees tomorrow morning and bring them to my office. Tell them we wish to pay everyone in advance and give them bonuses before we close our station in Rome. Have three soldiers with machine guns ready," he ordered.

He turned to The Monster. "You are to take them outside of the city and execute them," he declared. "This operation must be flawless and done with the utmost care. No witnesses. Have them dig their own graves in a spot that will not be detected easily. Do you understand?" he said to The Monster. He nodded in agreement. "Tomorrow night, you are to go to each house and kill the families. Shoot them in the apartments and leave the bodies," he explained.

"Empty the jails, first thing in the morning. All prisoners are to be eliminated. Include them with the Italians. We should do this in one operation," he insisted.

"What about Rita?" inquired the assistant. Up to now she had been treated as a special employee who was neither German nor Italian.

"I will take care of her, personally," replied The Monster. He winked and smiled as they left the room.

CHAPTER 227

SACKS OF SALT

Rita continued to destroy documents. She took care to separate the confidential and secret ones from the rest. The useless papers were burned. The incriminating ones she dumped in trash cans and covered them with magazines and newspapers.

Pandemonium was raging. The Nazis realized the end was near. Each person was seeking a way to survive.

Rita packed goods and papers the Gestapo wanted to take with them. Boxes of wine, cigarettes and cigars, and cases of Italian food were treated just as valuable as confidential documents.

German troops created a caravan to travel along the Tiber to the north, hoping to reach Kesselring's forces. Rita got the plan out to Joe and Tom. The news reached the Allies.

Nearly all Nazi personnel left the building before the night of June 3rd. Rita worked incessantly to hide materials that could be of value to the Allies.

When she left that evening, there were five soldiers, The Monster, The Devil, and his assistant present. They were sending secret telegrams and dispatches to Berlin.

Rita slept on a sofa in one office instead of going home. Partisans were coming out of neighborhoods, searching for Nazis and collaborators. She felt it was not wise to be on the street.

It was 2 AM. Four German troop trucks were lined up on Via Tasso.

They were unguarded.

A City of Rome police car drove up to the building. Two uniformed officers got out while the third took out his pistol to stand guard.

The officers opened the trunk. Sacks of salt were next to firearms, explosives, and hand grenades.

They took two packs each and went to the trucks. The vehicles were 1944 Opel Blitzes, used extensively to move soldiers and prisoners to be murdered. The policemen poured a kilo of salt into each tank. They got back into their car and drove off.

The Allies were one hundred kilometers away.

CHAPTER 228 ━━━━━━━━━━━━

CARE PACKAGES

"Add two more bags of coffee," said Silverio. "I have already put in three. I cannot make it too heavy. This box goes to Giovannina," responded Lucia. "It has sugar, flour, chocolate, cookies, and aprons for the girls and socks for the boy, coats, and sweaters. The cotton sack on the outside can be used as a pillowcase. She can stitch it together with the others we sent to make a sheet," explained Lucia, as she finished the latest parcel for her sister in Rome.

Each was wrapped in white cloth with the printed image of two arms joined. Written on it was, "A Gift from the People of the United States of America."

It had to be weighed carefully before it was brought to the U.S. Post Office. The boxes were collected, sorted, and delivered to the port of New York and loaded on ships bound for Naples.

Lucia sewed the edges, so that the covering sealed the box inside to protect the contents on the long voyage from America.

Even before Rome was liberated, families sent food and clothing to their loved ones in Italy. Some went through the American Red Cross, but most traveled via the US Government program of relief for Europe that began before the end of hostilities. Millions of packages were carried in Liberty ships and freighters.

In mid-1944, the war continued to thunder across the continent as the Allies drove the Germans from conquered countries. Vessels on the high seas risked attack by U-boats or striking Nazi mines and maritime explosives.

American cruisers and battleships accompanied convoys of boats, bringing vital provisions and supplies for the starving millions of Europe.

Countless lives were saved by the generosity of the Italians in America and the U.S. government.

CHAPTER 229 ━━━━━━━━━━━━━━━━━━━━━━━━━

LA STORTA

Sunday, June 4th.

"Sir, the Italians have disappeared," explained the assistant to The Devil. "We went to their apartments and no one was there. The families are gone," he reported.

The Devil ground his teeth in anger. He grimaced with rage. His face was red with fire in his eyes. "Someone tipped them off!" he screamed. "Get the prisoners into the trucks and move them out immediately!" he commanded.

Scores of famished, tired, and tortured men were in cells throughout the building. Some were left behind since there was not enough room in the vehicles and not enough time to shoot them in the jails.

No food was given to inmates for days. Soldiers opened the chambers and dragged them out. At gunpoint, they were forced into the four trucks to take them to the killing fields. The Devil and The Monster supervised the operation. SS officers were with the prisoners to carry out the executions.

The trucks traveled north out of Rome to the Via Cassia. The Germans were desperate to flee the Allied advance.

The salt crystals poured into the gas tanks needed less than thirty minutes to take effect. The mineral dissolved in the water below the gasoline in the gas tank. The fuel pump sucked the salt into its filter. After a few minutes, the filter was clogged. Gasoline stopped flowing into the carburetor.

Fourteen kilometers into the trip, the vehicles stalled. The trucks stopped near an area known as La Storta.

The Germans realized they were without wheels to advance their escape.

The vehicles with the prisoners were abandoned, except for one.

Nazi officers paraded fourteen into the forest. One by one they shot them in the back of the head.

The Germans ran off on foot.

The next day they were captured.

CHAPTER 230

ESCAPE FROM GESTAPO HEADQUARTERS

Rita was shattered. She looked at the prisoners being taken away with horror in her heart. She was powerless, as she watched these innocent victims carried to their death.

The Devil rushed to his office. He emptied his safe. He filled two black leather travel bags with small and large bars of gold and silver, valuable jewelry, and stacks of Lire, dollars, and Deutsche Marks.

He removed his uniform and boots and slipped on a brown suit, white shirt and tie, a hat, and shoes. He stuffed passports, papers, and letters into the pockets of his jacket and strapped a holster and pistol to his chest.

He ran out the door and got into the car with his driver. "To the home of the Ambassador," he commanded. He sat securely in the backseat and held onto his suitcases.

The Devil was promised safety in the hands of the German Ambassador to the Holy See. He was the intermediary between the Vatican and Berlin who negotiated to keep Rome safe from German destruction, although it was rumored that mines and time bombs were planted to destroy monuments, once the Allies entered the Eternal City.

As The Devil raced to the home of the diplomat, rifle carrying partisans and common people filled the streets. The freedom fighters were searching for Nazis and enemy soldiers to capture or kill.

Several partisans spotted the German limo as it turned a corner. The driver panicked. He made a wrong turn and was lost. "Stop!" yelled The Devil. "Get in the back," he commanded. The Devil got behind the steering wheel. He stepped on the accelerator and sped through one street after another. Tires skidded as he rushed to reach safety.

He turned into Piazzale Flaminio and raced up the road through the City Park of Villa Borghese. The home of the Ambassador was two miles away, off Via Veneto.

Halfway up the street, a band of partisans emerged. They had machine guns, rifles, and pistols. They made a sign for the car to stop.

The Devil turned into a side path toward the Borghese Palace.

Two men with automatic weapons came out of the park and pointed guns at the car.

As he passed them, they opened fire.

A swarm of bullets hit the doors on both sides of the auto, penetrated the hood, hit the motor, shattered the windows, and entered the car. The torrent of fire punctured the right front and two back tires. The vehicle stopped. The motor was dead. The Devil was near the rear gate of the Villa. His driver was in the backseat. A bullet entered his right temple. He slumped over.

The partisans ran to the car. They were twenty meters away. The Devil raced to open the back door and retrieve his bags with his ill-gotten wealth. He could not open it. It was locked from the inside and the bullets sealed the latches.

In desperation, he ran as fast as he could to the exit of the Villa. The freedom fighters watched him as he raced into a side street. In one bag left in the car was a small box of cyanide capsules.

He wanted them now, thought The Devil, as he fled like a rat into the bowels of the Eternal City.

"Let him go," said one patriot to the other. "He was only a driver. Let's see who the dead Nazi is," he said as they pried open the rear door of the car.

CHAPTER 231

"COME WITH ME"

The Monster stuffed his Gestapo uniform into the stove. He watched it burn along with his medals and decorations, as he changed into civilian clothes. A pistol was strapped to his belt, under his jacket.

His suitcase was packed with hundreds of thousands of dollars of riches, stolen from the people of Rome. In his pocket were diplomatic passes and a false passport. He bribed functionaries to arrange safe passage to South America. His plan was to reach Rimini, hide for a few days, travel to Genoa, and board a ship for Argentina.

His car and driver were on the street at Via Tasso waiting for him. The building was empty, except for Rita and The Monster.

She wore a black outfit with a jacket.

Rita was sorting through papers when he walked up to her. He dropped his bag. "Come with me," he said. "We will go to South America and start a new life," he insisted.

Rita turned. She was three meters from him. She took two steps back and clenched her teeth. "You filthy bastard! I hate you and all you stand for. I will see you rot in prison, if it is the last thing I do!" she spit out. Her voice was bursting with anger and determination.

The Monster's eyes widened, first with shock, and then with fury and hate. He reached for his revolver. Rita anticipated the move. She quickly went into the pocket of her jacket and pulled out a pistol. It was a small Colt 45 with a round barrel. Joe gave it to her. He said at close range it would blow the heart and lungs out of a man.

"Give me a reason why I should not kill you," she stated coldly. Rita wanted to shoot him. She could not. 'I am a human being. I will not put myself at the level of this monstrosity,' she thought.

She wanted to take him prisoner, but she was alone. It would not work.

"You have one minute to get out of here before I put a bullet through your head, like you did to others," she said, staring into his frozen eyes. He sneered at her, grabbed his suitcase, and marched out of the building, got into the car, and disappeared.

Rita slumped into a chair and nearly fainted.

CHAPTER 232

"THE AMERICANS ARE HERE!"

She could barely walk. Rita was drained physically, mentally, and morally.

It was dark as she left Via Tasso. She was not aware of the time or the day. She wandered down the street in a daze. She needed rest and peace.

For years, Rome had been quiet. Suddenly, church bells rang. Cars came out of buildings and coaches with horses trotted along the street. People were walking, talking, singing.

A young man ran past her screaming, "The Americans are here! We are free!"

It seemed anticlimactic. She had waited for this moment. Now that it had arrived, she was too numb to absorb it. She reached her building. It seemed a mirage. Was it real, or part of a dream, a nightmare? Was she awake? Was she alive?

Sensations and thoughts filled her confused and exhausted mind.

Rita opened the main door and went up the steps. She stopped. She sat. Tears poured down her face like a cascade.

Images and voices overcame her. They were families taken from the ghetto, weeping children separated from parents, and men and women loaded into trucks and murdered in the Ardeatine Caves. She heard pleading and cries from the bowels of Via Tasso.

A hundred scenes and sounds raced through her mind.

She screamed, and sobbed uncontrollably.

CHAPTER 233 ━━━━━━

ITALIAN BAKERY

"**I**sn't it magnificent?" said Luigi. Carlo and Helena held hands. They watched as workmen on ladders hung up a sign over the shop next to Luigi's General Store. It read, "Italian Bakery," in bright colors.

Two flags decorated the logo. One was of the U.S. and the other of Italy.

Luigi bought an oven and used bakery equipment, installed it in the basement of the shop, and prepared a display cabinet and even a cash register. "We will open it the day you return from Italy," said Luigi emotionally.

Carlo squeezed Helena's hand. She looked at him and smiled. "All we have to do is make sure everything works well," said Luigi. "No problem," responded Carlo. "I will look it over and fix it, if necessary," he said.

"Luigi, how can we thank you?" asked Helena. Her eyes were gleaming with warmth and joy. She saw a life with Carlo and even imagined children, family gatherings, and moments of love.

"All I ask is please make my brother happy," responded Luigi with tears in his eyes. He loved Carlo and dreamed of his return from the war and settling in West Virginia.

"I promise," replied Helena, looking at the man she adored. Carlo smiled at her, embraced his brother, and kissed Helena.

Carlo felt blessed. 'There is a God!' he thought. The Almighty saved him on the battlefield, brought him to America, put him in the arms of the most wonderful girl on earth, and gave him the love of a brother beyond limits.

'How could I be so lucky?' he wondered. He was liberated from anxiety, and his nightmares were gone.

Carlo knew dreams come true through effort. Sacrifices were ahead before he and Luigi could turn the key on their bakery and before he could marry Helena.

He needed courage.

The Allies liberated the area of his home and fed the multitudes of survivors. Temporary shelters were constructed to protect them.

His family lived in tents.

Carlo earned enough money in the camp to care for them until they could reach America.

President Roosevelt prepared laws to bring refugees to the United States when peace was secured.

Among the millions displaced were hundreds of thousands of orphans to be adopted by American families. These children would find a life and future in America.

Thanks to Luigi, immigration attorneys were ready to file papers.

Still, it would take time.

"When you return in June," stated Luigi, "we will drive to New York for the feast of San Silverio, now that Gabriela is engaged to Richard. His parents came from the Island of Ponza, and they say the feast is wonderful. Richard's cousins will take care of us during the holiday," explained Luigi.

"Their names are Silverio and Lucia," he said.

CHAPTER 234 ━━━━━━━━━━━━━━━━━

THE NIGHT OF BROKEN GLASS

June 5th.

Rita did not recall how she crawled up the stairs, opened the door, and got into her apartment. The memory was lost among so many others. Her mind seemed to erase traces of the past even if they were the present.

Rita remembered waking up to light flowing through a window. She was still dressed. Her head ached. She rose from the bed and went to the bathroom, dropped her clothes, and turned on the shower.

She felt her skin, her body was filthy, infected, and soiled by contact with the demons. She sensed the Monster's touch. It sent shudders, aches, and spasms through her organs. Rita washed and cleansed each tiny part of her being to eradicate the corruption and pollution of her time in the Underworld.

After thirty minutes of what seemed a waterfall of purification, she wrapped a white towel around her and walked to the bed. She sat and reflected. 'What's next?' she pondered. The wheels in her brain turned.

She heard a crash and the crack of glass. An object flew past her face. Startled, she stood up. A rock was thrown through her window. She flew to look out. People were racing along the street.

'Oh my God!' she thought. I am a target.

Rita looked at the pieces of broken crystal strewn across the floor.

A flash of terror chilled her. Memories came alive.

She was studying in Berlin in November 1938. She was eighteen. Her German was excellent. Her favorite place was Charlottenburg, a small community of homes and shops and manicured parks. It was near her school.

Each afternoon, she stopped in a bookstore. It was her oasis. The scent of ancient paper and brown sheets with words were a museum of culture. The shop was paradise.

The owner was Eli.

He was in his early sixties. He was a kind man who took a liking to this pretty Italian girl who spoke splendid German. She saw him as a father figure of tranquility and peace.

She spent hours in the store browsing. Eli often showed her rare books about philosophy, literature, history, and art. She bought what she could on her modest student budget.

Eli did not care if she purchased anything. He was delighted to see her.

"Good afternoon, my sweet Italian rose," he said, with the warm greeting he gave her each time she came into the store. "How are you this chilly day?" he asked. "I am fine," said Rita. "I am preparing for final exams," she responded.

It was Tuesday, the eighth of November.

"I have a birthday gift for you," said Eli. Rita laughed. "My birthday is not until May," she said, with a broad smile. "I know. But I want to be the first to give you a gift," he uttered, as he handed her a parcel wrapped in red paper. Rita was emotional. 'This sweet man is giving me a gift,' she thought.

She opened the package carefully, trying not to rip the paper out of respect for Eli, who she knew wrapped it personally.

As Rita removed the sheets, she saw four leather bound books. They seemed like first editions.

The collected works of Shakespeare, Dante's *Inferno, Purgatory and Paradise, The Federalist Papers of the American Constitution,* and *The Lives of Saints* were in her hands.

"Do you like them?" he asked. "I love them!" she responded, holding them to her bosom. She cried tears of joy.

"I know you are religious, so I thought the stories of these holy people would be of value. They were honest and courageous, just like you," stated Eli as he pointed to the book. *"The Federalist Papers* are the memoirs of three American patriots who fought the British to secure freedom for their people. The book is about the Constitution and what each thought and phrase meant to these insurgents who risked their lives and sacred fortunes for liberty," explained Eli. "The words of Dante will illuminate your soul with the wisdom of the ages," he asserted.

Rita hugged him. "Thank you. This is the most beautiful gift I have ever received," she said. "Enjoy them, my little flower," he said as she left the store.

She could not wait to read them. She opened the book of Shakespeare's plays and writings. On the first page was a note:

> *To my wonderful Italian flower: The universe gave you special talents to help make the world better. You will discover them in these stories and see yourself as a heroine and a person who will change the fate of mankind. God bless you,*
>
> *Eli, Berlin, November 8th, 1938*

Rita was excited and agitated when she woke the next morning. She picked a rose from a nearby garden. It was a small gift for Eli. She knew he would treasure it and seal it in a book forever.

When she arrived on the street of the shop, she saw hundreds of uniformed men in brown shirts. They were Nazis. They had metal pipes and bats and were racing from store to store, breaking windows and entering the stores.

Rita was stunned.

In the distance, she saw smoke. Buildings were burning. The young girl froze. The bookstore! Eli!' she thought. She ran. She got to the shop. Hundreds of shards of glass were strewn about the sidewalk. A huge pile of books was burning in the street. She smelled gasoline as the smoke from the flaming pages soared into the sky of Berlin.

She went inside. Rita recognized his grey suit. His yarmulke was pinned to his hair, covered in blood. Eli was lying face down. She went to him. He was motionless, lifeless. The young girl embraced him. She held him in her arms, weeping and sobbing, rocking back and forth. 'How could this be?' she thought. 'How could anyone hurt such a kind and warm human being?' she asked herself, unable to find an answer.

From November ninth to the tenth, thousands of Jewish citizens were murdered and attacked. Nearly eight thousand businesses and shops were wrecked and looted. Fourteen hundred synagogues were burned.

It was known as *The Night of Broken Glass.*

From that instant, Rita changed. She saw the cruelty of Nazism and Fascism.

Words from Eli's books were emblazoned in her soul. Her mission was to fight for truth, justice, freedom, and save the weak from the clutches of tyranny.

Quotes from those pages became her guiding light:

> *Give all the power to the many, they will oppress the few. Give all the power to the few, they will oppress the many…Those who stand for nothing, fall for everything.*

> Alexander Hamilton

A foe to tyrants, (is) my country's friend.

Shakespeare

These are the tyrants, who plunged their hands in blood and plundering.

Dante Alighieri

CHAPTER 235 ▬▬▬▬▬▬▬▬▬▬

RETURN TO VIA TASSO

Rita picked up the pieces of glass in her room and disposed of them.

She composed herself.

Her task was not complete.

She needed to return to the scene of the crimes.

Hidden in Via Tasso was proof of murder and mayhem. She had only minutes to retrieve it. Mobs would storm the building, free the prisoners, and torch the hideous symbol of Nazi rule.

Rita rushed out of her apartment, made a call on a pay phone, and ran up the street.

It was early morning. She arrived at the building. The doors were open, and people were streaming in and out. The clang of cracking metal echoed in the halls as jail locks were broken to liberate prisoners held in the dungeons of the Gestapo.

Rita ran down a flight of steps to the basement. The furnace was cold and silent, the pile of coal untouched. She shoveled. Dust flew into the air and blackened her face. She saw a piece of the sack. Rita grabbed it and pulled it out.

She put it under her arm and raced up the stairs. As she crossed a hall to the exit, a woman looked at her and yelled. "She worked for them! You helped the butchers kill my husband!" she screamed at the top of her lungs, pointing to Rita. Men and women rushed toward her. Rita clung to the sack.

"I recognize her," said another woman. "I passed her desk when I went to see the head of the Gestapo to spare my son!" she cried. "He killed him! *You* killed him!" she shrieked.

The woman slapped Rita. Someone pulled her hair. Her dress was ripped off. She felt a blow to the stomach. She was kicked in the legs. A violent punch to her face threw her to the ground. The mob struck her ferociously. Rita felt her ribs crumble with pain.

She was almost unconscious when she heard a siren.

Three police officers ran to the scene.

They blew whistles to stop the crowd.

The officers pushed aside the horde.

One of them picked up Rita in his arms.

He carried her outside as his colleagues held back the throng of crying families whose faces were imbued with hatred and wrath.

They got her into a police car. She had fainted from the terror and the blows to her body. Her face was black-and-blue.

Joe took out a small vial of smelling salts. He opened it and put it under Rita's nose. She grimaced and opened her eyes.

"How are you?" asked Joe. She could not respond. Her mouth was swollen and sore. She looked around. "Where is it?" she demanded.

"Are you looking for this?" asked Tom. He gave her the sack. She held it close to her.

Rita looked at Joe, Tom, and Fabio.

"This will send those fiends to hell," she said, as blood dripped from her lips.

CHAPTER 236

ROME IS FREE

"You are a strong young lady," said the doctor.

Joe and Tom waited outside the physician's office while he took care of Rita.

Fabio was near the police car. He watched as thousands of German soldiers left Rome in trucks, motorized vehicles, and armored cars pulling military equipment. They went north to join Kesselring's army.

American troops enter the gates of Rome, *Courtesy, US National Archives*

The relentless onslaught of the partisans, combined with the intelligence and aid of the Allies, debilitated the Nazi occupation of Rome and helped weaken the German forces in Italy.

The invincible Teutonic war machine became a blind, exhausted Cyclops searching for invisible enemies who tormented and chipped away at its strength until it was forced to retreat.

As the Nazis departed, American soldiers, tanks, and artillery poured into the ancient city and entered the gates in the south of Rome.

They marched in the footprints of legions and crossed the paths of the Caesars.

Thousands of Romans greeted the liberators who freed them from the shackles of the Fascists and the Nazis.

Courtesy, Rome Tourist Board

As troops paraded passed the Coliseum, a soldier went to Gianicolo Hill. He laid a wreath at the statue of Anita Garibaldi.

His grandmother was from Brazil. She came from the same town as Anita. He promised to pay homage to her when he went to Rome.

The young man was moved by the sight of this girl riding a horse, with a pistol in one hand and a baby in another.

Giuseppe Garibaldi,
Courtesy, Republic of Italy Archives and Wikipedia Commons

In front of the image of Giuseppe Garibaldi, the American laid down his rifle and pistol. He took off his helmet and saluted.

"General, we are here," he said.

CHAPTER 237 ━━━━━━━━━━━━━━━━━━━

BROKEN AND BRUISED

Rita and the Americans were not celebrating, as the Fifth Army marched through the Eternal City.

She was in pain. Her ribs were broken. They were taped.

She had bruises on her face and body. She could not walk or talk.

Internally, she was bleeding. Damage was done to her liver, stomach, and spleen, as well as her mind. The shock of the final days at Gestapo headquarters settled into her psyche, never to leave.

She knew she had saved many lives.

Rita informed the OSS and the partisans. She created false documents, forged signatures, and reproduced German rubber stamps used by freedom fighters to frustrate the enemy and free people from the clutches of the Nazis.

The risks and sacrifices, she felt, were not enough. She wanted to do more, but was impotent.

Those moments, where she watched and could do nothing, hurt the most.

Rita gave up years of her life in her struggle against the Nazis. She was older. Her face was wrinkled and her hair was turning grey and white.

The young woman looked in the mirror and stared at her eyes and ears. She had seen and heard too much. For the rest of her life, Rita would recall the faces of prisoners and their cries for help as they were tormented and tortured by The Devil, The Monster, and The Beast.

It was over, now.

Fabio brought her to the family home in Trastevere. He carried her up the stairs and put her on the bed. Furniture was covered with sheets. The apartment had not been lived in for years.

He moved Rita's goods from the apartment near Via Tasso. A nurse was assigned to help her while she was convalescing.

It would take months to heal her broken and battered body.

She needed rest and recovery.

Rita did not realize it, but the greatest challenges of her life were still to come.

CHAPTER 238 ━━━━━━━━━━━━━━━━━━

THE FEAST

It was the morning of Tuesday, June 20th, 1944, the feast of San Silverio in Little Ponza in the South Bronx.

"Did you iron my sash?" Silverio asked Lucia, nervously. "Of course. I also got your new suit cleaned. You will look splendid," she responded. Silverio was one of the founders of the Societa' Ponzese di San Silverio in New York. The organization united immigrants and families from Ponza in America.

They came for the celebration of their patron saint from all parts of North and South America and, most of all, to unite with their families and friends in New York.

Silverio wore a sash that carried the colors of Italy and the United States across his body to signify the union of these two nations in brotherhood and sisterhood.

He led the procession.

It started with a band of trumpets and horns playing the U.S. and Italian national anthems. Silverio put his hand on his heart as he listened carefully to each patriotic song.

He became emotional and cried. His love for Italy and America was strong and deep.

The procession began with the statue of San Silverio leaving the Church of Our Lady of Pity after the noon mass. It was a great honor to help carry it.

Next came the priests, dressed in white and gold garments, holding the Blessed Sacrament.

Thousands of friends, relatives, and people from the neighborhood followed, walking and singing hymns as they marched on the cobblestones, giving witness to faith, love of God, and affection for Italy and America.

The procession lasted hours.

They passed hundreds of stands selling toys and souvenirs and cooking food for the feast. The holiday went on for three days. Beds came out of closets and mattresses appeared miraculously in those tiny apartments in the tenements of Little Ponza to welcome relatives who came from afar to be together and share love and memories.

Courtesy, Bronx Historical Society and Ponza Racconta

That day in 1944 was a unique one. It honored the eight hundred and fifty thousand Italian-American men and women called upon to defend the United States in Europe and the Pacific.

Hundreds of them gathered in uniform outside of Our Lady of Pity Church. Some were on their way to the battlefield.

Others returned home, filled with wounds and psychological and physical scars they would carry forever.

In each case was a story, a life, and a chronicle of duty, courage, and liberation.

CHAPTER 239 ━━━━━━━━━━━━━━━━━━━━━━

SHOES

Joe and Tom hugged Fabio. The three men and their partners in the resistance had made life very miserable for the Germans in and around Rome.

They sat at a bar and reminisced over cups of espresso.

"Do you remember the warehouse?" said Joe to Fabio. "Oh my God!" said Tom. "I was sure we were done for that night!" he responded.

"It was my fault," insisted Fabio. "I should have gotten you the right shoes," he laughed.

It was an attack on a German stockpile. The building contained fuel, arms, and ammunition. It was on the outskirts of Rome and guarded by two soldiers.

Joe, Tom, and Fabio had wanted to avoid bloodshed.

"I will use my Gestapo passes. Once we are in, you and Tom can set up the charges," said Fabio.

They drove up to the entrance.

Two Germans in uniform were on guard.

"Heil Hitler!" said Fabio. The warriors saluted. They spoke little Italian. Fabio showed them his pass. It was signed by The Monster and sealed with a Gestapo stamp. A German eagle and swastika were on the letter.

> *By order of the Fuhrer, the bearer of this document is a trusted aide to the Greater German Reich in Rome. He is to have access to all facilities occupied by forces of the Third Reich, to conduct inspections and report to Fascist authorities for complete coordination of efforts to assist in the occupation of the Capital.*

Fabio had a backup permit, if this one did not work.

The soldier read the letter. He looked over Fabio and opened the door of the warehouse.

His comrade kept his machine gun unlocked and ready for any eventuality.

Joe and Tom walked in behind Fabio. Under their jackets were sticks of dynamite and clocks.

As they went by, one soldier looked at their shoes. They were wearing brightly polished GI boots.

"Halt!" he said. He pointed his rifle at them. Fabio and Joe spoke some broken German. The soldier knew some words in Italian. "Where did you get those boots?" he asked. "American prisoners in Rome," explained Fabio. "We exchanged the boots for cigarettes," said Joe.

Tom put his hand on his pistol.

The soldier and his partner looked at the shoes. "They are excellent and comfortable," stated Joe. "Do you want to try them on?" interjected Tom. "Yes," replied the German. Joe and Tom took them off. The soldiers removed theirs.

The Germans tried them on. They fit well. Remarkably, the four men had the same size foot.

"Splendid," said Joe. "They are yours," he insisted. A smile crossed the face of the young combatants.

The enemies exchanged shoes.

The German soldiers, Joe, and Tom shook hands.

For a second, Joe thought of peace.

'Someday we can celebrate as brothers who are part of the same world, and not foes wanting to kill each other.'

The three police officers went into the warehouse alone. It was packed with boxes of ammunition, grenades, and drums of fuel oil.

Tom and Joe planted the sticks of dynamite with timers deep in the depository. They were set to go off in three hours.

The policemen waved good night to the German fighters.

As they drove away, the boys from the Bronx and their Italian comrade spoke about the two young men wearing their boots. They hoped they would not be hurt.

Several hours later, an explosion rocked that corner of Rome.

The soldiers survived the blast.

CHAPTER 240 ━━━━━━━━

FREEDOM RINGS

A friendly sun was bathing the island in light.

It carried hope, openness, and a new beginning.

Peace and freedom reached Ponza.

It was June 20th, 1944, the Feast of San Silverio.

Samuele was on his balcony in the center of the port with a bundle of bamboo shoots. He was creating traps. It was an art.

The sticks were twisted, tied, and wrapped to make an elaborate, conical basket. It attracted fish and lobsters. Once they swam in, they could not escape.

From the veranda, he greeted passersby.

"Good morning, Samuele," said an American sergeant from the Bronx. "Boston lost to New York yesterday in a tough baseball game," he explained. "As long as we have the New York Yankees, there is hope in the world," remarked Samuele, grinning.

The sergeant brought him sports scores, copies of the *Stars and Stripes* military newspaper, the *New York Times*, and magazines.

"Emma, you make the best espresso on Ponza," said the young soldier. "Have a piece of the chocolate cake. Thank you for the oatmeal." she responded. Emma loved American oatmeal. "Thanks to you and Samuele, I have put on ten pounds," he said, laughing.

Their home was the center of Army and Navy gatherings. Soldiers and sailors loved meeting these witty, intelligent, lively, and patriotic people who adored America and Italy. The couple showed warmth and hospitality to these liberators who would soon be gone. Meals were social events, and moments of friendship and chances to enjoy Samuele's excellent wine.

"As soon as we organize an Italian administration on the island, we will leave to fight the Germans in the North," declared the sergeant. He was an African-American. He was tall, handsome, kind, and brave.

His great grandparents were slaves.

Samuele and Emma knew this warrior and others like him would face danger and death in the days ahead.

Food, commerce, and normalcy were returning to the island.

Samuele heard news and gossip. He saw ships enter and exit the port. Vessels returned filled with lobsters. Freighters, protected by the Allies from German guns, ventured into the waters to carry goods to and from the mainland.

A twelve-year-old boy named Livio visited Samuele. His father was a mariner. When he was not fishing, Livio helped the Americans. He did odd jobs and carried letters, notes, and food around the island. The soldiers paid him in dollars. Each day he took home flour, bread, and cans of vegetables and fruit to his family.

"Italy, Germany, and Japan will become American colonies," he told Samuele. "Really. Who told you that nonsense?" he asked. "Oh, people assume it will happen," the boy replied, innocently.

"Son, Americans fought to restore liberty. Imperialism is not in their blood. Once we have peace, they will go home. They will rebuild the lands of their enemies and bring democracy," he responded.

The boy went off, satisfied he learned something new.

Samuele turned to Emma. "For the first time in twenty years, we are free," he said. "We can talk, think, and act on our own, without someone looking over our shoulder or spying on us. We will argue about politics, choose our leaders, and make a better, richer, and wiser country," he remarked with conviction.

"Women will count for more than just being wives and mothers," responded Emma, hopefully.

"Let us not go too far!" quipped Samuele, laughing. His wife smiled. She knew her husband well, that he was joking.

Don Gabriele and Don Lorenzo prepared for the feast.

It was the first real celebration since the start of the war.

The churches were mute with sorrow as young men died on the battlefield. Bells were silent under the shackles of Nazism.

Now, chimes rang every hour.

People sang and danced in the streets. Radios were heard broadcasting music in foreign languages.

In the past, gatherings were watched and controlled. Short wave radios were prohibited. But now Fascists were no longer there to command and persecute.

The people marched in the procession as they demonstrated liberty, faith, and brotherhood. American soldiers and sailors walked with them.

The Jewish families strolled in the noonday sun for kilometers, from the port to the end of the island. They held hands with their new families.

The air seemed especially sweet that day as they celebrated freedom from fear.

Ten-year-old Adah asked her mother, Esther, "Who was San Silverio?" "He was a Pope and a hero who died for his beliefs. The Emperor demanded Silverio do things he felt were wrong. He refused. He was taken to Ponza and killed. Silverio was named a Saint for his courage and miracles. Today we honor his bravery and example of resilience in the face of Evil."

The ceremonies and fellowship were beautiful and unforgettable.

CHAPTER 241

LITTLE PONZA

On the other side of the Atlantic, a family gathered in Little Ponza to prepare for dinner.

Carlo, Helena, Luigi and his wife, and Gabriela and her fiancé, Richard, arrived from West Virginia.

"Angelina and Gennie will take care of them," said Lucia. "They have plenty of room. Yolanda and her daughters are helping me with the meal," she told Silverio.

"Go get the mozzarella. We need three kilos of ravioli," she explained. "Make sure the bread is fresh. Yesterday, the baker gave me a loaf that was a day old. I need another kilo of sausage," she said, anxiously. Silverio went off to shop in the Italian stores that lined the main streets of Little Ponza.

Lucia cooked her sauce early in the morning. It simmered for six hours before she thought it was ready. It was packed with meat balls, pork, beef, and pieces of lamb and sausage. The scent was incredible. The fragrance reached around the building.

The neighbors provided tables and chairs for a special family meal that happened once a year for Silverio and Lucia. The feast was Silverio's only holiday. He took off from his job on the waterfront. The store was closed.

At 6 PM, the guests arrived. Maria, Lucia's cousin and her husband Enzo, came with their daughter-in-law, Sofia, and Anna, Tom's fiancé. Carlo, Helena, Luigi, Antonietta, and Gabriela and Richard came a few minutes later.

After warm hugs and greetings, they sat around the table.

Silverio stood up to say a prayer. He closed his eyes. His thoughts flew to the battlefields, the seas and skies where the war continued.

He wondered about his family and men and women in uniform in Italy and America engaged in the greatest conflict ever known.

Silverio was grateful for life, liberty, and family:

> *Father in Heaven, protect our families, our boys and girls in combat. Safeguard America and Italy as we search for peace. Bless our family and friends gathered to celebrate this feast of companionship, and, most of all, love. God bless us all. Amen.*

Everyone clapped as Silverio poured wine and made a toast to San Silverio.

CHAPTER 242 ━━━━━━━━━━━━━━━━━━

THE NEW EMBASSY

The Americans bid farewell to Fabio. It was an emotional departure of three men who risked their lives together for freedom.

Joe and Tom removed their police uniforms and went to the headquarters of the Fifth Army at the Excelsior Hotel on Via Veneto.

The head of the OSS was waiting for them. "Men, you and the people you worked with have been magnificent. Your heroism saved lives and helped end the war. We will recognize them and you for your bravery," he said.

"By October, a new Embassy will be in place on Via Veneto. In the meantime, you are to organize an office of the OSS in the Consulate Building. You will have all the support you need, a budget and authorization to hire an Italian to help us in our work," he explained.

"Yes sir," responded Joe and Tom.

For the next three months, the boys from the Bronx set up the new special office of intelligence at the U.S. Mission to Italy.

It was a daunting task. It required extensive contacts with Washington, Rome, and the occupation forces.

The head of the OSS visited Joe and Tom in September.

Libraries with documents were in place. Safes to handle classified material and special communications equipment were installed.

For the first time, a sophisticated American intelligence program existed in Europe.

"My compliments. You have done a great job," he stated.

"Sir, allow me to present our office manager and admin assistant," said Joe.

The OSS commander met a young lady.

"What is your name?" he asked.

"Sheila," she said with a smile.

1971

Silverio slept for three hours. It was his first trip on a plane. His anxiety was not the journey. It was his past, meeting the present. His memories of life on the island were of adventure, poverty, and danger.

His slumber was a nightmare. He was in the cold water of Palmarola. He felt it again as he did when he was sixteen in February 1929. His boat sank in a storm. Five of his companions lived, and five died. He clung to an icy rock for three days and nights, surrounded by sharks.

He moaned, screamed, and woke up sweating as the plane bounced in the windy clouds and brought him back to reality.

In a few hours, he would land. He got up from his seat. He walked to the back, passing his fellow travelers, sound asleep. He watched a few. Some snored as if singing songs.

He stood by the round airplane window, thinking about the years of the war, with its worry and work, and those of the fifties and sixties, filled with progress and opportunities, all passed by in a parade of memories.

Silverio celebrated his sixtieth birthday, a few days before departure. Life was hard but good. He had a lovely family and true friends. All he wanted was peace and love for the time left.

He returned to his seat. Lucia and everyone were awake. He fastened his seat belt. The landing was full of bounces on the runway, and then a slow stop. A loud applause for the pilot came from the passengers.

They waited for their luggage. Silverio was amazed at the size and weight of the suitcases of other passengers.

'Perhaps they are smuggling in bars of gold, or their rock collections,' he smiled as he watched travelers struggle with oversized and weighty baggage.

He took his valises and put them on the cart. Carlo, Helena, and the others, who he had chatted with at JFK and Dublin, were up ahead, exiting.

Lucia pushed the wagon, while Silverio rolled a leather bag filled with gifts for relatives.

They followed the green sign. It said, "Nothing to Declare." They went out.

Lucia saw him. He was older, stout, and seemed shorter, but no one could mistake the face of Don Lorenzo.

He broke from the handshakes of Joe and Tom and ran to her. She and Silverio cried with joy.

This middle-aged priest was the center of attention.

Helena, Carlo, Gabriela, Richard, Luigi, and Antonietta gathered around him.

Joe and Tom were ecstatic. Don Lorenzo was their bridge of memories. He carried them to Rome and Ponza, to relive unimaginable exploits of risk and bravery.

Soon, the travelers from the New World would be on the island to celebrate the feast of a Saint who brought them together as heroic, loving, and liberated people.

A young man greeted Tom and Joe and their wives. "Sir, I am from the U.S. Embassy. The Ambassador sends greetings and invites you to lunch with him tomorrow, if you have time," he stated. "Wouldn't that be wonderful?" said Helena to Anna.

"Thank you, we will be there," responded Joe.

"Sir, I have a note for both of you," said the young man. He handed them a white envelope.

Joe opened it.

It was an exquisite card. Engraved on it was the Colosseum.

A short message was written in elegant calligraphy, with carefully drawn letters and words — "Dear Joe and Tom: Welcome Home!"

It was signed, "Sheila."

Epilogue

Joe and Tom received the Bronze Star for heroism, and each left the military service with the rank of Colonel.

They returned to New York in September 1945. As their ship came into the port, Silverio and Antonio were hauling cargo in the Brooklyn Navy Yard. The longshoremen watched as the vessel carrying thousands of soldiers and sailors landed in Manhattan.

They stood up to salute the returning warriors.

Joe and Tom were greeted by their families and hundreds of loved ones. Tom married Anna shortly after arrival.

Carlo departed the United States in early 1946. He returned to Italy. Helena joined him. They were married, and then they returned to Wheeling, West Virginia. In three years, they brought the entire family to West Virginia. Luigi and Carlo created a splendid Italian bakery that lasted several generations.

The people protected by the nuns and monks went to visit them over the years. The meetings were moving, beautiful, and memorable. Sister Cristina and Sister Chiara had fruitful lives, educating thousands of children to be ethical and courageous citizens.

Don Gabriele and Don Lorenzo served their flocks in Ponza. Don Lorenzo became pastor when Don Gabriele died in 1949.

Francesca went into medicine after the armistice. Colonel Lukas and other partisans returned to private life.

Five years after the end of the war, on May 8th, 1950, the most famous conductor in the world, Arturo Toscanini, celebrated the fifth anniversary of the Victory in Europe (V-E Day) with a special concert at Carnegie Hall in New York. He played Giuseppe Verdi's monumental "Hymn of Nations" and concluded it with the national anthems of France, Britain, and the United States.

In the audience that evening were Joe and Tom and their wives, plus Silverio and Lucia, Carlo and Helena, Luigi and Antonietta, and Gabriela and Richard. Anna, Tom's wife, sang in the chorus and did a solo performance.

The families enjoyed long, happy lives in America and raised their children in peace and prosperity.

Thanks to the documents saved by Rita, numerous Nazis and Fascists were brought to justice. Trials were held in Italy and throughout Europe.

The Devil was captured by the British. He was tried and condemned to death for the Ardeatine massacres. His sentence was commuted to life imprisonment. The Devil spent thirty years in jail, escaped, and died of cancer a year later.

The Monster fled to Argentina. He was a fugitive for fifty years until he was apprehended, tried, and sentenced to life imprisonment. He died under house arrest at the age of one hundred.

When the Allies arrived, The Beast fled Rome for Milan. He was arrested in 1945, tried, and sentenced to death. He was executed in Rome one year after the Eternal City was liberated.

The head of the Fascist Party was tried and executed. During his trial, the Director of Regina Coeli prison was a witness for the prosecution. He left the courtroom and was killed by a mob, who drowned him in the Tiber.

Rita worked for the American Embassy for nearly fifty years. She believed her mission in life was to fight tyranny. It continued with the Cold War and the struggle against Communism. For decades, she fought for freedom and liberty.

She married a physician in Rome. They had four children. Rita retired and moved to a small town outside the capital. She never spoke of her time in the War and accepted no honors or decorations for her service.

Despite what she saw and experienced, she believed people were essentially kind and good.

Her favorite quote was from Abraham Lincoln:

> *Though passion may have strained, it must not break our bonds of affection. The mystic chords of memory will swell when again touched, as surely they will be, by the better angels of our nature.*

About the Author

Emilio Iodice is a former senior official and diplomat for the American government.

He was an executive with a major multinational corporation operating across the globe, a professor of Leadership, and vice-president and director of a well-known U.S. university in Rome, Italy.

He is a distinguished author and public speaker, and he has written several books about leadership and history. His latest work, *The Commander in Chie*f, was a *Wall Street Journal* Number One Bestseller.

http://www.iodicebooks.com/books